\*

# THE
# GREAT
# BLIZZARD

\*

# ALBERT E. IDELL

\* \* \*

# THE
# GREAT
# BLIZZARD

\* \* \*

*New York*

## HENRY HOLT AND COMPANY

In Memory of
Eugénie Mather Cadwalader
(the Gene of this book)
whose stories of her family, told
to me while I was courting her
daughter, furnished the inspiration
for the Rogerses

✳

Lines from Father McGlynn by Edwin Markham
on page 96 reprinted by permission.

✳

# CONTENTS

PART ONE:   January, 1884 to May, 1885          1

PART TWO:   May, 1886 to September, 1887          95

PART THREE:   March 10th to 15th, 1888          185

# CHARACTERS

JESSE ROGERS—Philadelphia Quaker who married "out of Meeting."

AUGUSTINA ROGERS—Called "GUSSIE" by her husband and "TINA" by her sister. Daughter of an impecunious Italian nobleman, Count Borelli, who was a member of the entourage of Joseph Napoleon as "Mr. Repetto."

TERESINA (ZENIE)—Their eldest daughter.

JULIA and PHILIPPE LASCALLES—A married daughter and her husband. JESSE and TITI, their children.

GEORGINA and DR. AUGUSTUS PALMER (GENE and GUS)—A married daughter and her husband.

HENRY—Georgina's twin.

OHIO BALLOU—Who has taken the stage name of MAGGIE.

CLINTON WEATHERBY—Suitor of Zenie.

TERESINA LASCALLES—Sister of Augustina Rogers, called "AUNT ZENA" by everyone. The widow of Philippe Lascalles' uncle, who had been a rich French merchant.

WILLIAM MADEIRA, ESQ.—An old flame of Mrs. Rogers and employer of Henry.

FATHER DUFFY—A priest and friend of the Rogerses.

NORAH and TONY ANGELUCCI—The Rogers' living-out girl and the young man she marries in the course of the book.

THE BURTS—Next-door neighbors.

ABE—The stableboy.

Ladies and gentlemen of the Saulsbury Troubadours

The Rogers' pets

# PART ONE

* * *

January, 1884 to May, 1885

* * *

"Faith and philosophy are air, but events are brass."

HERMAN MELVILLE, *Pierre*

**Chapter 1**

THE NEW YEAR had begun inauspiciously, there was no doubt of it. Being an ex-railroad man, Mr. Rogers read with a personal eye of the terrible wreck on the Pennsylvania, at Bradford, and next to it, the report of a catastrophe of a different sort—the Northern Pacific Railroad was in receivership and Mr. Villard, its President, bankrupt!

'Eighty-four didn't augur well for his own prospects! He turned to the classified advertisements—a section of the Brooklyn *Eagle* which he had always disregarded prior to these last, worried months, and he mumbled through his beard, finally throwing down his paper in disgust. "Doesn't anyone want to employ a full-grown man? 'A cleanly lad to open oysters . . . Boy of eight to work on farm . . . Brother and sister between eight and fourteen . . . A half-grown boy . . . Neat boy . . . Likely lad . . . A young boxman . . .' What is a boxman, anyway?"

Mrs. Rogers was fashioning an embroidered cover for a footstool and held off the ribbon-decorated confection to appraise its effect. "It's nothing you could do, I'm sure of that. You need a new position, goodness knows, but I declare, I almost hate to see you pick up a newspaper, you get so wrathy."

Retrieving the *Eagle* from the parlor Wilton, Mr. Rogers rearranged its pages and turned anew to the advertisements. An item held his attention and he cast a sidelong glance at his wife. "I wish, Gussie, that you'd reconsider your decision about selling. I believe that salesmanship might very well be my forte. There appear to be good openings for responsible parties to sell sewing machines. A nice way to buy them has been worked out. One doesn't need to plank down the whole amount in cash but can pay a little a week. . . ."

Mrs. Rogers sniffed, and her husband again gave up the idea of

3

being a salesman. Instead he launched into a tirade about the kinds of jobs that were being offered. "One would think there was a world-wide shortage of shoemakers—'Shoe finishers . . . edge setters . . . heelers . . . lasters . . .' AND 'A man to side up boots.' " He gave an explosive laugh, "No less than a dozen finishers on galloon shanks. How many different men does it take to make a pair of shoes, anyway?"

On the whole, however, there was a paucity of positions open in this New Year of depression. Indeed, there were more people asking jobs than offering them. He counted sixty advertisements from laundresses alone. In scanning over them he was amused by something he noticed. "Gussie—this is good. All but one of these advertisement cards say 'A respectable woman wants washing and ironing,' but the sixtieth says 'Washing and ironing wanted by a good laundress.' She is the one I'd pick. Who cares a whoop whether a laundress is a respectable woman or no, so long as she does shirts the way you want them?"

Mrs. Rogers threw her hands high in the air. "If something doesn't turn up pretty quickly, it's quite likely I'll be taking in washing myself, and let me tell you, Jesse Rogers, I'll advertise as a respectable woman, whether you like it or no."

"Here is an interesting business card—Dr. Townsend's Oxygenated Air. 'Caution: Persons in Boston are putting up a bogus liquid and trying to pawn it off. Agents wanted.' You know, Mother, that might be a good thing. It must be a fine product or it wouldn't be imitated by those quacks and there is no more solid and respectable business than the sale of patent medicines—they are a boon to humanity as well—the good ones. Look at the Jayneses—they own a good slice of Philadelphia—Quakers, too."

His wife was becoming impatient but she spoke most reasonably. "Now, Father, there is no use talking—we can't live on odds and ends coming in from commissions. What you need is a good position where there is a job to be done and a pay envelope weekly."

With a profound sigh, Mr. Rogers protested, "You don't seem to realize, Gussie, the condition of the country. It's hard enough for a man of my years to be looking for employment. Who knows, if I had stayed with the Philadelphia and Reading, instead of com-

4

ing here to Brooklyn, we mightn't be in this fix now—but no, you insisted."

Mrs. Rogers' needle flew faster and her lips shaped themselves uncompromisingly, "At least you've had your pay regularly from the bridge people and more than you ever got on the railroad. Don't try to blame me for the way things are. If I hadn't spoken up when I did, we'd probably have been paupers years ago."

Mr. Rogers' beard had become folded between two pages of the newspaper and he ran a stout hand under it to free it. "Listen to this—'Five hundred loaves of bread will be distributed to the poor by the Iroquois Lodge of the I.O.O.F.' "

"What in the world does that stand for, Jesse? I find initials so distracting."

"The Independent Order of Odd Fellows. . . ."

"One of those awful lodges? Odd Fellows, indeed! They must be pretty queer looking fish, or I miss my guess. Why don't they use their name, instead of those initials?" At the exact moment that her husband prepared to explain, she went on, "Besides, if they are having O's at all, they should have three of them—Order of Odd, don't you see? It seems that way to me, at any rate."

Mr. Rogers moved heavily and the Turkish rocker creaked. It always groaned under his weight, so he paid no attention as he voiced his exasperation, "I declare, Gussie, there has never been a female living who can distract a man from his subject the way you can. It is quite beside the point how the I.O.O.F. chooses to designate itself. The important and terrible thing is that groups of our citizenry must exist on free bread, given by the charity of a lodge."

"It is better than folks starving, I should say. Surely you wouldn't prefer us to be uncharitable heathens, would you?"

That was the trouble with Jesse—they couldn't even sit in the parlor on a Sunday afternoon without a harangue on the condition of the country. Mrs. Rogers laid down her embroidery and swept to the window, parting the sateen-lined velvet draperies with a motion of her small plump hand. She peered with feigned anxiety through the floor-length curtains of ecru lace. "I don't know what is keeping Zenie. She should be back by now. She knows how worried about her I get."

Mr. Rogers hardly raised his head from the *Eagle*, "Why you

5

should worry about Zenie, I can't see. That girl can take care of herself."

His wife rested one hand on a bosom that did not need stays to give it roundness. "When a daughter of mine is out alone with a man, I'm always worried. I trusted Julia and look at the disgraceful thing that happened to her—there was a girl one could surely depend on. And the way Gene behaved! Zenie has gone stark mad over that Clint. Just let a good-looking man come along . . ." She paused to consider the effect of the male upon feminine virtue and then assumed a tragic, martyred expression. "It was my fault, I suppose, for allowing them to go out unchaperoned. No girl, however respectable, is safe alone in a man's company."

Mr. Rogers put aside his paper with a sigh while his wife watched with a birdlike expression, head tilted back and black eyes beady. Wasn't he going to come to the defense of his own family, refute the things that she had said? If he thought that her daughters *had* behaved scandalously, that she hadn't done everything a mother could to instruct them properly, she knew the course to take.

She tapped her foot impatiently, working herself up to blast his acceptance of her self-accusations.

Jesse Rogers had lived for too many years with his wife's fiery, Italian temperament not to recognize her moods. Let her stew in her own juice a minute or two longer, he thought, pretending a heavy Quaker stolidity. Finally he spoke with a slow, judicious air, "Julia is married to a man of respected family and considerable means. Gene has embarked upon a life of service to humanity as the wife of a doctor. If there is anything disgraceful about that, let the gossips make the most of it. As for chaperons, the whole business is an imported affectation, aping Queen Victoria's ideas. When I was a youth, girls were considered well able to take care of themselves without their elders snooping on them continually."

Mrs. Rogers snorted, "Quakers—in those ridiculous bonnets! Of course they were safe. Who'd as much as look at them in such outfits?"

"Quaker men, my dear." By Christopher, the retort was a good one. Mr. Rogers laughed, showing white teeth. "Believe me, Gussie, beauty requires no fancy raiment to enhance its charms. Some of the most attractive girls belonged to our Meeting."

6

"I notice you didn't marry one, all the same, though I often wish you had and spared me putting up with you. I never saw such a man. Here I am, distracted to death about Zenie and you start talking about Queen Victoria. What has she got to do with it, anyway?"

"This much, my dear—there is something wrong with the world when a narrow, intolerant female can impose her will and straight-laced ideas upon it. By what command of God has one dumpy German *Hausfrau* the right to rule three hundred million souls, or set standards of conduct by which we in America are expected to abide?"

This was worse than the newspaper! Mrs. Rogers sighed and busied herself with rearranging the furnishings, while her husband, conscious that he had gained peace for a while, returned to his reading. Gradually a feeling of contentment enveloped him. It was so seldom that he and Gussie could enjoy the intimacy of the parlor on a Sunday afternoon. Although they carried on an unending duel of words when they were together, it was a highly satisfying relationship. There was always pleasure in foiling his wife's conversational thrusts and if he could make a touch with his own heavy-handed feints, so much the better.

Mrs. Rogers took up her needlework. It was an unending task to conceal every useful article in the house underneath some decorative camouflage. No sooner were the tea and coffee pots provided with beribboned cozies than new covers had to be made for pillowcases and handkerchief boxes, for chair arms and knife baskets. Even the cuspidors, of which the house boasted a number, although Mr. Rogers was enjoined from chewing at home—even they were given decorative touches of ribbon-festooned crocheting, embellished with roses.

Yes, things were never done in a house, Mrs. Rogers thought, as her needle flew, but she found contentment in the notion that stretching ahead of her down the years there would always be something to occupy her mind and hands. That reminded her— she needed to make new covers for the slipper box. The old ones were quite worn out from years of use.

Mr. Rogers raised his eyes from the paper to enjoy a scene which always gave him pleasure. It was the vista of this room—center of the family's life—with his plump and still beautiful wife engaged in one of her little domestic tasks. In spite of the condition of the country, and their own immediate fortunes, he was able to forget everything in contemplation of his own parlor. His eye roamed lovingly over its contents. The Turkish corner, with its divan, luxurious pillows and hangings, scimitars and shields, was a gift from Aunt Zena, his wife's sister, Centennial year.

And the piano of opulent rosewood! He never thought of it without saying to himself, "a magnificent instrument." There was an eye-filling array of china and porcelain in the whatnot, and prized pieces of French and English ware stood on the mantel. There was a peculiar contrivance on another table that looked not unlike a fountain. Indeed, it was a fountain, a miraculous invention which Aunt Zena had also bought at the Centennial. Once charged with water it played for hours without attention. It had been Mr. Rogers' pride and plaything for a long time, but for years now, it had stood there, arid and neglected.

Then the pictures. With one or two exceptions he loved all of them. Enhanced with ornate frames of gilded or polished wood, they covered almost every inch of wall space and gave the room an effect of richness and solid respectability. The place of honor over the mantelpiece was occupied by a noble painting done on a grand scale, the work of a popular French artist. It represented the tragic retreat of Napoleon from Moscow, with the fire and smoke of the smouldering ruined city visible in the distance. Here and there an upturned cannon or the leg of a dead horse, stiffly protruding from the snow, furnished a symbolic reminder of the suffering of the forlorn and tattered men who filled the foreground. With utmost realism the painter had limned the hopelessness, starvation, and despair of those pitiful creatures. To the right, a small, implacable figure peered across the Rogers' parlor and hall. What could he be seeing? Mr. Rogers was reminded of a Latin quotation and mutilated it aloud, "Sic semper tyrannus mundi." He wondered further if "pluribus" did not belong in the phrase somewhere.

His wife looked up, startled. "I declare, Jesse, I wasn't listening," she apologized.

"Just a quotation in Latin to which I was moved."

Her eyes followed his. "Ah yes, poor Napoleon. As dear Father

8

always said, the Napoleons were never given their due. Just think, if things had only gone differently Father would certainly have been at court. And as for Zena and me, who knows? We might be sitting on thrones at this very moment."

When his wife looked back with regret upon her father's noble birth and subsequent exile, Mr. Rogers usually became impatient, but this afternoon he chose to be gallant. "My dear, you do occupy a throne. For a third of a century you have been queen of my heart. Napoleon never commanded a more loyal subject." He ran his hands through his beard with a pleased, fatuous expression. There, he had gotten that off rather nicely, and Gussie favored him with an appropriately arch glance before he returned to the solace of art. There was no doubt about it. While he had deplored the extravagance that had led his sister-in-law to send them "The Retreat from Moscow," he did derive the greatest satisfaction from it.

The mellow mood the afternoon had engendered was disturbed by the pleasant music of sleigh bells, signaling that their eldest daughter and her suitor were back from their drive.

"Gussie, they're back," Mr. Rogers shouted. "That's the bells on Mr. Quinby. I'd know them anywhere. And safe and sound, I'll warrant you, in spite of all your worrying."

Mrs. Rogers was first to the window, but within a split second she could feel her husband's beard tickling her neck as she took in the scene. The sleigh was crusted with rime, and Mr. Quinby was froth flecked. He pawed impatiently at the hard-packed snow while the occupants removed a welter of blankets and robes.

"That is no way to treat a horse of mine! Mr. Quinby is blowing like a locomotive." Mrs. Rogers stamped her foot in annoyance. "And not a word out of him today! What Zenie sees in him I can't tell for the life of me. Do you realize, Pet, that he has taken up all of her time for eight months now, and still no proposal?"

The horse seemed impatient, and Mrs. Rogers screamed in the general direction of the rear of the house, "Abe, you worthless good-for-nothing, get out and hold Mr. Quinby's head before there's a runaway."

The stableboy made his appearance almost immediately, to hold the bridle with one brown hand while he gently stroked the quivering muzzle with the other.

Mr. Rogers was so used to his wife's outbursts that he answered as though there had been no interruption. "How you can tell that he didn't pop the question this afternoon, I don't know, but I wouldn't worry. For my part, I don't think Zenie ever looked so beautiful. These last months have made a change in her."

"It is all that man! Zenie never did play her cards right, I admit, but she never allowed herself to be walked over. I tell you, Pet, I'm worried."

The front door opened and the young couple brought in with them the crisp cold of the January day. Mr. Rogers shouted, "You gave Mr. Quinby a good workout, I see. How was Prospect Park? By Christopher, I'd have enjoyed a nice sleigh ride myself, this afternoon."

Mrs. Rogers frowned. She had intended to say something about the way her horse had been misused, but Jesse's remark made that impossible. She drew up her short figure, and her face set in a smile that found no reflection in her voice as she inquired, "Well, Mr. Weatherby, I hope you have taken good care of my little girl this afternoon?"

Zenie hung upon her escort's arm in a manner that Mrs. Rogers thought quite shameless, although there was no denying that Clinton Weatherby was handsome, in his way. Her demeanor softened a trifle, as he displayed perfect rows of white teeth in a hearty laugh. She froze again when he responded, in tones only less powerful than those of Mr. Rogers, "That's a great nag. He's getting a little old, but he can still step out. We passed everything in the park, didn't we, Zenie?"

Although Mr. Rogers believed in heartiness, and approved Zenie's suitor as a man's man, he also disliked to hear the family's pride called a nag, but he could not be angry with anyone whose look was so open and who handled himself with such easy, athletic grace. While Zenie began an effusive account of the afternoon's adventures, he helped the young man off with his coat and piloted him to the central heating register, set in the parlor floor.

During the seven years they had enjoyed this modern convenience, Mr. Rogers had never grown tired of remarking the marvel of it. As Clinton Weatherby went through all the motions of a man before a pleasant stove—holding his hands out over the register, and then turning them over, and swinging around, like a fowl on a spit, to get all of himself toasted—Mr. Rogers boomed, "Come, Zenie, you had better take a turn here. Your skirt can trap all these pleasant zephyrs that arise from the cellar, and they'll warm you where it'll do the most good."

After his eldest daughter followed his suggestion, Mr. Rogers noticed how much she had changed since Clinton Weatherby rescued her during the Memorial Day riot on the East River Bridge. The belle of the Rogers family had been transformed in more than appearance and manner; her character had improved, as well. Gone was her aloofness, her petulance, and disdain. A year ago she would have been mortified to have suffered the least blemish to her perfect, ivorylike complexion. At the moment her skin was frankly glowing with a color that January winds had put there, and she appeared not to mind at all!

Teresina became conscious of her father's keen appraisal. Darting over to him, she threw her arms about his neck in a wild and impulsive embrace, planting a kiss on each cheek, and another, for good measure, full on his willing lips. It was a kiss such as Georgina might have imparted, and this led Mr. Rogers to a further thought, "By the Lord Harry, it never occurred to me before, but Zenie is growing more like Gene every day, except that she is dark."

More than he cared to admit, Mr. Rogers had missed Georgina's presence around the house since her marriage to young Dr. Palmer and their removal to Pottsville, in the anthracite coal regions. If only the young couple were with them the afternoon would have been complete. As was usual when Mr. Rogers had an idea, he gave voice to it. "It is too bad that Gene and Gus aren't around. We could have a real get-together!" Then, in explanation to Clinton Weatherby, "My daughter and son-in-law, you know. He's a doctor."

Teresina playfully slapped him on the arm, "Father, you old silly, of course Clint knows Gene and Gus. They met the day he rescued me—remember? And we've talked about them ever since."

She appeared unaware of her mother's behavior as she continued with unseemly proprietary pride, "And Clint plays! You should hear him!"

11

Clint modestly disclaimed, "Come, Zenie, old girl! I can barely pick out a tune with one finger."

"Oh, but the mouth organ, Clint! Really, Mother, he plays it beautifully."

Mrs. Rogers had to find immediate vent for her wrath. For any man to call Zenie an "old girl" was the last straw. It all went to show what a fool she was making of herself over that man, just because he happened to be good looking! She realized, at the same time, that any outburst would break her daughter's heart, so instinctively she sought an excuse to escape from the parlor.

"I'd better be seeing what kind of snack Norah is getting for supper," she improvised, as though she didn't know exactly, and marched off, her heels thumping heavily through the carpet padding of the floors. When the kitchen door swung shut behind her, she gave vent to her rage. Picking up a potholder, fortunately unbreakable, she sent it sailing across the room, while Norah, busy at the range, looked on in gap-toothed amazement.

"It's that young man of Zenie's," Mrs. Rogers explained. "I hate red-haired men, and don't ever get yourself tied up with one or you'll regret it."

Norah, all of eighteen, now, and with hair like burnished brass, but no more beautiful than when she first came to the Rogerses shortly after their move to Brooklyn—Norah had never accustomed herself completely to her mistress's tantrums. "But what about me, mum?" she wailed, "You said, yourself . . ."

"You're not a man, Norah," Mrs. Rogers interrupted, to be, in turn, cut off by Norah's protesting, "And the mister—his hair was red, before it began gettin' gray."

"No such thing! Mr. Rogers' hair is auburn—pure auburn, and hardly gray at all, I'll have you know." She paused, as the plaintive notes of a harmonica carried to the kitchen. Striking a dramatic pose, one hand on the kitchen table and the other lifted high overhead, she declaimed, "He plays the mouth organ! Next thing we know, he'll be bringing a banjo into the house. Imagine." Then, continuing a line of thought which should not have been apparent to her listener, but evidently was, "And no proposal yet, though Zenie's been throwing herself at him ever since they met. I declare, it is disgusting."

Norah's freckled, Irish face took on a look of native shrewdness that drew her pale, blue eyes into slits. With a nod of her head toward the front of the house, she suggested, "Couldn't she arrange to stay out too long with him, some time, mum? Nothin' wrong, I don't mean, but so he'd have to marry her."

The suggestion was well meant, and Mrs. Rogers accepted it in that spirit. "The morals of the Irish," she sighed. "You must understand, Norah, that Zenie comes of noble blood, even though Mr. Rogers is a Quaker—and besides, she would be just too stupid to manage it properly."

Further discussion between maid and mistress was interrupted by a fresh commotion that appeared to center at the front door. Mrs. Rogers spurred the girl with a "Hurry, Norah, and get the table set. That's Henry, or I miss my guess. There'll never come any good of working on Sunday, but there's no use telling him so, and meanwhile it'll do no harm to keep up his strength with a few victuals."

She sailed back into the parlor to welcome her only living son, who greeted her with a curt apology. "Sorry I'm late, Mother. I got tied up at the office."

It was easy enough to see what was eating Henry. He had never approved of Clinton Weatherby as a suitor for his sister, because he seemed to exist without working, while Henry, himself, did nothing else. Ever since his sweetheart had been lost at sea, more than a year ago, he had apparently locked his heart to everything but success in the coal business. It seemed a shame, especially when he was so handsome—taller than his own father—taller even than Mr. Weatherby, and filling out into a good, broad man, too, and none of your spindly sticks such as peopled New York and Brooklyn.

Much as she suspected the motives and character of Clinton Weatherby, Mrs. Rogers deprecated the rude way in which Henry avoided him, especially when Teresina's dark eyes became luminous and supplicating, asking for his help and understanding.

It was easy to appreciate the boy's feelings. He and Zenie had been at odds too long for him to realize how she had changed.

For another thing, Henry missed his twin sister, Georgina. They had always been close and Gene was like her father; no one could stay in bad spirits while she was around. Mrs. Rogers sighed. It seemed too bad that just because Gus Palmer wanted to make a martyr of himself doctoring those ignorant, foreign miners, a daughter of hers had to live in a coal town like Pottsville.

Shrugging off her regrets and assuming a gay and carefree manner, Mrs. Rogers announced, for Henry's benefit, "Mr. Weatherby has been entertaining us with a mouth organ. He plays it loud enough to hear clean in the kitchen. Supper's most ready, so hurry and wash up while Norah sets the table."

It was doubtful if Clinton Weatherby was at all affected by Henry's attitude. He was too thick skinned for that, Mrs. Rogers decided; but he pled another engagement and departed, leaving Teresina at the ungentle mercy of her mother's questioning. No sooner had Zenie turned around from the window, whence she had watched Clinton out of sight, than Mrs. Rogers began, "Him and his important engagements—who would he be going to see at this hour of a Sunday, and what does he do for a living, anyhow? That's what I'd like to know! Another day gone by—you've been out in the sleigh all afternoon and through the park, at that, which should certainly be conducive to a proposal, and not a peep out of him. Zenie, you made a great mistake throwing over a sure thing, like Mr. Hannigan."

Zenie's lower lip quivered, but she spoke firmly, "I hated Mr. Hannigan, and I love Clinton and always shall, whatever he does."

It would be impossible to say whether Mr. Rogers was more affected by mention of the greengrocer to whom his daughter had been engaged, by her being on the verge of tears, or by the pangs of hunger, as he went to her rescue. "Bosh, Gussie, I'm surprised at you, comparing a fine, upstanding, good-looking chap like Clint with that hairy ape of an Irishman and his brood of motherless children. I never approved of him in the first place, and love will find a way, I say! Now for supper, and an end to this foolishness."

This was one of the few occasions when Mr. Rogers had the last word in a discussion. He moved toward the dining room while Teresina, following, dabbed at her eyes with a dainty bit of handkerchief, and Mrs. Rogers stopped at the stairs to scream upward, "Henry, supper's late now—so hurry."

Soon all of the family were eating, to exclaim between mouth-

14

fuls, as they had been doing every mealtime for months, how strange it seemed for only four of them to be seated at the table—what with Aunt Zena gone back to France and Gene and Julia married and in homes of their own.

Chapter 2

THE WARM DAYS which had removed the last of the January snow seemed more suitable to April than to February. Young green dandelion leaves showed along the backyard fence, and one of the crocus bulbs that Mrs. Rogers had planted raised a courageous yellow bloom. In no time at all it would be a year since the East River Bridge had opened, and seven since the family had left Philadelphia and come to Brooklyn.

For all Mrs. Rogers' high hopes, their new home had proven not a whit more exciting than Kensington. In fact, it seemed hard to realize that they had ever lived anywhere but here on Cranberry Street. Mrs. Rogers sighed. They wouldn't be able to stay much longer, either, unless something turned up for Jesse. The Bridge Commission had been more than kind, keeping him on for six months after his work was practically finished, but he had been around the house now for a month or more—with nothing to do, which was bad enough in itself, in addition to which there was no money coming in.

She voiced the thought, "I declare, a man under one's feet all day is enough to try the patience of a saint." Her feeling of exasperation caused her to speak more loudly than she intended, and Norah, from the shed where she was laundering, stuck her head through the door to inquire, "What was it, mum?"

"Nothing—nothing at all!" Mrs. Rogers' curls shook in exasperation. "If you'd keep your mind on your business, you wouldn't hear the very last thing a body happens to think aloud."

15

Properly rebuffed, Norah banged the door behind her while her mistress nodded in satisfaction. "There, that will keep her for a while. Things have come to a pretty pass when I can't listen to my own thoughts without somebody snooping on them."

Returning to her previous reflections, she discounted her husband's belief that the New York aldermen whose lives he had saved some years before, would find a proper position for him. Memory was too short, for one thing, and for another, everyone knew that there were already ten times as many politicians as there were jobs for them.

Once the kitchen was redded up, she washed her hands and proceeded to the second story, while Moody and Sankey, the dachshunds, arose from their favorite corner beside the range and padded after her. As it was too much to expect Norah to do the washing and the beds; this latter task was taken over by Mrs. Rogers on Mondays, and she entered upon it with characteristic energy, shaking the sheets until they crackled, and by determined heaves changing slightly the position of the black walnut bedstead upon which she and her husband had slept for a good three decades.

Her thoughts continued while she worked. No, things couldn't go on as they were much longer. There were some well-invested remnants saved from the wreckage of an earlier Rogers' fortune, and she had various nest eggs, some in the bank and others in hiding places around the house, but the sum of all these would not keep them going. Without Henry, who was making a good salary for a boy barely come to a man's estate, the family would have had hard sledding before now. She pummeled the eiderdown pillows to give emphasis to one determination: no matter what happened, they were not going to become a burden to Henry, who would need all of his savings for future capital.

As soon as spring came they would have to dispose of Total Eclipse, what with the cost of grain and hay. Mr. Rogers' once favorite horse had grown old and heavy, and suffered considerable lameness, which she was certain would cure itself if the black were given the run of some country meadow. "I'd work my fingers to the bone before I'd sell Total Eclipse," she insisted to herself—

16

using one of her favorite phrases—"but if I could find a nice home for him with some farmer on Long Island, I'd do it."

They'd keep Mr. Quinby, of course, but perhaps they could find a smaller stable at less rent, or even board him at a livery, where Abe, the colored boy, could keep an eye on him. She was interrupted in this planning of new economies by the sound of her husband's voice, whooping from below. "Oh, Gussie, is dinner ready?"

With a gesture of annoyance, she mitered the last sheet, tucked it in hurriedly, and hastened downstairs. She noted at once a change in the expression her husband usually had when coming back from one of his work-hunting forays. "Jesse looks like the cat that swallowed the canary," she thought, but when she asked, "What has happened, Pet? You look real excited about something!" he dissembled, and with an appearance of complete innocence, replied, "Nothing has happened, except that things have been getting steadily out of whack in this household." Then holding up an admonishing hand, "Not that I blame you, my dear, it is this ridiculous business of the new time. No wonder trains are running late and there are accidents. No wonder the country is going to the dogs, when a man doesn't know what hour it is. I tell you, time is too serious a matter to trifle with. . . ."

These objections had been common since last October, when New York and Philadelphia had been put on the same time, but Father's protests were becoming increasingly vehement. It was a sign that he was feeling more like himself. Mrs. Rogers listened patiently as he went on, "According to my watch, dinner ought to be going on the table right this minute, but by that atrocious monstrosity standing on the sideboard, it is still eight minutes. . . ."

Why this was wonderful! Something had happened! Jesse hadn't fussed about the French clock for months! It was necessary, though, to offer some show of opposition so Mrs. Rogers exclaimed, "Good heavens, Pet, if you'd only change your watch, like everybody else has done, you wouldn't be mixed up at all. As for me, I never could see the sense of having so many different kinds of time. It seemed unnatural that things in Kensington might not have occurred yet, when we knew all about them."

"A misapprehension, my good woman," Mr. Rogers roared, but with no trace of irritation in his voice.

Something had surely happened! Mrs. Rogers prepared herself to meet either really good fortune or only one of Jesse's brainstorms as she called to Norah, "Get Sunday's leftovers out of the ice chest, and be quick about it. Father's early for dinner." This was at once a command to the domestic and a last, subtle dig suggesting that he was wrong about the time. This latter ordinarily would not have gone unchallenged, as the master of the house was too conscious of the fleeting minutes—but today he accepted it with the same equanimity he was according the usual Monday meal of ice-chest gleanings.

No one appreciated the value of suspense more than Mr. Rogers, but occasionally he overdid it, so that the interest of his listener was turned into exasperation. The family finished a tureen of steaming soup, the end of a roast of beef, a ham hock and assorted cold and heated-over vegetables without Mr. Rogers' rising to his wife's conversational baits. When he could no longer contain himself and came out with his news, there was little wonder that it was not more favorably received.

He wiped odd bits of food from his beard, threw his voluminous napkin on the table and proclaimed, "Well, Gussie, I've had quite a day and as I've always said, everything works out for the best. I answered a most interesting advertisement this morning—for a man of substance . . ."

Mr. Rogers' long-winded explanation did nothing to increase his wife's amiability. He announced, finally, "You see before you the Eastern District Representative of the U. S. Spring Motor Company," and withdrew from his pocket a boldly printed circular which he prepared to read when Gussie snapped it from his hand.

That was the trouble with women—you never knew how they were going to take things. Somehow he had gotten off on the wrong foot. Before he realized it he was on the defensive. "It is not selling at all but distribution," he tried to anticipate her objections, "and there'll be a good regular income after the first few weeks."

It did no good. Mrs. Rogers threw her head forward in her angriest manner. With every curl shaking, she began to read aloud from the circular and the words dripped venom. "'Successful spring motor to drive sewing machines.' Indeed! 'Ladies need no longer dread that deadly device, the treadle, with its unending train of disorders . . .'"

Her voice became even more strained as she read on, "'Backache, stooped shoulders, spinal and womb diseases, with weak ankles, and a hundred other complaints.' Jesse Rogers, you must think I'm raving crazy if you believe I'd let you go traipsing around to discuss womb diseases with God-alone-knows what females."

There was no use pursuing the matter further with Gussie in such a mood. Mr. Rogers escaped from the dining room while her tirade continued. Someday when the howls of the wolf were really at the door, he'd remind her, sadly but firmly, of the opportunities he had missed because of her senseless prejudices. Retrieving his hat from the rack in the hall, he quit the house—a man of lesser girth and stature might have been accused of sneaking from it. Slowly, almost majestically, he walked up Cranberry Street to enjoy his favorite view—the East River Bridge—which, now that he had completed it, required his services no longer. There it was, a glorious sight, indeed. Gradually, as he gazed at it, the wounds upon his spirit healed.

2

ALTHOUGH Mrs. Rogers always expected the worst, she forestalled trouble when she could. Two more weeks had gone by—spring was almost upon them and there was still no sign of a proper job for Father. It was time to make some plans of her own and with this in mind she set out for the family stable several blocks distant. Moody and Sankey, the aging dachshunds, walked sedately at her heels with none of their old scamperings. Even when Beecher, the mongrel Dalmatian, ran to greet them, as they turned the corner near the stable, the older dogs contented themselves with sniffs at the youth. Neither showed any sign that Beecher was his progeny, although dachshunds were so scarce in America and Beecher so obviously partly of the breed that one or the other must have fathered him.

Mrs. Rogers stooped to pet the little monstrosity, as Jesse always called him, and straightened again with a sigh—she couldn't bend over as she used to. The dachshunds had lost their old friskiness, Gene was married, and Julia possessed two children she had never even seen! She entered the dark stable, warmed by the presence of the animals. Yes, they were all getting old. Jesse would never get a job again at his years—she might as well make up her mind to it. The children had their own way to make. At least Julia's husband was wealthy, thank goodness—she had known how to make her bed in spite of convent upbringing. But Gene would have a hard enough time of it with Gus Palmer, even though he was a doctor, and if Zenie ever married that redheaded rapscallion . . .

The horses were nickering in pleasure at her arrival, and here she was, mooning over things that couldn't be helped. She threw her arms around Mr. Quinby's head and kissed him along the warm, velvet smoothness of his muzzle, inhaling his hay-sweet breath as though it were a perfume which she had been denied too long.

Mr. Quinby also was not as young as he had once been, as Mrs. Rogers put it, but at fourteen he was still a horse of which one could be proud. There were few animals in Brooklyn that possessed his distinguished lines and ease of gait. And how he loved his mistress! His forefeet beat a regular dance on the wooden floor of his stall and he gave soft neighs of ecstasy as though this embrace were of rare, instead of daily, occurrence.

In the next stall, Total Eclipse was almost overcome with jealousy. He threw his head wildly, rubbed against the separating partition and made other pleas for recognition. Finally his luminous dark eyes caught Mrs. Rogers' glance in a look so reproachful that she exclaimed, "I'm coming right over and give you a hug. Quinby, I've mushed over you long enough."

She bustled out of Mr. Quinby's stall and into the other, heaving her short, plump figure up on the manger, so that she could hold the black's head in her lap—careless of the golden dribble which began to spot her morning alpaca. "My poor, lame old boy . . ." Mrs. Rogers began a refreshing, sentimental cry which Total Eclipse exerted all his equine powers to assuage. "You'd never be happy with anyone else—even out in the country. So long as I have a thing to say in this family, you'll stay with us and you can count on it."

This was a promise which Mrs. Rogers was not to keep, although it eased her conscience for the moment. She slid down over wood that had been worn by years of contact with hay, grain and the questing noses of horses. Straightening her clothes, she tsch'd over the damage done to her dress by the black's slobber. "Well, it's old anyway and don't much matter."

She gave her shoulders a Latin shrug. "I come out here to think and this is what I get into. If only I had someone with whom to talk over what I have in mind," she wished, aloud. In the manner usual to her, she had been formulating a plan for some months, allowing it to simmer in the back of her mind like soup on the far end of the range.

"It stands to reason that things can't go on as they are. We're under too much expense—and the house is bigger than we need with Gene and Julia married, but not big enough to rent rooms and make it pay. If we could find a larger place in New York it wouldn't cost much more than here. If we couldn't buy at once we might rent for a while. I could get an upstairs girl to help Norah and with Zenie and myself we could manage the housework. Father could do the marketing and keep everyone in spirits—he'd like that. I do believe we could make a go of it."

Yes, the plan was a good one, if Father and Henry could be won over. Mrs. Rogers began her daily inspection with a new peace of mind. She had never been satisfied with the stable and hoped that they might find one in New York that had more light and air. From habit she ran her hand along the carriage and looked in shocked surprise at her smudged fingers and the dust marks on the varnish. Where was Abe? She'd have to give him Hail Columbia. She called his name at the top of her voice, then remembered that for the last week he had been working in the garden, in anticipation of spring, so there was some excuse for his negligence. She intended to give him a dressing-down nevertheless, and began to think back over past derelictions to work herself up to a proper pitch of anger.

The boy's arrival defeated her purpose. He ran in, greeting her with a hasty, "Mornin', Mis' Rogers. Just come up to give this

21

place a lick. It ain't as clean as I like to see it." The expression on his smiling, cocoa-complexioned features was one of love and devotion. He observed the dust on the carriage, but there was no sign that he feared a tongue-lashing.

Mrs. Rogers looked with secret approval at the healthy, well-built youth who had grown from the thin, tattered street urchin she had taken in years before. A mixture of charity and practicality had impelled that action and Abe had always earned his keep and sleeping place in the stable, but she felt nevertheless a warm glow of self-satisfaction. Abe was a credit to her generosity, and a good servant. As he stood there, dressed in clothes that Henry had outgrown, he looked almost handsome. Instead of the tirade he expected, she limited herself to a few well-chosen remarks on the subject of laziness among Negroes, whistled for the dachshunds to follow and set out for the house, conscious of a morning well spent.

### 3

Mrs. Rogers chose with great care the proper moment to present her plan. Father had just finished the first chapter of his regular evening peroration on the widespread condition of unemployment. Teresina was still toying with her dinner in a manner unbecoming a girl who wanted to keep up a fashionable weight. Henry was hurrying through a second dish of home-preserved rhubarb—a dessert in which Mrs. Rogers had great confidence as a blood purifier. Norah was in the kitchen—out of sight, but not beyond hearing. As part of her plan depended upon the young maid-of-all-work, Mrs. Rogers was quite content that she eavesdrop.

In another minute Henry would be off to his room, so she had to talk rapidly and without any of the little introductory remarks, relevant or irrelevant, with which she usually began long tirades. "Why anyone would want to stay over here in Brooklyn when there's New York to live in. We'd make a handsome profit if we sold here—enough to put down on a larger place. I have some nice brownstone in mind, uptown. Around Twenty-third Street, maybe."

Henry appeared unconvinced, so she turned toward him. "And

look at the hours you would save. Every time you take the ferry of a morning I wonder if you'll come back safe."

She had gotten on touchy ground with Mr. Rogers. "Why Henry should want to use those antiquated craft after I spent seven years of my life building a bridge . . ."

"It's the cars, Father. Either the engines or the cables are always getting out of order. If they had put in trains in the first place . . ."

"I advised it," Mr. Rogers began. This was not strictly true, but instead of arguing the matter, Mrs. Rogers agreed. "Well, they wouldn't listen to you and Henry can't afford to be late all the time. In New York he'd be closer to the office and rent from the extra rooms would keep us nicely."

Mr. Rogers objected. Hooking a thumb through his watch chain, he proclaimed, "If you are intimating that we start a boarding house, I'll hear no more of it. I refuse to end my days in that last resort of the indigent and ineffectual—in that . . ."

While he searched for a further comparison, his wife interrupted, reasonably, "Not a boarding house at all, a . . ."

"A rooming house, then. Redolent with the odor of insecticide."

"How you do snap one up, Jesse. I had in mind a genteel residence where we could extend the privilege of our home to a few guests—paying ones." Never had Mrs. Rogers expressed a thought more neatly and she gave a little smirk of satisfaction, holding her head sideways like a particularly pert and plump English sparrow, while she observed with bright, black eyes the effect upon her husband and children.

In a manner which showed again the great change which had taken place in her character, Teresina exclaimed, "I think it is wonderful, Mother. We'd be right in New York—in the heart of things—and making money besides. I could help with the housework. . . ."

Henry also approved—in more restrained fashion. "It might work at that. I'd save time, certainly. And we better face the fact that Father will never get another job."

The brutally frank words were said before Mrs. Rogers could create a diversion, so she launched into a spirited defense. "Henry Rogers, I have never heard anything so outrageous. Your father has had the most splendid opportunities, but I have put my foot

23

down because I've had this in mind. We'd be in business for ourselves—and I've been counting on Father to act as host. No one
could do it better and it would be like old times having a big
family again. I declare, it gives me the creeps with only the four of
us at table. Besides, you're so wrapped up in business you might as
well stay at the office, for all we ever see of you. Of all the ungrate-
ful, unsocial, un-un . . . Henry, there are times when you make
me sick."

When his wife finally ran out of breath Mr. Rogers interposed,
with unusual gentleness, "No, Gussie, I guess Henry is right. What
with the condition of things I don't see much chance for an old
codger like me. If I can help, I'm quite willing. . . ."

Mrs. Rogers was shaken by his tone—and more so when he continued, "I've been feeling pretty blue these last weeks, under everything else. I just couldn't see any hope ahead, though I've tried to
keep up a pretense. I'm glad Henry saw through it and said so—
and I'm grateful to you, my dear. . . ."

For Jesse actually to admit that he was stumped was too much.
And he had been worrying right along, when she thought him perfectly content with the way things were. The poor dear! Suddenly
her lower lip began to tremble. Her bosom heaved in its tight confines. She jumped up, ran around the table and threw herself upon
his lap—less to his discomfiture than to that of the children, who
had never before witnessed so demonstrative a display of affection
between their parents.

Mrs. Rogers clung unashamedly to Jesse's broad form and copi-
ous tears saturated his beard as she wailed into it. "Oh, Pet, you
are the most wonderful man—and things are going to work out all
right, I'm certain of it."

The poignant family scene was ruined by a most untimely interruption. Clinton Weatherby appeared in the dining-room doorway, to see Mr. Rogers, with eyes suspiciously moist, comforting
his wife. Zenie was sobbing quietly and Henry's grave expression
contributed to the misunderstanding. "Hello, folks. Good gosh,
what's happened? Somebody die?"

Mrs. Rogers slid down, ashamed to have been caught in so intimate a position. If that wasn't just like Clinton Weatherby, walking right into the dining room without so much as a by-your-leave.

24

Actually, this was unfair, as the Rogerses had been too occupied with their emotions to hear the bell which Norah had answered.

Zenie ran to greet Clinton. Henry muttered excuses and disappeared into the hall. Mrs. Rogers dried her eyes and assumed what dignity she could, considering that her curls were awry and her dress rumpled. Putting on an expression of gaiety and throwing one hand high in a manner which was intended to be carefree, she exclaimed, "Mr. Weatherby! I'm afraid that I didn't hear your knock. I was telling Father about a scene from a play and clean forgot myself. I overacted, I suppose. . . ."

Teresina interrupted a stream of explanations, each of which was less convincing than the preceding one. Despite her mother's look of vexation, she blurted out, "Clint, you are just in time to hear the news. We are going to take a huge house in New York and establish a genteel residence for paying guests."

"Zenie," Mrs. Rogers cried, in what was little less than a scream.

"Why Mother, your exact words. Isn't it a wonderful idea?"

Even while Mrs. Rogers anticipated what was to come, she couldn't help admitting that Clinton Weatherby had a certain coarse and animal handsomeness as he shouted, "You bet it's wonderful. It's capital!" And then, as though struck by an inspiration, "I tell you what—you already have a guest. I'll rent the second floor front and be your star boarder."

Chapter 3

THE WAY in which he had acceded to his wife's plans was regretted many times by Mr. Rogers during the ensuing weeks. Sentiment had disarmed him. If he had refused to have anything to do with the project until a suitable house had been found, he would have been spared dreary hours of climbing up and down stoops and stairs, bumping his head in cellars, or peering into closets. He would not have had to

25

listen to Gussie discuss matters of freeholding and leaseholding, of deeds, mortgages, and titles, with a seemingly unending procession of real estate agents.

He was astounded at her apparent knowledge of all these matters and it was deflating to his own ego to listen as she talked with perfect ease about subjects concerning which he was most hazy. No doubt about it, Gussie was a wonderful woman, not only in the way she pursued negotiations over a dozen or more properties, but in her powers of endurance. After a day of house hunting he was completely tired out, ready to spend the evening in slippers and semi-somnolence until a nine o'clock bedtime.

Mrs. Rogers, on the other hand, could sit up all night and discuss the places they had visited during the day, comparing them with those seen yesterday, the previous Friday, or two weeks before. She always identified each house by some characteristic which was not recalled by her husband. "The house with the door" meant the one with some particular door. There was "the place with the areaway," and the one "without an areaway." There was "the brownstone with the windows," and "the brownstone—you know the one I mean."

Mr. Rogers' confusion at these terms should have been understandable enough, but his wife was irritated when he did not instantly recognize the house she had in mind. "Jesse, you are too annoying. I don't believe you care at all what happens to us and would rather starve here in Brooklyn than make a change. It was the only house that had such a lovely grille on the door—a grape design, most natural, and the tendrils went off into little springs that looked quite effective. Anyone coming to the door would recognize immediately that we were persons of taste and refinement."

"If my tramping down every sidewalk in the city isn't proof of my interest, I don't know what is. I tell you, Gussie, I'm tired and my feet hurt. Good taste or bad taste, those grape tendrils in wrought iron—which I remember now—didn't look very beautiful to me. Iron doesn't seem to be a proper material for representing something as delicate as vegetation of any sort and the springs appeared better suited for those new bedsteads."

Between discussions such as this, Mrs. Rogers pursued others of a quite different nature with Teresina, until Norah remarked to

26

Abe one day that she missed the peace and quiet which had hitherto always characterized the Rogers' family life.

The subject of Clinton Weatherby took second place only to house hunting. "What does he *do*, Zenie? If you hadn't lost all of your spunk you would up and ask him. With all his talk of important engagements I don't think he worked a tap last winter. Now not a sign of him since Tuesday. Don't tell me that you know where he is, because I can tell from your expression that you don't. He was away like that once before, too, and not a word of explanation."

"But Mother, Clinton has no need to explain. We're not engaged, though I wish we were. . . ."

"Not another word out of you. I've never seen anyone so spineless and shameless. If giving almost a year to a man doesn't entitle you to some consideration . . ."

"I owe my life to Clinton Weatherby. . . ."

"Pshaw, Zenie, I don't believe that he saved you at all. He was probably there just to prey on some unattended female. But that is neither here nor there. When we find the new house I won't have him in it. Second floor front! The very nerve of him. And you throwing yourself at him the minute he opens the door. No wonder he has never proposed. He looks on you as an easy mark, that's why. He's just waiting his opportunity. Never fear, I'll see that he doesn't get it."

"Clint has never been anything but honorable in his actions—I wish he had."

"Teresina Rogers! Talk like that from a girl of your years. If your father were here, I'd have him spank you."

"I wish you'd stop pretending that I'm still a child. I'm almost thirty and you know it. I don't care what Clint is or does. . . ."

By this time, both women were giving full play to their Latin temperaments. Never had Teresina looked so beautiful as now. She stood inches above her mother, with arms straight and hands clenched. Her oval face, flashing black eyes that were heightened by thick raven's wings of eyebrows, full lips twisted in anger, the narrow waist and rounded bosom all combined to give her an attractiveness that had always been proud and haughty, but in which richness and fire had replaced cold reserve. In a supreme

27

gesture, she concluded, "He is my only chance for happiness and I'd go to him any time or any place."

Although Mrs. Rogers had often chastised the other children, she had never struck Teresina, but this fresh defiance made her quite beside herself. "I won't have any daughter of mine talk to me like a hussy. Take that, and that—and get up to your room!"

Slaps on the mouth and cheek raised pink flushes on Teresina's otherwise flawless olive skin. For one unbelieving moment she felt the spots, then burst into tears and ran for the stairway while her mother watched in short-lived satisfaction.

Later, when Mr. Rogers noted Zenie's reproachful manner and commented upon it while both parents prepared for bed, Mrs. Rogers explained, "Nothing but a little spat we had over that awful Weatherby man. Young women are so impressionable."

Mr. Rogers interrupted with a roar that was slightly smothered by the nightshirt he was in the act of donning. "Indeed they are. I remember how you were at her age. That must have been about the time I first met you, when you were starry eyed over that little dude—what was his name?"

There was vinegar in Mrs. Rogers' reply. "I wouldn't be wearing myself out looking for a roof over our heads if I had married him, anyway—and if you think I was as old as Zenie is now you are very much mistaken. Perhaps you do not realize it, but that daughter of yours is practically an old maid. Not that you've ever tried to do anything about it. . . ."

There was much creaking of the oversized walnut bed as Mr. Rogers prepared for a well-earned rest. Finally, he answered blandly, "You were older than twenty-three, Gussie, which has been Zenie's age for a good many years, if one goes by the figures in our Bible—and surely the good old book can't lie."

2

WHEN, in May, Mr. Rogers' constant predictions of national disaster seemed about to be realized with the Wall Street panic, it had no adverse effect on the Rogers' fortunes—or lack of them. He hated General Grant too thoroughly ever to have invested in his firm, which was one of the chief sufferers. With the news of the

28

failure of the Grant and Ward partnership Mr. Rogers found vindication for his attitude toward the country's great general and still-popular ex-president.

"The man is a rascal and I knew it from the first. It's a sign of the low moral state of the nation that he wasn't impeached at the time of the gold scandal. The connection between Grant and his nephew was plain enough then, and a president who uses his office for the financial benefit of one of his family is as dishonest as though he used it for himself."

"Oh, Pet, how you do go on. That's all over and done with. . . ."

"Nothing's ever over and done with. Right now deserving investors have been flimflammed by General Grant and his partner. To say that Grant had no knowledge of what was going on is to say that he was an idiot, which I don't believe for a moment."

Within a few days, further disclosures brought Mr. Rogers dashing into the parlor. He gave the impression that his wife was the sole remaining defender of the ex-president. "Here Gussie, try and get out of this. A man named Fish—James D. Fish—has just made public a letter he received from Grant, giving the assurance that the Grant and Ward profits were genuine and came from lucrative government contracts. If that doesn't prove that he was a swindler, what could?"

Mrs. Rogers pursed her lips and fixed her excited husband with a glance. "I've heard of nothing but Grant and his stupidities ever since the Civil War and I'm heartily sick and tired of them. If you had as much sense as he had, you'd think of your family too. Take this affair of Zenie's, for instance. All winter long that man hung around this house almost night and day—but did you try to find out anything about him?"

Without waiting for an answer, she went on, shrewishly, "It was impossible to get shut of him most of the time. He couldn't have done any work and he's not a man of means, I'll warrant that. Wealth carries distinction. . . ."

"Perhaps he lives on air. If so, he thrives on it."

"He thrives on our good food, as you very well know."

"Oh, come, Gussie. You never begrudged any of the other girls' suitors a few meals. Besides, I haven't seen him around for a week or more."

"I'm surprised you noticed." The sarcasm was heavy and not to be ignored.

"First you complain because he's here all the time and now jump on me because he isn't here. By the Lord Harry, you females are incomprehensible."

"At least we care about things that are near and dear to us, instead of worrying over somebody we've only seen once in our lives. After haunting this house all winter, he hasn't been around for a week and not a word of explanation out of him. Poor Zenie is getting to look like a freak, from moping."

"Perhaps they've had a spat. You know, my dear, the course of true love."

"Bosh. Zenie hasn't confided in me, her own mother, but that's not it, I'm sure. I tell you, Pet, there is something very strange about him. Several times before he wasn't around for a few days, then came back without a by-your-leave and as fresh and insolent as ever. Couldn't you find out what he does—follow him, or something?"

Finally aware of the full measure of Gussie's apprehension, he patted her shoulder. "Now, now, I don't think there is a thing for you to worry about. I've always been adept at reading character and Weatherby's fine open features indicate high principles, but if it will satisfy you any, I'll engage in a little detective work. I'll trail him so that he shan't see me, and find out just what he is up to."

The idea that her husband could go anywhere and not be the most visible thing in the landscape so tickled Mrs. Rogers' sense of humor that she giggled, then laughed. When he began to think that she was becoming hysterical, she walked over and kissed him full on the lips. "Jesse Rogers, you do try a woman's patience at times, but you are a dear and I love you—much as I thought I'd never be able to."

This was a cryptic remark and better not explored. With a pleased grin on his face, Mr. Rogers forgot about family problems and gave himself up to the enjoyment of righteous indignation.

FROM THE VERY BEGINNING, Henry had disliked Teresina's newest suitor, and when he noticed Clint's prolonged absence, he expressed satisfaction to his mother. "I hope he's gone for good. I'm all for this move to New York, but I was dead set against letting that fly-by-night stay with us. I walked to the ferry with him one day. Not that I wanted to, but he insisted. Over a dozen people hello'd to him. A person so well known can't be respectable."

Mr. Rogers took this moment to make his appearance. "Why can't he, pray? I know more than twelve people. I suppose I'm not respectable?"

"You'd stand up for anybody. What does he do, that's what I want to know."

This was no time to take Henry to task for his increasingly disrespectful attitude toward his father, but Mrs. Rogers intended to do so later. She retorted sharply, "Your father has promised to follow him the next time he comes around—if he ever does."

"Eh, what's that?"

"Last night you offered to find out what he was up to."

"Oh, yes, so I did. But do you think it's altogether honorable?"

"Not honorable for a father to find out whether his daughter is being made a fool of?"

"All right, if you insist." Mr. Rogers paused as a sneer marred his son's expression. "As for you, Henry, I shall prove that your father, whom you have come to hold in such contempt, still has considerable power of judgment. I'll follow Mr. Weatherby to his lair just to prove that you are both making a mountain out of a molehill."

By the time that he had finished mixing his metaphors, Henry was on his way to the ferry and Mrs. Rogers was impatient for house hunting. "This is Norah's day off and she'll be gone as soon as I'm out of the house—though what she does with herself for a whole day is more than I can figure out. There's a place that sounds interesting, but it is pretty far uptown. You'll be in the way more than not, so you might as well pick up a lunch from the ice chest and hang around, just in case Clint should turn up, as he may. Personally, I think that Mr. Weatherby is much too smart for you to cope with."

The taunt was forgotten by noon, when Zenie—contrary to instructions—prepared a surprisingly good meal. "There'll be cold cuts for dinner, so I thought you should have something hot," she explained.

"But what about you? These luscious viands look too good to be eaten alone. . . ."

"I'm not hungry—and there are some things I have to do upstairs." She was gone before Mr. Rogers could do more than reflect upon the foolishness of females, who would shun good food merely because of a little heartbreak.

When Teresina closed the door to her room, a moment later, she did much more than shut out the world. For long years this chamber had been a temple dedicated to her own beauty, with herself the worshiper—but the old goddess was forgotten. Now, as she looked at herself in the mirror, she wondered how she had contented herself during those past, barren years. She thought of a long procession of beaux and regretted the cold remoteness, the cruelty and meanness she had shown them. A number of men had fallen in love with her, but there were only two for whom she had felt any affection. When Philippe married her sister Julia she had been outraged, but underneath there had been secret amusement that he had been satisfied with someone of lesser beauty. Later, when Georgina ran away to Pottsville and Dr. Palmer, she had been hurt and annoyed. In retrospect she was shocked at the false sense of values that she had possessed.

This had not been the full extent of her folly. Suppose she had married Mr. Hannigan out of fear of spinsterhood? To care for a brood of motherless little Hannigans! To put up with the awful greengrocer himself!

Then Clinton Weatherby had come along. She treasured that first memory of him as he had stood on the Brooklyn Bridge—laughing and fearless among a lot of puny, frightened creatures like Mr. Hannigan. That event had wrought so complete a change in Teresina's point of view that instead of believing that she must be loved by him because of her beauty, she wondered how Clint had put up with her conceit.

Probably it had taken this long for him to see through her. He had told her that he would be away for a few days, but had offered

32

no explanation. He did not intend to return and she couldn't find it in her heart to blame him. Then, having faced the most awful future she could imagine—one that did not include Clint—she began to console herself with remembered words, attitudes or looks that indicated he did love her and would come back. Hadn't he been gone on these mysterious visits before?

But they had been of only three days' duration. This was practically a week. And what was he doing? Resolutely, she closed her mind to speculation. Whenever he chose to confide in her would be soon enough. She had come to believe that any display of her former selfishness would drive him away.

She walked to the window and looked over the long, narrow garden, bright in its green spring dress, and reached a decision. If Clint did not come back she would actually do what Julia had once talked about. She would become a nun and spend the remainder of her life making up for her early, intolerable pride. This sudden resolve brought fresh prickings of conscience. She hadn't been to Mass for months. All during their youth, the Church had played a large part in the lives of the Rogers' daughters—a reaction partially due to their father's lax Quakerism. Some of the happiest occasions she could recall had been those when she had worn a new dress to a service. Neither humility nor the desire to worship had taken her there, but pride in her appearance and the desire to display her beauty before the congregation.

When they had moved to Brooklyn, going to Mass had become a bore. The new priest harangued them with long, dull talks—about the immodesty of feminine clothing, the frivolousness of the times. Perhaps with Father Duffy there it would have been different. Even Father—who hated priests—loved Father Duffy.

Then Sunday mornings began to make her realize that both beauty and the hours were fleeting—that of desperate necessity she must attract an eligible man among the worshipers. She knew now that she must have cut a pathetic figure. Among men, proper appreciation of religion belonged to middle age and not to youth—and her very manner must have driven away the more desirable among them.

No, Church had held too much unhappiness. Since meeting Clint she hadn't gone at all. Besides, Mr. Hannigan belonged to the parish and she couldn't bear the thought of even seeing him again. It was one of the few things about which her mother had shown understanding. Not only had she avoided the subject with Teresina, but she rarely went herself. Teresina wondered if this growing carelessness were not the insidious effect of their religiously divided household. She said a little prayer of contrition, another that included her parents and a last, impassioned plea that she might see Clinton Weatherby just once more.

Some might say that prayers are not answered. Here was ample proof that they are. From below came the familiar boom of her father's voice, talking to someone. Mother was out and Norah gone for the day. Who could it be? She answered the question to her own satisfaction as she fled to the stairs, then made a frantic effort to compose herself as Clint's voice turned her knees to water. She caught a phrase he was saying. "Out of town a few days." A few days! It had been a millennium. The reserve expected of women seemed impossibly cruel, but she managed to stand erect and smile shyly as Clint said, "I stopped around as soon as I got back, Zenie. I have to run along now, but I was wondering if I could see you this evening?"

She found herself saying, "Of course, Clint, of course," and could hear her father's hearty invitation, "It's Norah's afternoon out, so there'll be a pot-luck supper. I hate it myself. I believe in hot food and plenty of it. Cold things don't fill you, but you are welcome to share with us. . . ."

"I don't think I'll be done in time, thank you." Clint smiled infectiously. "I can't tell you how much I feel at home here, Mr. Rogers, and how good it is to see you again—and you too, Zenie."

He was gone, but Teresina was too full of her immediate happiness to be regretful. Then Father began to behave peculiarly. He had started to resume his seat at the table, from which Clint's visit had stirred him, when he appeared to think better of it. Dashing to the clothes rack in the hall, he reached for his best hat, hesitated a moment, and snatched his gray felt stovepipe instead. Teresina watched after him in amazement as he hurried down the street in the same direction in which Clinton Weatherby was fast disappearing from view.

34

**Chapter 4**

FOR THE LAST HALF-HOUR Mr. Rogers had been regretting the impulsiveness that caused him to volunteer as a detective, although he complimented himself that he was doing a good job in shadowing his man. Once the gauntlet had been thrown down and he had taken it up—once the quarry was pointed out and he sniffed the scent—once embarked upon a course, through fair weather or foul—with these, and other comparisons he drummed up the volition to continue what had become a long and wearying chase. He seemed further from the end of it than ever, as Clint disappeared into a rough, wooden structure far ahead.

A barefooted boy trotted past and Mr. Rogers intercepted him. "My lad, what is that meadow—those buildings?"

There was unconcealed contempt for his ignorance in the answer—which helped him not at all. "Washington Park."

"Indeed! Washington Park. A locality new to me . . ." This was the prelude to a further question, but his informant had broken into a trot and was half a block away. He followed the way Clint had gone, so intent upon catching sight of him again that he was completely taken aback when someone seized him by the arm and spoke in a nasty and menacing voice. "Oh, no you don't, mister. Twenty-five cents admission or out you go—on your ear."

At another time, Mr. Rogers would have disputed with this fellow for his uncouth behavior, but the last thing he wanted was to bring attention to himself. He held out a twenty-five cent coin and retorted in a voice which was, for him, most restrained, "I apologize, sir. I had no idea that an admission was required to enter here . . ." and was hurried along by an impatient line of men behind him.

Ahead was an open field, framed by wooden grandstands already well filled with spectators. It required no great acumen to realize that this was a baseball field, a sport held in such low repute that Mr. Rogers knew almost nothing about it. To avoid further jostling he took an empty seat on one of the lower benches, while he up-braided himself for coming thus far only to lose his quarry. A hawker came through the stands, selling steins of beer, one of which Mr. Rogers purchased while he considered what to do next. Much as he hated to return home and admit failure to Gussie, there seemed nothing else to be done. He drank the beverage and balanced the empty stein on his knee while he mopped his fore-head, sweaty from his exertions and the late May sun. Almost be-fore he knew it, all hope of exit was cut off by a late influx of spectators. A dozen or more players in uniform dashed out upon the parklike field. He was conscious of various unmannerly cries of "Remove that tile," and glanced around to observe the reason. Someone jabbed him in the back and someone else bellowed into his ear, "Take off the lid," before he realized that the references were to his own high hat, which towered above less distinguished bowlers and caps.

He removed the offending headgear, placing it carefully on his knees, but he was already in the bad graces of the people behind him. Hatless, Mr. Rogers was still an obstruction to those un-fortunates. "Does that old codger think he's made of glass?" and "Hey, mister, got a pane in your back?" were only two of the witti-cisms which he chose to ignore.

Attention again reverted to the field, where the players threw balls aimlessly backward and forward, and Mr. Rogers' discom-fiture was forgotten in his surprise at the skill exhibited as the men reached out unerringly to catch the speeding missiles. He ques-tioned the man next to him. "I presume that these are the teams that are about to indulge in a game. Would you be good enough to tell me who is playing?"

Without removing his eyes from the scene in front, the man spoke out of the corner of his mouth. "Toledo."

"And who is opposing them, may I ask?"

"The Brooklyns, of course. Who would it be?"

There was no use in taking offense at the other's laconic manner, for the game was now under way. At each corner of a cleared-off, diamond-shaped track a player moved restlessly. Further out, three other men ranged themselves. A short, stocky fellow, with mutton-chop whiskers, took his place in the center of the diamond and a man with a bat faced him. Someone who was not in uniform took up a position behind mutton chops, who suddenly hurled a ball at the batter. There was a sharp crack, the ball went high in the air and was caught with ridiculous ease by one of the Brooklyns.

Another batter stepped up and again mutton chops threw. The un-uniformed man shouted something and there was a roar of disapproval—shouts of "Murder the umpire," and "Robber."

Mr. Rogers found himself yelling with the rest, and much more loudly, because of superior vocal equipment. Then there was a change of sides and further unfortunate decisions to be objected to. Gradually the pattern of the game became clear. One had so many opportunities to hit the ball and then was out. A certain number of outs changed the sides. Circling the bases after a hit meant a run. The man who threw the ball was the pitcher and the one who received it was the catcher. The basemen were named in numerical order and between second and third base was an extra man called a short-stopper. Those beyond were outfielders.

By the fourth inning it was evident that the two teams were well matched. Then the Toledoes seemed to be getting a little the better of it, much to everyone's disgust—including Mr. Rogers'. By this time he had practically forgotten the reason for his presence. Then a huzzah went up at the appearance of a man whose red hair was instantly recognizable. By some quirk of the game, Clint did not immediately take part, but began to toss balls to another player.

"Why don't they put him in?" Mr. Rogers asked his neighbor.

"Warming up . . ."

"Warming up?" That didn't make much sense, but the laconic one made no further explanation. There was another sharp crack, the ball disappeared beyond a distant fence and a Toledo player raced around the bases. This wouldn't do at all. If it kept up, Brooklyn would lose, and Mr. Rogers didn't intend that to happen. His hitherto taciturn neighbor furnished an inspiration by shouting, "We want Weatherby! We want Weatherby!" and Mr. Rogers took up the cry.

His voice, dwarfing all others, boomed over the playing field. A startled Clint recognized the familiar accents, and waved in the general direction of a wildly disheveled, bearded giant who remotely resembled Zenie's father.

Suddenly Mr. Rogers remembered that he was supposed to be inconspicuous, but consoled himself with two thoughts: he *had* discovered Clint's occupation; and it was impossible that he could be identified among all those wildly cheering men.

There was another crack of bat against ball. Another Toledo player sped around the bases. Apparently the Brooklyn team was becoming demoralized. The players went into a huddle on the field. The man with the mutton chops threw down his glove and walked disconsolately away. Clint took his place and tried a practice pitch, while Mr. Rogers, careless of recognition, again found himself shouting.

In spite of his apparent coolness and deliberation, Clinton Weatherby's thoughts were in a turmoil as he faced the next batter. So at last his secret was out. He might as well give up all hope of Teresina Rogers. Her mother didn't like him anyway and when she found out he was a baseball player he wouldn't be allowed in the house. And Zenie herself—he should have told her long ago and been done with it. No really nice girl, as she was, would want a sporting man for a husband, even one who had reached the pinnacle.

He spat on the ball and slowly measured his adversary, standing with poised bat, when again Mr. Rogers boomed forth. Did ever a player deserve so able a rooter? The old man was on his side, anyway. Though everything was lost so far as Zenie was concerned, he'd show *him* what he could do. He whipped his arm under in a throw so fast that for a moment everyone thought the ball had been hit by the wildly-swinging batter, because of its impact in the catcher's mitt. He threw a second ball with equal speed and accuracy—a third, and the side was retired.

It was now the turn of Mr. Rogers' neighbor to question him. "Good old Weatherby. Struck him out on three straight pitches. You seem acquainted with him, mister?"

Mr. Rogers smiled quietly into his beard, shrugged his shoulders in deprecation, and explained, modestly, "Just a friend of the family's."

38

THE HILL up toward the Heights always winded Mrs. Rogers before she reached the Cranberry Street house, but she climbed it today with no lessening of pace. Her short, quick, determined steps beneath her ample skirts, carried her forward without any apparent means of locomotion, like one of the new screw launches under full steam.

While she looked placid enough, she was bursting with excitement and with the feeling that she had, this day, fought destiny singlehanded and vanquished it. Subject to Jesse's approval and signature, she had actually purchased a house. And such a house—at a price so much lower than they had expected that it was almost unbelievable. Why if they could sell Cranberry Street for anywhere near the price it should bring they could swing the whole deal without anything but a little assistance from Zena. Her wealthy sister had always offered financial help and now, for the first time in her life, Mrs. Rogers was going to accept it—on condition that any small loan would be scrupulously repaid. She was so full of her plans that she did not realize how rapidly she was walking. By the time she reached her own front door and pulled the bell she was short of breath. She pulled again, then remembered that that was Norah's day off. But where was Jesse? Or Zenie? She fumbled through her bag, searching for the key.

Impatient at the absence of her family and the anticlimax of being unable to tell her news immediately, she let herself in, shooed the dachshunds from her dress as they greeted her, had a word for Jenny Lind, the canary, who began to trill his loudest, then plumped into a kitchen chair. There was a sound of movement from upstairs. "Mother, is that you?"

"Of course it is. Who did you think it was?"

Zenie made her appearance almost immediately, and Mrs. Rogers said, impatiently, "You might at least have answered the door when I rang. You know how much trouble I have finding a key."

"I didn't hear, Mother. Truly I didn't. And Mother, Clint stopped in after lunch. I'm so happy."

"What explanation did he make for his behavior?"

"I didn't ask. He's coming this evening. Perhaps . . ."

"How a girl with your looks can be so bamboozled. Well, your parents intend to know what is going on. Your father is going to follow him and will have a pretty story to tell."

"Is that why Father behaved so queerly? What an awful thing to do, spying on someone I love."

"We are determined to find out what Clint does with himself. A man ought to be working in the daytime, and not be on the loose."

"But Clint can't help notice Father, if he follows him. He'll never speak to me again—never, never."

"He's probably leading your father a merry chase. Suppertime and not back yet. What can have happened? And there is Norah at the back door."

Instead of Norah it was Mr. Rogers, the reason for his choice of the back entrance immediately discernible. The crown of his hat was dented, his collar was undone and tie awry. A scratch on his temple was backed by the saffron of a bruise.

"Oh, my goodness, Pet. You're hurt."

"Nothing at all, my dear." There was a deep, vibrant thrill, a strange excitement in Mr. Rogers' voice. "We were robbed, that's what—and in the excitement a few of us began to throw beer steins."

"Robbed? Beer steins? Jesse Rogers, are you in your senses? Who was throwing beer steins at who, I'd like to know?"

"We were robbed." There was righteous indignation in Mr. Rogers' voice. "The Brooklyns were robbed. Do you lack civic feeling, woman? The steins were thrown at the umpire, although I'm afraid that several hit me, inadvertently."

Mrs. Rogers sank back in the chair, her mouth slack, but in a short time she gathered her wits while Jesse went on about strikes, runs, fouls, and other incomprehensibles. Once, long ago, he had come home in a state that was suspiciously like this. She rose, faced him and sniffed, but except for an odor of stale beer, for which the steins might account, he had not been drinking. She commanded sharply, "Stop this gibberish. You left this house to follow Clinton Weatherby. Where . . . ?"

"You haven't a thing to worry about—or you, Zenie." Mr. Rogers

40

struck the pose of a Fourth of July orator. "Even in defeat, Clinton Weatherby was a hero. The pride of Brooklyn."

Never had Jesse been so exasperating, speaking first in one kind of riddle and then in another. Norah would be home any second and shouldn't see her master in this state. Mrs. Rogers therefore pushed him out of the kitchen and up the stairs while he continued his voluble, though incomprehensible explanations.

"He doesn't know that I followed him, of course. I managed quite adroitly to keep out of sight. I was discretion itself in the park—though I may have become a trifle excited after the umpire called Clint out when he was palpably safe. It gave the game to Toledo."

Mrs. Rogers' voice rose to a wail. "Zenie, see if you can make your father talk sense. What is he raving about? What does he mean?"

"I mean, my dear Zenie, that your suitor, and the man I hope will be our future son-in-law, is the finest baseball player in Brooklyn, a credit to the city and to us."

## 3

It wasn't what Jesse had reported that was so important, but the outrageous state in which he had come home. Taking part in a free-for-all with beer steins—admitting throwing them, no less. It proved the debasing character of baseball better than any argument that she could have used. Mrs. Rogers harped on it all through dinner.

"How much does a ballplayer make, anyway?" Henry asked. "Four dollars a week, maybe. Why I get twice as much right now."

"Who cares what he makes? He's a ragamuffin consorting with other ragamuffins. Look at the way your father came home—his second best hat ruined—and then for him to sit there . . ."

Mr. Rogers tried to stem what was becoming a full-fledged tirade, directed against him and not at Weatherby in the illogical manner of his wife. It was time to assert himself, which he did by drowning out everyone else. "Understand once and for all that Clint is not just an ordinary player. He is the one who hurls the pellets. His skill is known to everyone in Brooklyn. We have been

41

harboring a famous man whose innate modesty alone has prevented him from revealing the truth."

"A fig for everybody in Brooklyn!" Mrs. Rogers screamed, her hands lifted high in an Italian gesture of rage. This was a sign that she was at her most dangerous, and Mr. Rogers returned to the cold neat's tongue that eked out the pot-luck supper.

Having silenced her husband, Mrs. Rogers turned her barbs upon Teresina, who had been listening to the discussion with an expression of such sweet happiness that she could hardly have been recognized for the sullen, disappointed beauty of a year before. "I suppose you are satisfied, now that I've been proven right. Wasting almost a year upon such a man—a common baseball player! I tell you, Zenie, his whole character is written on his face. . . ."

She paused and then was suddenly stricken with compassion for this daughter whom she really loved the best of her children. "There's no sense in not eating some of those potatoes. You are falling off in weight terribly and you shouldn't. Things happen in everyone's life and you'll forget Clint in no time. I know this must have been a blow."

"It is not a blow at all. It seems almost like good news, in fact. I always expected that Clint did something so much worse that he had real cause to be ashamed. Something like—well, something that an unmarried girl might not be supposed to know about. I didn't know just what, but I had some horrid ideas, really horrid ones. Not that anything would have made any difference to me, but this is just a kind of relief, a wonderful relief."

Toward the end of this impassioned statement she began to cry, then jumped up, ran to her father and kissed him. "I'm so obliged to you, Father, I can't tell you how obliged." She turned and ran from the room, while Henry showed his disgust for the whole proceeding.

It was at this moment that Mrs. Rogers remembered her own news. "Good grief, Father—Henry. I clean forgot."

Mr. Rogers feigned bewilderment at the way excitement succeeded excitement. "Henry, I shall have to ask you to assist me upstairs; the Italian temperament of your mother and sister is too much for my phlegmatic Quaker blood. After thirty years I can't withstand it any longer. Come on, Gussie, out with it. What has happened now? Has Gene had triplets and you've forgotten? . . ."

"Oh, Pet, be quiet. You've made me get off the track once to-day. I bought a house."

"You've bought a house?"

"Yes, Jesse, I've done it. And a wonderful place, too."

"You've bought a house without consulting the head of the family—or this paragon of business who sits at my left?"

"I put a hundred dollars down and got a receipt, but if you don't like it, I'm to get it back. It is the greatest bargain and I was afraid somebody else might take it if I waited to talk it over. I know it is awfully far uptown, especially for Henry, but it has nine bedrooms. And two baths, imagine! That means nobody will have to wait—very long, leastwise. And the agent says that it is well plumbed. But the best thing is the price—only seven thousand! The way I figure, we should get four for this at the very least, and with a mortgage—I even thought I could ask Zena to lend it to us."

While he thought of himself as a very astute man of affairs, Mr. Rogers actually was bored by discussions of a business nature. When his wife mentioned the plumbing, he intimated by his expression that he'd not take an agent's word for it, and would make a personal examination of each drain and tap. The suggestion of borrowing from Aunt Zena gave him his first real opportunity to assert himself and he burst out: "Not a penny from your sister! We both agree that she is an estimable woman and generous to a degree, but we'll stand upon our own two feet or not go through with this."

"We'll have to cut our suit to the cloth and I'd rather be beholden to Zena than to some stranger."

Henry interrupted. "Instead of talking about ways and means, I think I should get someone to appraise the place. Right off, I would say that it is so cheap there must be something wrong with it. In the second place . . ."

"Botherations with your places. The only thing against it is that it's way up at Fifty-second Street."

It was Henry's turn to be offended. "You were asking my advice and I was trying to give it to you as a businessman—which you are not, after all. When something is too cheap it's time to look out."

"And if it isn't cheap you shouldn't buy it because it's no bargain."

"Exactly! Unless the place is a bargain, I wouldn't consider it."

## 4

AT THE TIME that Clinton Weatherby rescued Teresina Rogers during the Memorial Day riot on the Brooklyn Bridge, he had been amused by her simplicity, delighted with her beauty, and not a little annoyed that she did not recognize his name. Later, when her family displayed equal ignorance and ranked baseball with cocking mains and fisticuffs as something for men of low or sporting natures, he became ashamed of his occupation and hesitated to reveal it for fear of losing Zenie's regard.

That would have been a blow indeed. Used as he was to the ways of the women who frequented the meeting places of the sporting fraternity, Zenie's extreme conventionality had seemed artificial to him at first, but she had quickly gained his respect and then he came to love her ardently. What was more, in spite of the apparent hauteur in her manner, he suspected that she also loved him. To test that suspicion he would have proposed long since except for this matter of his profession, in which he had hitherto taken such pride.

For Clint knew that until age or disability forced him, he would go on playing. He loved facing the batter and outguessing him, the tensing of his muscles under a hot, summer sun, the thrill of victory and the plaudits of the crowd. These were sensations which the Rogerses did not know and therefore could not understand. Another thing, he was at the peak; the future could hold nothing better for him. Although he probably made several times as much money as Henry, Clint secretly envied him. Suppose he could have gone to Zenie's father and said, "Mr. Rogers, I want to propose to your daughter. I have excellent prospects in the hay and feed business—something with a wonderful future, if anything has." The old boy could have done nothing but give him permission to try his fortune.

On the other hand, he couldn't say: "Mr. Rogers, I'm the most important pitcher on the Brooklyn baseball team—a sport attended

44

by rowdies who throw beer steins when they don't agree with the umpire—a purely man's game, one that no women, even the free and easy ones, would dare attend—one which will cast me off someday, when I'll have to find another job. . . ." He couldn't even say in his favor that he was a hero to Brooklyn's small boys and treated as a great and famous man in every sporting rendezvous.

Many times he had gone to the house on Cranberry Street determined to make a clean breast of everything, following it with an impassioned declaration which might sweep aside Zenie's prejudices. Each time he had lost his nerve. The Rogerses were right; baseball was an ignominious profession. This year he might be making a huge salary, more than he could ever hope to earn elsewhere; next season a sprained tendon might end his career. Or the game itself might change. Look at that fellow Radbourne, who threw the ball overhanded, instead of properly. Suppose the leagues allowed him to continue? Could he adjust his muscles to this new style which had such obvious advantages—and unfair ones—over the underhanded delivery?

These and many other thoughts occupied Clinton Weatherby's mind when he dressed. Now that the cat was out of the bag, what should he do? How had Zenie's father come to be at the game? Surely it must have been by accident, and yet baseball had never been mentioned between them. Could Mr. Rogers have learned of his connection with the Brooklyns and gone for confirmation?

The old fellow had proven to be a good sport, anyway. My, what a voice he had! Then to have lost the game after practically winning it. That had been more of the day's bad luck, which Clint continued to regret as he left the park, walked to the horsecars, and swung on the first to come along, hardly aware of the greetings and commiserations of the driver and his passengers.

When a mean grounder was hit in his direction, Clinton Weatherby usually fielded it himself and took his chance at making an error, instead of leaving the ball for the infielders to stop. He intended to follow the same procedure now. He'd eat, then go to Zenie's house, as he'd promised, face an angry girl and her parents and take his medicine.

The saloon at which he turned in was the very one to which he had taken Zenie for emergency repairs the day of their meeting.

Again he was treated as a celebrity and consoled for the loss of the day's game. Helping himself liberally to the free lunch, he took a seat at a table and motioned to a waiter.

Maisie, the girl who had gone to Zenie's assistance, walked over. "Hello, Clint. What brings you in here? I haven't seen you in a coon's age."

After ordering beer for both of them, Clint answered, dispiritedly, "Oh, I don't know . . ."

"You can't fool me. You've been out with that brunette. I saw you in a sleigh with her a couple of times during the winter. Quite a turnout, if you ask me. What a horse—and what a girl!"

"Yes, what a girl! You're right, Maisie, but it is over now. She has just learned all about me."

"All about you?"

"That I play baseball, I mean."

"I like that! Famous as you are. If she didn't know, she's the only woman in Brooklyn who didn't."

"You don't understand, Maisie. Sports are something that people like the Rogerses know nothing about. They live in a world of their own where business—and church, I guess—mean everything."

"And precious little fun they have, if you ask me."

"Fun enough! I've had some of the best evenings of my life just sitting around in their parlor and singing. Mr. Rogers—that's her father—is a great old chap. He was a railroad man, years ago. Used to have some wonderful adventures he's told me about. Then he helped to build the bridge over the East River. He was practically second to Mr. Roebling. And Zenie—that's the girl—well, she's beautiful, you saw that, and refined. Honest, Maisie . . ."

The girl whistled. "Willikens, Clint, you're taken bad."

"Guess I am, might as well admit it. But it's finished. Her father came and saw me play today. . . ."

Clint drank a second beer, as his resolution weakened. Two hours later he was still explaining to Maisie why he couldn't face Zenie Rogers, while only a few blocks up the hill toward the Heights, Zenie cried herself to sleep, certain that Clint was through with her forever because her father had been set to spy upon him.

46

*Chapter 5*

IT IS downright indecent of you, Zenie," Mrs. Rogers insisted. "Whoever heard of a young lady taking a walk by herself at this hour of the morning? If you are accosted, you can't blame the man. He has the best of reasons for thinking that you are inviting it.

"And you look ghastly; your eyes are puffy, too."

"If I look such a fright, I'll be left alone, anyway. Honestly, Mother, I just have to get some fresh air and be by myself. My life is over, I might as well face the fact. I know you and Father meant well, but it was a horrible, underhanded thing, all the same. I don't blame Clint. . . ."

"Pish and tosh. Like as not he'll come crawling back like a whipped cur, making excuses for having deceived you. If we are really shut of him, it's good riddance as you'll agree before long."

Teresina closed the door against her mother's continuing diatribe and walked up the hill to the Heights, which was also Mr. Rogers' favorite walk when troubled in spirit. She found a bench from which the bay could be seen, and watched a large, four-masted ship whose sails were being slowly raised. She idly wondered about its destination and how it would feel to leave behind Brooklyn with its heartache and begin life anew in a distant clime. The trouble with heartache, though, was that one couldn't leave it. Wherever she went it would be locked in her breast, until the day that she died.

The ship became a distant white blot on the water, but she no longer followed its passage. She started crying again, although she felt drained of tears, after spending so many during the night. Her dainty cambric handkerchief became a sodden ball, with which she dabbed futilely at nose and eyes.

Through a paroxysm of sobs she became aware that someone had taken a seat on the other end of her bench. With her mother's warnings still dinning in her ears, she feared that it must be some unprincipled man, seeking to take advantage of her distress. Without looking in his direction, she stemmed her tears and started to walk off, still sniffling.

"Zenie . . . you have every right to be angry. Please let me explain. . . ." She could hardly believe her ears. It couldn't be Clint. But it must be! And he probably thought that she was crying on his account. But she was. And he sounded upset and contrite too. What had *he* done? This succession of conflicting thoughts might have continued indefinitely, if he had not jumped up and placed his hand on her arm, misunderstanding her attitude as completely as she did his.

"I beg of you, listen. I should have told you long ago, but I was afraid—afraid of losing you. Then yesterday, when I saw your father in the grandstand . . ."

"You knew he was spying on you. It was a horrid, horrid thing to do, but I didn't know about it, you must believe that."

By this time, Zenie had turned and her deep brown eyes were gazing imploringly into his blue ones. They began to talk at once. While Zenie said, "I came up here to get away from the house for a while—I felt so miserable," Clint said, "Your mother told me that you had gone this way. She was pretty short, and I don't blame her. . . ." Then they both were saying in unison, "I'm so sorry. Please forgive me."

It was perfectly silly, of course, as they realized immediately.

Clint began to laugh first, and then Zenie joined in. It seemed to her that she would never be able to stop. She clung to the lapels of Clint's coat and tried to smother her laughs against his chest. They returned to the bench they had quit and sat down, still laughing. . . . Right there, in broad daylight, for all the world to see, Clint reached over and stopped her laughter with a kiss.

It was a long one, and when it was over, Zenie exclaimed, "Oh, I am so happy!"

Clint nodded his head, keeping his arm around her waist. "So am I."

2

AT TWENTY-TWO, Henry Rogers had every reason to congratulate himself. He had been advanced until he was now next to the manager in the New York branch office of Madeira and Company.

48

He would never have believed that a part of his success came from a friendship which existed between his mother and Mr. Madeira. He would have said that it was the result of working longer hours and with greater concentration, of spending the firm's money more charily than his own and of keeping at heart his employer's interest. He never gave a superior a chance to complain about his actions; he dressed conservatively and with great care. He considered each word he spoke and he was a Republican in politics. In short, Henry was a model young man and thought of himself as such—a model young man and a conservative one. He deplored the growing use of the telephone and was certain that the typewriter was made for laziness. He insisted on going to work by ferry, not because the cable cars on the bridge were undependable, but because the structure had represented a fantastic misuse of money.

This morning, as he stood toward the bow of the ferry and twisted his mustaches, he thought of the day's tasks and planned a time for looking at the house which his mother wanted to buy. He was convinced that in a few minutes he would discover enough things wrong with the place to support the decision he had already made regarding it. How could any woman be expected to know a good purchase when she saw one?

The ferry overtook a busy little tug with a tow of loaded coal barges and Henry felt a pain at his heart. Until recently his work had taken him to the coal slips and he knew many of these craft, their history, tonnage, and the families who lived on them. It was the last barge in the tow which affected him. It was smaller than the others, with something about it . . .

He knew that it could not be the *Lissa*, whose foundering had changed him from a lovesick youth into a hardheaded businessman. But its lines were similar; probably it had been built in the same yards along the banks of the Schuylkill. He imagined that he could see Melissa Heil, the captain's daughter, stride along the barge's narrow decking, her short, ankle-length skirts whipped by the breeze. She was looking at him with laughing brown eyes that were filled with love. She called, and waved an arm in farewell.

Suddenly Henry felt an almost uncontrollable desire to jump the rail and swim over, so that he might run his hands once more through her curly hair. Then she was gone.

49

He left the ferry at the Wall Street slip, walked up the street
to the office and took his place at a familiar desk. No one could
have suspected that his air of smug respectability concealed an all-
consuming hurt. He worked even harder than usual: letters, in-
voices, and manifests passed over his desk in a continuing stream.
Five hours later, with the noon whistles, he glanced up from his
labors in surprise. A fool's errand, undoubtedly, but he had better
run uptown and see the place his mother had picked out.

To save time, he took a hack, and when it stopped before a
modern brownstone house, with an imposing, high stoop, he
thought that there was some mistake. But this was the only empty
house in the block and the number tallied. He let himself in and
observed the spacious rooms, the attractive, up-to-date mantels,
tastefully decorated with green tiles around the central-heating out-
lets, the parquetry floors. There were brass lighting fixtures more
elegant than he had ever seen, with a multiplicity of gas jets. Dashing upstairs, he saw enameled tubs instead of zinc ones in the
bathrooms, and the water closets were adorned with roses and lilies-
of-the-valley in most artistic style. Why, at the price, the house
was more than a bargain; it was a steal, a real steal.

Then Henry's caution reasserted itself. Perhaps it was entailed
or there was a cloud on the title. He'd have to go into it pretty
thoroughly.

His fears were to prove unfounded. Mr. Madeira's New York
attorney attended to everything. The Cranberry Street house was
readily salable. Without the need of calling on Aunt Zena, the
Rogers' genteel home for respectable (and paying) guests seemed
well on the way to realization.

A week before the moving, the family descended upon the new
house. Only Henry was exempt. Mr. Rogers, his large person encased in an apron, scrubbed paint, protesting the while at the use-
lessness of the task, as it was all to be covered over, anyway. Norah
took apart the kitchen range, soaking each section in lye before
replacing it. Mrs. Rogers and Zenie, clad in old skirts that were
folded up and tied at the side, scrubbed floors. As both women's
ankles were equally trim, the effect of the six inches of limb thus

50

exposed was commented upon by Mr. Rogers with an accompanying leer whenever he saw either of them.

After the first day, when Abe brought over the family in a carriage that was otherwise loaded with cleaning materials, the horses and dogs were boarded out with a farmer who served them with butter and eggs.

Clinton Weatherby also went over to help. He arrived at the new house in time to hear Mrs. Rogers objecting to Zenie's insistence upon scrubbing, an occupation she was already pursuing with zest. "I've reached an age when hands don't matter, but it would be a shame for yours to get red and wrinkled," she protested. "You shan't scrub a minute longer."

"But I like to, Mother, I really do, and it won't hurt my hands a bit."

Apparently Clint thought otherwise. A discerning student of human nature might have found an index to his character in his subsequent actions. He did not take brush and bucket forthwith but left shortly after, to reappear that evening carrying a small parcel.

Teresina opened it with a series of fluttering gestures of excitement and drew forth a pair of queerly shaped, suede gloves. What was the purpose of making them so large, and with flat steels down each of the fingers?

Clumsily drawing a glove over her hand, Clint explained, "You see, Zenie, you're supposed to put on plenty of cold cream first, which the glove keeps in, so you won't mess up the bedclothes. The man in the store says they will keep your hands nice and white; besides the steels will stop you from bending your fingers during the night, so you won't get wrinkles at the joints. Here, let's try the other one. . . ."

After he had tied them at the wrists with the dainty pink ribbons, Teresina held up her hands for general examination and exclaimed, "Clint, they are just the thing! Mother, look, aren't they marvelous? I feel exactly like a seal and these are my flippers. Does anybody have a piece of fish to throw me?"

Then, in a more serious vein, "I do thank you, though how in the world I'll sleep in them I don't know. But if wearing these is the price of my helping Mother, I'll do my very best."

"WE CAN'T MOVE on Friday, that is certain," Mrs. Rogers proclaimed. "A Friday flitting means a short sitting."

Her husband combed his fingers through the curling froth of his beard and pretended a most serious view of the situation. "That leaves no day but Sunday, Gussie. Do you think the neighbors would approve breaking the Sabbath?"

"What in the world are you talking about?"

" 'Monday moving never done roving.' And 'Tuesday travel leaves much to unravel. . . .' " While he searched about for an appropriate rhyme for Wednesday, Mrs. Rogers interrupted his series of imaginary adages with an impatient, "I wish you would be sensible, just for once. . . ."

"I am being eminently sensible. If you find Friday the most suitable day for moving it is ridiculous to be deterred by an old wives' saw—or just as sensible to suppose that there are sayings for every other day in the week. . . ."

"I've decided on Tuesday," Mrs. Rogers interrupted, without further explanation, and proceeded to outline a plan of campaign for the moving that would have been worthy of a military strategist.

Everything worked out reasonably well. Two hours before the vans' arrival on the morning of the great day, Abe and Norah set off in the carriage, behind Mr. Quinby, who had been brought in from the country the previous evening. The back seat was packed with precious articles which Mrs. Rogers would not entrust to the movers, and they drove away to the tune of threats of what might happen if anything were broken.

Mr. Rogers was to accompany the first load, while Teresina and her mother superintended the packing of the second. "When you get there, have the carpets put down first thing and whatever you do, don't let them scratch the piano."

"Now, Gussie, that's silly. If anything gets scratched, it certainly won't be by deliberate intent. . . ."

"I never saw such a man for argument. You get me clean off what I have to say—oh, yes, and leave any upstairs things downstairs until I get there, as I haven't decided yet how I'll furnish the bedrooms. Don't let the driver gallop the horses, but get back just as soon as you can."

Mr. Rogers took a glance through the front window, where the four great Belgian horses made a brave show of brass-decorated harnesses, braided manes, flowing tails, and yellow fly nets. "I don't think you have to worry much about those fellows setting off at any breakneck clip. I fancy they're a little like myself—built for strength and endurance, not for speed."

"Meanwhile Clint has promised to come around and help, which I could do without. In addition to everything else I'll have to keep my eye on them all day. It is too bad I can't be two places at once; I should really go along with you. . . .

"There, they are putting up the tailgate now, so you better hurry."

Mr. Rogers was glad enough to seize his hat and escape. Gussie in her present state was someone to keep away from. Holding his umbrella with one hand and clinging to the dray with the other, he climbed up while the driver shouted encouragement and advice. Reaching the high seat with no other mishap than the loss of his hat, which was rescued from beneath the horses' hoofs by one of the helpers, Mr. Rogers looked over the broad backs of the draft animals, held out his umbrella like a sword, and proclaimed, "All right, my good fellows, on to New York."

An hour later, after the second van had been dispatched, Mrs. Rogers performed a sad, but important duty. Distraught by the breaking up of an old home and the making of a new one, she dashed out to the back yard, where a bed of hollyhocks was fast going to seed, and paused before a scarcely perceptible mound. "Good-by, Nellie. You know how sorry I am to be leaving you here with strangers. I do hope they keep up the flowers real pretty. . . ."

It was years since the old Dalmatian bitch had died, but the memory of each of Mrs. Rogers' pets was very dear to her. She sniffled, dabbed at her eyes with a bit of handkerchief, remembered that Clint and Zenie were alone together in the house, and hurried back to find them innocently engaged in trying to force the hall costumer through the front door. This had suffered one of those mysterious changes which occasionally take place in furniture. Mrs. Rogers recalled that when they had moved from Philadelphia it had come through the doorway quite easily. Now it was stuck half-way, where the impatient movers had left it for a later trip.

"What has happened to it, I can't understand," Mrs. Rogers repeated for the third or fourth time, while Clint pushed and Teresina tugged at the recalcitrant oak.

"It's no use, Zenie," Clint finally decided. "I saw a screwdriver somewhere upstairs and I'll have it apart in a jiffy."

While Teresina went along to aid in the search, Mrs. Rogers began an appraisal of the remaining effects. "I declare I don't see where all the things come from, anyway." She threw her hands high in one of her characteristic gestures. "Another load here and the bedrooms still to clean out."

This statement was addressed to a room that bore little resemblance to the Rogers' parlor. The piano, Turkish corner, whatnot, and love seat were gone. All the pictures were down and arranged in rows, according to size and shape. The marble mantelpiece looked naked without its chenille scarf. Barrels of bric-a-brac, each piece carefully wrapped in newspaper, choked the doorway.

Mrs. Rogers listened for sounds of activity from the second floor. When there were none, she dashed up the stairs and burst into the front bedroom, to find, this time, what she had expected.

The lovers were in a fervent embrace, from which they hurriedly separated. Zenie's face was flushed, her lips still moist with Clint's kisses. "So this is the way you go on behind my back. I'm ashamed of you. Mr. Weatherby, I think that you had better leave now, moving or no moving. It is no more than I expected of you, I must say—taking advantage of a young girl's innocence. I'll have you know that this is a respectable house in which you can't take a cut off the lamb just when it pleases you."

Mrs. Rogers' voice rose to a shriek, but Zenie faced her proudly, with head high. "You mustn't blame Clint, Mother. It was my fault. I knew the old screwdriver wasn't here, but I said I thought it might be. I behaved shamelessly, I know."

"Don't listen to her," Clint interrupted. "She looked so beautiful sitting on the washstand I couldn't resist."

"On the washstand?" Mrs. Rogers' voice achieved a new shrillness.

54

"I wanted to rest a moment. The chairs are gone, and the bed . . ."

"You are positively depraved to even mention that article of furniture in front of a man you're not married to and who has no intentions that way, or I miss my guess. Why, I would no more have mentioned a bed in your father's presence. . . ."

Mr. Rogers burst into the room at this moment, intent upon announcing the return of himself and the empty van. He stopped short to take in a scene in which each participant appeared to be trying to talk faster and louder than the others. Clinton Weatherby was saying with great earnestness, "But I do intend to marry Zenie whenever you give your consent. Life without her . . ." Zenie was proclaiming dramatically, "I love Clint and I'm not ashamed of being caught kissing him." His wife was screaming something about a bed.

With that peculiar ability of his to say the wrong thing, Mr. Rogers ignored the remarks of the young people and appeared to misunderstand that of Mrs. Rogers. He drowned out all three of them with a hearty, "Yes, indeed, a wonderful bed. They don't make them like this any more." Walking over to it, he patted the high and richly carved headboard. "Solid walnut, through and through. I'm glad to add my recommendation to yours, Gussie."

It was seldom, in recent years, that Mr. Rogers had felt in such fine fettle or seemed to be enjoying himself so hugely. He turned toward the young couple with a benign smile. "We've slept on it for more than thirty years and though it has been well used, I warrant you, shows nary a sign of wear. When you two get married we'll present it to you, won't we, Mother? We'll get along with something else. May you enjoy it half as much as we have." Pompously, as though he had just disposed of a kingdom and that anything that he might say further would be anticlimactic, Mr. Rogers turned and left the room, hurriedly followed by Clint and Teresina, while Mrs. Rogers, in exasperated impotence, heard their footsteps descending the stairs from which the carpet had been removed.

WHILE NORAH STRUGGLED with a range that was completely unfamiliar in its burning habits, her mistress commented, "You know Norah, I'm not at all sure that this was a good move. Everything seems so large and strange and not like home, somehow. It is so different from when we moved to Cranberry Street. That house was as like ours in Kensington as two peas in a pod, but here there is nothing the same. I doubt I'll ever get used to it.

"And the noise! I never heard so many strange sounds in a house. I wanted to get up and look several times, but I was afraid to; and Mr. Rogers slept like a log. I was so provoked with him."

Norah began to poke at the recalcitrant coals, spurred by Mrs. Rogers', "Hurry with that range. Henry will be down in a moment and you know how he hates to be kept waiting for breakfast."

The maid's forehead creased and her lips twisted in determination. "I'm doin' the best I can, ma'am, but I ain't used to this fire yet and that's a fact. It don't seem to draw right."

"Well, hurry anyway . . . and the traffic! Did you ever hear so many drays? I believe every last horse in New York pounded over the cobbles outside. The agent said Fifty-second was a quiet street. I'd like to tell him a thing or two. Then when I got up, things turned so still, and the house so unfamiliar. I declare I believe I'm homesick for Brooklyn, much as I thought I'd never be."

"Beggin' your pardon, ma'am, I felt the same way meself. It was too noisy all night and too quiet this mornin'. I came down to get the fire started and what with none of the creatures comin' a-runnin' for their breakfast . . ."

Mrs. Rogers let out a cry of pleasure. "Why Norah, that's just what the matter is. Moody and Sankey! And Beecher, too. No wonder I feel lonely, without them around. I was afraid they'd trip somebody and they are always under foot so. Or they might have gotten out what with the movers . . .

"Here, give me a hand with that poker. I hear Henry now and the coffee not boiling yet." Mrs. Rogers tackled the fire with vim —too much of it, for there was a sudden rumble of coals, a clang of iron and the whole grate fell into the ashpit. "Botheration. Now I've done it. Well, Henry will have to go to work on a cold breakfast. He ought to be glad to get anything, considering the state of my nerves. . . .

"And when that worthless darkie comes around, tell him to hitch up Mr. Quinby. I've a million things to do, but I won't stay in this house one more day without my dogs. We'll pick them up and lead Total Eclipse. Poor dear, I'll bet he's grieving right this minute. No, a place just doesn't seem like home without animals around."

Within an hour she had written out a set of long, confusing and contradictory instructions for Mr. Rogers and Zenie, had given as many more oral ones to Norah and was off, with Abe driving so smartly that in another hour they had crossed the bridge and were on the way to the further reaches of Flatbush. Well out in the country, Mr. Quinby was watered at a roadside brook, when Abe assured his mistress that the farm was not much farther.

They turned off the dusty main road and sped down a narrow, winding lane that led to a farmhouse. There was farmer van Duym, whom she hardly recognized without the long, white apron in which for many years he had sold her butter and eggs in the market. As he came forward to greet her, there was a sudden, high-pitched wail from one of the outbuildings. Mrs. Rogers smiled in satisfaction. "That's Sankey. He sang like that the first time we ever saw him, which was why Father gave him the name. He knows it's me, which is real smart, I think.

"Abe, run ahead and let them all out, will you? I'm most as fussed as they are, not seeing them for almost a week."

In a moment the elongated creatures dashed toward her, all three now in voice, with long ears flapping and bodies squirming. Mrs. Rogers knelt down and took their kisses on both cheeks, until gradually they quieted and threw themselves in her shadow. She rose, wiped her face with a handkerchief, and remarked, "There is nothing like a dog's wet tongue to make you feel good; and now, how is my horse? If I know Total Eclipse he's off his fodder completely."

Mr. van Duym's huge body shook in a hearty laugh. "No such thing, Mrs. Rogers. He's out to pasture, and grazing nice as you please. Romping like a colt he was, this morning." He gave her a side glance. "He's better off here than in New York. Leave him for the winter. I'll only charge for feed."

Although it was the sensible thing to do, Mrs. Rogers protested. "He'll never forgive me. No, we've come to take him and we shall, but I'd like to see him where he is."

They followed a path through the barnyard and into the field beyond. The big black stood out among a group of roan and gray farm horses and at Mrs. Rogers' whistle walked forward to meet her, but with none of the exuberance that she had expected. He whinnied in recognition, put his head down to have his ears scratched, then kicked high and dashed off through the lush grass to rejoin his fellows.

His attitude answered the problem of caring for him, but as his fat rump disappeared behind some bushes, Mrs. Rogers' voice was annoyed and peevish. "Well, I guess you're right, Mr. van Duym; besides, I can always come out and see him on the N. Y. and S. B. steam trains. It is too far to come often by carriage."

As they drove back, she held a hotly panting dog in each arm, while Beecher snuggled at her feet. Reaching forward, she confided in Abe, "I've never lived without horses and dogs and I'd never want to, but a horse has to be broken to man's use and never forgets it, I'm afraid, while dogs were born only to love and be loved in return."

Abe nodded his head, as Mrs. Rogers glanced at each of the dachshunds for further confirmation of her statement.

Chapter 6

IT WAS a sad day for this family when Clinton Weatherby came into this house," Mrs. Rogers remarked to Teresina. "Look at the effect he has had on your father. You'd think we still lived there, the way he goes on when the Brooklyns lose. He used to be a gentleman and he's become a rowdy. It is all Clint's doings. Just as he has changed you from a girl with some spirit into a floor mat."

This was ground which had been covered many times and Teresina did not answer immediately, which only made her mother more furious. "When they get in tonight they'll get a piece of my mind. Not that it will do any good. . . ."

"Oh, Mother, I don't think it does Father any harm to go with Clint. He gets very lonely having nothing to do and you must admit he is more like his old self."

That was true, but not to be admitted; and the tirade continued for another quarter-hour until the errant pair finally made their appearance. The season was almost over and Brooklyn out of the running for the league championship, a circumstance which Mr. Rogers charged to improper umpiring. If proof were necessary, today's game supplied it. "The fray went twelve innings, which is why we were delayed," he explained. "A daring attempt of one of our runners to advance himself on the bases—stealing, it is called —resulted in our downfall. The theft was eminently successful, as everyone saw but the umpire. . . ."

Mrs. Rogers sniffed, but decided to hold her fire until after the meal. One of the hardest things to get used to in the new house was having the kitchen in the basement, so that either she or Teresina had to serve the food as Norah sent it up on the dumbwaiter. It was a convenience, though, to have the servant beyond earshot when she intended to have so personal a discussion.

While Teresina collected the plates on which not a vestige of mince pie remained, Mrs. Rogers began, almost sweetly, "I suppose, Mr. Weatherby, that today's disaster will have an unfortunate effect upon your prospects with the team?"

"Oh, I don't know. I can't win them all. . . ."

"He's the best in the league—except Radbourne, who doesn't pitch fairly, so shouldn't count," Mr. Rogers interrupted.

"But if you began to lose regularly, surely they wouldn't continue to hire you to do whatever you do do?"

The statement was on the involved side, but its meaning was plain and Clint was about to reply when Mr. Rogers broke in, impatiently, "He is the man who hurls the pellet. Let me explain the game to you, my dear. . . ."

"Let's scheme a way for you ladies to see one; what do you say? Right now, though, I think I should answer your question."

Mrs. Rogers wanted to protest violently against the idea that either Zenie or herself would be interested in such a purely male sport, but she stifled her feelings as Clint continued, "When I can't win games for the Brooklyns any longer, I can still pick up a few years' work with a lesser team, but in the end—ten or twelve years from now, if I have luck—I'll be finished."

He held up his hand as Zenie and both parents began to talk. "Just a word more, and I'll be through. . . .

"In the meantime, I propose to save my money and turn it over to Zenie every week, so that when the evil day comes I'll have some capital."

Henry, who took no trouble to hide his dislike for the man who was now accepted as his sister's fiancé, listened in glum silence up to this point, then inquired, "Just how much do you make a week, Weatherby? As a businessman I know it takes a whacking good salary to save anything, especially with a wife to support."

Mrs. Rogers secretly applauded. Trust Henry to come to the point. If Clint thought he was not going to have to support Zenie, once he had married her, he might as well be disillusioned right now. Henry's question had hit home, all right, from the way Mister Weatherby was frowning!

"Clint's salary is his own affair, Henry Rogers, and I think both you and Mother are behaving most rudely. . . ."

Clint gave Zenie a glance of understanding before disagreeing with her. "No, Henry and your mother are right. I only earn fifteen hundred. It will be hard to save much over a thousand a year out of that. I've been planning to get some other employment during the winter. I might be able to make enough to pay our expenses and sock away all my baseball earnings."

Fifteen hundred dollars for a summer's play? It was preposterous! Over three times as much as Henry was paid for the whole year for twelve hours a day, instead of two or three hours several times a week. As the full injustice of their relative salaries grew upon him, his strong dislike for Clint turned to a jealousy very close to hate.

Mrs. Rogers did not believe a word of Clint's statement. So he

60

was a blowhard and a braggart in addition to everything else. Why Father hadn't made that much salary with the railroad, and only a few dollars more during the opulent years of building the Brooklyn Bridge. She kept her thoughts to herself, however, as Clint continued. "That's not all that worries me. I do hope we can go on living here after we're married. I'll insist on paying well, of course. I'm on the road so much when the team is traveling and I don't want Zenie to be lonely. . . ."

"Oh, Clint! Can't I go along? I was miserable every time you were away this summer."

For a moment there was a return of Clint's usual happy-go-lucky manner as he ran his hand through his upstanding red hair. "Sure you can, if you want to. We travel by Sullivan Sleeper; think you would like that?"

"If it is at all like Mr. Pullman's I shouldn't mind. . . ."

Clint laughed uproariously at his own joke. "That's the name for the smoking cars that ballplayers use. I'm afraid if we went by Pullman there wouldn't be much of my salary left. No, for a while, at least, you'll have to stay here."

"Of course she'll stay here, and you too, my boy, when you are playing at home," Mr. Rogers shouted, anxious to get back into the conversation, "but we'll adjourn to our commodious parlor. There's some claret in the cellar; let's drink a toast. Gussie, call down to Norah and have her scout around for a bottle. I remember putting it away, but can't recall just where."

Clint left them with the explanation, "I'll run down to the corner for a paper with the out-of-town scores. Save some of that wine for me." Mr. Rogers descended to the basement, too impatient to wait for Norah to find the claret, and the others trooped into the parlor. They were just seated when there was a peal of the front doorbell and Mrs. Rogers arose with an annoyed, "I guess I will have to answer. I declare, it will take a corps of servants to run this house properly." But before she had finished wondering aloud who could be calling at that hour, the agile Norah had dashed up from the basement, given final pats to apron and hair and gained the vestibule. There was a moment of silence and then one of what Mr. Rogers called "Norah's banshee cries."

Only Father Duffy could have occasioned such an outburst. As

61

he appeared in the wide doorway to the parlor, escorted by a doting Norah who held his hat in her hand while she worshiped him open-mouthed, he looked nearly as young as when he first came to Kensington. He had probably been in his middle forties then, for Patrick Duffy was no priest who had gone directly from college to seminary. He had been educated in the hard school of railroading and had entered the priesthood from some inward force of maturity rather than from youthful dedication. His brown hair had always been sparse, although it completely covered his scalp, and his full, sanguine face was unlined. He bulked almost as large in the doorway as did Mr. Rogers, but, perhaps because of his black clericals, seemed to overshadow them to an even greater extent.

At times Mrs. Rogers disapproved of the priest, especially when he insisted upon talking politics with Jesse while both of them chewed at hearty plugs of tobacco. In fact, it was only when Father Duffy was around that Mr. Rogers thought of the weed, he had been for so long forbidden its use in the house. To that extent he was undoubtedly a bad influence, but he was a wonderful man nevertheless, and she ran to greet him with both hands outstretched.

"Well, Father, this is a surprise! But how did you find us? I've been meaning to send the new address . . ."

Before he could answer, she exclaimed testily, "Instead of gaping, Norah, hang up Father Duffy's hat. I'll call Jesse, who will be overjoyed to see you, though you mustn't mind if he still calls you Duffy. He is stubborn as a mule about some things and that's one; though as a Quaker it is no more than you can expect from him, of course. Now do take a chair, and Norah, tell Mr. Rogers to come right up and stop rummaging in that dirty cellar."

There was no need for Norah to go on the errand for the sound of tramping feet indicated Mr. Rogers was ascending the basement stairs. He burst into the parlor triumphantly bearing a cobwebby bottle. "Imagine a house without a proper wine cellar, but I found it. . . ." And then, as he saw the priest, "Duffy! By the Lord Harry, you are a sight for sore eyes."

As soon as the two men had finished their greeting, Mr. Rogers inquired, "And how do you like our new house? We've come pretty far, wouldn't you say, for a stick-in-the-mud family from

Kensington? I never thought of it until this moment, but we've lived in the country's three largest cities. There is a record for you!"

"It is indeed, Rogers." Father Duffy's eye took in the familiar furniture that seemed almost lost in the long, narrow room. "And a step up in the world, I'd say. Things must be going good for you, for which I am happy, as you deserve it. Most of the people I know are feeling the sad rub of extreme poverty."

Mr. Rogers' smile was rueful. "I'm afraid that outward indications belie the true facts. This house was an idea of Gussie's. With the bridge finished, there seemed to be no suitable market for my services, so we took this to embark upon a new venture—a genteel home for paying guests. In other words, a boarding house, though I swore I'd never live or die in one."

"Oh, come now, boarding houses can be very happy places. I've lived in a number of them and I know."

The conversation veered as Mr. Rogers thought of the claret, and shouted to Norah as though she were a house-length away and not right there, "Bring a corkscrew, girl . . . we're drinking a toast to Zenie's future. Gussie, you haven't told Duffy yet. . . ."

Mrs. Rogers hid her annoyance. "Teresina is marrying a very nice young man, Father, an—an athlete. . . ." She paused, torn between confiding her real opinion or sticking to platitudes, when Mr. Rogers broke in again. "He pitches for the Brooklyns and tosses a most confusing spheroid. If you'll be in New York long we must watch him perform."

"Indeed we shall. I enjoy baseball—used to play a little myself, in fact—and I'll be in New York permanently. I've been transferred here."

This was news, and it was not until after a chatter of questions and explanations that Father Duffy could inquire, "And who is the lucky man?"

Zenie, who sat by, silent but glowing, spoke up proudly, "His name is Clinton Weatherby. He's wonderful, Father, and I'm so happy."

"Tall, good-looking, and redheaded? Of course! I remember when he brought you home, Memorial Day. So that horrible catastrophe was productive of some good."

Mrs. Rogers could not forbear adding spitefully, "That remains to be seen. They'll live with us after they're married, anyway. He'll be away half the time tossing his spheroids, which isn't proper work for a man, I don't believe."

The jangling tones of the front doorbell floated up from the kitchen and Mrs. Rogers finished resignedly, "I suppose that's him now."

Zenie was at the door before Norah reached the hallway, and welcomed Clint with an embrace. Father Duffy shook his hand most heartily and a moment later Mr. Rogers shouted a regret that no one played the piano. This was a signal for Clint to whip out his harmonica and suggest, "Won't this do for a substitute?"

He began to play "Marriage Bells" while the others joined in:

> Oh marriage bells are ringing,
> What a glorious peal to me.
> The present hour is bringing, love,
> My fondest thoughts for thee.

The song was a toast in itself and the wine was drunk to its strains while Norah was dispatched for a second bottle. Instead of a mere get-together, the evening had grown into a real occasion and Mrs. Rogers began to think of food to serve with it. She objected to the harmonica as an instrument almost as lacking in respectability as a banjo and several times tried to bring the song-fest to an end before the neighbors should hear the strains of so unfashionable an instrument. Intercepting Norah with the claret, she put the girl at work upon a collation which would surely interrupt the racket.

Alas, the approaching elections caused politics to displace music and conversation turned to the possibilities of a Democratic president after more than two decades of Republicanism. Out of deference to the ladies, no mention was made of Mr. Cleveland's bastard child, but each man wondered about the effect this child might have on the church-going public.

Henry, who had retired for a while, came down during the singing and actually unbent so far as to join in a chorus or two. He was all out for Blaine, although he realized the futility of arguing with his father or Father Duffy. If personal scandal would defeat Cleveland, so much the better. Along with most businessmen he felt

64

that the great James G. Blaine had been smart to feather his nest at the expense of the stockholders of an obscure western railroad, whereas adultery came in another classification entirely.

Mr. Rogers was for Cleveland, but Father Duffy was not entirely persuaded. "I suppose I shouldn't say this, as one of the stipulations of my transfer was that I'd refrain from politics. I'm not yet sure that I was right in agreeing, and here, in the bosom of this family where I feel so completely at home, I'll say what I think. To me, the major political parties are both dedicated to greed and self-interest. I'll agree that Cleveland is the better man, though perhaps I'm too tolerant of human weakness.

"What the country needs, though, is a man—and a party—dedicated to the good of all. The industrial revolution has done evil things to America. It is pauperizing our people so that soup lines seem a permanent part of our lives. Pick up your paper any day and read the heartbreaking accounts of women with babies starving to death, or freezing in some makeshift room, and you'll admit that we need some new concept. I was working a little along that line in Kensington, but I had a bishop who objected.

"Not that there aren't a great many forward-looking, truly Christian men in the Church—Cardinal Manning, for instance, and my late good friend, Cardinal McCloskey. . . ."

When Mr. Rogers broke in to observe that apparently Duffy was being infected with the ideas of Altgeld, the Westerner, the priest caught him up quickly. "The salvation of America lies in men with similar philosophies. I see a great new political party that will include the Knights of Labor, the farmers and humanitarians like Altgeld and Henry George, whose ideas I particularly favor.

"But there is no use for me to get started. I'd rather hear from you, Mr. Weatherby. I saw you bring in the evening paper; what were the scores today? I suppose there is no chance for your team to win the championship now?"

Father Duffy proceeded to talk baseball in a manner that showed him to be a real follower of the game. When Mrs. Rogers sailed in, piloting Norah, who bore the hastily-contrived refreshments, she found a completely happy, amiable group which seized eagerly upon her offerings.

It was much later before the good priest arose. He exchanged resounding thumps on the back with Mr. Rogers, took Clint's hand in a hearty grasp, looked him squarely in the eye and announced, "I like you, Weatherby, and I'll tell you now that you're getting something pretty fine in Zenie, here. When the two of you set the day, I'll do the marryin', if you'll allow me."

Chapter 7    THE WEDDING, set originally for late October, after the close of the baseball season, suffered a postponement when Clint, because of his local popularity, was hired to help Mr. Cleveland in his campaign against Blaine. Both Clint and Zenie rebelled. The latter proved to be endowed with a good share of Quaker practicality, however. After taking a more reasonable view herself, she won over her fiancé with a telling argument. "It will only be a month, Clint. You couldn't take enough time off from electioneering for a proper wedding, which Mother has set her heart on, even if it is at home. Both the other girls eloped and you can see for yourself that Henry is becoming an old stick, who'll never marry, so there is nobody else to make a fuss over. Besides, I want a real honeymoon, just with you and away from everyone, which we can't have if you're on the go day and night getting Mr. Cleveland elected."

Never had the Rogerses been so much in the swim of things. They were provided with special tickets to watch the cornerstone laying for the Bartholdi Statue of Liberty, soon to be on its way from France, and attended Brooklyn's welcome to Governor Cleveland, of which the high point was the great barbecue at Ridgewood Park. Indeed, while Clint was busy rousing the sporting contingent to proper enthusiasm, it was time-conscious Mr. Rogers who established the astounding fact that the Democratic candidate shook hands at the rate of thirty shakes to the minute until exhausted.

66

In the early morning hours of November 5th, Mr. Rogers and Clint, soaked by the rain which had been falling all night, returned home jubilant with the glorious news. Grover Cleveland had won!

Later, after breakfast, all but Henry accompanied Clint to Printing House Square, to watch the celebration from the *Times* Building. Teresina, hanging upon Clint's arm, vibrant with his nearness, felt that the scene was not only a tribute to New York's great Governor, but to the popularity of her fiancé. Her eyes filled with tears of happiness as she gazed down from the dizzy, fifth-floor height, upon the lines of stalled horsecars foundered in a wildly-cheering sea of humanity—upon the boldly-lettered banners that flaunted the end of Republicanism.

Once the excitement was over, a new date was set for the wedding and this time the lovers vowed there would be no postponement, not for any reason whatsoever.

But the reason developed—one which those most concerned accepted only after much discussion, and Mrs. Rogers exclaimed, with a sigh, "I declare, I don't believe the Good Lord ever intended Zenie to get married, from the way things are working out, yet I don't see what else could be done, under the circumstance."

It all began with a letter.

## 2

PROOF of the poet's contention that hope *does* spring eternal was the manner in which the family awaited the daily appearance of the mailman. Mr. Rogers always became restless a half-hour ahead of time and dashed for the front door at the first note of the postman's whistle on their block. It was usually a race that he won from Gussie, handicapped by skirts and shorter legs. Teresina would open the door of her room and call down, "Is there anything for me?"

Even Norah, who had never received a letter, so far as anyone could remember, and who had but one relative, an elder sister in Ireland, hovered around in anticipation when something was left.

There was a delightful moment as the missive would be turned over and its contents anticipated. Foreign stamps, accompanied by the familiar handwriting of Mrs. Rogers' sister, or of Julia—still traveling with her husband in far corners of the world—would end most quickly the serving-girl's hopes. But occasionally there would be a strange letter, when Norah's mouth would gape open and she would watch in suspended animation until Mr. Rogers would thunder, "Gussie, a bill from Stern's. What have you been wasting money on now?" or "Addressed to me. I wonder what it can be." Then Norah would remain out of curiosity to share whatever there was of good news or bad. . . .

This morning there were two letters and as Mr. Rogers seldom had such an opportunity to excite the family curiosity he made the most of it. Finally, Mrs. Rogers spoke in exasperation. "You can't fool me, Jesse. One is from Julia. Hand it over this instant."

"Quite so, my dear. I was merely taking a moment to identify this other. It's postmarked from Kensington, but it has me stumped."

"In that case you might try opening it," Mrs. Rogers snapped.

For a time that seemed unending to Norah and Zenie, who had run out breathless, there was no sound but that of mumblings in both bass and soprano as the letters were perused half aloud. There was a shriek of joy from Mrs. Rogers followed by something very much like a moan. "Jesse, I can't believe it. Julia and the children are coming to America—with Philippe, too, of course. We'll see them, Jesse, really see them. . . .

"But how awful . . . their money . . . conditions in France . . . dear Philippe excited about prospects in the States. H-m-mph, I'm not so sure about *that*. And Zena. My poor, dear sister. Julia says she has lost almost everything."

The news completely overshadowed that in Mr. Rogers' letter, which otherwise would have provided days of conversation, and he waited in a dither of impatience to read for himself.

Never had tables been turned upon him more completely. Mrs. Rogers clutched the letter determinedly, feeding out little morsels of information to tease his curiosity. "Zena poor? Impossible! Let me see. . . ."

"I am quite able to read my own daughter's writing. From what Julia says, they're not poor, exactly, but things have been going from bad to worse on the Continent and suddenly they aren't rich any more. . . ." Another pause, and she went on, " 'both Philippe and my dear Aunt are turning their assets into funds which they will send over by draft,' so they can't be completely poverty-stricken. It will be January before they arrive.

"They'll live here, of course. . . ." Then, as the full significance of this descended upon her, "Pet! Our home for paying guests. Julia and Philippe will need most of the third floor, with the children—and Zena the second-floor front! There'll be nothing else to rent out, what with Zenie staying at home. . . ."

As she thought of all the plans she had made, the advertisements she had composed while Jesse snored, the appearances of the guests themselves as she had conjured them up in her mind, behaving genteelly and respectably in the parlor on quiet evenings, her pleasure at the thought of seeing her grandchildren was succeeded by vexation, to which she gave vent.

"Bosh, Gussie, I'm surprised at you. If Zena and Julia move here, they'll contribute to the household just as Clint intends to. We'll get along famously. . . ."

A near-shriek interrupted him—one that caused Norah to dash for the safety of the kitchen while Zenie hurried forward and assisted her mother to a chair in the parlor. When Mrs. Rogers quieted, finally, she began to explain the reason for her outburst. "I was just going over in my mind again where we'd put everyone when I suddenly thought of Zenie. . . ."

"Me? Now Mother, what in the world? . . ."

"You'll just have to postpone the wedding again. I can't see any way out of it. Julia and your Aunt would both be hurt. Zena would be furious as well, if you were married while she is on the high seas. . . ."

"Again? Oh, I can't. I can't. And what will I tell Clint? It doesn't seem to me that I'll ever get married. . . ." In the nearest thing to tantrums that Teresina had displayed in a long time, she suddenly dashed for the door and up the stairs toward her own room, while her mother, her wits leaping ahead with accustomed agility, cried after her, "If he *really* loves you, he'll do as you say and besides, Julia says clear enough that your Aunt's not a pauper yet, so you better think which side your bread's buttered on."

69

Mrs. Rogers felt almost herself again as Jesse said, "I know you can't guess who my letter is from."

"Pet, I'm just in no mood for games. . . ."

"From Sol Peale, my dear!"

"The Peales! Why we haven't heard from them since we left Kensington. How are they?"

Mr. Rogers' face fell a trifle. "Why, all right, I suppose. Sol doesn't say. He's interested in the movement for an eight-hour working day. You know, he's in the Knights of Labor."

"Oh, pshaw, as though I cared. Jesse Rogers, I have more important . . ."

"Hold your horses, Gussie. My news is quite different. It's by way of explanation . . ."

"Bother your explanations!"

". . . Of a matter that has aroused my curiosity."

"With this house to get in order and Zenie to straighten out . . ."

"Sol has been working with Al Naylor."

"That Socialist—or worse!"

"Is there anything worse to you than a Socialist, my dear? Not that I necessarily approve. . . ."

"Of all the men! If you have any news to tell me, spit it out, otherwise I have a million and one things . . ."

"I'm coming to the news, my dear. He and Al and Duffy have been working together."

"Father Duffy?"

"If you insist upon calling him that. Duffy's a fine man, for whom I have nothing but respect, but he's a little young to be the parent of either of us." Even Mr. Rogers tired of this verbal fencing. "You'd never guess. Duffy took the stump for the eight-hour day and the ideas of Mr. George."

"And who, pray, is Mr. George? . . ."

"He has a philosophy that you might find it somewhat difficult to understand, Gussie. It lumps taxes together. Sol sent a clipping along—from the *Record*, a good Democratic sheet, so it must be dependable—that says Duffy's bishop was opposed to his views, which is why he was transferred. . . ."

"I don't see anything to get excited about . . . nor does it help

70

the pair of you sitting around evenings talking about Mr. Blaine and the bonds he stole, or something about Mr. Cleveland—who is no fit man for President, I might as well tell you—and his . . ." Mrs. Rogers was just about to add "bastard child," when she remembered that Norah or Zenie might overhear, so she substituted "escapade" instead.

## 3

THE WORLD was in a distraught and upset condition during this winter of 'Eighty-four. Trouble between the Irish and their masters led to explosions in London that damaged the House of Commons and the city's famous Tower. It spilled over into New York, where O'Donovan Rossa, the American Fenian, was shot by a hysterical young Englishwoman. In Egypt the rebels had captured Khartoum and the great General Gordon was killed. War between England and Russia appeared to be certain after the latter made advances toward Afghanistan and people wondered why, in this modern day and age, civilized nations could not settle their disputes amicably instead of resorting to force.

At home, the death of Dr. Leopold Damrosch, manager of the Metropolitan Opera House, caused general mourning, though his son, Walter, was well equipped and willing to carry on. People were amused by the remarriage of Mrs. Tom Thumb to "Count" Magri, at the Church of the Holy Trinity. The bride, a plump and womanly little figure, and her sturdy miniature groom spent their honeymoon at the brand new Murray Hill Hotel. The country excited itself over the roller-skating fad and many a public-minded citizen wondered if it were not an exercise which the female should avoid.

Ordinarily these and other questions of the moment would have occupied the attention of the family, but its interest was given over entirely to the arrival of the relatives from abroad and Zenie's wedding, which was to follow.

Zenie sewed frantically all winter, not only upon clothes, but on linens and doilies and the hundred and one kinds of covers that a bride considered necessary. Her old trousseau, which Aunt Zena had given her at the time of her engagement to Philippe, was

71

taken out and examined by mother and daughter, but after much debate was in the main discarded as hopelessly old-fashioned.

Late in the fall, Father Duffy took Mrs. Rogers to task when she told him of the postponement. At that time she had rushed forward to greet him, exclaiming, "Oh, Father, I am so happy! Our family is coming home to us. You can't tell the feeling of a grandmother who has never seen her grandchildren. We get photographs of them every year, but they are not the same. To think that little Jesse is six . . ."

This statement coincided with Mr. Rogers appearance. "He is close to eight, my dear."

"I must say, Pet, that I don't like the way you argue with me continually . . . and they call the little girl Titi. Her name is Teresina Augustina after my sister and myself, but the child found it hard to say. . . ."

"As well she might."

Disregarding her husband's remark, she went on, ". . . and she said 'Titi' all of herself. Wasn't that smart of her?"

"Once you have done with the names and ages, Gussie, I will go on with the story. . . ."

"Story? There isn't any story. It is just that Julia is coming home, and high time, too. Zena is sailing with them. They've had some financial losses and with this awful war coming between England and Russia they have determined to settle here, lock, stock, and barrel."

At this point, Mr. Rogers began to laugh and received an angry glance. "I don't see that I said anything funny."

"No, my dear, I am not laughing at you, but at my own error." As even Father Duffy looked puzzled, Mr. Rogers explained, "My good wife is master of certain phrases which I've learned to know and anticipate before she says them. I was certain that she was going to say 'bag and baggage,' which I claim would have been more suitable under the circumstances, but instead she comes out with 'lock, stock, and barrel.' It is this unpredictability which endears her to me, Duffy."

Mrs. Rogers gave him a blank stare and went on as though there had been no interruption. ". . . Of course we've postponed the wedding until they get here . . . Zena would feel hurt—and Julia would like to see her own sister married."

It was then that Father Duffy became grave. "I am not at all sure that I agree. Human desires are a gift from God, which shouldn't be put off too long in their fulfillment. If you want my advice, I think Zenie has waited long enough."

In spite of Mrs. Rogers' "Zenie is perfectly content to wait until the rest of the family is here," Father Duffy attempted a second protest later in the winter, but to no avail. Then, for a considerable time they saw nothing of him, when little items in the daily papers reporting that the Reverend Patrick Duffy was speaking here or there, accounted for his continued absence.

## 4

ZENIE was in tears when she greeted Clint on the front stoop, where she had been waiting to intercept him for these past fifteen minutes. It was an action which her mother would have considered unmaidenly in the extreme, but she just had to talk to him alone. Once inside there was certain to be one of the family around.

As Clint took the steps of the brownstone stoop in his usual three-at-a-time manner, she threw herself into his arms. "Oh, Clint, dear, everything seems to go wrong. Mother had a letter from Julia this morning and they won't get here until May. What with the conditions in France, things are taking so much longer to wind up."

Clint responded with a hug as he asked, grimly, "I suppose that means we have to put it off again? Well, Zenie, old girl, I still think you are worth waiting for, but I have something to propose. I'm getting pretty tired of coming over from Brooklyn every day and it seems silly for me not to stay here, especially as you have so much extra space and your family needs the money. I'd like to be where I could see more of you. . . ."

"And I of you, dear. . . ."

". . . Once the season begins I'll be away so much of the time. I'll put it up to your folks."

Teresina was enthusiastic, but fearful. "Oh, Clint, it would be just perfect, but Mother will never give in to your living here until

73

we are married. 'What will the neighbors think?' she'll say. You know how people are at the hint of scandal. . . ."

"You let me talk to your mother. I'll take care of her," Clint promised with more confidence than he actually felt. "I love you, Zenie, and all this delay is more than I can stand. At least this way I could put up with it."

As proof of her own feeling, Zenie kissed him without once looking around to see who might be watching, although there was no light but the soft gleam of the gas street lamp a third of a block away. She re-entered the hallway and announced, in too-spritely tones, "Here is Clint, Mother. Imagine meeting him on the stoop quite by accident when I went out to see if the weather was taking a turn for the better."

Not a bit taken in, as she had observed half a dozen such trips since the lamplighter had made his round, Mrs. Rogers listened to Clint's suggestion which was quickly forthcoming—he was never one to put off decisions—and calculated that with Clint as a paying guest she could avoid placing too heavy a burden on the Rogers' finances until the others arrived. Of course there was the matter of appearances, but let the neighbors think what they would. She'd see to it that there were no goings-on in her house until the rites, duly administered by Father Duffy, gave them the approval of Church and State.

With this resolve, her lips narrowed into a straight line so that her daughter and prospective son-in-law, watching the changes in her expression, expected a refusal. They were surprised when she said, with seeming matter-of-factness, "I don't see why not. Your expenses will be much less certainly, and you can take it from me that a young married couple will need all they can scrape together to live on in this day and age."

Clint spent the next day in moving his possessions, in spite of an all-night fall of snow which tied up bridge traffic and made walking difficult and treacherous. With him living in the house, waiting was more easily borne. There were shy glances at breakfast, across Norah's great stacks of golden-brown pancakes and full platters of steak, chops or bloaters, according to the day. Then Zenie helped him on with his ulster, picking off threads, real and imaginary, just to feel his sturdiness beneath.

Mrs. Rogers was indefatigable in keeping her eye on them and Mr. Rogers was always eager to involve Clint in a discussion about the exploits of John L. Sullivan or next year's chances for the Brooklyns. In spite of these difficulties, there were treasured moments when neither parent was about and a palpitant Zenie was caught up in Clint's athletic arms.

At night, Zenie received a pleasurable thrill merely from hearing Clint's footsteps in the room over her own. She waited with passionate intensity for that time—long after nine o'clock—when two thumps from above, in rapid succession, indicated the dropping of his shoes as he unlaced and kicked them off, preparatory to retiring.

After he left the house in the morning, in pursuit of one or another of the vaguely described projects which engaged him, Zenie, in her role of assisting with the housework, aired Clint's room first of all. There was a satisfaction just in tracing on the mattress the place where he had lain, the depression from his head on the rumpled pillow.

Henry bore Clint's presence with the worst possible grace. Whenever Clint mentioned any of his ideas or plans, Henry made disparaging remarks. "Apparently they have perfectly good baseballs already, so why should you want to design one that could be hit a longer distance? Harebrained, I'd say. Don't see any money in it." Or again, pontifically, "The only way to make your way in the world is by good hard work, Mr. Weatherby. You'd be well advised to give up these schemes of yours."

When he was home, Henry seemed forever slipping past Zenie and Clint with averted face, or pretending some interest in the parlor when they happened to be in that room together.

After a week that seemed particularly long, in which occurred none of those chance favors which made living endurable, Zenie ran upstairs one morning, certain that Clint had long since left the house. She burst into his room, quite unprepared to find him there, in the act of changing his shirt. Clad in his heavy woolen undershirt and trousers, he was no less surprised by her entrance, but when she hesitated a moment, then dashed into his arms, careless of all possible consequences, he caught her to himself, declaring over and over the impossibility of continuing to keep his love in check. The door closed behind them while Zenie sobbed out her own affection and its frustration.

Neither was conscious of how long they stood this way until Zenie pushed Clint away, horror-stricken at the thought of anyone of the family surprising them. "Clint, my love I must go—I'm being perfectly shameless," she gasped, agitatedly. Desperately she tried to pat out her rumbled house dress and opened the door. Her worst fears were more than realized. Henry stood there, his face a study in scorn and loathing.

After the first moment of shock, she threw her head up proudly. "Henry Rogers, I know what you are thinking and there is no use in telling you it isn't so. I've done nothing I'm ashamed of and you can tell Mother if you've a mind to. . . ." Clint appeared in the doorway behind her, his woolen undershirt above his trousers confirming all of Henry's suspicions to his own satisfaction. "Run along downstairs, and I'll settle this," Clint suggested, but Henry turned without a word and walked toward his own room.

Chapter 8

THE MEAL was practically over when Clint reached into his inside coat pocket and brought out three brightly colored tickets. "Look what I have, folks—three ducats for the Ryan and Sullivan engagement. How about it Henry? Would you like to go and see old John L. meet his match? I know you'll come, won't you, Father Rogers?"

While Mr. Rogers boomed his assent, Henry shook his head. So Clint thought that he could bribe him to forget the stain upon his sister's honor! Coldly, Henry replied, "Fisticuffs? No thank you! I have better ways of utilizing my time."

Clint looked disappointed. He was so anxious to make friends with Henry, but nothing ever succeeded. Surely any man would want to see the great John L! "Oh, come on, Henry. I'm sure that you'd enjoy it . . ."

Henry's "No!" was so uncompromising that Teresina suggested wistfully, "I don't suppose you could take me, could you?"

Even Clint was shocked by the idea, which had been suggested more to bridge an uncomfortable moment than from any hope of acquiescence. "I'm afraid, Zenie, old girl, that a fray such as this would be too much for a refined girl," and Mr. Rogers backed him up emphatically. "Indeed yes, the bloodletting will be terrific with good, old John L. in the arena—but if Henry won't go, I suggest we ask Duffy."

"The very idea!" Mrs. Rogers shrieked. "Father, will you never learn sense? Don't you dare to ask Father Duffy. It would be just like him to accept, too."

"Of course he'll accept, if he isn't otherwise engaged. I met him on the street last week and he said to me, 'Rogers, John L. makes me proud of the Irish.' "

"If you've made up your mind to it, I guess there is no holding you back. Three of a feather, I'd say. . . ."

Mrs. Rogers' prediction proved correct. In spite of further argument, on the clear, cold evening of the twentieth—a perfect January day—the three men were at an entrance of Madison Square Garden.

Rebuilt since the tragic collapse of a wall several years before, the Garden was brilliant with light. Surely a thousand jets illuminated the spacious structure, while over the raised square blazed a veritable sun of burning gas. It was the first time that Mr. Rogers had ever attended a match, while Father Duffy admitted that his only experience had been at several clandestine affairs between rival Kensingtonians. To evade the police, the matches had been held in barns, giving them a surreptitious air.

"It is a change for the better, having the coppers supervise the matches," the good man remarked. "I should say that the whole police force of New York must be on hand."

While they were walking down the aisle, Clint explained, "They want to make sure that Ryan gets a square deal. That's Captain Williams, head of the force, getting into the ring."

The seats filled up rapidly while the officer, his uniform heavy with gold braid, posed within the ropes. He continued to strike various attitudes while the audience smoked or chewed, at first contentedly and then with rising impatience. What had happened? Wasn't the great John L. going to show up?

A movement at the back of the Garden caused the restlessness to subside as two men in trunks and short jackets made their way toward the ring, escorted by a whole squadron of policemen. When it was seen that these were not the famous gladiators, the boos and catcalls were only stilled when a third man entered the ring and announced, "Gentlemen, there is no need for excitement. Sullivan and Ryan will surely appear. The preliminary engagement brings together Pete McCoy, to my right, and Mike Gillespie, of Brooklyn, to my left."

The latter contestant lost, much to Mr. Rogers' chagrin, as he had loudly proclaimed a belief in Mike's victory all during the three rounds of the fray. Next came Japanese wrestlers, who butted their heads together until the crowd again became restless and Father Duffy observed, "We came to watch a couple of good Irishmen fight, not to see two heathens push each other around. Clint, my boy, I think you should complain to the management."

Clinton grinned. "I would, Father, except that my tickets were given to me by the promoter. . . ."

A cheer went up as the great John L. Sullivan stepped into the ring, his green stockings and white trunks showing beneath his short pea jacket. Then Ryan appeared, similarly dressed, except that his stockings were even greener. Clint whispered to Mr. Rogers. "They both look fat to me—too fat, I'd say. The last time they met, Sullivan must have been thirty pounds lighter."

Captain Williams was joined by Inspector Thorne and both police officials posed in statuesque attitudes while the gloves were being tied on. The contestants advanced to the center of the ring and the officials withdrew. "What two magnificent brutes," Mr. Rogers whispered, while Father Duffy chewed away, excitedly nodding his head in complete agreement.

The fighters feinted a time or two and then John L. let fly a blow that would surely have toppled Ryan had it landed. Ryan countered, but his fist slid harmlessly by the champion's mustache.

78

Sullivan again set himself for a haymaker, when Ryan, instead of awaiting it, drove a punch over his adversary's heart.

A roar went up and an amazing thing happened. Apparently Police Inspector Thorne had become jealous at no longer being the center of interest, for he climbed back through the ropes and separated the sweating athletes. Pandemonium broke loose, but the official was adamant. The grand championship match was over! There had been but one minute of inconclusive fighting and there was to be no more.

Clint was adept at escaping from unfriendly crowds. Before either of his companions quite realized it, they were beyond the turmoil of the thousands of angry men who had been cheated of their spectacle, and outside the dressing room door.

A little man with knobby ears said, "Hello, Clint. Want to talk to John L.? He's inside."

"What do you say?"

"Lead the way, my boy," came in a duet and the next moment proved a great one for both of the older men. Sullivan stood, stripped and smiling, showing no sign of the recent conflict except for a red spot on his chest where Ryan's single blow had landed. It was not until Clint introduced them that Mr. Rogers realized that the great John L. Sullivan was no bigger than Duffy, and that both Clint and he were taller.

In response to Father Duffy's question, John L. said he did not know the reason for the sudden end of the bout, but he shouted a hearty farewell and "It's a great night for the Irish," to the priest as the three went on to the next room, where Ryan was talking to a flashily-dressed youth who also knew Clint.

"Bill, meet Mr. Rogers. Bill, here, is a reporter on the *Tribune*. Father Duffy, Bill Trimble." Both men shook hands with the representative of the press and then with Ryan, who was still angry that the fight had been stopped. "If the coppers hadn't stepped in, I would have won hands down. I tell you, Father, when I got that heavy blow in on Sullivan, I could not help thinking of my old mother—and the thought gave me renewed determination."

It seemed to Mr. Rogers that he had almost become a part of history when he read the account in the next morning's *Tribune* and saw the very statement, just as it had been taken down by the reporter, printed for posterity to see. Somehow it increased his belief in the factuality of the news, and proved also that beneath their rough exteriors men like Ryan and John L. Sullivan had loving and sentimental natures.

**Chapter 9**

Proof of Aunt Zena's reduced financial status—if any were needed beyond her constant references in her letters—was provided by the choice of steamer upon which she and her nephew's family were arriving. A far cry, this, from the palatial six-thousand-ton vessel upon which she had first crossed the Atlantic during Centennial year, when the family had gone all the way from Philadelphia to New York to meet her. Now, while the rusty, tubby *Wisconsin* backed gingerly into its berth, Zenie and her parents discussed that former occasion—how it had required a whole parade of hansoms and hacks to convey Aunt Zena's luggage to the Astor House, the opulence of their own entertainment there, the extravagant dinner at Delmonico's, all of Aunt Zena's fabulous history.

It was just two years since Aunt Zena had returned to Paris after a second visit to her sister's family, when she had traveled with a less complicated entourage—one more suited to the chase, as Mrs. Rogers had once remarked in a vindictive mood. The comparative simplicity of her wardrobe and the lack of personal maids had combined to rob her of some of the earlier glamour, but the family still could not visualize her without the great wealth to which she had so long been accustomed.

Mrs. Rogers voiced the thought of both Zenie and her father when she said, "Really, Pet, I'm so anxious to see Julia and the babies that I can hardly wait. My knees are shaking, truly they are, from nothing but excitement. I dread meeting Zena, though. Poor dear, I'm afraid to think what her loss may have done to her."

They threaded their way between hogsheads and packing cases to a point where they could glance up the rusty sides of the old vessel and see the passengers lined along its rail, but these looked too poor and forlorn to be companions of the Lascalles, even in their present state. Mr. Rogers was the first to grasp the truth and he snorted with disgust. "Come Mother, this is an immigrant boat and those are steerage passengers. Another boatload of Fenians, I suppose, come to throw their bombs over here."

This statement seemed hardly fair to the group of tattered children, shawl-clad women and square-shouldered men who were looking for the first time upon a land of new opportunity after having escaped the tyrannical British yoke, but it did express the feeling which Mr. Rogers held in common with most other Americans toward the poor Irish just come to their soil.

He shouldered his way forward, and as they came opposite the cabin section, shouted, "There's Philippe—I'd know him anywhere."

Philippe saw his father-in-law at the same moment and waved frantically in return. A tall, dark, slender child, his head fringed with long curls, stood next to him, and then Julia made her appearance, holding a fair-haired girl. The sight of her daughter and grandchildren put Mrs. Rogers in such a state of ecstasy that she waved her handkerchief with one hand while she clung to her husband for support with the other. "Oh, Pet, the baby is the spitting image of Gene at her age—but it really breaks my heart to see little Jesse. Who does he remind you of?"

"That's easy! Julia, of course."

"Oh, Jesse, don't you see? Isn't there someone else?"

At her husband's blank look, she went on, "He's exactly like Raphael just before he died—exactly. He is breaking my heart, indeed he is."

Mr. Rogers realized, as he had done many times before, how little he knew this woman with whom he had lived for so long. Why Raphael was no more than a vague, distant memory to him. The tragedy which had taken away their first-born some twenty years before had been grievous enough at the time, but except for Gussie's reminder he would not have called it to mind. To think that she carried that image alive in her heart all these years!

81

A spirited conversation had begun between rail and wharf, but everyone became impatient as time passed and no one was allowed ashore. Little Jesse became restless and tried to climb the railing. The baby cried and had to be comforted by its mother. Philippe, who had grown considerably stouter, shouted descriptions of the voyage and Mr. Rogers bellowed back platitudes as though the oceans still separated them, but even their lungs gave out while the interminable business of the customs officials continued. Gradually there came long periods of restless quiet that were punctuated by infrequent observations, as when Mr. Rogers cried, "Did you pass the Bartholdi pedestal?" and it turned out that though living in France, Philippe was in complete ignorance of the Statue of Liberty that was being built there.

Mrs. Rogers called upward, "Where is Zena?" and missed Julia's reply in confiding, "I'm so worried about her. It wouldn't surprise me at all that she'll go into a decline—if she hasn't already. I just can't imagine that sister of mine without money."

She had no more than uttered the words when the passengers were allowed to descend the gangplank and it was Zena Lascalles who led the way. Mrs. Rogers changed her worried look into a grimace and complained, "Zena was always a one to make an entrance. Just look at her, will you?"

More stunning to the eye than ever, she was brave in a diagonally striped dress of cream and brilliant green. It was set off by a bonnet in which green roses and yellow ostrich tips mingled. Yes, indeed, if anyone thought that Zena Lascalles would be dismayed by the loss of a few million francs her appearance was proof to the contrary. When she reached the wharf she hugged Mrs. Rogers, kissed her brother-in-law on both cheeks and then, daringly, on the mouth, and greeted Zenie with a "Well, my dear, dear child. You are more beautiful than ever! And where is your handsome Clinton?"

Before any answer could have been made, a divertissement was created by the frantic cries of little Jesse Lascalles, frightened by the way his strange grandmother suddenly pounced upon him, nibbling at his olive cheeks, suffocating him against her bosom. With Latin effusiveness, Mrs. Rogers laughed, cried and shrieked in almost the same breath and the more little Jesse tried to wriggle and scream the closer she pressed him.

Julia extricated her offspring, soothing him with a soft, "Why Jesse, darling, that is your dear, dear grandmother. She is collecting all the crosses you made on the bottom of my letters to her—don't you remember?

"And Mother, this is Teresina Augustina—aren't you going to make a fuss over her?"

Of course Mrs. Rogers was, and did—and over Julia as well—but it was easy to see that little Jesse was her real love. That youngster, though, continued to protest her attentions and instead ran into the arms of Zenie.

Zenie embraced him with mixed feelings. Except for her own conceit, years ago, Jesse might have been her son—that stoutish, baldish man her husband. A succession of barren days might have been filled with exciting adventure in parts of the world that were only names to her. Instead of frugal living in Brooklyn, she might have enjoyed all the luxury Julia had known. But she would not have met Clint!

The bitterness toward her sister which once had filled her heart was replaced by intense gratitude. Why there was just no comparison between Philippe's fleshiness and Clinton Weatherby's lean strength, between Philippe's amiability and Clint's vital directness. She unloosed little Jesse's fingers from her dress, ran over to Julia and in each other's arms the sisters discovered a love they had never known before.

While the women laughed and cried together, the men arranged the opening of trunks for the customs and procured the necessary drays and hacks for their conveyance uptown. When they returned, Aunt Zena was telling with gusto of the days when she thought an Indian lurked behind every tree on Broadway. A remarkable woman, Aunt Zena, Mr. Rogers told himself. Surely she possessed the secret of eternal youth. Why it didn't seem any time since Gussie had been furious with him—and with Zena—over the latter's advances. That had been over nine years ago, but she looked younger than ever. . . .

"A penny for your thoughts, Jesse. I declare, you have become an old bear. You need me around to liven you up." There, that was

83

Zena for you, taking up with him right where she had left off, in spite of Gussie's furious glances.

They arrived home to find Gene and Gus, apologetic that the lateness of their train had caused them to miss the *Wisconsin's* berthing. While Mr. Rogers intimated that the Pottsville express had never been behind time during *his* years with the Philadelphia and Reading, Gene told about her life in the coal regions, the gradual increase in her husband's practice and the terrible poverty among the miners.

Mrs. Rogers' discerning eye noted that Gene was wearing the dress in which she had eloped two years before, but that it had been done over with a few extra ruchings of ribbon; that Gene's hands were suspiciously red at the joints; that Gus had a gaunt and worried air. There was more here than appeared on the surface! Things were not going as well as Gene pretended!

After the newcomers had made a complete inspection of the house and exclaimed over its size, convenience, and elegant appearance, Gene suddenly cried out in dismay, "But where is Henry? He isn't sick or anything, is he, Mother?"

"Oh, Henry!" Mrs. Rogers made a gesture of disgust. "I suggested that he should take the day off, but no . . . business comes first, he says."

"And he is right, Gussie." Mr. Rogers broke in. "Your brother, my dear, has just been made the manager of his office. Not bad for a youth of Henry's years, I should say. One of these days he'll be branching out for himself. . . ."

Although Georgina's face lit up at the news, she was disappointed. Then with her usual buoyancy, she inquired, "Where is the lucky man? Wait until you see him, Julia! He's better looking than Philippe and would make two of my Gus—though he couldn't be sweeter. . . ."

This new camaraderie among the three sisters was pleasant to each of them, but it was sweetest of all to Teresina. She glowed with an inward light in which pride had a part, but a newly-discovered pride that came from thinking of Clint's endearing qualities and not of her own beauty. With more vivaciousness than the others had ever seen her display, she cried out, "Oh, Gene, stop! You are making him out to be a regular paragon—

84

which he isn't, or he wouldn't have fallen in love with me. And whatever you do, don't ask how the game went. Today is his turn to pitch—which is why he isn't here—and when he loses he hates to talk about it. If he won, Father will worm it out of him quick enough. . . ."

Henry arrived home before Clinton Weatherby; and proof that he still possessed a human streak and was not given over completely to business, was the manner in which he ran to his twin sister and embraced her, then grasped Gus's hands in his own until the doctor winced and objected, "If you want me to play tonight, you better stop crushing my hands in that grip of yours, Henry, old man."

This reminded all of them how long it had been since they had enjoyed an evening of Gus's songs—that in fact they had not all been together this way since the Centennial. Aunt Zena cried, "If that charming priest were only here—what was his name? Too handsome a man ever to have taken the cloth, anyway."

Two or three voices screamed at once, "Father Duffy, you mean," and Mr. Rogers went on to explain that he was probably at the baseball game this minute, with Clint. . . . "By one of the vagaries of the sport it sometimes requires more than the usual nine innings, which adds to the excitement. . . ."

Mrs. Rogers silenced him with one of her most forbidding glances of disapproval, but as dinner was about to be served, of which the main dish was collared eel, he was soon launched upon a description of each of the reptilian-like fish which he had selected the day before at the great eel market between Water and South Streets. "Sometime I must take you down there," he confided (at the top of his voice) to Aunt Zena. "There are some less desirable markets, so don't be misled. The best eels are sold at the Catherine Street Slip—great, beautiful, slippery fellows from Canarsie Bay. . . ."

As they were already partaking of them, Mrs. Rogers felt it indelicate to describe them in such detail and interrupted to give her recipe. "First you wash them real well—after they are skinned, of course—and cook them in well-seasoned water. Just before they are done, when the liquid is most boiled away, add some sour white wine—I like that better than vinegar, myself—then jar and cover close. They'll keep all winter, that way, but mercy, that doesn't mean that we have ever been able to, the rate we eat them."

Dinner was over before Clint made his appearance with Father Duffy. Neither victory nor defeat had delayed them, but a twelve-inning tie, which should have been won, except for the Brooklyns' unexampled bad luck with umpires.

Father Duffy exclaimed at the weight Philippe had taken on and teased Julia about the effect of happy marriage upon the male. The children had already been put to bed, over which he expressed disappointment and then went on to flatter Aunt Zena, upon whom the family turmoil had a tonic effect. In her most provocative manner she proclaimed, "Anyone so gallant as you are, Father, is simply wasted as a priest. If you ever put away your clericals let me know. I'll capture you before any other woman can even get close."

For a moment, Father Duffy's expression became almost grim. "There's been many a true word spoken in jest, dear Madam Lascalles. I can think of no happier fate than to fall into your hands. . . ."

Clinton Weatherby, meanwhile, was assuring Zenie that it was not necessary to set places at the table. "We've both eaten, as we knew we'd be late," he explained, when Father Duffy interrupted, "Collared eel! Hush your mouth, Weatherby. It is my favorite dish. You have such delicious viands daily, while with me 'tis a rare privilege."

He was still gorging when Gus Palmer, at the piano, lured him into the parlor with a rendition, in his clear light tenor, of the minstrel yodeling song of untrue love:

> One night when I got all the babies to sleep
> I took a short walk down the street,
> And to my surprise I saw with my eyes
> My wife with a soldier six feet . . .

There was no end to Father Duffy's accomplishments. He rushed in, wiping vinegared eel from his chin and completely outdid Gus at yodeling, with all kinds of involved effects, as to-

86

gether they "Rocked the Baby to Sleep," while the faithless wife continued her shameless doings elsewhere.

It was the most memorable songfest ever. Georgina was prevailed upon to do several of her elocution numbers and Gus sang a plaintive song of the miner who spent all his time, "Digging dusky diamonds underneath the ground." Clinton Weatherby, after taking much good-natured raillery over the fast-approaching nuptials, pulled out his mouth organ and played some Irish jigs that set everyone to tapping. He finished with a reel—when Father Duffy jumped up, seized Aunt Zena and danced with her until both were dizzy.

The high point which ended the gay evening turned out to be Mr. Rogers' barnyard imitations. As he stepped forward, stroking his beard with a heavy hand, Father Duffy was intrigued by the thought that the two Rogers' daughters who were dark and Latin in appearance and temperament—and who both had so often been at loggerheads with their father—should have fallen in love with men so much like him. On the other hand, Georgina, the fun-loving, blonde female counterpart of himself, had married the thin, nervous, highly idealistic Dr. Augustus Palmer.

Mr. Rogers cleared his throat once or twice, bellowed forth "Little pigs lay upon very good straw," and squealed and grunted with appropriately piglike noises, then waved his hands as a signal to them all to join in the nonsense chorus.

Mrs. Rogers screamed, "It's been wonderful, but what will the neighbors think?" over the final, exuberant refrain:

> Feed him on bananas and he'll never get the gout
> Bless the darling little nigger's woolly head . . .

as Father Duffy left the happy family group, promising that he'd be on hand early for the wedding two days hence.

2

MRS. ROGERS struggled with the blue silk foulard that had been her best warm-weather dress ever since they had first moved to Brooklyn. "Jesse, will you come here and help me with this? My fingers are all thumbs. I've never been in such a state and now one of the hooks is caught in my hair. I can't move either way."

Mr. Rogers was wrestling with his own collar that refused to be impaled upon its button and as most of his wife's plea was smothered in a welter of silk and crinoline, he retorted impatiently, "I can't hear a word you're saying, Gussie—besides, this collar would try the patience of a saint. Why Norah starches them until they are like cast iron . . ."

There was another wail from beneath the turrets and puffs. "*Please*, Pet . . . I'm suffocating, indeed I am. I can't get in or out. . . ."

Mr. Rogers let go of the ends of his collar, which sprang apart like a steel spring, dashed over and began the intricate task of freeing various hooks that were caught in curl or under-bodice. "There, I've got you all unhitched. If you can wriggle, I'll pull." A series of contortions followed, but the dress stubbornly refused to budge. "When is the last time you encased yourself in this sausage skin?" Mr. Rogers asked, accusingly, wiping his brow, and an answer came from the depths, "How should I remember? But you will have to do something besides asking stupid questions, or I'll faint. I think that you are deliberately trying to keep me from going to my own daughter's wedding."

Mr. Rogers began a new series of yanks and pulls, accompanied by warnings of "Look out, Jesse, don't tear it—be careful of the ruching," and so on. " 'Deliberately trying to keep' you from going! I like that. Did I invent this confection of folderols? Did I add ten pounds to your frame? Ten pounds that makes this garment almost impossible of slicking on. But if you'd only keep your breath instead of talking, I'd make it at that."

"Hold everything, Pet." A flushed and panting Gussie examined herself in the mirror with appraising eye. This had always been her favorite dress; thank goodness that she had been able to get into it. For a moment she had expected to have to sit down then and there and make alterations—with the wedding only an hour away.

The wedding! She gave up her critical examination of the skirt, trimmed with its narrow kiltings and fine shirrings, and of the bodice so effective with lace and jet, sat down in the rocker by the bedstead, and gave way to tears. "Zenie is the only one of our daughters to be married at home—and then it has to be to a man of whom I disapprove. When Julia ran away, I would have preferred a respectable wedding, of course, but it was easy to reconcile oneself to a man of Philippe's fortune. As for Gus Palmer, while he is throwing away his talents, I always did like him and anything that went wrong there was because of Gene. . . .

"But to think of Zenie, the most beautiful of our daughters, marrying a baseball player—even going to Cincinnati on her wedding trip with his team . . ." Words failed her for a moment or so, while she sniffled. "I fully expect to get a telegram saying he's deserted her. Married or not married, I wouldn't put it past him."

"I never saw your like for borrowing trouble. For a year you kept repeating that Clint would never marry her; now that they'll be hitched in a little while, you say he'll leave her the next day. You are being silly, I think. By the Lord Harry, women . . ." Exasperation gave away to sympathy, as he noted her woe-begone expression. "Come, Gussie, pull yourself together. We've the three girls married at last—which should satisfy you—and only Henry to think about. A pretty good record, if I do say so myself. In a few years there will be little Titi. I envision for you a most delightful old age worrying about every boy who comes to the house calling on her. Right now, though, I think you had better go back to Zenie's room and see how she is coming. . . ."

Zenie's dress! Norah was supposed to be helping, but there were certain to be little things that a shiftless Irish girl couldn't be expected to notice. Constrained somewhat by her own elegance, Mrs. Rogers patted cold water on her eyes—Zenie mustn't see that she had been crying—and hurried down the hall to the bride's room. Her smile was a trifle hard and set, but that she managed to achieve one at all was in the nature of a miracle. "What! Your dress not on yet? Child, what are you thinking of? Heavens above, not those drawers—the ones with the pleats and the lace. So long as I am well and in my right mind, no daughter of mine is going to be married in drawers that look as if they just came from Hearn's."

After this shot, she bustled off downstairs to make certain that the hired potted palms had been properly placed. Julia, meanwhile, descended toward the first floor, followed by her young son, who walked with the utmost consciousness that he was on good behavior and dare not race or slide down the walnut balustrade. Mrs. Rogers glimpsed him through the portieres and rushed forward to embrace him with the fervency that the child disliked. He turned his head sidewise to avoid the too-loving kisses, then Mrs. Rogers surveyed his colorful costume and gushed, "Julia, where did you get that lovely hat? You look charming in it, Jesse. The way it sets off your curls . . ."

The child, his perverseness increasing, snatched off the little gray felt, with its red band and streaming ribbons, and shouted, "I'm not going to wear it any longer."

There was tremendous handclapping from the direction of the stairway. Mr. Rogers also disliked the trousers of red, blue and gray striped linen, with the contrasting coat and red striped waistcoat, the blue cravat and ruffles. "Bravo, Jesse. I shouldn't wear it either. They are trying to make a namby-pamby of you and the first chance I get we will slip down to the barbershop and clip off those long curls."

With an anguished cry, Julia ran to little Jesse's protection. "My precious child! Mother loves his curls, and you do too, don't you?"

"I don't like them—I hate them."

Mr. Rogers applauded again. "A real boy, even if he is Frenchified. If I were you, Julia, I'd save a costume like that for a masquerade."

"Father! I see you are still impossible. That is a peasant suit; it was most expensive and the latest thing. I think it is terrible of you to egg on Jesse this way. He always loved this suit so."

While little Jesse screamed, "No, I did not. I never did," Mr. Rogers was shouting, "The answer is that Jesse isn't a peasant, but is to grow up into a good American boy, which he won't if you keep him tricked out in curls and ruffles."

The altercation had grown so loud that it frightened Titi, who was being borne downstairs by Philippe, and she began to cry. As little Jesse was still airing his distaste for peasant costumes and curls, it was no moment for the first wedding guests to arrive. Twelve large and broad, mustachioed and whiskered gentlemen filed in, bowed toward Mrs. Rogers with an excess of good manners, then looked around curiously. At her expression of surprise, one of them proceeded to introduce himself and the others. It was the Brooklyn baseball team!

<h2 style="text-align:center">3</h2>

THE CEREMONY was simple and the guests were few. In addition to the Brooklyns, of whom Smith—the catcher of Clint's "pellets" —acted as best man, the groom produced two maiden aunts. As she was introduced to them, Mrs. Rogers thought how little she really knew about Clint and tried to gather some clue of what his family might have been by one of her appraising studies— studies more obvious than she imagined them to be. There was nothing to be gained from this examination of the rather colorless, but respectable-looking aunts. When she tried to question them she met with no greater success and ended up by excusing the small number of their own friends who were present. "We've moved here so recently, of course. In Kensington my husband was very well known—his father was in the shipping business there— but then we had to move to Brooklyn because of the bridge people needing his help. As soon as *that* was finished, we came to New York, so we've lost touch. . . ."

Her own family should have made such trumpery explanations unnecessary. Mr. Rogers was a triumph of impressiveness in tailed coat and winged collar, which he identified, respectively, as "shadbelly" and "gates-ajar." He gave the bride away with a masterly portrayal of the father at once saddened by his own loss and happy over the bride's joy to come.

Gus was called "Doctor Palmer" almost more often than necessary and Gene's lush beauty compensated for the made-over look of her dress.

Julia was gowned in a Paris creation of cream-colored ottoman silk, decorated with clusters of appliquéd pansies. Before and during the ceremony, she conversed with Philippe in French, which added no little *éclat* to the affair, and Jesse, as page to the bridal couple, looked like Cupid himself (in peasant costume).

Henry was handsome, but forbidding, as though he disapproved of the whole affair. His feelings were mixed. Clint was really going through with the marriage, so Zenie would become an honest woman; on the other hand, he was no proper husband for her.

It was Aunt Zena, though, who really established the tone of the occasion. She wore a dress in varying shades of purple that the family had seen before, but it had been enhanced by even further decoration, until she billowed with ribbons and puffs, ostrich plumes and tips, flowers and laces and other furbelows. The presence in the parlor of twelve athletic and handsome Brooklyns made her more vivacious than ever, so that while the only other guest outside of the family was Al Naylor, the room seemed to be alive with people and movement.

Georgina had greeted Al in a fashion that was almost scandalous, considering that she had once run away with him, when they had spent most of the night asleep in the same train seat. She had rushed to him, kissed him resoundingly on the cheek and otherwise had been most unladylike. Not that Gus Palmer seemed to mind. He and Al were friends of years' standing, and had the same political convictions, which were pale pink or deepest red, depending upon one's point of view. Henry's greeting of Al was almost as warm as his sister's; in fact, it was the only time that he unbent at all, and they sat together, with Georgina next to Henry, while Father Duffy performed his task.

Zenie, dressed in simple white, was ravishing. Indeed, Mrs. Rogers wondered if the dress were not a trifle too simple. In addition to the veil which misted her black hair, and a small bouquet of lilies-of-the-valley, the only decorations to her costume were the box pleats in front and the rather heavily braided side panels, with the loops of silk cord that fastened the drape on the right side. Mrs. Rogers had planned to add some baby-blue silk ribbons, which she had put away for just such an occasion, and only lack of time prevented her, before Zenie entered upon the arm of her father.

Meanwhile, Father Duffy had been keeping the group in good humor by his fund of Irish stories, one or two of which seemed almost too risqué for a wedding; but even Henry laughed and relaxed, his old constraint returning only when he was compelled by proximity to talk with the groom.

92

Nervousness had made Clint more boisterous than usual before the ceremony took place. His red hair gleamed against the palm fronds and Zenie floated in accompanied by a figure so blurred and distorted to Mrs. Rogers that she felt the whole thing was unreal, a dream from which she would shortly awaken.

Clint kissed the bride and Father kissed the bride and Father Duffy kissed the bride, the maiden aunts began to cry and Norah, viewing the scene from the doorway, began to cry, and Mrs. Rogers began to cry.

The men were not affected by this excess of tears. There was much laughter and many knowing smiles among them, followed by a tiptoeing to the front door, when in came a man with a camera, his arm draped in green and black cloths, followed by two of the Brooklyns bearing sundry mechanical contrivances. The clamps were screwed tight, and Clint and Zenie stood rigidly while the photographer fussed over knobs and cloths and plates. One pose followed another, until a complete record of the affair had been taken for later fond recall, and Zenie dashed upstairs to change for breakfast and the train.

4

IT WAS a happy party that took the ferry over to Jersey City. The bride and groom rode behind Mr. Quinby with a beaming Abe at the reins, and special livery carriages conveyed the rest of the wedding party. Fortunately, the ferry was practically empty and they were all accommodated. The photographer made some more shots while the vessel churned out from the pier. The first attempt proved a failure, as Zenie, lovely in a shrimp-pink suit, was too excited to hold still for the required time. The photographer posed them in silhouette, against the rail, not looking at the distant shore, but toward each other, in a way that everyone felt was highly artistic and symbolic.

The Brooklyns possessed a good quartet that rendered "When You and I Were Young, Maggie," which did not seem altogether appropriate, but received enthusiastic applause. Aunt Zena flirted outrageously with the second baseman, who turned out to be a

Lothario quite able to deal with the Continental manner of Clint Weatherby's new aunt.

After the voyage was over and Clint and Zenie dashed into one of Mr. Pullman's sleeping cars to the accompaniment of a shower of rice and another rendition from the quartet, and after the train had pulled out of the station and was a blot in the distance, Aunt Zena confided to her sister, "Tina, dear, I've never known the intimate friendship of an athlete. Aren't they wonderful! Such muscle, and so light on their feet. I quite envy Zenie. I think baseball players are thrilling."

They were well out from shore on the ferry's return trip before Mrs. Rogers spoke. "At least they are more of gentlemen than I should have suspected. But oh, it is terrible to think that all my girls are married. No one can tell what troubles they may be in for later. . . ."

# PART TWO

\* \* \*

*May, 1886 to September, 1887*

\* \* \*

"To love and lift was all your creed:
 Child-bold, you went the way of it:
You crammed your doctrine into deed,
 To bring the golden day of it."
                    EDWIN MARKHAM, *Father McGlynn*

*Chapter 1*    **M**UCH as they all loved Father Duffy, it had never occurred to any of the Rogers family that he would ever be a famous man—or an infamous one—if *The New York Times* was to be believed. They had grown used to seeing his name in obscure corners of the newspapers. Then he spoke in Pottsville on the same platform with Mr. Powderly, of the Knights of Labor, and the *Times* reported that he had been "guest of Dr. Augustus Palmer and his attractive wife."

Mrs. Rogers was dismayed. "If Father Duffy is going to be a Communist it is his own affair, but when he gets our own kith and kin involved it is too much. It is not fair to Gus and Gene, putting up with a notorious character and getting their names in the paper just because of an old friendship."

"You forget, Gussie," she was reminded, "Gene made a speech too, and it was a humdinger."

"That came from your idea of having her take elocution. . . ."

Rank untruth though this was, Mr. Rogers had let it pass at the time. Since then there had been nothing but news of strikes and meetings of one sort or another and he also began to doubt the wisdom of his daughter and son-in-law identifying themselves with workingmen's causes. Yesterday there had been May Day celebrations everywhere, including a great mass meeting in Union Square. A new railroad strike had begun. No wonder the papers became frightened and launched a violent attack upon Anarchists, Communists, Socialists, and Single Taxers. In the *Times* editorial, venom was loosed against the Reverend Patrick Duffy, D.D. "Here is what it says, Gussie. 'No man can serve two masters. There is Scripture for it. This is what Dr. Duffy has to do. He is either a priest of the Roman Catholic Church and then his allegiance is

97

due to the head of the Church; or he is a private American citizen and then he must walk out into the world on his own merits.'

"And listen to what Duffy replied. Be patient a moment, until I find the place. . . . 'God is Father of his children and he has given them all equally his bounties.' A well-put sentence that. I don't know that I altogether approve of Duffy mixing in politics, but he is a man of great conviction and a fighter. The nearest to a really Christlike man I've ever known, which is a funny thing to be saying about an Irishman."

He shook his head while Mrs. Rogers continued with a variety of tasks. "This is a serious matter for Duffy, though they say that he has already become the most popular priest in New York."

Three days later came the horrible news. The radicals and the workingmen were in open insurrection against the government. While several thousand workmen were listening to a speaker in Chicago's old Haymarket Plaza, they were charged by a column of police. The workingmen threw stones and the police answered with pistol fire. Then came an explosion. When the smoke cleared away, sixty-four workmen had been seriously injured, two policemen were dead and others hurt. The forces of law and order had been massacred! This was what came of allowing irresponsible rascals to speak in public! This was what came of permitting men like Henry George and Father Duffy and similar misguided persons to incite the masses.

"I'm afraid Duffy is in for it." Mr. Rogers shook his head sadly before he turned the page in response to his wife's, "What I want to know is, what does it say about the President's marriage? She looks a real sweet girl, though for my own part I'd be ashamed to be married to Mr. Cleveland, knowing the past he'd had."

"Now, Gussie, I think you're too hard on our President. He is a good man, I'd say, and not just because he's a Democrat. He stood by the girl he wronged and accepted his responsibility, which is more than most do. . . ."

By the next day there was more in the papers about the Haymarket massacre; and Mr. Rogers' capacity for sympathy was such that at one moment he was believing in labor's side and then agreed with the *Times*' editorial, which objected, "Forcing employers to grant eight hours work for ten hours pay has resulted so far in the death of five policemen and six workingmen. Fully 30,000, earning on the average $1.50 per day, have been idle for a week."

The clergy was also rallying to the side of the poor employers. "Hear this, my dear. . . . No, I've the wrong line. Here it is. The Reverend Swing preached a whole sermon on the way things are going. 'Over the graves of our brave policemen, many of us are longing with Apostle John for a new Jerusalem. We need a careful definition of what freedom is. If it means a license to proclaim the gospel of disorder the sooner we exchange the Republic for an iron-handed monarchy the better. America must be Americanized!' That's aimed right at Duffy. . . ."

When the house was otherwise quiet, and the children out with their parents, why should Jesse keep ranting about Father Duffy's backsliding into Communism or something? Mrs. Rogers slipped out of the parlor to go upstairs, but Mr. Rogers didn't notice. "They should get rid of Germans like this Haymarket bunch. . . . 'Schwab's eyes are covered with heavy, puffy lids and he shields them behind a pair of steel-rimmed spectacles.' Chris Spies is a chucklehead and his brother has a furtive look. Fielden 'chewed savagely on a toothpick.' With Germany the center of Communism, every member of that benighted country who comes over here should be examined. The government has been remiss letting them run around loose. . . ."

The government did not continue remiss. Within the next two weeks most of the known radicals were arrested and probably only his cloth saved Father Duffy, who continued to plead for the Haymarket prisoners. But his was a voice crying in the wilderness. A bomb had been thrown from behind the red flag—so people believed, and their belief was not to be changed.

One morning, when Henry and Philippe had gone on a short trip together and little Jesse was dispatched to school—free these six months of the curls that had made his first days in the classroom a torture—Julia and Zenie set off for the park with Titi in the perambulator. They were no sooner out of the house than Mrs. Rogers queried her husband, "I hope you noticed the way that Zenie is looking? I've recognized from the first that Clint would never bring happiness to her and proof of it is before your eyes right now, if you'd only look. But no, you are like she is. Anything the man does is all right. Why before he left for the West he wasn't home more than one or two nights a week. Zenie is eating her heart out, though she is too proud to say anything. Pet, I think you should get him aside and talk to him, indeed I do."

Mr. Rogers grunted, still intent upon his paper. "The President's new wife must be a darn good-looking female. 'Tall, graceful, blue-eyed and fair, blushing like the morn beneath her misty veil, Miss Folsom looked an ideal American bride.' She'll be a credit to the White House, too. I've always felt that the country needs a married Chief Executive. . . ."

"If you'd think more about your own family and less about other people! Here is Zenie miserable because Clint is away so much, but instead of helping, you are either out gallivanting with him yourself or talking about the new Mrs. Cleveland." There was truth in the accusation and Mrs. Rogers watched intently to see how Jesse would take it.

Mr. Rogers chose to be grandiose. "The male, my dear Gussie, finds it difficult to occupy his mind with the piddling details of domesticity which appeal to the female. While Clint and I have spent a few evenings together, they have been of an educational or worth-while nature. The other night we attended the meeting to raise funds for the Statue of Liberty pedestal—surely a laudable project which citizens should support. Yesterday we watched Professor Gleason, the world's greatest horse educator, as he handled vicious animals. If Mr. Quinby ever gets rambunctious, I . . . ."

"Piffle! Mr. Quinby hasn't been fractious in his life, so he won't begin now. And I suppose it was highly educational to go all the way out to Coney Island just to watch the roller skating in the Elephantine Colossus. . . ."

"At least it is a change from sitting around the house all the time and doing nothing. I tell you, Gussie, I get bored. . . ."

"I don't see why you should be bored. I'm around the house all the time and so is Zenie. If we can stand it, you two should be able to."

"Clint's position is different. He has to stay in the public eye. It's part of his business. Zenie will have to grow used to the idea that he is a public figure.

"Besides, things aren't too pleasant for him here when Henry is home. The boy is downright disagreeable. . . ."

"Henry is concerned about his sister's welfare and will hold Clinton Weatherby in line when he can. And that's a poor excuse to use now, with Henry traveling all the time. I don't think you realize what a responsibility he has, practically running all of Mr. Madeira's business. In another year he'll be making as much as Clint—and with better prospects."

Aunt Zena's entrance put an end to the discussion. "Now, Tina, there is no use making a face. For years I had my breakfast served in bed at eleven. I think I've made concession enough crawling downstairs at nine-thirty.

"And Jesse, if you dare look at me I'll never forgive you. What a hag I must appear at this moment!"

"On the contrary . . ." While Mr. Rogers launched into an elaborate bit of flattery that wouldn't sound too much like that of yesterday and the day before, his wife pursed her lips. Zena always appeared in *déshabillé* too provocative to be accidental and Mrs. Rogers dispatched Norah to the neighborhood store, where she had intended going herself for the perishables among the day's provisions.

NORAH had fitted into the life of the family so completely that it seemed as though she had always lived with them and there were times Mrs. Rogers rattled on about Kensington when both of them forgot that Norah knew it only by hearsay. Then some little point would be raised and there would be a "What say, mum?" from Norah and an explanation beginning, "The place at the end of Richmond Street," or "You remember the picnic, Norah! When we took the steamer up the Delaware? . . ." and then they would be amazed to rediscover that Norah had been with them only since Brooklyn days, when she had come as a frightened child, fresh from Ireland. Why it was Mary who had been with them in Kensington—poor rheumatic Mary, doing for them as she hobbled around on her lame leg, working her toothless gums.

That was one of the tricks that memory played, for Mary's spirit had merged somehow with Norah's.

There was a time when the young girl had been terribly afraid of Mrs. Rogers and her scoldings, but as she learned to love her mistress she also began to stand up to her, so that now life between them was largely a duel of words in which Norah's sharp Irish wit was more than a match for Mrs. Rogers' shrewishness.

The family accepted Norah so completely that the idea of her leaving them for any reason whatsoever never occurred to them. She appeared happy and devoted and certainly no man would ever be interested in her, for her ugliness had become almost proverbial. She had brassy hair and a freckled face. Her small features, up-tilted nose and intensely blue eyes were so completely undone by bad and irregular teeth that when she smiled one was conscious of little else. Of course most of the other Irish immigrants suffered from a similar defect because of malnutrition in the old country, and Norah's countrymen might see nothing unusual in her unsightly teeth, but her own countrymen she treated with the greatest contempt. "A bog-trotter tried to see me out of church this mornin' but I'd have none of him," she'd told Mrs. Rogers on more than one occasion.

Then, a few weeks ago, a change had taken place in Norah's appearance—one which had been noted vaguely, but was later recalled in detail. She had appeared at dinner one evening with the brassy tresses done up in a very creditable chignon similar to that affected by Julia and had borne the soup tureen with an air of grave triumph in place of her usual gap-toothed smile.

Today, after depositing her marketing in the basement kitchen, she went upstairs, presumably to do the chamberwork. Later Mrs. Rogers went up to the catch-all room on the fourth floor and heard the sound of deep, uncontrolled sobbings from next door. In her usually impulsive manner, she rushed down the uncarpeted hall, burst in and surprised Norah, who was crying her heart out.

She lay in her muslin underthings, face downward, and on a little table next to her cot was strewn—as though she had just been counting it—a pitiful hoard of coins, of which several for twenty-five cents were the largest in denomination. Her black uniform and white apron were removed so as not to muss them, and hung in the open closet along with the pathetic articles of finery which constituted the girl's wardrobe.

Mrs. Rogers lifted the girl's head. "Norah, my dear child, what in the world has happened?" Then she saw the reddened, hopeless eyes and woe-begone expression. Her always ready suspicions caused her to inquire more sharply, "You haven't let any . . . Norah, you're not . . ." and the usual search for a word that would do duty for the one on the tip of her tongue, ". . . you're not in trouble?"

A most positive shake of the collapsed chignon satisfied her on that score and gradually the story was unfolded. Between snifflings, Norah explained, "It's the down-payment on me teeth, mum. I been a'savin' and a'scrapin' for months and it's still not enough— when I was sure I had it together. . . ." She brought out a much creased and handled clipping of a business notice from one of the papers, showing the before and after appearance of one of the patients of a certain Dr. Richards, who pulled bad teeth without pain and provided new porcelain ones that in their glistening whiteness and regularity were far superior to anything ever put by nature into human skull.

"It's a fine man I've met, and with nice teeth like them he'd have me sure, but he won't wait forever, that's certain, good-lookin' like he is and not Irish, either."

In spite of the poignancy of the moment, Mrs. Rogers could not refrain from commenting, "If he's good looking it goes without saying that he isn't Irish."

"There is a livin'-out girl down the street is makin' eyes at him right now. I'd like to tell her off—and I will, too, if she keeps it up. . . .

"And it's two whole dollars I'll be needin' for the down-payment on the plates before the dentist will even begin pullin' the old ones. The twenty-five cents a week afterward I can manage."

As the whole story unfolded, Mrs. Rogers rocked back and forth on the cot, holding as much of Norah's person as she conveniently could while she alternately patted her damp forehead and "tsch'd, tsch'd." Gradually she came to see Norah with new eyes. With teeth, Norah would be downright pretty, having beneath her maid's costume the kind of figure men most appreciated. Short she was, and not of sufficient weight, but her waist was tiny and blossomed rearwards in most adequate hips while her breasts were firm and creamy white. Her petticoats revealed trim ankles that swelled into compact calves. Why, if Mrs. Rogers knew anything—and she was certain that she did—Norah would suit male taste to a T. It was tragic to think that the girl had been denied the happiness which she might have enjoyed so easily. Mrs. Rogers blamed herself for a lack of imagination—for downright cruelty to someone in her care.

"This Richards is a quack, obviously. You'll pack off tomorrow afternoon to Mr. Rogers' dentist in Brooklyn and have him start work on you. We'll foot the bill and you can pay us every week as you get it. I declare, child, I never thought of your teeth worrying you." She held her head back, the better to observe the sobbing girl. "With plates, I wouldn't be surprised but you'd look real pretty, which I wouldn't have thought possible, knowing you like I do." Then her voice turned waspish as she suddenly thought of Mr. Rogers alone in the house with a Norah transformed by new and pearly dentures. "And you better remember your place and confine your attentions to your policeman, or whoever he is. . . ."

Norah looked up, round-eyed. "Policeman, mum? Well, I never. How'd you get such an idea? I'm sure I never suggested it. It's the lamplighter—and handsome he is. Eyetalian, though I don't hold that against him meself."

"Against him? I should think not." Mrs. Rogers went to the defense of her own Latin blood. "My own dear father was Italian and a wonderful man. You couldn't do better, though *he* came from the northern part of the country while yours is undoubtedly a southerner."

"Eyetalian is all I know, mum. He's not given to talkin' much. We just look at each other most of the time and me tryin' to keep me mouth shut."

"Well, Norah, we'll help all we can, of course, and you shall go to Dr. Smith's tomorrow, though we shall hate losing you."

"Losin' me, mum? Not at all. I hope to stay right on, but I thought perhaps . . . well . . . if Antonio *is* willin' . . . which I'm hopin' he'll be when he sees me with me new teeth . . ."

Because Mrs. Rogers was giving signs of impatience, Norah burst out, "It'd be wonderful if we could share this room—we'd be proper married, of course, and he'd be no trouble. . . ." She paused, while her inward eye gazed into an imagined future that was a vista of unutterable bliss. Then she had a further thought. "You don't think I could get down today and get the worst pulled? I'd hurry back fast as I could to get Master Henry's dinner."

Her mouth gaped open, showing the sorry snags, when she saw that Mrs. Rogers' eyes were filled with tears that she brushed away hastily, without recourse to a handkerchief. "It is nothing, Norah. Get your street dress on and be off with you. I'm only crying with shame at my own thoughtlessness as I think of the heartbreak you've suffered over what we've made fun of instead of doing something about."

## 3

ON AN ESPECIALLY WARM AFTERNOON late in June, Father Duffy dropped by the Rogers house and was admitted by the Master himself. After the first, exuberant greetings were over, during which both men delighted in using old railroad phrases, Mr. Rogers exclaimed on the change in his friend since last he had seen him. Father Duffy was whitening perceptibly at the temples. His jaw had grown lean and there was a strained look about his ordinarily calm and placid eyes. He slumped into a chair, but with his old grin suggested, "Rogers, do you have a chew of that jawbreaker plug you used to save for me? I feel the need of it."

Mr. Rogers scurried off to bring it from its hiding place. They bit off larger quids than they would have otherwise—a kind of bravado that was also left over from their railroad days—and Mr. Rogers chewed monotonously, waiting for Duffy to unburden himself, which he began to do very quickly.

"My good friend, I had no intention of stopping here, but suddenly I felt that I needed you more than anything else. Rogers, your willingness to talk man to man and forget the cloth—of which I'm proud, understand, but which defeats itself as often as not—is a boon to me that's greater than you know."

Mr. Rogers chewed on and the priest continued, "I know how closely you follow events in the papers, so I'm certain that you're familiar with the struggle in which I'm engaged. It is much more than a fight for the eight-hour working day and the welfare of the poor souls who are entrusted to my care—and to that of my

Church. We'll win that battle eventually, although the employer can be vicious when his profits are in danger. The operations of the Pinkertons are an example of what to expect. In the end, though, we'll win.

"My worst fight is within my own Church—and that hurts. It was Cardinal McCloskey who first made me aware that the physical needs of our people are as important as the spiritual—that slums breed sin and that poverty breeds slums.

"He is dead—good, dear man, but there are others. When I was transferred to New York after promising that I'd stop getting involved in politics and stick to matters of the Church, it was the example of Cardinal Manning that gave me courage.

"A priest owes a duty to his superiors, and if Archbishop Corrigan ordered me to go as assistant to the lowliest parish of his diocese I would obey unquestioningly. But when he orders me to stop fighting for what I believe is right I can't do it. There is something in the soul of Patrick Duffy that shrivels when it sees the homeless seeking shelter of a night at the Oak Street Police Station. In the shadow of the bridge that you helped to build, long before the doors open at six o'clock, women form lines on one side of the street and men on the other to wait for free lodgings in the cells and rollrooms.

"And the tenement tobacco workers! Twenty-four thousand children alone, making cigars for sixteen hours a day. They are tubercular and half-blind before they're grown men and women. As priest of God, I must cry out against such misuse of His children."

Mr. Rogers had never heard Father Duffy speak so strongly. He nodded his head once in a while, as though in agreement, then cleared his throat. "The mistake you make, Duffy, is in getting yourself mixed up with that man Marx, who's an irresponsible German—and this George chap, who wants to confiscate property. Why there is something sacred about property—about what is yours. . . ."

"The Master to whom I owe allegiance said to give it away. . . ."

"Your trouble is that you believe in the things you preach and I honor you for it. But you can be true to yourself—which is good Quaker philosophy—without giving offense to others."

"When you have truth to tell you will always offend those who

106

think they will suffer from it. The Quakers who stood up in church pews and denounced preachers were less cordially received than I am. Also I feel that people are confused about men like Marx and George. Their ideas have little in common, except interest in humanity. Marx was opposed to religion, more's the pity, but I can understand how he came to feel as he did. It's a matter of confusing the real thing with the spurious. I see nearer eye to eye with Henry George, who, by the way, is running for mayor. . . ."

There was a long silence which Mr. Rogers finally broke. "All I can say, Duffy, is to follow your own light, wherever it leads you. In my own case, it has guided me down some pretty hum-drum paths into this blind alley, where Gussie is occupied with household affairs, Henry and the others furnish a good part of the wherewithal, and I try to keep them all amused. I'm like an engineer on a limited who is consigned in old age to keeping up round-house steam on some broken-down yard engine. Several times, when I've read of your doings I've felt like joining in—for the fun of a good fight, I suppose. Then my good sense reasserts itself—or perhaps it is just a little Quaker practicality."

Father Duffy arose. "This may have been only a simple and pleasant little chat to you, my good friend. I assure you that to me it was much more. I know no one else in the world to whom I can talk in the way that I can to you. . . ."

Actually, Mr. Rogers was paying very little attention to what Father Duffy was saying, except that his voice was warm and the words appreciative. He laughed heartily, and was about to shout some platitude garnered from the daily press when Clinton Weatherby came in the front door, bearing a long package done in wrapping paper. "Don't go yet, Father Duffy. You'll be interested in this."

Clint untied the package with nervous fingers. "I've been working on this evenings—over at a woodworking shop. What do you think of it?"

"A baseball bat! But you've cut out a chunk?"

"It's a flat-sided bat." Clint became enthusiastic. "It will practically do away with foul balls. Once the ball is swiped on the flat surface it can't go anywhere but straight."

"A brilliant idea . . ." Mr. Rogers began, to be interrupted by a question from Father Duffy. "But the rules, Clint, my lad—don't baseball bats have to be round?"

"There's no rule about it. I've already arranged with the manager of our team to try them out against the Providences. If Radbourne can pitch overhand, we can hit with a new kind of bat."

The idea seemed a good one. While Father Duffy wished Clint success with his flat-sided bat and departed, Mr. Rogers narrowly missed wrecking the whatnot and all its contents in trying its feel.

"I believe you have something," he cried out. "It stands to reason that a flat surface will pound your horsehide globules a whole lot straighter than a round one. It's strange that someone didn't think of it before."

**Chapter 2**

FOR A LONG TIME, neither of the Rogers' sons-in-law felt that he was getting ahead. Philippe had become enthusiastic about a variety of businesses, all of which turned out to have vital defects which Henry pointed out. Philippe had never worked in his life, unless his sojourn at the Centennial could come under that category, and he sought a pleasant and profitable business to which he need give little attention. Meanwhile, he was living on his capital, which worried him.

Clinton Weatherby was even more unhappy about his affairs. Like the ball with the gutta-percha center, with which he had experimented, the flat-sided bat turned out to be less satisfactory than the kind in use. It was a case in which theory did not work out in practice, for Clint hit nothing but foul balls during the game in which he tried it out.

Henry, whenever he was home, made a point of bringing up the fiasco—out of jealousy, no doubt, that Clint's salary had been increased to $2,000 just when Henry was coming close to a hundred a month.

"Don't worry, Clint," Mr. Rogers consoled. "Hard times are

definitely over, or will be soon. Russia and England are bound to go to war; neither country can back out and save its honor. It is a practical certainty from which America cannot help but benefit. Look at the way the stock market is going up. One good war and the underpaid masses that Duffy talks about will be on easy street."

Underneath the irony that came of his Quaker heritage there was more than a hint of earnestness. With the collapse of the war scare and the signing of the treaty between the two great powers which was to remove war forever from civilized life, there came a deflation of American hopes of gain from the conflict so narrowly averted. This was followed by despondency and unrest and again Father Duffy's name came to the fore as he continued to advance Henry George's philosophy.

Mr. Rogers felt that it was an unfortunate thing for him to be doing just when the furor over his earlier activities was dying down. Then Father Duffy called when Gus Palmer and Gene came for a visit, and the house was transformed into a very nest of radicals.

The surprising thing was to find that Gene and Dr. Palmer were rabid revolutionaries. While this knowledge perturbed Mr. Rogers, his wife was more upset by Gene's appearance. She had lost a great deal of weight. "Next she'll be getting consumption or I miss my guess," Mrs. Rogers confided to anyone who would listen.

Gus had always been slender, but in the last years he had grown thin to the point of emaciation. During their visit a pattern of their existence in Pottsville became clear. Gus was working day and night and Gene, though not really a trained nurse, helped him in caring for patients, as well as in the office. For all these long days of work they were rarely paid because their patients were too desperately poor.

In the meantime, Gus had become interested in the Knights of Labor and in spare moments—if he could be considered to have any—assisted in its fight against the more recently organized American Federation of Labor. Again, in this field, Gene was at his side and to listen to her talk, she had become no mean advocate of the cause. Her round prettiness had been succeeded by a forthright expression which Mrs. Rogers deprecated as being too nearly masculine, but which undeniably gave her an attraction of her own—

one that set her apart from those women whose concern was only in their home and children.

"I wish you could see the way that things really are," she attacked her father's defense of the status quo. "Every steamer from Europe brings in more people who have been fooled by wild promises. The shipping companies work in cahoots with the mine operators and railroads to get as much labor as possible so that they'll have cheap sources to draw from. The immigrants are transported like cattle; they're sent all the way from New York to Chicago for one dollar a head—less than for a pig.

"Up around where we are, the poor Irish live in homemade shacks on the mountainsides and exist on berries and small game that they trap. Those that are lucky enough to find work in the mines get asthma or consumption. Gus does what he can and I help, but two people can do so little."

"But speaking in public," Mrs. Rogers interrupted, "making a show of yourself the way you've done—is certainly not ladylike. . . ."

"I've done with being ladylike—if I ever was. You don't realize how defenseless these poor creatures are. Since the end of the Mollie Maguires there isn't any organization at all to protect them, not even an illegal one. Now the Knights of Labor are helping and I think they are wonderful. They believe in equal rights for every man and woman regardless of color or sex and think that a common laborer has as much right to live as a skilled mechanic.

"That is what makes me so furious with the A. F. of L. people. They've just elected a man named Samuel Gompers as their President. I wish he had to work down in a coal mine for a time! What he wants to do is create a third class who would trample down the starving poor just as the mine owners are doing."

When she paused for breath, Father Duffy clapped his hands and Mr. Rogers shouted, "Bravo! It's unusual to hear a female speak so persuasively about a matter which might be supposed to be beyond the understanding of womankind."

Father Duffy took him up. "There's nothing lacking in Gene's understanding, Rogers. You should hear her at a miners' meeting."

Both Henry and Philippe had been listening and the latter now spoke. "It is giving the workingman too much freedom which has been the ruination of France. Look at Julia and myself. At this season we should be enjoying Biarritz. Instead, here we are, living en famille, while I try to find a suitable business. That for your Knights of Labor. Georgina, you used to be a little brat—I fear that you've grown into a big one."

His smile took the edge off his remark, but Henry, who backed him up, was angry with his sister and made no bones of it. "Here I am in the coal business—which depends upon getting it for the lowest price possible—and my own twin fights against me. There'll always be poor in the world, I say, and it's not very nice of you to stir up trouble."

"I'm disappointed in both of you. The idea, Philippe, of even wanting to live off the work of others. And Henry Rogers, I never thought that you would place your own welfare over that of the needy after all the things Father used to tell us about Christian charity. . . ."

Although Mr. Rogers was taken completely by surprise—when had he inculcated such sentiments?—he beamed nevertheless. Trust Georgina to remember episodes of her childhood which he had long since forgotten. As usual, he ended by taking a middle-of-the-road course, commending the selflessness of Father Duffy and Dr. Palmer while enlarging upon the part played in American life by intrepid young businessmen such as Philippe and Henry. Before he knew it, he was comparing free enterprise with the restrictions of monarchy-ridden European states, which in turn set him off on a dissertation concerning human liberties. He had just coined a neat phrase (he felt) about not agreeing with the radicals' point of view, for instance, but fighting to the last ditch for their right to express it, when he recalled how many of them had spent the summer in prison.

To change the subject and avoid further uncomfortable thoughts, Mr. Rogers brought up a matter which seemed pertinent. Who was going to the unveiling of the Bartholdi statue? The great occasion was only a month away and Clint was certain to receive a number of tickets.

That was another advantage of being a public character—one that Henry envied so much that he disparaged the whole affair.

111

"The idea of a statue that large is crack-brained, I'd say. A waste of money. Philippe, I'm surprised at your countrymen. . . ."

Philippe shrugged his shoulders. "I'm not surprised at anything that goes on in France these days. However, if Clinton is given tickets for the grandstands I think we should see the parade, though I doubt that it would be wise for the womenfolk to risk chill on the water. Don't you agree, Julia? . . ."

In true wifely fashion, Julia proclaimed her dislike for steam launches, their soot and smell and general unhealthfulness. "Completely, dear. Besides, the children couldn't go, and someone will have to stay home with them."

Zenie made a little grimace. "It's so seldom I see Clint at all, I certainly intend to enjoy his company in public when I can."

Georgina also wanted to go steam launching, if possible, and began a discussion with Gus concerning his expectant mothers, to see if it would be feasible to leave Pottsville on the date of the great occasion. Their frankness so disturbed Julia, who retained her delicate mindedness in spite of double motherhood, that she retreated to the kitchen and assisted Norah in the preparation of a late snack. Julia and Zenie had become really devoted sisters, now that they were no longer rivals, but Georgina was still a bit too forthright and earthy for someone of Julia's sensibilities.

By the time that Julia and Norah returned—the latter bearing a tray containing an oddment of cookies, cake, and sandwiches—various plans for Bartholdi Day had been decided upon, while Clint reassured them of his ability to procure the necessary tickets. Chiefly because of his efforts, Brooklyn was still in the championship race and across the Bridge he was a real hero. At times he became increasingly annoyed that at home only his wife and Mr. Rogers so considered him. On other occasions, as now, he tried good-naturedly to impress them all with his importance. "If I win six more games before the season's over, Brooklyn will make the twenty-eighth into Weatherby Day, if I asked it."

Mr. Rogers shouted, "And you'd deserve it, too," but Philippe thought that such boasting showed bad sportsmanship and Henry maintained a stony silence.

Norah passed her tray, happily unconscious of the tension. Her new teeth—two perfect, gleaming rows, with a display of most naturalistic waxen gum above the uppers—transformed the girl. The dentures were still a novelty and were exclaimed over by everyone present, until Norah moved about in a state approaching ecstasy. She had been holding in the news all day, waiting for this occasion and was now overcome with shyness.

Finally she summoned courage and made a prim little curtsy before Mrs. Rogers. "I've been tellin' you about Tony, mum. . . . He saw 'em last night—the teeth, I mean. He took to 'em right off . . . and mum, it's engaged we are. I'm so happy and I had to share it. I hope you don't mind, mum, for it's all your fault, in a manner of speakin'."

2

THREE WEEKS before the day of the great unveiling, a picture of the Statue of Liberty showed it to be headless and torchless—a condition symbolic of the low state of human liberties, if one believed Father Duffy.

Eleanor Marx Aveling and her husband had arrived in New York to address a Haymarket defense meeting at Cooper Union. There had been an influx of ideas foreign to American thought and morals: the English translation of *The Heptameron*, seized by the customs as full of impure suggestion, and Captain Burton's nasty translation of *The Arabian Nights*. Why had Karl Marx's daughter to choose this moment to invade the land of freedom? . . .

It could only be part of a deep-laid plot and the answer was to arrest and detain her. Henry George, who had the effrontery to run for Mayor of New York City, was another radical who needed to be confined under the theory that less liberty for those who advocated it made for more liberty for those who found the condition, if not the name, objectionable.

There seemed nothing incongruous to the Rogerses in a Statue of Liberty although men languished in jail for advocating freedom; the crowds who attended the street parade with them were even more carefree.

The day was not an auspicious one. The fog that hung over the streets turned into rain just as the family loaded into the carriage.

Fortunately, Mr. Quinby was well shod and clanged over the slippery cobbles at his usual speed.

At the last moment Henry was called West on one of the business trips that were becoming constantly more frequent, and Philippe—still on the lookout for a location—accompanied him. To their disappointment, the Palmers were also unable to come because one of Gus's patients did not hold to schedule. Mr. Rogers took the reins, with Aunt Zena beside him—trust her to find a place beside the only man in the entourage—while Mrs. Rogers, Julia, Teresina, and the children were loaded uncomfortably into the rear. Mrs. Rogers fumed, not so much at her squirming grandchildren as at her sister's freedom from inconvenience, and by the time they reached the reviewing stand on lower Fifth Avenue she was in a murderous frame of mind.

Clinton Weatherby was supposed to meet them, but there was no sign of his towering figure. The women gazed about uncertainly while Mr. Rogers drove off to hitch Mr. Quinby on one of the side streets. Even Aunt Zena felt a bit intimidated by the preponderantly male crowds and Mrs. Rogers fumed. "That's Clint for you! Neither hair nor hide of him. Zenie, I don't see how you put up with the man, indeed I don't. He was to meet us right here by the reviewing stand. . . ."

Teresina assumed a look of patient resignation which infuriated Mrs. Rogers the more. Then Zenie's face brightened and she waved frantically. "There's Clint, down at the other end of the stand. I believe he's been there all the time, waiting for us. Now you must admit that you've been most unjust."

Mrs. Rogers sniffed, and was not completely mollified when Clint, after forcing his way to them, announced, "We'll all be on the second row—right behind the Mayor. I'm sorry if you've been kept waiting, but I did say the south side of the stand, you know."

Clint *had* said the south side—even Aunt Zena remembered, and the blame was shifted from Clint to Mr. Rogers, for depositing them at the wrong place. When he came back he met the concerted feminine reproaches with characteristic aplomb. "Well, here we are anyhow. Clint, my boy, lead the way and Zena and I will bring up the rear."

This was something for which Jesse would have to answer later!

114

For the moment, Mrs. Rogers only pursed her lips the tighter and allowed herself to be assisted by Clint's right arm, while Zenie hung upon his left. The day was going completely wrong. To add to everything else, Zena and Jesse were up to their old tricks. There was a moment of gratification when Clint introduced them all to Mayor Grace, who looked very imposing in high hat and Prince Albert coat. Then Mrs. Rogers returned to nursing her grievances as her husband said, "A pleasure, indeed, Your Honor. It was through the offices of Mr. Low, the Mayor of Brooklyn, that we first removed to that city. I am, sir, nothing but a plain Philadelphia Quaker of no pretensions. . . ."

He paid no attention to a kick on the shins that was delivered with wifely accuracy. "I also had the good fortune to know an ex-mayor of my native city rather well. He and I used to bet on the same races, although not on the same horses, which was fortunate for me."

All this talk of other mayors had not interested the Honorable Mayor of New York to any extent, but when horses were mentioned he suddenly became affable. Reaching over, he whispered into Mr. Rogers' ear while Rogers tried to look knowing as possible, though actually he'd risked nothing on the races since that summer at the seashore when he'd won all of a dollar or so while Mayor Warwick of Philadelphia had lost but little more.

A good horse to bet on? By the Lord Harry, where were they racing at this late date in the year? Mr. Rogers thought of the only horse whose qualities he fully appreciated. "As a fine piece of horse-flesh, sir," he boomed, "I recommend to you a horse that I know well. Bet on him and you'll never go wrong. . . ."

The arrival of the parade's vanguard made it impossible for the Mayor to question further, but as he stood up to acknowledge the salutes of the marchers, he filed away the name of Mr. Quinby in his memory.

Meanwhile, the Rogerses took their seats, determined to view all of the spectacle despite the drizzle which continued.

It was an especially satisfying time for Teresina. There were so few occasions when she could be with Clint in public and take pleasure from the notice he received. It was wonderful to sit by him and notice someone turn around idly, fix his attention and perhaps nudge a companion, after which both would either stare at Clint, or shout to him in recognition.

Clint accepted this interest without thought, although it could not be said that he disliked it. He was constantly waving to this or that admirer, so that Zenie began to feel, complacently, that the stand had been erected wholly for the purpose of showing off her handsome husband. Her pride grew to bursting when a brigade of Brooklyn policemen marched past. One among them must have spotted Clinton for immediately the guardians of the peace broke it with a roar that brought Mayor Grace to his feet in acknowledgment, only to sit down shamefacedly when he discovered that it was Clinton Weatherby's name they were shouting. Apparently, Clint knew each of the policemen by name, for he called to them in turn, much to the mortification of Mrs. Rogers, who felt that they were making a spectacle of themselves in the company of anyone who behaved with so little dignity. She had been working herself into a mood against Clint ever since they had left the house, and felt that she had fully achieved it when he cried out, "Hello-o-o Moriarty. How's the wife and kids?" Wait until she got Zenie alone and told her what she thought of her precious husband's behavior!

Her bitter thoughts were interrupted by a bellow that could only have come from Jesse. After the first shock upon her eardrums she gave him a nudge and tried to gaze genteelly upon the paraders, but Mr. Rogers was proving more exuberant than Clint had ever been. "Gussie! Philadelphia's finest! Have you ever seen such policemen? Look at the way they're performing. The Brooklyn police aren't one-two-three to them."

As she watched the once familiar, gray-uniformed men go through their intricate drills, Mrs. Rogers became conscious of a slowly welling nostalgia. These men were from Philadelphia, all the way from the city in which she had married and brought up her family! Why there was . . . no it couldn't be . . .

But it was. It was. There was no forgetting the deeply carmined cheeks and fringe of gray beard that distinguished Mr. Baumgardner, who had helped her across Richmond Street on many occasions. Suddenly she found herself on her feet, screaming piercingly, while a bewildered policeman gazed around, wondering who recognized him in this strange and distant city.

## 3

EVEN MR. ROGERS did not feel up to braving the weather further, so only Teresina and Clint attended the second part of the ceremonies designed to welcome the Goddess of Liberty to American shores. Alas, the day did not augur well for her stay. At one-thirty, when the naval parade was to start, Mr. Bartholdi's statue was lost in the fog—not that Zenie minded. All that mattered to her was that she sat in the bow of a tiny launch, protected somewhat by Clint's greatcoat, which was thrown over both of them, and was sharing in the esteem which his athletic prowess had won him.

Their host was a compact, bearded man, most vivacious, who had designed the launch's steam engine, as Clint explained while he introduced them. "This is my wife, Zenie, Mr. Maxim. Zenie this is Mr. Hiram Maxim, who invented the electric lights—like those on the new bridge."

"Oh . . . I thought Mr. Edison . . ."

Mr. Maxim's eyes almost flashed sparks. "Don't mention that robber's name in my presence, Madam. *I* invented the incandescent electric light, among many other things, as my present legal action * to establish my rights will eventually prove.

"But look—the fog is lifting a little. And here they come."

It was a glorious sight to watch the vessels, which had assembled in the Hudson, steam down the bay toward the open harbor and Liberty Island. With consummate skill, Mr. Maxim swung their own launch into position and they followed in the wake of some three hundred others. Zenie had never seen so imposing a display. "Oh, Mr. Maxim, we are more indebted to you than I can say. . . ."

"Nonsense. It is fitting for you to be with me. The greatest baseball player and the greatest inventor. I wish I were half as good a pitcher as he is an inventor."

* Which Hiram Stevens Maxim lost, although he may have been right at that.

117

It was Clint's turn to protest. "My baseball and flat-sided bat. Failures both—and they never meant anything, anyhow. Certainly not compared to yours . . ."

"Which they're trying to cheat me out of. . . ." Mr. Maxim interrupted. "If Thomas A. Edison wins this suit for the most valuable invention in the world, I'll leave the States and go to England, where patent rights have some meaning. A word of advice to you, Clinton Weatherby, I'd patent that rubber-centered ball of yours before Edison steals it from you. That's got merit, I'd say; the present fault is in the wrapping of the twine; might even be the kind of material you use. . . ."

Further discussion was prevented by the sudden shrieking of steam whistles as a large and handsome launch passed at great speed. "That's the Vixen," Clint cried. "And that's the President, or I miss my guess. . . ."

"The old gentleman must be Count de Lesseps!"

"And the sculptor is next to him."

Pandemonium broke loose as the warships, anchored lower in the bay, let go salvo after salvo of artillery in salute to Cleveland, de Lesseps, and Bartholdi; then the fog closed in again, and only Mr. Maxim's expert seamanship kept them from being run down by one or the other of the larger vessels. Gilmore's Band played patriotic airs, both French and American. From a previous announcement they knew that after a prayer, and speeches by de Lesseps and Mr. Cleveland, the sculptor himself would pull down the tri-colored veil that shrouded the Goddess; but of all this nothing could be seen for fog continued to cover her.

They made the run up the bay ahead of the flotilla, while Zenie, shivering from the dampness, snuggled close within Clint's protecting arm.

Their host noticed her chattering teeth and suggested, "Here—get up close to the boiler." Then, after he had made a place for her and thrown more coal into the miniature furnace, "How's that? Better, isn't it?"

"Indeed it is. I'm warm as toast already. All I need is Moody and Sankey and I'd feel right at home." Zenie was quite unprepared for Mr. Maxim's reaction to her feeble little witticism. His eyes opened wide and his pointed, black beard seemed to curl forward into a kind of inverted question mark. "Did I understand you to say Moody and Sankey?" he shouted, in what appeared to be extreme anger.

When Clint explained that it was only the family dachshunds to which Zenie had referred, Mr. Maxim burst into a laugh louder than even Mr. Rogers could have achieved. "That proves, Weatherby, that it's a delusion ever to believe you thought of something first. Several years ago I tamed two crows out on our country place at Fanwood, New Jersey. I thought those two old fakes would make highly original names for them and here your father thought of the same thing years before. . . ."

An extra burst of speed brought their little craft into a dock on the Brooklyn side, close to the Bridge entrance. After they had left the eccentric Mr. Maxim, following an effusive exchange of thanks and protestations, Zenie declared, "Oh, Clint, it has been a wonderful day. And Mr. Maxim was so wonderful—like Father, in a way, always excited about something or making fun. And most wonderful of all was having you to myself, without the family, or people knowing who you are and calling to you. . . ."

"Too bad it wasn't a nicer day. Why Zenie, old girl, we didn't even see Bartholdi's statue. Do you realize that?"

"I don't care. I had you. Honest, Clint, when I look at Philippe, who's growing fat and stodgy, I can't help think how lucky I am. I wouldn't trade you for anything."

There was the first discordant note of the afternoon when Clint answered, with just a shade of bitterness, "I wish the rest of the family felt that way about me. But never mind, you are all that matters."

"But what about Father? He thinks you are even more wonderful than I do. . . ."

"That's right, we mustn't forget him. Which reminds me, the editor of one of the newspapers says that next season they plan to put a man on just to write up the baseball games. Imagine, he wouldn't do anything else. I think I could get the job for your father; think he might try it?"

Teresina laughed softly. "Poor dear. I never appreciated Father until I met you, Clint. I think he'd love it. But be certain about it before you ask him . . . and perhaps I better sound out Mother

first. She likes to keep her finger on Father—even at his age."
Then, with a touch of roguishness new to her, "And I intend to do
the same for you, Mr. Weatherby, so you better begin to get used
to it."

Chapter 3 OVER EIGHTEEN MONTHS had
passed since Philippe had
arrived in New York with
Julia and the children, and he had not yet found a suitable business. He regretted that they had ever left France. Things were even
more unsettled in the States than they were in Europe. How foolish they had been to flee the specter of Republicanism in the Old
World by coming to its materialization in the New. Now that they
were uprooted, however, some kind of decision would have to be
made—and that shortly.

Philippe paused to consider a matter which was almost more
serious—the gradual thinning of his hair. He examined himself in
the mirror from several angles, brushed his scalp thoroughly, gave
a stroke or two to his beard and decided complacently that he had
a beautiful wife, who still loved him, and two adorable children.
Everything would work out for the best; hadn't it always done so?

If he could entirely trust Henry Rogers' judgment. He seemed
to be doing extremely well—traveling all over the country, but he
was so young. Philippe could remember him as a child and that
couldn't be more than . . . no, it was longer—over ten years, in
fact, since he had first set foot in the tempestuous Rogers' household. It seemed hardly possible that Henry was so old. Perhaps he
should acquiesce to Henry's proposal that they go into the coal
business together. Each time the suggestion had been made,
Philippe had put him off. It seemed a hard bargain that Henry
would put nothing into the partnership—nothing but knowledge
and business acumen. These were the very qualities which Philippe

lacked, but compared to wealth—cold cash in the bank—they seemed trivial and lacking in substance.

With Gallic shrewdness, he decided that perhaps he could cajole Aunt Zena into sharing a part of the risk. After all, wasn't her money to come to them eventually? Why not some when it would be of the most use?

Now that he'd made up his mind—partially, at least—he determined on an immediate further discussion with Henry, and to that end ascended from the second to the third floor and walked down the hall to the rear room which Henry had made into an office for himself and incidentally, a sleeping place.

Philippe knocked, and in response to a gruff sound from within, pushed open the door. Henry sat at a table, reading a chart of precisely penned figures, but when he saw his visitor he sprang up cordially and indicated another chair. "Glad to see you, Philippe. I thought you and Julia were giving Mr. Quinby a workout. He's a wonderful horse for sleighing."

"B-r-r, not for me. Your American winters were designed for savages. I am surprised that Aunt Zena stands the cold. She's gone with Julia in a shabby old sleigh that belongs to the livery. I don't see what possessed your father to sell yours."

"It was my idea. Since we haven't a stable here in New York, the cost of storing the sleigh was all out of reason for the use we get from it. Even the board for Mr. Quinby is disproportionate, to say nothing of carriage upkeep. I've urged Mother to sell them off and depend on hacks. It would be cheaper in the long run, and we'd get some real use of Abe, who always pretends he's grooming the horse when there's work to be done."

Even Philippe was horrified. "Your mother worships Mr. Quinby. Indeed, we all do. What an end for a noble horse—to be pulling some ragpicker's cart. It's been hard enough for your mother to put him in livery. I think you should have some sentiment, Henry."

"Sentiment means nothing to a businessman. . . ."

"Which reminds me—I've decided to help you out with the money you need. This kind of weather convinces me that coal is indeed a necessity."

Henry hid his jubilation behind a mask of indifference. "I wish you had made up your mind when I broached the matter. I've since given assurances that I'd stay on where I am. Of course that is the safest and most advantageous thing for me to do anyway. I had thought, though, that by going in with you I might be doing a favor for Julia and yourself."

After first complimenting himself on a rather neat opening of the conversation, Philippe was distressed by Henry's apparent lack of interest. "Can't you be prevailed upon to change your mind? I've really become anxious to get to work, though the coal business is less romantic than I could have wished for."

"But safer—and with more future than most things. Look at the success I've made."

Henry hadn't achieved very much compared with Philippe's grandiose ambitions, but as they talked he became more impressed than ever with Henry's business qualities. Gradually, by making even more concessions than he'd intended, Philippe gained Henry's consent. Once committed, the latter had surprisingly complete plans to offer. It might not be necessary for him to break off connections with Mr. Madeira, his present employer, at all. "Cincinnati is the place for us, Philippe. I believe I could make a deal to represent the firm out there while we build up our partnership on the side. Mr. Madeira knows what I can do, so I'm sure I can persuade him. Such a connection alone will be worth as much to us as the amount you are putting up. Unless something unforeseen happens, like labor getting completely out of hand, our fortunes are as good as made."

Indeed, by the New Year the firm of Rogers and Lascalles was an actuality—under conditions more favorable than either of the partners had hoped. For the time being, Philippe was to stay in New York, right in Mr. Madeira's office, and learn the business under Henry's tutelage. By spring, Philippe should have progressed far enough to be left alone, when Henry would establish headquarters in Cincinnati.

Philippe was enthusiastic and only regretted that he had not approved the scheme long ago. The wonder was that Mr. Madeira behaved so generously—a circumstance which Philippe ascribed to his new partner's persuasive abilities, without knowing of a call his mother-in-law had made a few weeks earlier.

When the partnership agreement was first announced at dinner it was met in various ways by different members of the family. Mr. Rogers proposed a toast—in Croton water—and Aunt Zena suggested a theater party, to celebrate. Clint shouted "Hurray," and earned a frown from the senior partner. Julia left the table, on the pretext of seeing that the children were being properly fed by Norah in the basement kitchen. Once there, she broke into tears. The last months had been so happy—home with Mother, not having to worry about showing one's self to strange doctors, not having to sight-see and walk through dusty streets filled with dark-skinned natives of evil intent, or crawl around in ruined cities of the past.

A move to Cincinnati would mean beginning all over again. Julia found that more than anything else she wanted to be warmed at the heart of the family in which she had once felt a complete stranger; and this change would spoil everything. She wet her eyes with cold water and dabbed them dry before returning to the others.

As for Mrs. Rogers, she said nothing at all, but later, after everyone else had retired, she got out the portable secretary that she rarely used since the return of her family, and wrote a short note. She read it over several times, stamped, sealed the envelope and hid it away to mail in the morning.

The answer arrived by return post, though, as she said to herself, she had ". . . the Devil's own time to keep Father from grabbing it first." She arranged a daily errand in time to intercept the mailman before his arrival. The morning that the letter came she retreated with it into the corner store that had furnished the excuse for going out. She handed the milk pail to the woman behind the counter, and while it was being filled quickly opened and read the note:

Dearest Augustina: It was a pleasure to receive your letter. I think you are oversensitive in not letting Henry know that his employer is still your devoted servant. I am coming to New York on Monday and will stay at the Windsor, which is not far from your present address. Shall we set the hour at two-thirty?

Faithfully,<br>B. M.

A first smirk of satisfaction over the salutation was replaced by a frown. Botheration, he'd given no indication at all of what he thought. She took the full pail as it was handed to her, answered some remark about the coldness of the day and set off down the street. "Faithfully," that was nice of him. "Your devoted servant." Too bad she couldn't show the letter to Jesse, who took her for granted all these years, while an earlier swain wore his heart out.

She had always liked Billy Madeira—might indeed have married him if the Rogers' ships hadn't appeared more promising than a dingy office on Philadelphia's Third Street. Though the Rogers' fortune had faded and the Madeira business flourished, she had no regrets. Jesse, with all his faults, was twice the man Billy was. When she had interceded with him, years ago, to get a place for Henry, she had wondered how she could ever have considered him. Why Billy Madeira was a little man—hardly taller than herself, and bald—lacking the virile, billowing mass of whisker which always appealed to her feminine heart.

But Billy must have loved her truly, for he'd never married—and he'd been wonderful to Henry. Mrs. Rogers turned in at the basement areaway door to meet the avalanche of dachshund that always greeted her return as though she'd been away for weeks, and delivered the milk to Norah. "If you'd step lively, once in a while, I wouldn't have to run errands every whipstitch."

This was a completely unfair remark, as both women knew, but Norah realized that her mistress was up to something, and this was a part of the game.

Mrs. Rogers practiced further deceit the following Monday. She dressed carefully and was just leaving the house, when Jesse, who usually took an afternoon walk, returned unexpectedly. She was nonplussed for a moment by his "Gussie, where are you off to? I haven't seen you so dressed up since Zenie's wedding."

But only for a moment! She compressed her lips in simulated anger and slid by his intended embrace. "At this season of the year it's unwise to ask where anyone is going, and I can't shop on Twenty-third Street looking like a rag bag." She comforted herself that this was a statement of fact and not a lie at all, while she hurried off with her husband's surprised gaze still upon her.

It was only a short walk to the Windsor, at Forty-sixth Street,

124

but Mrs. Rogers was exhilarated as much from the exercise as from excitement. There was Billy Madeira now, waiting for her. He jumped up, like a little jack-in-the-box, and rushed over. "Augustina . . . you never change. Just to look at you brings back youth. How do you stay this way?"

"I don't believe a word of it. You'd be surprised how many gray hairs I have . . . and don't forget that I have a son who's . . . well . . . who's over twenty."

"Ah, Tina. And three daughters also, aren't there? It doesn't seem possible."

Ever touchy about ages, Mrs. Rogers explained, shortly, "I had my children very close together. And what I came to see you about is Henry. He's . . ."

Mr. Madeira held up a thin hand. "Come now! Let's visit a while first. I'm very fond of Henry—proud of him, too—but he'll keep. Let's sit here and I'll order some tea.

"Tell me, do you remember when we first met? Your father and sister were with you and you had just come to Philadelphia. The town was quite agog over the young Italian beauties. . . ."

"Zena is living with us now here in New York. She's been a widow for some years. And do you remember? . . ."

There were many cups of tea before the talk got around to the reason for the visit. "I hope it won't shock you, but Henry is planning on going in business for himself—with one of my sons-in-law. I wanted to know what you thought before I approved. Not that he asked me for advice, but I can do a lot sometimes, in little ways."

"Shocked? No indeed. He suggested the idea to me quite a long time ago—an astute plan that could be advantageous to both of us. He had some capital in mind, I suppose. I didn't realize it would be a family affair. I'm to see him tomorrow at the branch office here and I imagine he'll bring it up then."

Mrs. Rogers gave a sigh. "I must say I'm glad to know that. I expect Henry to be honorable, of course, but you've done so much for him."

"Don't worry about Henry. The hardest working man I know. With both feet solidly on the ground. I'd feel better about him if he wasn't quite so all-fired serious, though. What got into him,

Tina? He seemed a human enough boy when he first came with me."

Mrs. Rogers threw up her hands in a gesture of helplessness. "He fell in love. A girl completely without prospects—or money. Worked on a coal barge which her father owned, to be exact. It sank with her aboard. He's been different since. I often say I wish he'd marry a nice girl. . . ."

Looking down at his clasped hands, Mr. Madeira observed, gently, "I think perhaps I know how he feels—when nothing counts any more but getting ahead. . . ."

This was ground that might become dangerous, so Mrs. Rogers put on a sudden sprightliness. "Oh, la, I suppose so, but there is such a thing as being sensible. Now I must go . . . a man as busy as you are . . ."

"Not at all. It's been wonderful. Believe me, Tina, if there is anything I can do for you, ever, please ask me."

Mrs. Rogers hesitated. "Don't do this if you think it wouldn't be fair to Henry, but Philippe, who's going in with him, is married to my daughter Julia. They have two children that I adore—can you imagine me a grandmother?—and I'll be heartbroken when they leave. So will Julia, I know. If you can think of any plan that would keep Philippe here a while longer . . ."

Mr. Madeira thought a moment, then nodded. "I have an idea that I can arrange it—and in a way that will be helpful to the new firm."

With a sudden impulse, Mrs. Rogers kissed him, first on one cheek and then on the other, before fleeing from the lobby, abashed by her public display. "Well, I never," she told herself, as she walked homeward. "Imagine me, at my age, doing a thing like that. Anyway, I think I accomplished what I set out to." She got further satisfaction from another thought. "What if Jesse had seen me kissing Billy Madeira? He'd killed him on the spot, like as not, and given me a good talking-to, into the bargain."

2

"By the Lord Harry, Gussie, your genteel home for paying guests would never have been like this," Mr. Rogers shouted, while he carved the cod's head and shoulders that formed the *pièce-de-résistance* to the Friday evening meal. It required some dexterity to cut pieces that included some of the sound as well as a portion of liver, so it was a little while before he could pursue the thought. Finally, when all were served, and he had reserved for himself the choice jawbone and tongue section, he went on to explain. "We've never told you before, but it was Gussie's idea to buy this house—and rent out rooms. Providential, as it turned out, for there is nothing like having a family together and there wouldn't have been room enough on Cranberry Street."

To this, Mrs. Rogers cried, "Ten at table! Isn't it wonderful? Why it's weeks since we've all been together this way. And it is so nice, Julia, to have the children eat with us. They are behaving perfectly." She favored little Jesse with one of those fond-grandmother leers that always brought out the worst in the child, who was only restrained by the sudden pressure of his mother's hand as she diverted attention by inquiring, "And how were things in Cincinnati, Henry? You haven't said."

Henry gave the "h-u-u-mph" that was becoming a habit with him as prelude to a statement. "I hardly think that business is a matter to discuss at the table. . . ."

"Oh, but I didn't mean in a business way at all. Are things modern—the way they are here in New York, for instance? Is there gas street-lighting, for instance? And are the streets nicely cobbled, or muddy? I fear it will be most primitive."

"It's just a city, like any other. Not as up to date as New York, of course, but it's well situated for us. Coal from the Pocahontas fields, which we'll handle, can be shipped in by river boat and distributed over all of Ohio. . . ."

Clint spoke up to suggest, "What I think Julia wants to know is, what *kind* of a place Cincinnati is. I think you'll like it. There are steep hills back from the river, with the city nestled at their feet. It has a large German population, folks who enjoy spending the evening in one of the many beer gardens. It's a nice thing to do, too, for it gets pretty hot in summer."

Henry made no attempt to conceal his irritation. "I suppose you know more about it than I do, who've been there a dozen times at least."

127

"You forget that I've played ball there every summer for six years. The Cincinnatis have a good team, too. They beat us in the last series." Clint made a serio-comic expression of regret, but showed no resentment toward Henry. Instead, he smiled pleasantly and went on talking to Julia. "When you and Philippe move out there, just telegraph if you get lonely, and the next swing of our team around the western circuit I'll bring Zenie along to visit you for a while."

"Indeed you won't. What kind of reputation do you think our partnership would get if it became known that my sister was married to nothing but a professional baseball player?"

There was a moment of shocked silence and then a chorus of protests. Zenie jumped up first, to exclaim, angrily, "Henry Rogers, you've always been insufferable and now I think you're impossible." Without explaining what constituted the difference in meaning between the two adjectives, she hurried from the table and rushed upstairs.

Philippe, always courteous, said, "Julia and I will be proud to have you as a guest at any time, Clint. . . ." Then he was drowned out by Mr. Rogers' booming voice, "If we still had an outside shed, young man, I'd order you to step into it and pay for your discourtesy with a touch of the cat-o'-nine-tails. . . ."

Nobody in the family had ever seen Mr. Rogers in such a temper. Henry, who realized that he had gone too far, became really frightened as his father shook a thick finger under his nose. "It is unfortunate that this happy family group should be disrupted by your boorishness, an enjoyable repast ruined, your sister and her husband insulted. You'll either apologize right now or leave this table and not return to it until you've improved your manners. . . ."

"I don't believe Henry meant it the way it sounded," Clint interrupted, although for the first time in his many encounters with Henry, he kept his temper only by the use of will. "Let's forget the whole thing, Father Rogers. I've no ill-feeling toward Henry and I'm glad to shake hands to prove it."

This was heaping on coals of fire! Without a word, Henry folded his napkin, glanced regretfully at a remaining morsel of cod, arose and walked slowly and pompously toward the hall. His father's voice followed him. "Gussie, I often insisted I never beat that boy enough and this is proof of it. You've no one to blame but yourself that he's spoiled."

In the way that only she could do, Mrs. Rogers took command of the situation. "La, Father, there's no use going on with a spat after it's all over, especially as we've a trifle for dessert, which Norah made from a French recipe in *Harper's*."

Partially mollified, Mr. Rogers returned to sucking the glutinous bones of the cod's head, while his wife began a long explanation of the number of macaroons, the quantity of brandy, spoonfuls of jelly, custard, whipped egg whites, and wine that went into the trifle. Zenie, who had been coaxed back by Clint and was still red-eyed, pronounced the new dish a great success, but Mr. Rogers dissented. After finishing a third portion he shook his head and delivered his opinion. "I like shoo-fly pie better, but such is the blind folly of this age that you would rather be imposed upon by a French nincompoop than admit to the goodness of plain American cooking."

In spite of this pronouncement, Mrs. Rogers felt that the trifle had served its purpose. It had been intended for tomorrow's dessert, and quick thinking had been required to substitute it for the evening's less glamorous bread pudding, which would keep another day.

It had been a trying evening, though, as she confessed to Norah, who cleaned the table after the others had retired to the parlor. Again she gave voice to a thought which had been increasingly upon her mind of late: "I declare, I do wish Henry could find a nice girl who'd take him in hand and make him fit to live with again. He's become plain, unvarnished Quaker and more than I can put up with much longer."

*Chapter 4*

THAT STRANGE BREED of dog which Mr. Rogers called "the dash-hound" probably was first introduced to America by Aunt Zena, Centennial year, in the persons of Moody and Sankey, now grown old and so sway-backed that their bellies brushed along the carpet. They lived sedentary, old men's lives and had even given up climbing the stairs behind their mistress, except at bedtime.

The unfortunate dalliance of Nellie, the coach dog, dead these many years, with one of the pair, led to further indignity for the breed in the misshapen, truly dachshund body of a puppy with Dalmatian color and markings. This creature had been dubbed Beecher and during the years in Brooklyn, had lived in the stable. Upon the family's removal to New York it had taken up residence in the kitchen, sleeping on an old rug, to the side of the range.

While he see-sawed along with the others as they followed Mrs. Rogers around the house, he had become the special charge and pet of Norah, and her chief vexation. For Beecher possessed that same unfortunate and undisciplined desire for the other sex which had given the great preacher such notoriety. Furthermore, like all of his breed, he was unusually well equipped for venery, except in the matter of legs—a deficiency which apparently furnished no serious impediment to his efforts, from the number of short-legged puppies which began to make their appearance in the neighborhood.

Whenever Mr. Rogers was in an inquiring or scientific mood he was apt to discuss Beecher's problems with a lady Spitz or Pug and speculate quite shamelessly upon their solution—often to his wife's acute embarrassment.

A sport which Beecher enjoyed only second to the delights of sex was chasing along at the heels of dray horses. Whenever he was able to evade the vigilant Norah, he would streak through an open door and pursue the first team of Percherons or Belgians that passed. Perhaps a heritage from the Dalmatian side of his family gave him an extra alertness at dodging hoofs and wheels. If so, the coach-dog strain seemed not enough to compensate for his length of body and bow of leg. Often, the first knowledge that Beecher had escaped the house came with the furious noise of barking, the squeak of brakes and the shouts of an irate teamster, when Norah would dash out the basement entrance and fly to the dog's rescue.

As Norah always accompanied these rescues with her usual Fenian cries, anyone else at home was quickly brought flying to door or window—as were any neighbors who were dog minded.

This morning the scene was being repeated—with a single difference. There was Beecher's furious barking, the clatter of hoofs and rumble of steel tires over the cobbles, Norah's screamed threats at a completely bewildered drayman. Perhaps Beecher had slipped on a remnant of snow left from the last fall, several days earlier. Perhaps the near horse had been unusually nervous for a Percheron, who could say? Instead of a lively, wriggling, speckled creature, joyous at having vanquished two such giant intruders to the street, Norah, tears streaming from her eyes, picked up a limp, polka-dotted body that seemed entirely devoid of life.

Only Mrs. Rogers and Zenie were at home and they assisted Norah to the kitchen. Zenie dashed upstairs for blankets, and the old deal table was transformed into a bed. Norah, still crying, was dispatched for the nearest veterinarian, down on Fiftieth Street and Mrs. Rogers administered her standard remedy—brandy—a drop at a time. There were no marks on the plump, clean little body to show where it had been hurt, and after the first drop of the liquor, the long, red tongue that had lain inert between open jaws, made a slight, automatic licking motion.

When the brown eyes slowly opened, Mrs. Rogers' sobs mixed with a smile of pure happiness. "Oh, Beecher, I do believe that you're coming around all right. Take a little more of this, now, like a nice dog. . . . Good grief, Zenie, hold his head steady. . . ."

Beecher's long, slender tail wagged slowly, then his life ran out as they watched, helpless. In death, his grotesque, dappled body took on a dignity it had never possessed in life and as Mrs. Rogers clutched it to her, she realized that she was holding within her arms the final link with her first home, with Kensington, with the bearing and rearing of her family. Mary was gone and Nellie was gone; now Nellie's puppy was gone too. When Norah returned with the doctor, Mrs. Rogers still held the blanket-wrapped bundle, rocking it like an infant, while she whispered baby words to it, over and over, as Zenie tried vainly to comfort her.

An hour later, Mr. Rogers came in for lunch, so agog with his own news that he failed to notice the red-rimmed eyes of his womenfolk. "The intellectual blight which has existed in Brooklyn for so many years is in a fair way to pass. Beecher died this morning."

The opening phrases were lost upon all three women. While Norah began to wail again, Mrs. Rogers threw herself upon her amazed husband. "Oh, Pet, how did you hear? Isn't it terrible? Poor Beecher, I'll never forgive myself for not giving in to him oftener. He'd plead and plead for something that I could have let him have as well as not. . . ."

Here, here, what was this? Even Zenie was crying into her handkerchief—and Norah, who was supposed to be such a good Catholic. Had Henry Ward's seductions penetrated into the Rogers' household behind its master's back?

"Honest, Jesse, when he looked at me with those great brown eyes, my heart broke and my knees turned to water."

Elizabeth Tilton, one of his victims, had said much the same thing during the preacher's trial! Mr. Rogers found the perspiration starting on his forehead. His whole family had been corrupted without his knowing. What a complacent fool he had been!

The tragi-comedy might have continued much longer if Mrs. Rogers had not thought of another problem. "And where will we bury him, Jesse? I refuse to plant any dog of mine under the bricks of the back areaway, without a single flower over him."

There was still a series of misunderstandings to be cleared up, details of the accident to be gone over and plans of interment to be made, when everyone marveled at the strange coincidence that resulted in the passing of both Beechers at almost identical hours.

The next day, Lincoln's Birthday, while 40,000 people passed an open casket in Plymouth Church, a melancholy little party took carriage to farmer van Duym's, there to commit the world's only dappled dachshund to the soil. Afterward, Mrs. Rogers visited with Total Eclipse, who, though fat, had completely lost his lameness, while Mr. Rogers talked politics with the amiable Dutchman.

When, homeward bound, they drove across the bridge again, even Mr. Rogers was depressed, although he pretended complete lack of sentimentality where animals were concerned. But neither sorrow nor a sense of loss could long affect his irrepressible spirits. As they turned into Fifty-second Street he let out a whoop that startled Mr. Quinby, used though he was to the strange noises that emanated at times from his carriage.

"My lands, Jesse, if Mr. Quinby gets skittish in his old age it will be your fault."

"Nonsense. I merely wished to call your attention to that strange creature by yonder cottonwood." All eyes turned toward a puppy with flecks of gray in its long, white hair. Obviously poodle in most respects, only its short, bowed legs gave it away. Father was undoubtedly right when he shouted in triumph, "Beecher may be dead, but his spirit will live on for a long time in this neighborhood."

2

During the winter Clinton Weatherby had become increasingly dissatisfied with living in the Rogers household and only the pleas and arguments of his wife kept him from searching for a small home of their own. "I'd be so lonely," Zenie said. "When you're away for whole weeks at a time, what would I do? And it would be dangerous, too, with a lone female in the house.

"Then look at the money we're ahead. Even after what we pay to Mother we're saving three-quarters of your salary. Can't you put up with it for just another year, darling? We do have some wonderful times, too, you must admit."

"It's this attitude of Henry's. I'm sorry, Zenie. Some day I'll lose my temper with him—then we'll both be sorry. I almost did the other week when he made that scene at dinner."

"But he's been away all the time since. . . ."

"Your mother isn't exactly in love with me, either."

"That's just her way. Look how she is with us and with Father—always fussing at us, though she loves us dearly. Please try it a while longer, Clint. Soon Julia and the children will go West, when we can take over their rooms. That will help."

It was probably not any of this argument which persuaded Clint, but something quite different. Zenie held out her arms impulsively. "Oh, my dear, dear man. You are so wonderful and I love you so— and here we are, almost fighting. We must stop this minute and I'll do whatever you wish. . . ."

Under these circumstances, Clint naturally gave in, but he looked forward to the new baseball season with greater anticipation than ever. He would have been happier if he could have found a wintertime position, as he'd tried to do both winters since he and Zenie had married, but the offers seemed so small as compared with his summer salary, that despite her urging he had never accepted any of them, generally with the excuse—and sometimes a valid one—that it would hurt his prestige as a player. His attempts at inventing new and better baseball equipment continued equally unsuccessful. Time hung heavily on his hands and more and more he spent it in the company of the sporting element that looked up to him as a hero. At times Mr. Rogers accompanied him to special events, but more often than not he went alone to some Brooklyn saloon or billiard parlor, returning late redolent with the odors of tobacco and stale beer.

He realized that for the first time in his career, he would not be in perfect condition for the opening games, but told himself, knowing the while it was untrue, that a few days on the diamond would put him back in shape.

The growing irregularity of Clint's habits and his evident unhappiness in spite of their intense love for each other, worried Zenie, but at the same time made it more difficult to leave home. As her mother had always predicted, she began to lose weight and took on a wan, distracted air. She felt that spring would never come, though actually the weather grew mild so early that almost before everyone had done with exclaiming that it was 'Eighty-seven and not 'Eighty-six any more the streets began to bloom with the first summer bonnets.

When Aunt Zena invited her to go shopping—along with Julia —she was only too glad to escape the house. Once Aunt Zena would have gone in style, with a footman to carry their purchases through Mr. Wanamaker's store (recently purchased from the Stewart heirs by the Philadelphia merchant) and would have wound up at Tiffany's for a bauble. Today she set out with her nieces on foot to brave the mobs of other women shoppers in the cheaper stores.

It was a long walk down to Twenty-third Street, but the day was so warm and springlike, though it was still March, that none of the excited trio minded. Indeed, the clothes of other shoppers provided them with ideas of what they might like to purchase for themselves.

"Look, Zenie," Julia exclaimed, "mohair is coming back. They haven't worn mohair since we were small. Do you remember that Mother had a suit of it when we were in Kensington?"

Aunt Zena nodded her head in satisfaction. "There's nothing like good English mohair for wear—which reminds me, girls, I've several suits of it and a cloak or two in my trunks. With a little altering I think they'd look most modish and up to date."

Ah, Aunt Zena's trunks! Since she'd come to live with them permanently on Fifty-second Street, Julia and Zenie had outdone each other in thinking up wiles to lure her to the fourth floor room where those fabulous trunks—huge, French ones made of wicker and covered with heavy fabric—were stored.

What occasions those were when Aunt Zena acceded to their sly hints and both girls ascended to the upper regions, when Aunt Zena opened this or that trunk and spread before their eyes a wealth of European fashion. There would be dresses of tightly crocheted jet beads, there would be others of cut velvet, of heavily watered satin, of China silk. There were feathers and plumes and buttons, yards of laces, and more yards of braids. One whole trunk was filled with nothing but flowers: roses more luscious than had ever bloomed in garden, sprays of white or yellow daisies, blue cornflowers, spikes of tuberoses, mixed bouquets that could "make" any bonnet.

In another trunk were startling natural-looking birds, some of them whole and of others a wing, a breast, or aigrette. Ribbons? Aunt Zena had them in every conceivable shade and material.

Although the trio continued their walk down Fifth Avenue, the two sisters would have been content to turn around then and there, while their aunt was in a trunk-opening mood. Gradually, though, they again caught her enthusiasm for the day's shopping and even suggested that they should take one of the omnibuses

135

which went careening past, its horses froth-flecked, in order to reach their goal the sooner.

Aunt Zena suspected all public conveyances, however, and preferred the walk. She never tired of this handsome avenue with its elegant homes that reminded her, to some extent, of those in the fashionable parts of European cities.

The racing omnibuses and the beautiful turnouts of fine carriages and high-spirited horses, the impeccably clothed gentlemen and beautifully dressed ladies—all helped to fill Aunt Zena with unusual sparkle and animation. More than once she was certain that some fine gentleman who stood idly at a street corner, swinging his cane or stroking his mustache, had eyed her in an interested manner. Then, with almost schoolgirlish excitement, she would ask her nieces to glance around and see for certain if the man's eyes were still following her.

It never occurred to Teresina Lascalles that the masher might be ogling either of her very personable companions, nor did the girls think it, for neither Julia nor Zenie was flirtatiously inclined. Aunt Zena's excitement would become intense when Julia would report, after a discreet glance backward, "He's looking! I do believe he's looking. Oh, Aunt Zena, suppose he should follow us—what would we do? Zenie, isn't it awful? Aren't men horrible?"

Twenty-third Street was thronged with shoppers. When they turned west and entered Stern's, that emporium was crowded to the doors. The millinery and dress departments seemed to be the principal objectives, and these were also the ones toward which Aunt Zena turned. Her attention fixed upon the new French faille, a silk poplin that was all the rage. There was a suit made up of it that was trimmed with gilt braid and enhanced with elaborate designs in lace. This the three women examined with the most intense care, so that the details might be indelibly impressed upon their minds, in case they should decide to duplicate the costume at home.

There was another suit of estamin, with plush bands in Scotch plaid. Zenie liked a gorgeous and unique material in two tones, called frieze and the interest of all three was captured by a very handsome wool crepe that closely imitated the Chinese material,

136

but came double width instead of single, and cost only seventy-five cents the yard.

With the thought of Aunt Zena's offer in mind, everything in English mohair was given serious attention for ideas as to how her suits might best be utilized. Her real interest, however, was in the millinery department. "They are selling small, close-fitting bonnets this spring," madame in charge said, but in these Aunt Zena had no interest. She preferred a model that made more of a splash and tried on a confection called "The Equestrienne," of green split straw that was faced with a puffing of olive velvet. It was trimmed with a fan of gilt lace and olive chenille, topped by a handsome bunch of flowers, to the side of which nestled several gilded aigrettes.

The question was, whether Johnston's, at the corner of Fifth Avenue and Twenty-second Street, might not have something even more fetching, though Stern's values were traditional. Aunt Zena laid "The Equestrienne" aside with the excuse that they would be back later if she saw nothing that she liked better. As she did so, she recalled the old days, when she would have bought half a dozen much more expensive creations without another thought.

"I suppose I can be glad that I'm not completely a pauper," she confided to the others, taking the optimistic view. "No wonder people are so unhappy in the world when they can't buy what they've a mind to. It should depress me too, but I don't allow it to. I'm certain that Henry and Philippe will retrieve my fortune and make their own, when I'll go on a real spree and just buy and buy until I drop."

The parasol department next claimed their interest and when Zenie opened a lovely French model and walked down the aisle holding it, Aunt Zena cried, "It is ravishing, my dear, you must have it. Call the salesman at once."

It was a gorgeous creation and Zenie's classic beauty took on new effectiveness as she gazed out from under its mushroom-shaped white satin body, covered with puffings of white lace tied with gay ribbon bows.

Both girls protested that their aunt should not spend her money so foolishly, especially as she felt the need of a new hat, but Aunt Zena shushed them with a "Now children, I assure you that the greatest pleasure in buying is not in getting things for yourself, but in giving them to others. I have ample hats at home, anyway. There are three trunks full of them and Zenie does not have a decent parasol, so that's settled."

## 3

AFTER THE FIRST, pre-season game—one with the Metropolitans—during which he had pitched but a single, disastrous inning, Clint boarded one of the bridge cars in an unpleasant frame of mind. Then, as so often happened, the cable was out of order and another quarter-hour passed before a steam engine was coupled to the train and puffed Manhattanward. By this time, the late afternoon rush was under way and there was another long wait until Clint found a place, right behind the engine, on the Sixth Avenue Elevated, where he suffered from cinders and smoke. To cap everything else, he became so preoccupied with his thoughts that he missed his station and had to walk back from Fifty-ninth Street. The upshot was that Clint missed dinner entirely, but ate an abundant meal of leftovers in the kitchen, served by an anxious Zenie who realized that he was edgy.

Mr. Rogers came down to question about the day's game and for the first time since he had known Clint, received a short and irritated answer.

Later, Zenie and Clint had very different ideas as to what led up to it, but the fact remained that they had their first serious quarrel—not in the presence of the family, for which Zenie was glad, but in the privacy of their own room, where the necessity for keeping their voices lowered gave a feeling of the most intense passion to all the unkind and unmeant things they said.

The next morning Clint was all contrition. "Zenie, old girl, I've behaved like a fool all winter, but wouldn't admit it to myself. I'm out of condition and knew it, but just let myself drag along. Beginning today I'm starting real training, but first we're going to stay right here in bed until I make my peace with you the best way I know. Am I forgiven?"

"Oh, Clint, of course. I've been so miserable all night. It's my fault, really, wanting us to stay on here. . . ."

"You were being sensible, that's all. Nobody knows better than I do that I can't go on forever as a pitcher. Then we'll need what we've been saving. It won't be long, either, if I give many exhibitions like yesterday. . . .

"Say, Zenie, that reminds me. I clean forgot. You remember I spoke last winter about a job for your father on a paper? I talked with the editor yesterday before the game, and Father is to go see him this afternoon."

Thus casually was Mr. Rogers about to be introduced to the third phase of his career. Right now, Clint reached over to find Zenie beneath the blankets. "Let breakfast wait, I don't even care if I have any, as I need to take off some weight anyway. You do love me? . . ."

When, an hour later, they descended to the dining room together, Zenie's face held an expression that caused Mrs. Rogers to look sharply at her for an instant, with head to one side, and then give a little sniff that spoke volumes of disapproval.

Zenie understood her mother well enough to imagine exactly what she was thinking, but although she colored slightly, she spoke firmly. "Clint has the most wonderful news, Mother. A position for Father on the *Times*. Won't he be excited?"

The children took this moment to tear through the house, pursued by Mr. Rogers in shirt sleeves. The interruption was welcomed by Mrs. Rogers as a means of covering up her excitement. If Zenie and Clint thought she'd excuse their lateness easily, they were very much mistaken! Pretending to include Jesse and the children in her wrath, she exclaimed, "Good grief, Pet, what a racket! I declare that you're worse than Jesse and Titi, egging them on. Besides having breakfast at all hours, I'll have the whole house to re-arrange. . . .

"Zenie says something about a position for you on the *Times*— not that I think it will come to anything, but you've spent so much time and money on newspapers it would be poetic justice if they paid you for a change."

Contrary to her prediction, the position on the *Times* did come to something. Punctually at three o'clock Mr. Rogers presented himself at the *Times* office on Printing House Square, attired in a manner that might be considered fitting to a gentleman of the press. In addition to his best high gray beaver, which did not look a bit old-fashioned, he carried the gold-headed cane that had been his father's, and wore in his cravat the large, coral pin that had once been treasured by Count Borelli, Mrs. Rogers' parent. Although this latter was completely hidden by luxuriant beard, the mere knowledge of its presence added to Mr. Rogers' feeling of well-being.

The editor seemed impressed by his visitor's size, amplitude of voice, and splendor of dress. "It's all in the nature of an experiment," he explained, "but an increasing number of our readers appear to be interested in sporting events. I understand from Mr. Weatherby that you are not only a student of baseball, but a close observer of pugilism as well.

"I must say that I am rather surprised that a gentleman of your evident attainment should find interest in amusements that inculcate so little of culture or moral tone. . . ."

Mr. Rogers puffed out his cheeks. "After retiring from a long and active career, my good sir, I found that the boredom of ease was not so much mitigated by cultural pursuits as by contemplation of our clean-limbed youth engaged in athletic endeavor." There, that should hold even a *Times* editor!

Apparently it did, for he took a new tack. "More and more people seem to think as you do, so we intend to give greater space to the news of these encounters. Instead of taking the scores as reported by the teams themselves, you would give an eye-witness account. Have you any idea, Mr. Rogers, what aspects of the game you would stress?"

"I've given the problem considerable thought. It appears to me that the mere recital of the score and the number of hits fails to impart to the purchaser of your excellent sheet any of the drama which takes place. I think I should try to develop the characters and thoughts of the contestants, couched in as close an approximation of the *Times*' literary style as I could achieve. While I have never written for publication, I've always striven for grace and variety of diction. . . ."

"As I can very well perceive," the editor interrupted, politely. "To coin a phrase, you believe in the human touch—and so do I. Before we make final arrangements, I propose that you cover the game between the New Yorks and Brooklyns tomorrow. If your contribution is half as good as I expect, we'll reach an agreement easily."

The following afternoon, Mr. Rogers and Clint left the house for the ball park. Again Mr. Rogers was resplendent in clothing befitting his new position and in addition had supplied himself with a plentiful supply of pencils and paper for the taking of notes.

The *Times* had reserved a seat for him in the stands, on the first row, right behind the batter's box, so that he could pass upon the umpire's accuracy in calling balls and strikes. As his career progressed, Mr. Rogers became a highly partisan observer, his greatest fealty to Brooklyn, then to the Metropolitans, and finally to the Giants. Whenever the Phillies or the Athletics played any of these teams he was apt to be unpredictable, depending on the degree of nostalgia the men from Philadelphia happened to arouse in him.

Today, with Clint not playing, Mr. Rogers applauded with complete impartiality, so that the game was almost over before he remembered to make notes. Afterward, he greeted his son-in-law, who had spent the afternoon in a workout beyond the players' bench, with the promise that his trust had not been misplaced. "I've all the facts here, my boy, and shall spend the evening in polishing them into a diverting and literary account. . . ."

"But Father, hold on a minute. The *Times* will want to print that article tomorrow morning, not the day after. . . ."

"That's impossible. I shall require a proper choice and variety of adjectives. This is too important a task to perform in a slipshod manner."

"Suppose you picked up tomorrow's paper and didn't see anything about the game in it? . . ."

"H-m-m-m, I can see what you mean. I shall have to concentrate immediately."

"I suggest we drop off at the *Times* office. I'll go with you. Maybe I can help with an idea or two."

Why couldn't Gussie see what a sterling fellow Clint Weatherby was? Mr. Rogers debated this question all the way to Printing House Square. Within the busy office, from which his friend the editor had departed, Mr. Rogers accosted a worried little man with a green eyeshade. "I am Jesse Rogers, your new sports correspondent. If you will be good enough to show me to my desk? . . ."

The man looked at the gold-headed cane and tall beaver, then made a kind of choking noise, followed by a vague gesture toward a further room, where men scribbled away furiously at badly-battered walnut desks. Clint suggested, "If I were you, I'd take that empty one. I guess this is a pretty busy time." He sat on top of the desk itself, in a confident manner that seemed a bit out of place to Mr. Rogers, who had always held newspapers in awe. He drew up a rickety chair, nevertheless, cautiously seated himself and sought vainly for inspiration.

"Maybe it would be a good idea to say how many people were there," Clint prompted, finally.

"Excellent!" Mr. Rogers set pencil to paper. "How's this? 'Three thousand persons wended their way to Washington Park yesterday afternoon . . .'"

"I don't think the gate was over seventeen or eighteen hundred."

Suddenly Mr. Rogers was completely self-assured. "Round numbers, Clint, my boy." He wrote on with great rapidity, repeating aloud lines that particularly appealed to him. " 'The men began to play soon after three o'clock. . . .' I don't like to have to say that—they should have started promptly on the hour. 'The New Yorks were the first at bat. Brady, the first batter, led off with a hit. . . . A neat play doubled him and ruined what looked like a sure run for the boys from the metropolis.' Pretty good, that, I think."

After relating Brooklyn's three runs in detail, he thought a moment. "I have it. 'The New Yorkers were discouraged and started their second inning without the vim and vigor which distinguished them a few minutes before . . . they were desperate in the third inning. Defeat stared them in the face and they responded to Captain Brady's call for a grand effort.' " The pencil sped on, until " '. . . by a fine spurt they managed to tie the Brooklyns, to the delight of the New York people in the assemblage, who yelled themselves hoarse in cheering their favorites as the game was called on account of darkness.' There, that's an account with some zip to it, I'd say. . . ."

Clint was as enthusiastic as the fledgling reporter. "Indeed it has. Why you could sit at home and recapture all the excitement of the game, just from reading the paper. It should bring in lots of extra pennies, but I'm not sure it will do baseball any good. If people can read all about it maybe they'll stop going."

"Nonsense. It will make those who've never seen an exhibition desire to attend. I can visualize a time when seven or eight, perhaps even ten thousand persons will be present at a single game."

Apparently the Times was satisfied, for there the account was, in full, on its last page, the following morning. Mr. Rogers read it over to himself, and then aloud. "Listen, Gussie, to this. . . ."

Hearing Mr. Rogers read each of his efforts was a small price to pay for having him working again and out of the house during the daytime. Mrs. Rogers confided as much to Aunt Zena during one of the latter's late breakfasts. "There were times when Jesse was around that I could just scream. He always wanted attention and me with a houseful of work to do. Then there's the money, of course. You could have knocked me over when I learned his salary. There's something about baseball that drives men daft, I declare. Not that I should complain under the circumstances. Philippe and Julia leaving will make quite a hole in our finances."

"Oh, Tina, I am so glad for you. Wasn't it thoughtful of Clint to make it possible?" Aunt Zena volunteered smugly.

"That's all that gripes me—being beholden to him. . . ."

"But why, Tina? Of all your sons-in-law I prefer him. He is so strong—so—so virile. You know what I mean?"

"I do indeed," Mrs. Rogers replied grimly, and then softened. "Though I shouldn't hold it against you, when I guess I was the same." She then went on with a further confidence which she was to regret for the rest of her life. "Which reminds me, Zena. Do you remember Billy Madeira who used to live in Kensington? I saw him the other day and he asked about you."

"Madeira . . . Billy Madeira . . ." Mrs. Rogers could see her sister shuffling through mental pictures of men as though they were postcards. Suddenly she came to the right one. "Ah, yes. Billy Madeira. A little man—with wavy black hair."

"He's bald now—and rich. He proposed to me a number of times, but I took Jesse—for the same reason you like Clint

143

Weatherby, I might as well admit. Billy has never married, whereas, Jesse would have run off with the first lifted skirt he saw, if I hadn't been around to keep an eye on him. I hadn't thought of it before, but I guess that's why I dislike Clint so; he's just the kind of man girls like Zenie make fools of themselves over."

Aunt Zena's face had taken on an expression of speculative cunning. "Madeira . . . Mr. Madeira . . . a-a-ah. The man that Henry worked for! I begin to see."

There was no mistaking the uncompromising truth in Mrs. Rogers' sharp, "Not what you think, you don't. After a body has lived with someone like Jesse for years, you're glad to sleep nights, after a while, and not go gallivanting. If Mr. Madeira helped Henry along a little because of me I see no harm in that."

"My dear Tina, of course not." Aunt Zena began to make a slight humming noise between her teeth, then stretched her arms in a catlike gesture. "It's such a beautiful day. I think that I shall take a walk this morning."

**Chapter 5**

IF, in the long days of early summer, there was one evening when the street lights were late in being lit in a section north of Forty-second Street and west of Fifth Avenue, it probably passed without notice. Certainly the Rogers family paid no attention, for the day must have been the occasion of Norah's marriage.

Originally it had been planned to have the simplest possible ceremony, to spend the day at Coney Island or go on an excursion to one of Starin's groves, along the Sound, and to return in time for Tony to make his rounds.

When Mrs. Rogers was informed of the plan, which was to take place on Norah's day off, she threw up her hands angrily. "You'll do nothing of the kind and I don't know what you can be thinking of. You'll not be married in chapel by some strange priest you've never seen before if I have anything to say. After I practically raised you from a freckle-faced shanty-Irish brat into what you are today I don't want Tony nor anyone else to think you're entirely without a family. You'll be married right here in the parlor, decently, as becomes a decent . . ."

She caught herself suddenly, realizing that only one of her daughters had been married at home. To cover the awkward moment she proposed a generosity she had not at first intended. "And on your day off, of all things! What can you think of us? An outsider might believe I was a female Simon Legree the way you go on. You'll need your day off for shopping. There's always last minute things a bride needs. Besides, a Thursday is no day to get married on; we'll make it the following Tuesday."

"Yes mum . . ." Norah's heart was too full to say anything else, so she repeated the phrase she used a thousand times a day, then added, ". . . and what will you be after me doin' now?"

The morning of the fateful day, Mrs. Rogers herself attended to the arranging of Norah's hair, which had the habit of coming down at the wrong time. Before she succeeded in anchoring the brassy coils in place with myriad hairpins, she observed, from exasperation, "Norah, you must use that tonic the Seven Sutherland Sisters put out. I've never seen so much hair. If it stays until Father Duffy is finished with you, I'll be surprised."

Julia helped with the bridal costume, which had been altered from a summery white-lawn dress out of Aunt Zena's trunks. The Lascalles had planned their move to Cincinnati for the first of June, but Julia had insisted upon the postponement, much to Philippe's annoyance. "It isn't the same as with the rest of the family, who've lived with Norah so long. We hardly know the girl," he had objected, but both Julia and her mother grasped at any excuse that would put off their parting.

A surprise was the presence of Henry, who admitted gruffly that he had come all the way from the West Virginia mining country just to be there. "I don't see why you make all this fuss about it," he complained. "Norah makes the best hot cakes I ever ate, bar none. For another thing, I always liked her. There's a present for her coming. A couple of pieces of furniture to begin housekeeping with, some day."

It was the first time since their scene of months ago that Henry made his appearance in the same room with Clinton Weatherby. The latter waited an opportunity to explain that he bore no grudge, but Henry avoided him.

When Father Duffy arrived, everyone remarked how he had aged. His hair was almost white and his face had grown thinner. For the first time, as Mrs. Rogers observed, he looked almost as saintly as some people thought he was. But the greeting between the priest and Mr. Rogers was as boisterous as ever, with Father Duffy looking quizzical when asked what he was doing that kept him from coming around. He appeared to think a moment before answering, "I think I can truly say that I'm following your advice, Rogers, my friend. I'm obeying my own inward light."

Mr. Rogers let out one of his best freight-yard shouts. "Then I've succeeded in making a true Quaker of you, Duffy, which is more than I ever accomplished with any of my family."

Suddenly Father Duffy appeared to be on the verge of collapse. He caught hold of the back of a chair with one hand and passed the other over his forehead. A moment later he seemed well again and smiled at Mr. Rogers' distress. "A flash of headache, that's all. I've been working too hard lately. Between the Henry George campaign and the defense for the Haymarket men I've had a full life in addition to my parish duties; knowing beforehand that we'll fail is what makes it harder. . . .

"But no more of this now. I suppose that is the young man who has won our little Norah?"

Tony looked remarkably handsome in a four-button cutaway that the bride had helped him buy the Thursday before; and a decided bargain it had been, for not only was the suit reduced from $18.00 to $10.00, but Mr. King, the store proprietor, had given with it, as he had advertised, a bronze and silver mantel clock. When Mr. Rogers heard of this shrewd shopping, he suggested that Tony was duty bound to carry the clock with him to the altar, and proposed setting it so that it would ring twelve as the fatal words were pronounced.

Neither member of the bridal couple had relatives in this country, but a fellow Italian stood for the groom. The family sat around in a semicircle and Abe, the colored boy, watched from the doorway. Later he accompanied Zenie down to the kitchen to help with the surprise collation, while Henry again proved unpredictable. Withdrawing rice from a side pocket, he pelted Norah with almost boyish vim.

By the time the food was consumed and Father Duffy had gone, a dray stopped out front and an oddly-styled old cupboard and chest were carried into the front hall. Mrs. Rogers, who preferred new furniture to old, wondered where Henry had purchased two such pieces. But Henry explained, "I saw these up in Pennsylvania, Norah, and thought you might like to have them. They're very old and no Dutch girl would think of getting married until she had a bridal chest and if possible, a water bench, which is what the other is."

Since the one-day honeymoon was to include a steamer excursion and picnic there was no time to be lost. Under another deluge of rice the newly-married pair dashed down the steps to the curb, where Mr. Quinby waited impatiently, Abe at the reins. Tears of happiness marred Norah's already ruddy complexion as she cried from the carriage, "God Bless all of you for bein' so wonderful."

Abe clucked to the horse and they were off for the Cortlandt Street Pier, on the North River, for the most glorious day ever. The Rogerses watched them out of sight, feeling to the full the warmth of heart their kindness had engendered. Then Henry left them and quietly moved his presents up to the two fourth-floor rooms that had been given over to the newlyweds.

He alone understood the secret urge which had led him to buy the chest and *Wasserbank* at a country auction sale. They had reminded him of others, almost identical, that had been treasured heirlooms of Melissa, his first and only love. A chest and *Wasserbank* that had been lost at sea with her.

2

"THE WHOLE FAMILY is breaking up—after we'd been so happy together again," Mrs. Rogers moaned. "Something tells me I'll never see the dear children any more."

"Cincinnati isn't very far away. We may very well visit them later this summer. Meanwhile, may I suggest, Gussie, that you stop waving that handkerchief—the train's been out of sight a full five minutes." Mr. Rogers revealed his impatience.

As they left the Grand Central Depot, Mrs. Rogers' steps lagged. "You know, Pet, I just had an awful thought. When I looked up at you against the sunlight coming in that window, I saw that your beard is real gray. We're old, Jesse, old. I just can't get used to it. I'm knocked all in a heap."

"I was beginning to feel old myself, a few months past, but the increasing success of my journalistic endeavors has renewed my youth. I have always known that my forte lay in self-expression; I don't understand why I didn't take it up years ago."

Mrs. Rogers was not to be deterred from indulging her emotions. "That's all very well, but it can't keep up long—you're getting on, you know. And look at poor Father Duffy. When I saw him I was shocked, without realizing that our appearance must affect him the same way. And have you noticed Zena? . . ."

There was malice in Mrs. Rogers' voice. Her sister was several years older than herself and showed it, despite the liberal use of the creams, emollients, and toilet waters that filled her dressing table. If Mrs. Rogers had known what Zena was about at this very moment, she would have found less comfort in the thought that however much age was catching up with her, Zena was at least several years older.

Teresina Lascalles had given her little parting presents to Julia and the children before they left the house, pled fatigue as a reason for not seeing them off on the St. Louis Express, and as soon as the others were gone, sent out the new Mrs. Angelucci in search of a hackney.

After the death of her husband, Aunt Zena had considered love as a pleasant pastime, to which variety added an exciting spice. Then came a period when she toyed with the idea of marrying again, but could not fix with certainty upon a particular suitor. Later still she engaged quite frankly in the pursuit of a husband, but failed, if rumor were true, because of too-generous impulses before attaining the goal. Finally in desperation, she was even willing to purchase a husband with her wealth, but her excessive ardor frightened away several candidates. With her fortune depleted, she had, apparently, lost courage. During the past two years in New York, as guest (paying) of her sister, she had been very circumspect, except for an occasional flirtation on the street or in a restaurant, when an impartial observer might have felt that Aunt Zena responded to glances that were either completely innocent or meant for someone else.

Meanwhile, she never admitted to herself that she was, actually, an old woman. She spent hours at her mirror, massaging upward the sagging flesh of her neck, dabbing her cheeks with rose water to prevent wrinkles, making tiny O's with her mouth, to keep it from becoming slack. At night she stuffed quantities of cotton between her gums and cheeks and suffered its presence until morning to round the contours of her face. Weekly she applied a mask of mud that was supposed to come from Egypt. In short, because she did all the things that beauty experts recommended for keeping youth, according to her reasoning, she still possessed it.

The trouble was that the Rogerses knew so few eligible men. Theirs was an existence that centered in the family. Aunt Zena's great opportunity, she told herself, had been Mr. Rogers' old friend, Louis Havemyer. But she had awed him with her European manners and extravagant clothes, and he had married another. If only she had acted a simple and unsophisticated role with him! Well, it was too late to think of that now.

Tina had let drop a remark, a few weeks before, that aroused Aunt Zena's hopes anew. Billy Madeira was a bachelor, wealthy, near at hand, and he still remembered her. Of course Tina would think that he had stayed single on her account. How like her sister. Actually, wasn't it more probable—almost certain, in fact—that he had carried a different picture in his heart all these years? No doubt he had been shy and too slow to come to the point before the glorious Teresina Repetto returned to Europe. Then, a year later —or was it longer?—he had read of her marriage. A dagger had turned in his heart. Like her similarly wounded nephew, he had devoted himself to the accumulation of wealth. Now what more natural than that he should want to spend the last days of a wasted life in the company of the woman who had so unwittingly hurt him.

149

It was high romance, as Aunt Zena conceived it. So much would depend upon his first view of her. Mature handsomeness had replaced the girlish beauty which he would remember. Somehow she needed to bridge that change.

This was the problem over which she had been mulling. Then, in an idle moment she began to read the advertisements in a paper that Mr. Rogers had discarded and found what might very well be the solution. She read the advertisement again:

SOMETHING NEW! The Pompon Pompadour $2.00 upward. The Marie Antoinette Wave for front and back. All the rage, requires no nets or hairpins, and imparts a marvelously youthful appearance, $5.00 and upward.

Eugenie's Secret of Beauty—our Transparent Enamel for the complexion is unsurpassed. Imparts a brilliant transparency. Removes all wrinkles and all other blemishes. Recommended by physicians. Exclusively used by the belles of Europe. Tested and applied on premises.

L. Shaw, 54 West 14th Street, 3 doors from Macy's.

Why it sounded wonderful! Aunt Zena wore a secret smile as she set out for the Shaw establishment. There she allowed her enthusiasm to run away with her. She bought both the Pompon Pompadour and front and back Marie Antoinette Waves—then in a burst of genius, Madame Shaw suggested dyeing the *tout ensemble* a glorious shade of red.

After the application of Eugenie's Secret of Beauty, Aunt Zena hardly recognized the gorgeous creature that stared back at her from the mirror. She surveyed herself with greatest satisfaction and elation. Let Billy Madeira resist her now! Ho, for Philadelphia.

First of all, though, she'd have to make some excuse for leaving New York. She couldn't let Tina know at this stage of the game. She'd be furious, as she always used to be when Zena sailed in and took a man from her. While Teresina Lascalles gazed out of her returning hansom with unseeing eyes, she allowed her thoughts free rein. This time there must be no mistakes. She must restrain her impetuous nature. She must proceed with the utmost caution.

When they turned off Fifth Avenue, she called to the driver through the little door in the roof of her vehicle and instructed him to pull to the curb. After tipping him generously, in her old manner, she continued her way on foot, steeling herself the while for the questions which she felt would be inevitable.

Surprisingly enough, there were none, not even through dinner, when she was at first subdued and retiring. Then, when not even Jesse remarked upon her appearance, she began to talk and gesticulate with increasing vivacity. Where were everyone's eyes?

Afterward she retired to her room in disappointment, but no less determined upon her plans. When she had gone, Mr. Rogers questioned his wife, "Did you notice anything about your sister, Gussie? She acted to me as though she'd been drinking!"

To which Mrs. Rogers answered spitefully, "Jesse, where are your eyes? She's dyed her hair and done it differently. With rouge on her cheeks! At her age I call it pitiful."

*Chapter 6*

MRS. ROGERS felt that it was bad form for the members of her family to speak to any of their neighbors until they were first spoken to. Therefore, she always put on her most forbidding expression as she approached her house, and if the short, stoutish woman who lived next door was on her front stoop, managed to look straight through her while taking in every detail of her appearance.

Since the short, stoutish woman put on a similarly blank yet perceptive expression, Mrs. Rogers thought that her neighbor to the east was unfriendly and given to airs. "If that Mrs. Burt thinks I care she is very must mistaken," she'd say, in an aggrieved tone. "I have plenty to do without having truck with neighbors, especially the kind you have in a place like New York. That's the trouble with a city—the folks in it don't care an aye, yes or no about anyone else."

The Burts kept a German living-out girl, and the coolness extended to the servants. Indeed, when Mrs. Rogers was employed at some task in the kitchen and in a merry mood, Norah would regale her with imitations of Bertha's accent as heard over the back fence. Considering that Norah spoke with more than a touch of the bog and made a fizzle of her new name of Angelucci, it was doubly ludicrous.

Because the house on the other side was closed most of the year, while its owners traveled, all of Mrs. Rogers' frustrated sense of neighborliness centered in the Burts, and more specifically, in Mrs. Burt, as her husband left the house early every morning and generally returned long after dark. Mrs. Rogers spoke of her as "that woman." "That woman had on a dress today that takes the cake."

Apparently Mr. Rogers had never paid much attention to these remarks, for one day he interrupted a particularly spirited "That woman puts on the most outrageous airs . . ." to inquire, "Who do you have in mind, Gussie? There are a few too many women in New York for me to know instinctively the subject. . . ."

"Of all the men! That woman next door, of course. I just ran over to the store for something Norah forgot. Of course she had to see me carrying the package and gave one of those stares of hers. I looked right back, as though to say 'I'll carry my groceries if I feel like it.' Oh, she is hateful. I don't know what her husband does, but you'd think from her airs he was President."

"No, he's in the shoe business. A very fine chap, too. I think you must be mistaken about his wife."

"Jesse Rogers, do you mean to stand there and tell me that you have known that man all this time and never said a word to me about it? After all I've told you about her, too!"

"I had no idea your relations were strained. I meet Charlie Burt in the barbershop right along and often speak to his wife on the street. She seems a pleasant woman to me."

"Well! You take the cake! I wish you could have seen her stare at me, just now."

"And you stared right back. I suggest that you try smiling the next time."

"Indeed I won't. I've never been a woman to make advances."

"Well then I'll make them for you. We'll invite them over for the Fourth and make an occasion of it. Write up to Gus and see if he and Gene can come. We haven't had a clambake for a long time—I'll buy a bushel of them down at the slip."

Mrs. Rogers said, "You'll do nothing of the kind," but the objection lacked force. Her husband disregarded her remark. "I'll invite Duffy, too, if he's around town. Both Henry and Gus would enjoy seeing him . . .

"Now I have to dash away. There's a rumor that a man is going to jump from the bridge today, for a wager, and I'm asked to do what I'm pleased to call a 'human interest' story on it."

He was gone before Mrs. Rogers could raise further objections to his plans. Since Robert Odlum had lost his life, several years earlier, in jumping from the Brooklyn Bridge to publicize his Old Point Comfort swimming pool, there had been other attempts equally disastrous.

Mr. Rogers reached the bridge, in which he always felt a proprietary interest, pleased to discover that there was no sign of excitement. After paying his penny toll, he strolled along the pedestrian walk and took a position in the shadow of the great stone pier that carried the cables. An hour went by, during which he scrutinized the passersby—both those on foot and in conveyances. During the second hour he began to tire of inaction and was almost ready to give up the story, when suddenly he saw a man already perched on the railing. How had he gotten there without being seen?

Mr. Rogers ran forward, waving his cane and shouting. The poised figure was about to plunge, but then he hesitated. Other bridge passengers saw him and came running, but Mr. Rogers reached him first. With a firm grasp upon the man's belt he hauled him back to safety. A more cynical person might have suspected that this tall, quaking creature was not the stuff of which heroes are made. Mr. Rogers thought only of his story.

"Your name, if you please?"

"Irwin Fleischer."

"Address?"

"Staten Island . . ."

"What street?"

"Just Staten Island . . . we're squatting. I made a little place."

Mr. Rogers voice became stern, partially out of real feeling, but

153

also from a consciousness that he was the center of attraction. "And why, may I ask, did you contemplate so perilous a step?"

By this time, quite a crowd had gathered, all of whom were listening intently. The man said firmly, "For my wife and children, who are desperate for food. A successful jump and I would be famous."

There were murmurs of "Poor man . . . children, he said . . . a real hero, to take a risk like that." Somebody began to take up a collection, to which Mr. Rogers contributed the largest piece of silver in the hat. A man of obvious means suggested, "I'll gladly give you a job. . . ."

A farmer with a wagonload of produce presented Mr. Fleischer with bunches of carrots, beets, and turnip greens. A housewife, crossing over to Brooklyn, said, "Staten Island! Imagine! The poor soul," and handed over a whole market basket filled with victuals.

Then, as though by magic, the man was gone—not that Mr. Rogers cared very much, for he had all the notes he needed. Back in the *Times* office he invented a new word, Odlumism, and observed that in these days of hardship, men would do anything to earn an honest dollar for their families. He elaborated the kindness shown by the people more fortunately situated. "A job at eight dollars a week was offered Mr. Fleischer, which should maintain him, his spouse, and their eight children in considerable comfort." He deprecated the human impulse which made heroes of those who took unnecessary and foolish risks.

It was a good story, but when the editor read over Mr. Rogers' large, round script he shook his head. "No . . . I'm afraid you had better stick to baseball. The wager we had in mind has been called off. This man Fleischer is a flim-flam artist. He's pulled that stunt every day for a week."

Mr. Rogers was very chagrined, not only at being taken in by a trickster, but at revealing his own gullibility. Until now his journalistic career had been a succession of triumphs. In addition to baseball, he had covered a number of other sporting events: the six-day roller-skating races in Madison Square Garden, a lacrosse game, and the dog swimming events at the 116th Street Beach on the East River. He had interviewed the lady pugilist, Hattie Steward, and dubbed her "The Female John L. Sullivan."

154

Somehow he would have to retrieve his prestige, because he was determined to make his position a year-round one, not limited to the baseball season. At the moment, though, he had plans to make for the party on the Fourth of July.

The Glorious Fourth! Mr. Rogers had an inspiration and rushed to a desk. As he wrote, a smile broadened his features. This would show them! Just the right humorous touch. He read the heading over: "Information for persons who wish to escape from the small boy and the noisy firecracker." Then, half aloud, he continued with the charms of Long Branch and Rockaway, Fire Island and the various picnic groves, inserting an adjective here and there, or striking out a comma.

He had saved the best for last. "Coney Island will be the Mecca of a million. Although a great army of pleasure seekers will demonstrate their patriotism by hieing to other wave-washed watering places or to the mossy dell, and will return in the gloaming, laden with mementos of rural joys or saturated with sea water and other liquids, at Coney the thousand and one sights and sounds that can be seen and heard nowhere else will be magnified in honor of the day, and the festive clam will make desperate but futile efforts to dig himself into his sandy habitation beyond the reach of the voracious multitude he hears tramping over him." There, that was a sentence embellished with all the graces of literature.

With almost a swagger, Mr. Rogers gave his piece to a copy boy, placed his hat at a rakish angle and went marketing for his clams.

2

ANY OTHER WOMAN might have been intimidated by making a trip to Philadelphia alone, even in one of Mr. Pullman's Palace Parlor Cars, but in pursuit of romance Aunt Zena was dauntless. Just before she announced her intention of leaving the city for a few days, Mr. Rogers read in his usual tones of impending doom that the Ute Indians were on the rampage again. Aunt Zena's notions of American geography were still vague. Except for a few Shinnecock Indians that had once been pointed out to her, she had never seen any of the American savages either in Philadelphia or New York, and she had been assured on many occasions that they were too far away to worry about. Speaking as casually as she could, she said, "I am glad they are out wherever they are and not in Philadelphia. I'm making a little visit there next week and I should hate to encounter an Indian Redman with nothing on but those little things they wear."

While Mr. Rogers wondered what picture of Indians had left its impression in Aunt Zena's mind, Mrs. Rogers questioned sharply, "To Philadelphia? Zena, what in the world for?"

All the elaborately prepared excuses were discarded as Aunt Zena realized they would not pass muster with her sister in this mood. Instead, with sudden inspiration, she assumed an arch air. "Ah, my dear Tina, it is something I had contemplated doing when I visited you there and had a lot more money than I have now. Circumstances prevented, but I've never forgotten. Please let it be a surprise. . . ."

The implication was obvious, and Mrs. Rogers put up only a half-hearted objection. "Now Zena, don't spend any money foolishly. I can't think of anything we need. Besides, you can't go alone. . . ."

"Why can't I? The Utes would not come that far. Jesse always said . . ."

"Oh, lands no, not Indians. But what about strange men, Zena? A lone woman is their prey."

"Yes, Zena, I think you should think twice," Mr. Rogers added his warning. "If you insist, I have a suggestion. The Pennsylvania Railroad is providing female companions for ladies compelled to travel alone."

"Nonsense. I used to travel with nothing but maids—and practically all over the world. I enjoy it. I used to find it most exciting."

"I dare say you did," Mrs. Rogers agreed, drily. "Well, if you've set your mind to it I guess there is no use arguing."

"I have it," Mr. Rogers shouted, with sudden inspiration. "You won't go until after the Fourth, when Gene and Gus will be over. You can go back with them and they'll see you safe in a hotel. That will cut the danger in half, at any rate."

Aunt Zena thought rapidly. Yes, that would work out all right, just so she had a free hand in Philadelphia, and accordingly she agreed.

When her plans were again discussed at dinner that night, she realized to the full the disadvantages of a too-loving family, for Clint burst out, "Why we'll be playing in Philadelphia then. There's a morning game on the Fourth. . . ."

It was Mr. Rogers' turn to look perturbed. "Clint, my boy, we were counting on you for our clambake. . . ."

"We'll be there. I promised Zenie that she'd see me play, and the crowds are more refined in Philadelphia than in Brooklyn, so she's going over with the team, but we'll be back for the party in the evening. Zenie will stay here when we return to Philadelphia the next day with Gus and Gene. Then I'll come home with you on the eighth. Now no arguments, it's all settled."

Aunt Zena sighed, then took a philosophic view. She could twist Clint around her little finger, and perhaps there would be an opportunity to meet again the charming second baseman of the Brooklyns.

Things worked out to plan—at least up to a point. Zenie accompanied the team to the city she had not seen for so many years. While the others sat up in the Sullivan Sleeper, she and Clint enjoyed Mr. Pullman's together. It was a new experience for both of them, although the broad and suggestive teasing to which they were subjected by Clint's teammates at the park, made Zenie wish that they had sat up and gone to a hotel with the others.

In spite of having dressed as inconspicuously as possible in the English mohair suit cut down from the one Aunt Zena had given her, Teresina looked so lovely that Clint felt a great surge of pride as all eyes turned in her direction.

It was a strange sensation to be the only woman among so many men. She sat in the grandstand close to the players' bench, with Brooklyns to each side of her, as protection against possible rowdies, and in a few moments forgot everything but the scene on the field.

Her excitement reached its peak when Clint took his place in the pitcher's box and hurled a ball to the catcher with such speed that it resounded in his mitt like a pistol shot. Clint had been having a poor season, and she said a little prayer under her breath that he should win, conscious that ordinarily a game of baseball might not be a proper subject for prayer.

Then came the first surprise. A familiar voice said "Hello, Zenie" right in her ear. She turned quickly and there was Gus Palmer. And Gene! "Did Clint know you were coming and never tell me? Wait until I give him a talking to."

She fancied that Gus's voice still held a special note of regard for her as he answered, "No, your mother's letter said you would be here, so we decided to keep you company. Neither of us have ever seen a real game. . . ."

Gene interrupted, "And did we have trouble finding you among so many people. There must be a couple of thousand, at least." Looking toward the diamond, she pointed her finger and almost screamed, "Look, Gus, there's Clint. My, doesn't he look handsome in a uniform?"

There were hurried introductions to the few Brooklyn players who had not started to warm up. Before Gene could get done with explanations and an exchange of news the game had begun.

Zenie found herself in the role of expert and was surprised at how much information she had unconsciously picked up. She explained the windmill-like motions with which the Athletics pitcher wound up before snapping the ball with a peculiar, underhand twist toward the batter. When he stopped in the middle of a windup and threw to first base, she knew immediately that it was a balk that advanced the runner.

Evidently Clint had made up his mind to win. There were few innings in which even a single Athletics batter got on the bases. Then Zenie and Gene would scream themselves hoarse and Clint's long arm would whip the ball into the catcher's mitt with bullet force until the side was out.

The difficulty was that the other pitcher did as well. When the final inning came around, neither side had a score. In various turns at bat, Clint had not appeared to try very hard and Zenie explained that he had to save his energy for pitching. Then, when the Brooklyns came to bat in the ninth inning, the first batter hit the ball so far that the player in center field ran back to the fence before he retrieved it and the runner reached second.

"Smith is swinging now," Zenie explained excitedly. "He is known as a terrific swiper."

Apparently the Athletics pitcher was taking no chances, for in a minute, Smith threw down his bat and walked to first, showing in pantomime, that he would have preferred a hit to a base on balls.

The next man to pick up a bat was Clint and the irrepressible Gene screamed to him, "Swipe it clear over the fence, Clint! Swipe it hard, do!"

But wait, there was a discussion going on. Half a dozen of the Brooklyns milled around Clint and even Zenie had no idea what was going on. Apparently Clint was determined to take his turn and the others wanted someone else to bat for him. When, finally, he stepped up to the plate, there was a huzzah from all the on-lookers, even those who had been applauding the Athletics.

The pitcher studied Clint long and carefully, then leisurely helped himself to a chew of tobacco. "I hate that man," Zenie whispered. "There isn't anyone on the Brooklyns who looks so villainous."

"He's trying to make Clint nervous, that's all he's doing," Gene joined in. "And the way he's twisting his mustaches. Anyone could see that he's conceited."

The man threw the ball so suddenly that Clint didn't have a chance to swipe at it. There was no doubt at all that it was unfair, but the man in the blue suit cried out "Strike one!" No wonder the Athletics were in first place in the American Association, when the umpire was on their side. A good part of the girls' animosity was transferred from the pitcher to him.

Even Clint, who rarely lost his temper, appeared angry. They could see him run his hand through his brush of red hair, then grip his bat with renewed determination. Again the ball came over without due notice and Gene was quite ready to climb down on the field and tell the umpire and the horrible Athletics pitcher just what she thought of them.

This time Clint dug his cleats into the ground. Once more his opponent tried to be unfair but Clint was only pretending not to be prepared. His bat came around and caught the ball a sickening crack, then it became a little dot in the sky and floated high over the fence that enclosed the far side of the park. Clint ambled leisurely around the bases while the two runs came in ahead of him. Then he walked over to Zenie's place in the grandstand, made a deep bow and threw his cap up to her.

Zenie was certain that never in all her life could she feel more proud of Clint than at this moment, but when he stepped from the pitcher's mound after retiring the side in order, her heart was so full that she climbed down from the stand and ran across the field to greet him, with Gus and Gene close behind. Clint was sweaty from his exertion under the July sun and walked uneasily on his spikes, but Zenie thought that he looked wonderfully handsome and told him so.

He grinned a trifle sheepishly, "Easy, old girl, or I'll never hear the last of it from the rest of the fellows. Hello, Gus—and you too, Gene. I thought there was more noise from Zenie's corner of the stands than she could make alone."

"You mean that you didn't see us when you made your bow?"

"As that was my first home run for the Brooklyns I must have been dizzy. Did I bow to anyone?"

"Oh, Clint, you did. Of course you did, and you know it very well. I was so thrilled."

He left them to dress. Then they hurried from the Twenty-sixth and Jefferson Street field and caught the one o'clock train by a race down Ridge Avenue in a crowded hackney.

Before they reached Wayne Junction there had been a complete and excited resumé of the morning's game, after which Clint and Zenie heard all about life in the coal regions. In talking over the affairs of their individual households Gene and Zenie found a common meeting ground such as they had never before possessed. Zenie especially found herself admiring Georgina's forthright qualities. As with Julia, she felt glad now that she had not married her sister's husband, although she had felt jealous enough at the time.

Not that she didn't like Gus anymore; for the first time she really understood and appreciated his selflessness, his tolerance and lighthearted humor that so easily changed to seriousness. It was Gene, though, to whom she felt closest and they exchanged confidences about the problems of marriage and the characteristics of their respective husbands.

They reached their destination and exclaimed over the quick passage of the time. Gus had just finished reading a new book called *Samantha at Saratoga*, from which he quoted whole paragraphs in an indescribably funny manner. Josiah Allen's wife, who was alleged to have written it, delighted in homely Americanisms that sounded unbelievably strange to modern ears and everyone howled when Gus said to Zenie, "I kin see that you're one of the girls who would flirt with the town pump or the meetin' house steeple."

When they arrived home, long before they were expected, Samantha's dialect had become a private joke, so that when Mr. and Mrs. Rogers asked in concert, "How did you find Philadelphia, after all these years?" Zenie giggled and said, "It wuz dretful fashionable, but I prefer it here, 'cause it's more placider like."

Twelve months later all of America was repeating the pseudo-rural phrases of Josiah and Samantha Allen in which the whole family were to find so much pleasure that Fourth of July afternoon. Unfortunately Father Duffy could not come, and Henry left shortly after the return of Clint and Zenie, pleading a business engagement the next morning in Pittsburgh. Gene, particularly, showed her anger. "The first time we have been here in perfect ages and my own brother finds an excuse to rush away."

But the family disagreement was forgotten with the arrival of the guests of honor. Nobody would have thought that the Burts lived next door, and had done so for two years or more. At the moment of their arrival a giant firecracker exploded outside and Mr. Rogers shouted, "A salute from my private army! . . ."

"Or from the small boy with the firecracker, about which you wrote so delightfully this morning," Mr. Burt responded. How could one help liking a neighbor like that?

"Gussie, this is Mr. Burt, who has been reading my piece in the *Times*, anent escaping the city for the Fourth. He sees that we do not practice what I preach! And this is Mrs. Burt."

Mr. Burt was clean-shaven and pink-skinned, with a fringe of beard beneath his chin, in the style affected by Horace Greeley.

Mrs. Rogers gave him her most arch smile. "Well, this is a pleasure indeed. Jesse says that he has known you for months and I'm perfectly furious with him that he did not invite you over sooner.

"And Mrs. Burt! I've been simply dying to meet you, but our paths never seemed to cross. After all, I'm a pretty busy woman, what with a family to run. Not that things aren't easier now, with my daughter Julia and her children gone to Cincinnati. . . ."

She paused for breath and Mrs. Burt took the opportunity to insert her own excuses. "I've seen you dash by, of course. We poor women never do have any time, do we? My children are all married and in homes of their own, but a big house is chore enough. I declare that we are so tired after dinner we do nothing but go to bed, or play a little game of two-handed pinochle."

The unanimity with which both Rogers parents cried "Pinochle!" might have startled anyone but another devotee of the fascinating game.

"Why, yes. Don't tell me that you play?"

"Indeed we do. When we lived over in Brooklyn we played foursomes, twice a week, but since we moved Father and I have a two-handed game once in a while."

"It's not nearly as much fun as four-handed, I agree. Mr. Burt often says, 'I'd enjoy a game more if we knew another couple who played. . . .'"

Everything indicated that this was the beginning of an enduring friendship—one which could survive, right at its beginning, the next words of Mr. Burt. "Knock on the wall and we'll come over any time you say. And as a writer, Mr. Rogers, I wanted to read you a little something of mine, for your criticism. I write these for the *Times* too, but I pay for them." He withdrew a clipping from his pocket, and read: " 'Surely the *fittest* thing is a shoe. It may be trodden on, stamped on, kicked, cuffed, sworn at and abused and make no sign. It is questioned in vain by wives and mothers-in-law concerning the wanderings of them of uncertain hours. Dear friend of man, having eyes it sees not; having a *tongue* it speaks not. Though it raises corn it never raises the D. . . . It is a born tramp and never tires. It covereth alike the feet of the just and the unjust and will *last* until its *sole* is worn out. Blessed, thrice blessed, be the E. C. Burt Shoe. $2.50, Warranted.'

"I've never quite liked that last line. It sounds too commercial, what do you think, as a newspaperman?"

Mr. Rogers humphed a time or two, flattered not a little, but unwilling to commend in another the kind of puns which he was himself prone to make. Fortunately, the appearance of Norah, with the first installment of clams, caused a welcome interruption. These were none of your little Ipswich clams, or nanny-noses, but good-sized, hard-shell clams from the blue mud of Barnegat, baked on the half shell and plentifully supplied with melted butter and their own bouillon. Norah carried them to the table on the iron baking sheet, which she held at each end with pot holders.

"This is beach style, without the annoyance of sand or flies," Mr. Rogers proclaimed. "Don't touch the shells, as they're hotter than blazes, but spear them up this way—and the one with the longest reach gets the most!"

While the first panful disappeared, Norah returned to the dumb-waiter, where Tony, who had been pressed into service, had the next one ready for her.

It was a wonderful party, enjoyed by everyone, and especially by Aunt Zena, who had never before tasted the large and luscious Jersey shellfish. "I never went to Spain without enjoying a good dish of clams. Indeed, I always thought that nothing could compare with Spanish clams, saffroned rice on the side, a bottle of wine and a handsome Spaniard to share it with."

Imagine Aunt Zena saying something like that before neighbors they hardly knew! What could they think? Mrs. Rogers tried to silence her sister with a look, and when that failed, took Georgina to task, as loudly as seemed suitable to genteel behavior, for not eating more.

It was a completely false accusation. Clams were virtually coming out of Gene's ears. "Oh, Gus, why do we stay away so long? Isn't it fun to be home? Don't we always have the jolliest times?"

Gus agreed wholeheartedly, and for a few minutes there was no sound but the soft sibilances, rapidly repeated, of clams in the process of being consumed—that and Aunt Zena talking on about various Spanish men she had known, from which, Mrs. Rogers

163

knew, it would be but a short step to men in general, and then her sister never could be stopped.

As everyone was growing sated, Mrs. Rogers quickly proposed adjourning to the parlor, where refreshments would be served later, with coffee. This gave Mr. Rogers a chance to hold forth, as planned by his conniving wife, so Aunt Zena and her damaging account would be drowned out. But Father proved almost as bad! Following some obscure association of ideas, he got on the subject of the Rogers' fleet in its halcyon days and ended up by conveying the impression, without actually saying so, that he had once been a seaman himself, and dragged Gus to the piano to accompany him in a series of sea chanties.

It was always a cause for wonder where Father had learned such an assortment of songs and recitations and how he remembered them all. Certainly no one present had ever heard him sing a single "Heave-ho my lads" but now he blew the man down, hurrah-ed for Jenny, way-hi-lo-ed and cried for rum and gin in the manner attributed to sailors, until the Rogers' timbers were ready to shiver. Then—talk about Aunt Zena being indiscreet—he practically told the Burts (as he heard many times after) that sometime in the past he had had truck with a heathen hussy. No doubt he was in an expansive mood, when strict truth gave away to a desire to entertain, for he introduced his final effort with ill-conceived rashness. "Ah, yes, the Sandwich Islands. An idolator's paradise. I hate to think how this new Pearl River Harbor Naval Station of ours will change it; how our uncouth mariners will affect the gentle savage—the unspoiled daughter of nature. It was different when . . . well, there's another sailor's song I know, not exactly a chantey. It goes this way." He la-la-ed through a bar or two and then plunged into a plaintive, nostalgic refrain so realistically rendered that if Mrs. Rogers hadn't known better, she might very well have thought what Mrs. Burt couldn't help but think. "The Pretty Mohea" indeed. This was one Fourth of July night when there would be fireworks—of a kind Jesse didn't expect. She motioned to Norah to bring on the ice cream and coffee before Mr. Rogers reached the final verse:

> Oh the last time I saw her 'twas down on the sand
> And as my ship passed her she waved me her hand

Saying, when you get back to the girl that you love,
    Just think of Mohea in the cocoanut grove . . .
    Just think of Mohea in the cocoanut grove.


3


GENE AND GUS stayed over an extra day, chiefly because the young doctor got Aunt Zena's ear at breakfast and told her some of the hardships of the folk in upstate Pennsylvania. "The bands of homeless children are our worst difficulty," he began, with an earnestness quite different from his carefree attitude of the previous evening. "It just complicates the problem to send out posses of vigilantes after them, as they do around Philadelphia. What those children need is loving parents—although even in families conditions are terrible, the poverty is so extreme. Do you know that half of the people around us go barefooted all winter? That most of Schuylkill County is desperate for food and clothing?"

Aunt Zena had risen earlier than usual. She was convinced that she had been in love with a particular man for years without knowing it, and this was the day to begin remedying the oversight. At the same time, she was too sympathetic to be unmoved by Dr. Palmer's account and followed her habit of buying peace for her conscience by an act of impulsive generosity.

"Oh, the poor dears! It is awful, isn't it, when you think about it? I tell you Gus, there are two trunks upstairs that are filled with nothing but servants' liveries and uniforms. Most of them have never been worn, though a few date back to the days when poor, dear Mr. Lascalles was alive, and carry his crest—not that I don't think he invented it, for he was a very common man in many respects. . . . But here, I shouldn't talk about the dead. . . .

"I never could understand why I kept the things for all these years, but it must have been God's purpose for this very emergency. I always ordered uniforms by the dozen; they came cheaper that way. You might as well have them for those poor people."

"I assure you that they can use anything that is warm . . . and they'll be very grateful, I know. Shall we wait over so that Gene can go through them?"

"Do, by all means, though I shall go with Clinton now, as I

have some urgent business in Philadelphia. Heavens, look at the time—while we've been here talking." She removed two keys from the ring she always carried with her, hesitated a moment and then added another. "These are the keys to the servants' trunks . . . 10 and 11, they're numbered—and this is for number 5, which holds all my best summer things. Tell Gene to pick out a nice dress and a suit. She looked pretty tacky, I thought. Don't leave the key here, for if Tina and the girls get hold of it there won't be a stitch left. Mail it to me from Pottsville in about a week.

"Now I have to dash. You are a really good man and Gene was lucky to get you. If I'd known someone like you in my own youth things might have worked out differently." She interrupted herself to cry out, "Here I am, Clint, and practically ready. Good-by, everyone, and I'll see you soon."

When they arrived in Philadelphia, Clint accompanied her to the Bingham House, which she had decided upon as a clean and respectable hostelry, yet reasonable enough for her present means. As she signed the register, a thought began to grow in her mind. When next she stayed at a Philadelphia hotel it should be at nothing less than the Lafayette or Continental, as the wife of Billy Madeira.

When Clint had gone, Aunt Zena felt terribly alone—terribly alone in a way that she had never felt in her whole life. This in spite of the fact that her room was a corner one, high above the multiplicity of railroad and streetcar tracks on Market Street, with its throngs of passers-by. It was possible, then, to be lonely close to so many other human beings. It was an idea that had never occurred to her before.

She hastily applied some of Eugenie's Secret of Beauty, which imparted a brilliant transparency, as the advertisement promised. She adjusted the Pompon Pompadour and the Marie Antoinette Waves and then fared forth. She had discovered the address of Mr. Madeira's office and made a memorandum of it.

"Third Street—and let me see—this is Twelfth. Much too far to walk on a day as hot as this. And the difference between six cents for the horsecar and twenty-five for a hansom isn't enough to bother about," she thought, pleased that she had given due consideration to economy, which was almost like practicing it.

Chestnut Street! How vividly she remembered it. And the silly little buildings that Americans made so much fuss about and called old—where they'd signed some kind of Republican document. She could show them really old buildings! As for Republicanism, the less said the better, after what it had brought to France.

Below Independence Hall she found herself in a man's world. Indeed, her driver was surprised when Aunt Zena insisted she wanted to be let out in front of the Custom House. She paid him, remembering to give him a generous tip.

She glanced around uncertainly at the hordes of clerks and their employers returning from a late lunch. They in turn gazed at her with frank curiosity. What could a woman be doing in a business neighborhood during the daytime? Aunt Zena was not unaccustomed to masculine stares, but she sensed here more disapproval than interest. Perhaps Billy Madeira would also resent her intrusion into these male preserves and consider her bold or forward. That must be his office over there—but did she dare to go in as she had planned?

Talk about your coincidences! Here was fact stranger than any fiction could be. Aunt Zena said afterward—without ever revealing the reason for being in that neighborhood in the first place—that if one read such a happening in a book it wouldn't be believed. A slender, elderly man made his way toward her. He lifted his hat in a courtly manner and inquired, "You appear to be confused, Madam. At the risk of being misunderstood in my intentions, I would like to offer any assistance I can."

What a charming gentleman—and so polite. Aunt Zena could be excused for putting on an air of greater bewilderment than she felt. "I fear I lost my way. It is some years since I have been in Philadelphia—at the time of the Centennial, that was . . ."

"I was certain that no lady would intentionally be seen in this area. May I procure a hack for you?"

"You are very kind. So many men . . . the way they stare . . . I dislike feeling so helpless." As she talked in disjointed phrases Aunt Zena's thoughts flew. If the gentleman could be inveigled into walking a block or so, perhaps she could learn something to her advantage. She couldn't, of course, ask him to ride with her.

167

. . . She smiled most ravishingly. "A conveyance isn't necessary, I can't be very far from where I wish to go. It is what you Americans call the Independence Hall? . . ."

"Ah, you are French. I should have known from your accent. Slight, but delightful. You have come to see the Liberty Bell, no doubt, which means as much to France as it does to us."

Aunt Zena shrugged her shoulders. "French once, as I was married to a Frenchman. Italian originally, but I make my home with a sister in New York."

The gentleman's interest mounted perceptibly. "Indeed! No, it can't be possible. Do you remember me, by any chance?"

Aunt Zena had lived too long to place much belief in coincidence, but she also rarely missed a bet when chances were so markedly in her favor. "Ah, no. It is impossible. I have no acquaintances in Philadelphia whatever. Once, years ago, I was here with my father—and sister. I met a man then, but he is probably dead by this time. . . ."

With each word, Aunt Zena grew more Latin in manner, so that by now she was more emotional than suited staid Philadelphia's Third and Chestnut Street corner. Apparently unaware of what the gentleman was doing, Aunt Zena allowed herself to be squired into a hansom which he signaled. Nor did she pay attention when he said "Fairmount Park" to the driver and stepped in beside her. As soon as she could, she took up where she had left off, placing all her stakes, as she would have put it, on the red. ". . . Alas, I returned to Europe a heartbroken and disillusioned girl. One minute he paid attention to me, then to my sister." She sighed, lapsed into silence until her companion seemed about to speak, then she cut him off. "I fear he was just a Don Juan, as so many of you Americans are, but I shall always have a special place for him in my heart. I married a short time later, to kill the pain. It didn't. Dare I confide to you that I had no great grief in my heart when my husband died?"

Her companion began to mop his forehead with a large and impeccably white linen handkerchief. "Philadelphia in summer is abominable. . . ."

"Ah, Monsieur, a man seldom realizes what happens when he

168

trifles with a young girl's affections. It must be twenty years ago, but the name Madeira still raises a lump in my throat. . . ."

"Zena! Teresina Repetto. Look at me. Don't you recognize me? . . ."

"Ah—Billy! My dear! But not until this moment, I insist. I feel actually immodest, now. Speaking of this love locked in my heart so long is most foreign to my nature."

"Zena, I assure you . . ." Of what, exactly, did he wish to assure her? With a caution bred of years of bachelorhood, Mr. Madeira hurriedly changed the subject. "Evidently your sister never told you that Henry works for me."

Aunt Zena shrugged her shoulders. "No—but then what can you expect of Tina? Married to that great ox of a man. And with all those children. I fear that she has always been a trifle jealous, anyway."

She moved by almost imperceptible degrees until Mr. Madeira was suddenly aware that she was leaning close against him. It was then that he shouted upward, "Cabbie, to the Continental," and to Teresina Lascalles, "We'll have a bottle of wine, for old times' sake. . . ."

Chapter 7

As the baseball season progressed, Clinton Weatherby became increasingly worried over his performance. Except for the "Chicago" he had pitched on Fourth of July morning, he was suffering so bad a season that he had jokingly remarked that he needed Zenie's watching in order to win. Then, early in August, she had confided a secret that she had held some days, waiting to be certain.

He reacted as prospective fathers are supposed to do. He hugged and kissed her fervently, then asked, "Are you sure?" and "When do you think?"

With an excess of modesty such as she had never before felt

with Clint, Zenie whispered, "Some time in March, I believe."

In spite of himself, Clint felt a new concern. Another responsibility and increased expense. He overcame his fears—and Zenie's, if she possessed similar ones—by saying heartily, "This will bring me luck. Now I'll have to win to support my family."

He won his next two games—against the Louisvilles and the Metropolitans—which encouraged this superstition, but then developed a sore arm that kept him on the bench into September. Before his marriage he would have been philosophical about the layoff, but now he became worried and morose.

The trouble, he told himself often—taking a kind of stern satisfaction from self-recrimination—was in getting out of condition the previous winter. He had worked hard all summer, appeared extremely fit and seemed to pitch with all his former skill, but something was missing. For the first time he had won less than a majority of his games. The last time he had pitched, the spectators, instead of cheering, began to boo and hiss.

This had disturbed Clint deeply, for he fed upon the plaudits of the crowd. In games away from home, he could take boos, but not from the Brooklyn spectators. These he really loved. Almost as much as having to leave baseball altogether, he dreaded the thought of being sold to another team. Actually, part of his unhappiness in the Rogers' household was because it was in New York and not in the rival city over the bridge.

Everyone else was doing so well. Mr. Rogers was to stay on the *Times* during the winter and write about sleighing, skating, and similar activities. The new firm of Rogers and Lascalles was also coming along swimmingly, judging by letters from Julia and by Henry's guarded comments when he appeared occasionally at dinner.

Clint tried to console himself with the knowledge that Dr. Palmer didn't make money very fast, up in Pottsville, but in his heart he realized that Gus and Gene had a more enduring kind of reward. No—he was the only failure!

His dreary introspection was interrupted by the booming voice of his father-in-law, who, as a member of the press, invaded the players' locker room. In spite of his appearance, which marked him as a toff, Mr. Rogers was accepted and liked by all the teams, not only for his engaging personality, but because he wrote such fine items about individual players.

"Well, Clinton, my boy. How is the arm?"

"You've been making wonderful excuses for me in the paper, but it's not good. Soon everybody will catch on that you were unlucky enough to get me for a son-in-law and are making the best of it."

"Nonsense. I wouldn't be on the *Times* if it wasn't for you. When I used to come home from work I enjoyed the tasteful furnishings and restrained taste of our domicile. Then I had to spend all my time there and I got pretty tired of it. I got tired of *things*—which is something hard to understand, I suppose.

"Anyway, you gave me back the joy of living. My time is practically my own, I'm earning a good salary, and I can befriend people. That's important . . . to me, at any rate. When Otterwon made an error, yesterday, I could have said 'Otterwon stupidly missed the ball.' Instead, I said 'Otterwon endeavored bravely to stop the flying pellet, but it evaded his outstretched glove,' which was kinder and more literary as well."

Clint realized that Mr. Rogers was trying to talk him out of his despondency. He grinned at the older man. "I suppose if you were Kaiser Wilhelm, you'd be pinning medals on my chest?"

This thrust at Mr. Rogers' resemblance to the aged Emperor (which arose mainly from the similarity in shape of their beards) only drew a laugh. While Clint finished dressing, Mr. Rogers suggested, "The Metropolitans intend to play a Sunday game tomorrow, with the St. Louis Browns. They can't play at their regular field on Staten Island, of course, but will try at Weehawken. Shall we see the fun?"

"Not me. I'm sick and tired of baseball."

"Then how about the Labor Day Parade Monday morning? I have to do a piece on it. They expect 70,000 in the line and I'm to count noses. There'll be a picnic afterwards. . . ."

"And listen to speeches all afternoon?"

"No speeches. Grand Marshal Morrison says they are to be omitted—though I can't imagine labor unions getting along without them.

"I tell you! The races at Sheepshead Bay. I'm going there in the afternoon."

Again Clint shook his head. "Let's go home. Zenie's waiting, I know, and she's nervous, these days."

As the two men left Ridgewood Park, Mr. Rogers was still disturbed by Clint's somber expression. Mopping his face with his handkerchief, he made one further suggestion. "It's hot as mid-August. Let us pause at a wayside tavern and partake of the brew that refreshes, but doesn't inebriate."

2

HENRY arrived home unexpectedly, thereby causing Mrs. Rogers to delay dinner. "Whether Father likes it or not, things will have to wait until we get another pie baked. I can't have my son coming home without a proper dessert, even though, if he'd had any thoughtfulness at all, he'd have sent me a letter before time," she told Norah, who was rolling out the crust.

"What this house is coming to, I don't know. I used to get angry enough, in the old days, when Father wanted his meals on the split second. Now I think he was more right than I gave him credit for. I'd welcome a little routine, what with Henry coming in at all hours, and Jesse never being dependable since he got on the paper. . . ."

"And your sister at breakfas', mum. Some days it's at nine and others nearer to eleven."

"Always the days after she's been to Philadelphia! Norah, what in the world is she up to, do you think?"

"That I don't know, mum. I'm surprised, though, a lady like she is. It ain't safe, I'd say, alone on them railroad cars."

"Safe enough, I suppose, at Zena's age. What gets me, Norah, she's been content to set here, like a bump on a log, for two blessed years. Now she has to go to Philadelphia. A surprise, she says, which is all I can get out of her."

"Maybe she's buildin' a house. A place in the country against the old age of the mister and yourself, with a spot of garden where Tony could grow the vegetables whilst I did for all of ye."

There was no beating Norah for imagination. "She's not back yet, is she?"

"She's not, mum. But she said 'I'll be back for Saturday dinner, Norah,' and you can bank on it, come the train's not late."

Mrs. Rogers shut her mouth in a grim line. "This time I'll be ready for her and find out what she's up to, or my name's not Augustina Rogers."

Tony slipped into the kitchen for his supper and both women stopped their gossiping, as though it were not appropriate for masculine ears. Of medium height and good looking indeed, Tony had wavy black hair, oversized brown eyes, and what Norah called a "whiskful" expression. He fitted into the Rogers household beautifully, although he also contributed, in a sense, to the irregularity of hours about which Mrs. Rogers complained. Not that he wasn't as regular as the seasons themselves, supping in the winter at three to be on his lighting round at dusk, an hour later. But in the summer, he ate long after the family had finished and his breakfast was at four, to be as saving of gas as possible, come daylight. Now, in September, he had no need to leave until six in the morning, swinging along with easy stride, his long pole on his shoulder, to begin at the far end of his rounds and work toward home.

Tony spoke so little English that Mrs. Rogers always wondered how he had been able to propose. He and Norah never appeared to say much to each other and yet a perfect understanding existed between them. He was unobtrusive, with a smile that showed real teeth every bit as white and regular as Norah's porcelain ones.

After eating, Tony lighted his long-handled torch and was off before the pie had finished baking. "Of all husbands I ever heard of, Tony is the least trouble," Mrs. Rogers remarked, when the front doorbell began to vibrate noisily on its spring. "That's Zena now. I know her pull." She rubbed her hands on the apron, with grim determination in her expression.

Waving an evening paper, Aunt Zena exclaimed, as the door opened, "Oh, Tina, I couldn't wait until I saw you. The most awful thing has happened to dear Father Duffy."

"Land sakes, Zena. Father Duffy? He's not been killed? Do

come in instead of standing there screaming. What will Mrs. Burt think?"

"He's not killed, or hurt either. Tina, it's awful. He's summoned to Rome. For being a Communist, or something. And he always looked so sweet and saintly to me."

"Here, sit down. Jesse's not home yet and I won't have him bringing trouble on the house by talking about the Holy Father the way he would if he heard of this—liking Father Duffy the way he does." Mrs. Rogers closed the parlor doors while she made this rather involved explanation of her reason for so doing. "Now— let me see what it says."

There it was, on the front page. Father Duffy's espousal of Henry George. His defense of the Haymarket bombers. His objection to parochial schools. His statement that the poor had the right to steal to live. What could Father Duffy be thinking about, worrying himself and his friends over things that couldn't be helped?

"I'll run up and fix a little, for dinner," Aunt Zena suggested and Mrs. Rogers' eyes narrowed. Trust Zena to turn events to her use! She probably didn't care a hoot about Father Duffy but had been sly enough to see the article and use it to her advantage. Not that Mrs. Rogers cared at all what went on in Philadelphia. . . .

She thought of the second pie, and screamed down to Norah, to find that it was long out of the oven. ". . . And the dinner's ready to set, mum, exceptin' the Mister and Mr. Weatherby."

What had happened to Father this time? Mrs. Rogers had grown accustomed to certain stock excuses—that there had been a tie and the game had gone into extra innings, that the traffic on the bridge had been blocked, that the northbound horsecars were filled, or the steam railways stopped by a wreck on the elevated tracks. Now, though, it was six-thirty—high time for them both to be back, whatever the trouble—and a roast cooking to death in the oven. "Labor Day on Monday and only a few more weeks to the season," she thought. "I wish I had never heard of baseball." Suddenly she made up her mind. "We can't keep Henry waiting, just in from a trip on those horrid trains, and not a good meal since God knows when, eating around in restaurants, the way he does." She voiced the thought to Norah, down the stairway, word for word, and then, with slight variations, up to Henry in the third-floor back.

Henry waited until they were seated to look with disapproval at the two empty places. "I suppose they play baseball in the dark, with electric bottles to see by."

"Now Henry, no remarks out of you when they come in. Your Father has a position on the paper of which you should be proud. Like as not he's at the *Times* office right now. . . ."

"Or someplace with Weatherby!"

"What has Clint ever done to you, Henry Rogers? I don't think that you are a bit fair. He's wonderful to me and if it wasn't for him Father wouldn't have his job."

Aunt Zena added, "No indeed. He is a most handsome man, I say and I'm sure Zenie's son will be quite as good looking."

This innocently meant remark precipitated a new crisis. Henry's ordinarily pale complexion reddened and he inquired angrily, "You mean Zenie is . . . is? . . ."

"Honestly, Zena, can't you keep anything to yourself?" Mrs. Rogers spoke with harshness. She'd only learned about Zenie a few days ago, herself, and had promised not to breathe a word.

"I don't see why I should. Zenie is my namesake and I have every right to be happy in her good fortune. She's taken long enough, too, under the circumstances. . . ."

"Aunt Zena, please! This whole subject is revolting to me." Henry stabbed his napkin under his collar and put on his most forbidding expression.

"Eat your victuals and don't rile me. I'm saving what I have to say for your Father. In all the time we've been married he's never stayed out so long—well, not over once or twice, anyway."

"One of the nicest men I ever knew was like that. Delightful, but he'd ask you to dinner and not appear for ages. Then one time, he never came at all. I felt like a perfect fool. . . ."

"Zena, honestly, this is one time you might spare us your experiences. Zenie is nervous and worried, which certainly isn't good for a girl in her condition. And I'm in a state, you might as well know. Something must have happened. Perhaps Jesse has gotten in a fight with one of those awful people he's always talking and writing about. The empires, or whatever they call them."

175

The apple pie was served and Henry delayed long enough to finish his quarter section, then threw down his napkin, pushed back his chair and declared, "I'm going out to see what happened to them. I'll go to the police, to the fire department, to the morgue . . ."

"Oh, Henry, you don't think they could have been hurt?" Zenie caught her brother's arm as she pleaded with her eyes.

"Of course they haven't been hurt," Mrs. Rogers said. "But go ahead, if you've a mind to." Then, to Norah, hovering in the doorway, "I don't see what you're waiting for. Here we're all done long ago, and no wonder, what with the undercrust of the pie soggy the way it was. I haven't a word against your cakes, Norah, but I suppose I'll have to start making the pies again."

Contrary to her usual manner upon being reprimanded, Norah merely ducked, said "Yes, mum," and began removing the plates before Henry had time to put on his hat and slam the outside door behind him. When she got downstairs again, Tony was returning through the areaway entrance, his torch still smoking. With none of the Rogerses around, she hastily dumped her load of dishes in the sink, and threw her arms about him. "Tony . . . me dear . . . I'm glad ye come in when ye did. I can stand the Missus havin' tantrums, but when she calls me pie crust soggy it's hard to stomach, even when ye know she's beside herself with Mistress Zenie's man and her own not home yet and it most eight o'clock at this minute."

How much of this Tony understood was hard to say, but he caught her up, kissed her, and said something which Norah, in turn, could not understand, although it sounded nice, and entirely comforted her for the slight to her baking.


3


Mr. Rogers always insisted that it was not because he was particularly thirsty, but because he wanted to cheer up Clint that he had extended his invitation. If this was the case, the saloon into which they turned had an opposite effect. Not one of the half-dozen men at the bar appeared to recognize Clint, which was unusual in itself. Then the bartender asked disinterestedly, "What will it be, gents?" He slid over two seidels of the sudsy brew and then returned to an argument that did not concern baseball.

It seemed like a pointed affront, and Mr. Rogers chose thus to regard it.

"Oh, forget about it. Besides, I'm not the hero I was last year."

"I propose to find out. Another beer, bartender. . . ."

Two more seidels skidded across to them and Mr. Rogers said, "Apparently you don't recognize Clinton Weatherby, who . . ."

"Sure I do. Hello, Weatherby. The Brooklyns ain't doin' so good, are they? Still in third place."

"And I, sir, am Jesse Rogers. I write baseball news for the *Times*, *The New York Times*."

"You don't say. I read the *Eagle*, meself."

A most unusual barkeep, Mr. Rogers thought, but he held his temper. The interior of the bar was pleasantly murky, the beer was cool to the tongue and it was unseasonably warm outside.

"Come on, Father Rogers. You had better drink it down. It's late now and I don't want Zenie to worry."

From some obstinate quality in his nature, Mr. Rogers became most deliberate, carefully blowing away the suds after he took a sip, so none should stick to his whiskers. He hoped that the barkeep and the habitués of the place would be forced to some kind of interest if he and Clint lingered long enough. When they did leave, not even a "Good-by" floated through the swinging doors after them.

The episode bothered Mr. Rogers all the way on the streetcar to the bridge terminus. Clint had always met with adulation wherever they went in Brooklyn! "There's a conspiracy on foot, I tell you. I suppose you noticed that the driver paid no more attention to you than if you were one of his horses."

"When my arm gets well enough to win another game or two, everything will be all right. Now, let's try and get through the crowd. I'll be glad when they finish the Arcade Railway, underground. It will connect with the bridge trains and we'll get home in no time."

The rush hour was on. Mr. Rogers boomed over the voice of the train announcer, "The condition of bridge traffic is disgraceful. I propose, Clint, to compose an article on the subject."

A middle-aged, athletic-appearing man sidled up to them, and Mr. Rogers, in fear of pickpockets, felt his wallet. "Excuse me, sir. You are Mr. Weatherby, who pitches for the Brooklyns? I was almost sure, then I heard this gentleman call you 'Clint.' My name is Spalding."

"We should have recognized you from your portraits, Mr. Spalding. This *is* Mr. Weatherby and I am Jesse Rogers, of *The New York Times.*"

"This is fortune indeed. I went all the way out to the park just to see you. A moment ago I was cursing my ill-luck." Mr. Spalding glanced around. "Perhaps we could find a place to talk for a few minutes. I have a proposition to make which you may find of great interest."

Clint hesitated, but Mr. Rogers caught his arm and spoke with buoyancy which came from the feeling that all was again right with the world. "By all means, Clint. Allow me to guide you both to a spot where we can enjoy a leisurely glass and a mussel stew. If you care for good, Long Island mussels?"

While Clint explained, "Mr. Rogers is my father-in-law," Mr. Spalding said, "Capital. I suppose like oysters they are just coming in season."

In spite of his own wishes, Clint allowed himself to be led away to the second bar—one with which he was probably more familiar than Mr. Rogers, for almost every one inside had a welcome for him.

The great baseball player of an earlier day quickly came to the point. "Some gentlemen want to start a league in Jacksonville, Florida, and that vicinity. Also they wish to promote greater interest in the game in Cuba. You'll remember that the St. Louis Browns wouldn't play the Cuban Giants last week because several of the Cubans are Negroes. I hope you don't have such a prejudice?"

"Let the best players win, I say," Clint responded, while Mr. Rogers applauded silently.

"Good. Now my idea is this: After the present season you'll go to Jacksonville and help organize the teams. They'll need pitchers more than anything. Later on you would go to Cuba and play in a few exhibition games, perhaps . . ."

"Sounds interesting. But why did you pick me?"

"You've been on the bench for a month with a sore arm. You need it baked out under a tropic sun. You know what I think? One of these days every team that can afford it will send its members south for training!"

While Clint seemed to be considering, the steaming mussels arrived. After commenting upon their goodness, Mr. Spalding continued, persuasively, "There's a personal reason, also. You probably know of my interest in manufacturing equipment for the great American game. I've heard of several of your ideas and they are ingenious, very ingenious. Frankly, Weatherby, I'm looking forward to a long association. I hope you say you'll come with us. The salary would be a thousand and all expenses for you and your wife."

It was so much more than Clint had hoped for that he was afraid of appearing too eager. "It sounds all right to me, Mr. Spalding, but I would like to talk it over with my wife first before giving a final answer. Which reminds me, if I don't get home soon I won't have a wife, and that goes for Mr. Rogers, too. Where can I reach you, sir?"

"At the Murray Hill Hotel. It's rather far uptown and inconvenient. . . ."

"But not for me. We live on Fifty-second Street. I'll call upon you tomorrow and I'm sure my answer will be yes."

When recounted to their respective wives, the stories of both men were remarkably similar up to this point. Much too similar— according to Mrs. Rogers, who had a highly suspicious nature.

4

HENRY left the house with little expectation of actually finding his father, but he had felt too angry and frustrated to listen any longer to family talk. Ever since Weatherby had come to the house things had grown steadily worse. Mother was a fool for tolerating him and the sooner she gave Father a good talking to, the better.

Almost before he realized it, he turned into Fifth Avenue, stopped suddenly and moved into the shadow of a high stoop.

There were the culprits, descending from a hack. There was a chatter of feminine voices and now Father was assisting a handsomely dressed female, while the arc light picked out the form of another still in the vehicle.

Henry was beside himself. His father, his own father, led astray! He hadn't a single doubt as he watched the little group shake hands. Mr. Rogers paid the driver, explaining in an unctuous voice, "We live little more than a block from here. A few moments' walk will be settling." Henry anticipated an embrace, right there on Fifth Avenue, and was disappointed when the females only smiled, while Father, with a fatuous expression, made a gallant parting sweep with his gray beaver hat.

Their guilt was obvious from the way they hurried. Henry had trouble to keep within earshot. "Most engaging ladies," his father was saying, with a smirk in his voice. "Right now I want to see Zenie," Clint said, and well he might. Henry's keen nose caught a faint aroma of beer mingled with tobacco smoke. They were drunk as well as profligate. He wanted to take Clint by the throat and choke him. "I envy you your experience, my boy," floated back, with most evil connotations.

He waited until Clint and Mr. Rogers entered the house while he tried to control his agitation. He intended to expose them in as cold and distant a manner as possible, but he was too distraught.

"Whatever is wrong with Henry?" Mrs. Rogers asked herself, when he came in with face flushed and highly agitated air. She had just finished saying, "Well, Jesse, I think it is about time you two got home. . . ." and Mr. Rogers launched into an explanation that began in the middle and worked both ways, so that all she understood of it was something about Florida sunshine. Then Henry shouted, "Don't believe a word of it, Mother. They are both the worse for drink. They have been having a rendezvous with two—well—unspeakable females. I saw them saying good-by, so they can't deny it. I'm ashamed of you, Father, and I think Mr. Clinton Weatherby should be put out of the house tonight."

Instead of cringing before the truth, as Henry had expected them to do, the culprits attempted to brazen it out. Mr. Rogers sputtered in rage, but Clint spoke clearly enough. "Come now, Henry, don't make a fool of yourself."

No wonder Henry forgot all reason. While Mrs. Rogers began questioning about the women, and Aunt Zena listened avidly, Henry cried out in a voice that broke from tension, "Don't forget that I saw Zenie coming out of your room before you were ever married, you . . ."

Whatever else he intended to say was lost in the ensuing scuffle. Henry was as tall as Clint, but lacked his agility. He struck out wildly with both fists. The dachshunds began to bark and Aunt Zena to scream. Clint lunged forward with a left-handed swing that was intended more for protection than anything else, but his timing and skill were so automatic that the blow caught Henry squarely in the eye. Norah began keening and Mrs. Rogers started to wonder if fainting would not be the best way to end the melee when the front doorbell rang.

Almost before the last, fluttering tones of it had faded away, a casual observer might have thought that the Rogers family was enjoying an ordinary Saturday evening at home. In a stage whisper, Mrs. Rogers hissed, "It's the Burts, over for a game, sure as shooting. Jesse, you and Clint get into the parlor—I'll settle with the pair of you later. Norah, go to the door, but take plenty of time and hold them in the hallway long as you can." She began to push Henry stairward. "Hurry up with you. That eye is swelling by the minute. Soon's she can, Norah will make a beefsteak poultice to put on it. Zenie, look pleasant, can't you. . . ."

It was not the next-door neighbors, but Father Duffy who entered, and the forced looks of polite amiability gave away to genuine smiles of welcome. "I'm making a trip I'd look forward to under other circumstances, and before I left I had to drop in upon you. . . .

"The peacefulness of your family circle is always an inspiration, friend Rogers."

"Going away, Duffy? By the Lord Harry, I'm sorry to hear that. Have a seat, do, and tell me what's on the manifest."

Father Duffy's grin was the old one, though he looked worn. "I'm on the carpet—and not before any divisional superintendent, either. It's the big boss and the whole board of directors, if I may be forgiven for joking over something I take much to heart. I'm summoned to Rome. . . ."

"You're free, white, and over twenty-one, Duffy. I'm surprised at a good American like yourself taking orders from an Italian you've never so much as met."

Father Patrick Duffy looked really old, but with a set, purposeful expression he answered, "It's the inner light we talked about once . . . remember? And I haven't time to stay. I'll be saying good-by to all of you."

The following morning, after Mrs. Rogers and Teresina had discussed the culpability of their husbands until they had exhausted each other, Mrs. Rogers suddenly observed, "Can you beat it, Father Duffy coming in just when he did? I'm not admitting that you are right, but it was kind of providential. I liked to have died when he called us a peaceful family or some such thing, but he did keep Clinton from a bad trimming. I hate to think what would have happened to him, once Henry really got his dander up."

They were off again, as Zenie answered spiritedly, "He had no right to say what he did to Clint."

Mrs. Rogers sighed, then her eyes bored through her daughter's. "And how did Henry get such an idea, I'd like to know?"

Teresina answered, quietly, "It was true, in a way."

"In a way? You mean you did behave scandalously with Clint before you were married and that Henry knew?"

"He knew nothing of the sort, but he thought he did. He saw me . . . well, he got a very wrong idea then and started to make a fuss. You'll have to believe me that there was nothing wrong, really wrong."

"Wrong is wrong, I say, and this really wrong business is more than I can accept, Zenie, you might as well know, but it's beside the point now. I'll try to believe anything that doesn't have strange females in it, but . . ."

"It seems simple to me. Father and Clint took Mr. Spalding to the Murray Hill Hotel in a hack. There, as Mr. Spalding was getting out, he met two ladies of his acquaintance who were awaiting a conveyance. Father learned they were going within a block of here and offered to take them. Then, as they bade the ladies good-by, along came Henry. It is perfectly clear."

182

"Teresina Rogers, you are a perfect fool. Do you think you would ever have heard one word of such a fabrication if Henry hadn't surprised them as they were saying good-by to their lights-of-love? I expected the worst of Clint, but that Jesse should begin carrying on, at his age . . ."

She stopped abruptly as Clint made his entrance, and listened to his brusque and nervous speech without once cutting in. "The way Henry feels, and all, I think we ought to take a place of our own, Mother Rogers. I've found some rooms over in Brooklyn that will do until we go South. What say you put on a street dress, Zenie, and go look at them with me?"

It was difficult for Mrs. Rogers to maintain her expression of indifference, but she managed. Zenie jumped up, looked toward her in supplication, then followed her husband upstairs.

When they came down again, a very few minutes later, Mrs. Rogers was still sitting there, and Zenie said, "I'm sorry, Mother, but I think Clint is right. . . ."

"My goodness, child, don't disturb yourself." Mrs. Rogers' voice was unusually snappish. "It's high time your father and I began to think of ourselves, anyhow. I've put off long enough starting my home for genteel guests—I'll have him insert a card of advertisement in the paper tomorrow."

PART THREE

\* \* \*

March 10th to 15th, 1888

\* \* \*

"It is hard to believe in this last quarter of the Nineteenth Century that for even one day New York could be so completely isolated from the rest of the world as if Manhattan Island was in the middle of the South Sea . . ."

*The New York Times*, March 13, 1888

*Chapter 1*     Honest, Zenie, you've gotten as big as I was, the last time, when I had Henry and Gene. They say twins run in the family, and I, for one, wouldn't be surprised."

"Oh, Mother, you make me feel like a . . . a balloon."

"You look like one, that's certain. I don't see why you didn't have breakfast in bed. Norah would have brought it up to you. I'm not at all sure that all this running up and downstairs is good for one in your condition."

"I feel all right—and it is so wonderful to be home I don't want to miss a minute of it. Norah's breakfasts and pancakes instead of hominy. I was so homesick for you and Father and—well, and home. I hated Florida just because you weren't there."

"If you want to know what I think, Clint showed his usual thoughtlessness in taking you to such a benighted place."

"Mother, you should understand, loving Father the way you do, but somehow . . ."

"I love your father?" Mrs. Rogers questioned, in surprised accents, then caught her words. Of course she loved Jesse, but it seemed strange when Zenie said so.

"Well, Florida was wonderful and Mr. Spalding was the nicest man and I did like Cuba, where everyone was perfectly mad over Clint, though I did get seasick, and Georgia was nice too, especially Thomasville, where they have the grandest hotel. It's not benighted at all, but it is not like home. When we drove down Fifty-second Street yesterday . . ."

"I still say he should not have waited until now to bring you home. The very idea, traveling in your condition."

"He would have come any time I said, but I knew he should

187

finish the season if possible. After all, I still have a couple of weeks to go."

Mrs. Rogers examined Zenie with that professional eye which all mothers acquire with their first born. "Maybe, but it is a chance I would have disliked taking. Supposing you had been caught and would have had to go to a hospital, instead of your own home? I'd as soon have a child of mine mauled by nurses and strange doctors as . . . as . . ." After searching in vain for a fitting comparison, Mrs. Rogers returned to her original attack. "And there is no reason why Clint couldn't have stayed here, instead of in Brooklyn. I must say I hated to think of you over there among strangers last autumn, before you went South. It was pure stubbornness, I say."

"After the way Henry behaved? I don't think so, Mother. You just don't understand that Clint is proud. He *likes* playing baseball and you and Henry have made him feel that it isn't really respectable. . . ."

"It isn't—as you very well know."

"It is clean and athletic—and out in the open air. It takes a real man to play it, too. Then, where else could Clint make so much? Last winter everything he earned was clear profit. When I tell you the amount we've saved your eyes will pop. Besides, Clint has so much to do in Brooklyn. He'll be over every day, and stay when I need him."

Mrs. Rogers gave a sniff, but it was impossible for her to hide the disappointment she felt. "After I kept your rooms all winter, too, instead of trying to rent them. I can't abide outsiders in my home —sitting on my furniture as though it were their right. So long as your father goes on working I've made up my mind to leave things as they are, so my children have a place to come back to if they need it."

"Julia and Gene both have homes of their own. I guess you will have to get used to me having one. After little Clinton is born . . ."

Mrs. Rogers pressed her lips together and too casually reached for the newspaper which her husband had discarded before leaving for the *Times* office. "Little Clinton" indeed! Her feigned interest in the newspaper quickly changed to intense perusal—not of the news, but of the advertisements. "Macy's are having a sale of bonnets Monday. I wish you were able to go with me, but I think I'll go anyway. I haven't had a new summer bonnet in years."

"Perhaps Aunt Zena will go along."

"And I'd come home with a parasol, or some such foolishness, instead of what I set out for—like you did last year."

"Dear Aunt Zena. She is so generous and impulsive. The parasol turned out most useful. I carried it every day down South. Everyone complimented me on it. I just can't wait for her to come downstairs to tell her."

"Your aunt went to Philadelphia yesterday, before you arrived, and not a word about when she'd be back. She's gotten very queer, Zena has. Last fall she was over there every whipstitch—at least that's where she *said* she was going. Then she moped in the house all winter. It was almost impossible to get her out of the parlor except on Sunday mornings. She's started going to Mass, regular. Zena—who'd hardly been to church in years! You never saw such a change in anybody.

"Then, the day before yesterday, when it turned so warm, she announced at dinner that she'd be away over the week end. To look at her, you'd have thought butter wouldn't melt in her mouth, but she was up to something. She's my sister, so I ought to know."

It was so wonderful to sit dawdling over coffee, while her mother chattered on. Teresina gave a long sigh of contentment. Her face had filled out again over the winter and had taken on a placid, Madonna-like appearance. Her eyes had acquired an unfathomable depth, her lips held more color, the oval of her face had rounded. She gazed around at the familiar furniture, the pictures and objects of art with which she had grown up, then was suddenly startled by the sharpness of her mother's question.

"I said, 'Don't you think it is peculiar in your aunt?' but I declare, Zenie, it's hardly worth talking to you if you daydream this way."

"I'm sorry, Mother. I was just thinking how nice home is. . . ."

"Henry was there at dinner with us. He's got some business in Pottsville and is going to visit with Gus and Gene for a few days. He'll be back here Monday or Tuesday to see Mr. Madeira, who's been abroad all winter. His steamer docks today, I believe, in Philadelphia. . . ."

Suddenly a great light broke. Mrs. Rogers stopped in the middle of her chattering, and her lower jaw dropped. The whole thing was crystal clear. Every bit of the puzzle fell neatly into place. She'd have to do something, and that right away. She pushed back her chair and jumped up.

"Mother? What's wrong? What's happened?" Zenie also had risen before Mrs. Rogers could cut through her startled questions.

"Sit down and stop exciting yourself. I've been trying to figure Aunt Zena's behavior the whole winter and it just came to me, that's all." She bit her lips. How could she explain to Zenie without involving herself? "I've been too stupid. But it is nothing to bother about now. It's such a beautiful spring day outside, a little fresh air would do you good. I'll have Abe harness Mr. Quinby and we'll go for a ride in Central Park."

2

When Henry stepped off the train in Pottsville, he was reminded of his first visit there. It had been his first long trip away from home, and he had been young and in love. That had been seven or eight years ago and wintertime, instead of spring.

How far was it to Pine Grove, the little town from which Melissa had come? They had driven over by sleigh—it should take a much shorter time in a carriage. Sunday he'd hire a good, fast team, go over and visit the grave, high in the hillside cemetery, where Lissa's mother was buried.

He was startled from his reverie by the appearance of a dirty youth in maroon and cream-colored knee breeches. Henry usually carried his own bags—indeed, thought it spendthrift not to do so—but some obscure impulse led him to hand them over. With the pompousness befitting a successful coal merchant, he ordered, "The home of Dr. Augustus Palmer."

On the way, they passed two other men in similar costumes. Henry wondered if the Philadelphia and Reading Railway had become bereft of its senses and was uniforming all its porters in such livery. The grandeur of the satin-striped uniforms did not suit bare feet and emaciated faces.

After a modest tip, and a greeting from Gus and Gene that made him forget his feeling of sadness, he observed, "Queer clothes they're wearing up here. If it's an idea of the P. and R. they'd do well to save their money, I say."

Gus roared. "Come, Henry, don't tell me those outfits are strange to you—of all people," while Gene screamed, "They're from Aunt Zena. She gave us two whole trunkfuls when we were over to New York last summer and Gus has been doling them out all winter long. There are plenty of poor souls here glad to get anything. And don't they remind you of the old days—when Aunt Zena used to send things that weren't altogether appropriate, but which we kept anyway, because they were of some use, and expensive as well?"

This was the first time in years that Henry had seen his twin away from the rest of the family. He had always liked Gus, too, and the three spent an enjoyable evening talking over the time when Gus had courted Zenie and how the young Dr. Palmer had treated both twins for a summer complaint that was nothing but the ill-effect of having chewed tobacco. Then Henry reminded Gene of some of their earliest, harum-scarum escapades in Kensington. "When we rolled the barrels from the wagon, remember?" and Gene countered, "Father gave you a touch of the cat-o'-nine-tails after. He always blamed it on something else, but that was the real reason."

Those had been wonderful times! After Gus and Gene left him to treat a late patient in the front-room office, Henry wondered if he could ever enjoy life again. In spite of his business success he was not happy. The partnership with Philippe had turned out more profitably than either had expected. And the Lascalles were cutting a wide social swath in Cincinnati, which Henry deplored, though contacts made during Philippe's nonworking hours brought customers to the firm.

Henry was conscious of a growing sense of dissatisfaction as he contrasted his feelings with the evident contentment of Gene and Gus. They were not making out very well, that was easy to see, but they seemed to have a good time in spite of it.

The following day Henry accomplished his business with results so satisfactory that his doubts were forgotten. Of course he was happy. If things kept up the way they were going he'd soon be rich. As he hurried back to the Palmers, a man in one of the maroon and cream costumes ran in front of him. Somehow it was symbolic. Some day, not too far distant, everyone in Pottsville would be working for him, though they might not wear his family's livery.

A surprise came close to interfering with his Sunday plans. When he announced that he wished to take a drive on further business, and that it would require most of the afternoon, Gene was disconsolate. "Oh, Henry, why didn't you say something sooner? A friend of yours is coming over. We wanted to surprise you. Can't you wait just a little while? He's driving in from one of the mine patches and will be here most any time."

To Henry's guesses, Georgina shook her head. Then there was a jingle of harness, the staccato of shod hoofs and a familiar voice crying "Whoa," although there was nothing familiar about the driver hitching his team at the post in front.

"Here he is now," Gene cried. "I am so glad that he didn't miss you."

Henry still did not recognize the figure that strode toward the house, dressed in a farmer's blue denim overalls, with short coat and homemade fur cap. "Hello, Henry, my boy. Gene said you'd be here. How you've filled out this past year!"

"Father Duffy! This is a surprise." Henry rushed forward, genuinely pleased. But what was the priest doing in such clothes? And what had happened to make him appear so old and sad?

"I never before realized how much you resemble your sister. She is one of my best friends here, while I get accustomed to a new way of life."

"He says, Henry, that he isn't Father Duffy any more, but only Patrick Duffy—though he'll always be 'Father' to us, won't he?"

It took some time for Henry to learn the details of what had happened to their old friend. In spite of having grown up in a household that was more than half Catholic, he did not fully understand the term "excommunicate." Gradually, as the picture cleared, he proposed, indignantly, "But you don't intend to give

192

up without a fight, do you? Everybody knows that you are completely unselfish, though I don't hold with stirring up trouble myself. Some people are born to be poor and others rich, I say, and I
propose to be one of the rich ones. But—well . . . what ministers
and priests are for is to get the poor to be satisfied with their lot—
which is what you didn't do, manifestly. If you believed you were
right, though . . ."

Patrick Dufly's benign, priestly smile looked strangely incongruous with his farmer's clothes. "Spoken like a true son of your
father! I have no intention of giving up my calling, which is to
promote the brotherhood of man and protect the welfare of God's
children. If I was 'contumaciously disobedient,' in the words of
Holy Father, I am willing to rest my case with One still higher. In
the meantime, I'm living in the little mine patch where I first
learned to know God, to grow close again to His Earth and His
people. . . .

"But enough. How is your father, and good mother? I'm looking forward to a long visit with you, as I've seen few outsiders these
last weeks."

Gene pursed her lips in a way that startlingly resembled her
mother's. "Henry is going out this afternoon. On a business trip.
I was so glad you got here before he left."

"I never thought of you being up this way, Father. I have a rig
ordered, at one of the liveries. . . ."

"A hired rig when I have two of the finest horses in Pottsville?
Cancel it, man; tell them you're a friend of mine. It will be a
privilege to drive you about, and we shall be able to chat."

Henry had thought of this afternoon's mission as something not
to be shared with anyone. Now, however, he felt that he would be
unbearably lonely, and he accepted Father Duffy's offer eagerly.

It was not until they were well out of town that Henry explained
the real reason for his trip. It was a beautiful, warm, springlike
day, and the pair of gray roans kept a merry pace along the valley
road. Father Duffy handled them easily, depending less upon his
reins than on tone of voice, while the light buckboard rolled over
winter-packed clay or jostled against stones and ruts.

Henry did not realize how long and continuously he talked, or
to what an extent he unburdened himself. Father Duffy was an

excellent listener, who attempted no advice or observations, further than an occasional grunt of understanding. By the time they reached the little farmhouse where Melissa Heil was born, Henry felt a peace and content he had not known since her death. There were blossoms on a shrub in the garden and a vine that ran to the eaves to one side of the house was putting out new shoots; otherwise the place had the same slattern air that had disturbed Lissa on that earlier occasion.

Pine Grove, also, appeared unchanged, except that the trees were budding and there was no snow to hide the badly-rutted main street. Silently, they climbed the steep hill back of the church, stood for a while and returned to the tied horses.

On the way back, Patrick Duffy had his opportunity to unburden himself. "I'm a worker and of a family of workers. One cleaves to one's own, I suppose, and the souls of those who toil have always held the greatest importance for me. These are evil days in this country, when men are murdered legally for trying to improve the lot of the poor. No testimony—not a word—connected those who were hanged for the Haymarket tragedy with the throwing of the bomb, and for speaking in their defense I've been cut off from my Church, from all that I've held dear. . . ."

For a while, then, they rode in silence, content to enjoy the beauty of the afternoon, the banner of cloud that lay along Blue Mountain. The horses slowed to a walk, when Patrick Duffy spoke again, more softly than was usual for him. "Henry Rogers, I've known you since you were a small devil of a boy and I've loved you as I have all your family. Take a word from me; the past is behind you. It was beautiful, though sad. Maybe it was intended to make a man of you, but not to embitter you, surely. Your girl would not have wanted that.

"You are certain to have money and power; remember to share with those less gifted. You'll never rue it. And Henry, for the love of God, boy, get yourself another good, fine girl and stop eating your heart out."

When Father Duffy spoke in this manner, a slight brogue became noticeable in his speech. The cloud along the mountain had grown larger and more menacing, and he clicked to the horses. As they sprang forward, he concluded, "Above all, do your job. You might like to know that I'm better able to go on with mine as a result of our little excursion today. Perhaps I'll be seeing you and the family in the city. I shall be having to go to New York in a day or two."

It began to rain, slowly at first and then with increasing force. The horses' hoofs pelted the footboard with dollops of mud. At the Palmers' house, Father Duffy stopped to let Henry out. Refusing Gene's invitation to stay over until morning and clear weather, he was off at a gallop, careless of the buckboard's slithering.

### 3

AUNT ZENA was filled with misgivings as she departed for Philadelphia. During her first visits there, when she had maintained a discreet reserve, Billy Madeira had been most attentive. They had dined together and later he had squired her back to the hotel, but the fancied love of years ago had proved difficult to revive. When she closed the door to her room, smiling provocatively through the crack in a way that had always brought results, Mr. Madeira had remained a perfect gentleman.

Then, late in the fall, he had of his own accord invited her to see "Mazulm, the Night Owl" at the Academy of Music, and she had gone to Philadelphia with palpitating heart. It had been a wonderful spectacle, and certainly Aunt Zena was to be excused for pressing her escort's arm during the magnificent portrayal of the cemetery of Père-Lachaise by moonlight, when the shrouded inmates of the graves came forth and flitted among the tombs. Had she done or said anything further that might have startled the wary bachelor? Aunt Zena could only recall the joy of the occasion. What then had caused Billy's subsequent action? She might have taken a hint from Mazulm's subtitle, "Purity's Guardian Spirit," but she chose to think that he had run away in a moment of weakness—in an effort to escape a passion which was proving too strong for him.

It had required a series of little lies to explain to him why her letters should not be sent to the Rogers' address (where they would be seen by an eagle-eyed Tina), and daily trips to an empty postal box had been boring and mortifying. Finally, when a letter did come, it was from Paris. It had said nothing of importance. The pleasure of having met her again, the necessities of business, a vaguely expressed hope of seeing her in the circle of the Rogers family, as he'd always wished especially to make the acquaintance of Augustina's husband. "You know how fond of her I have always been," he had written and it was a phrase that rankled in Aunt Zena's mind. How like Tina to undermine her!

All winter there had been silence. Daily visits to the post office became weekly ones. When Henry casually mentioned his former employer's return, Aunt Zena had been afraid to question him for fear of arousing her sister's suspicions. She therefore obtained the necessary information from the paper. Only one passenger vessel was scheduled to arrive in Philadelphia on Saturday. That was the one that Billy must be on.

She had already stretched the long arm of coincidence to the breaking point in their original meeting. What excuse could she make for being at the pier to greet him? Men frightened so easily!

Teresina Lascalles felt less sure of herself than in any of her earlier adventures, though in many ways the occasion seemed auspicious. First there was the weather. Surely on such a springlike day, even Billy Madeira's fancy must turn to love. Then, she was wearing her most elegant dress—elegant, but simple. It was of olive green grosgrain, and though long one of her favorites, was still in American vogue. Trimmed with nothing but a pleated ruche lined with *tilleul*, it was draped with green damassé silk, joined with a revers of velvet folded to form a bandeau. A touch of dignified smartness was given by an agraffe and loops of thick, green silk cord, with a deep fringe of green chenille along the under side of the drapery. A similar fringe, with a plastron and revers of velvet decorated the square-necked waist.

The effect was sufficiently restrained to appeal to sober Philadelphia taste. A black velvet Japanese bonnet trimmed with four black ostrich feathers continued the somber tone, but the outfit was given a special flair—and just the right note of frivolity—by a lace-trimmed umbrella with a handle whose knob was carved in the shape of a poodle dog.

The ten o'clock Washington Express, which stopped at Philadelphia, was composed entirely of Mr. Pullman's Palace Cars. It carried the elite of the traveling public, but Aunt Zena was the most eye-filling person aboard. By this time, the trip had become a commonplace, so she passed the time in reading one of the earlier stories of Wilkie Collins, *My Lady's Money*, which had furnished her with literary entertainment for some months. The subject matter seemed appropriate to the occasion and almost before she realized it, they were passing through the suburbs of the Quaker City.

Aunt Zena had always been one to allow events to work themselves out, but this time they proved contrary indeed. Mr. Madeira was not a passenger on the ship upon which she had expected him. Frantic questioning developed that a collier was due the next day —had, in fact, been passed just outside the Delaware Breakwater. "Perhaps he has the owner's cabin, Madame." It was this last remark which won her informant a munificent tip in Aunt Zena's old manner. But how to take advantage of the suggestion? Not for nothing had she followed her loves to the ends of the earth. Besides, she was desperate. All day Sunday she considered plans, while, gradually, the weather turned colder again. Mr. Madeira was not on the collier either—not upon its arrival in Philadelphia, at any rate. "A launch came out for him at Wilmington, or maybe it was Chester," she learned from a steward.

By the time she had returned to the Bingham House it was raining. She closed the windows to her room, but got up to examine them, hours later, when she began to feel a draft. It turned out to be nothing but the wind, blowing around the sash. Outside it was snowing, and the street was already blanketed in white.

Chapter 2

WHEN MR. ROGERS entered his home he usually enlivened it with the force of his voice as well as his personality. There were times when prudence dictated the approach surreptitious, but generally, with the opening of the front door he expressed whatever was on his mind in loud tones. Sometimes it was no more than a greeting to Norah, who might let him in before he had finished fumbling through his keys. Again it might be the announcement of a rare bargain in beef (generally contingent upon purchasing half a steer) down in the markets. Since his employment by the newspaper, it was likely to be a tidbit of news; or, as this evening, a continuation of the conversation that had been in progress when he had left, earlier in the day.

In any case, he never waited to talk to his wife in the intimacy of parlor, hall, or dining room, but spoke in sufficient voice to reach her anywhere in the house. "If you ask me, Gussie, R. H. Macy is being a little previous about their grand spring opening. It is raining now and if it gets much colder we'll have snow by morning, sure as shooting."

Mrs. Rogers was upstairs, fretting over Zenie, so that although she was immediately aware of her husband's arrival, she could only make out, here and there, a word of what he had to say. By the time that he had repeated his remarks several times, with editings and emendations, and she had descended the stairs far enough to lean over the balustrade, all that carried to her was the prediction, ". . . snow by morning."

"Oh, Pet! Snow? It's hard to believe, the way the weather has been. And me wanting to look at spring bonnets tomorrow. Not that I'd any intention of buying one, but I might get a good idea for doing mine over."

"And I have to go to Wall Street in the morning. The paper believes the bears are going to chase the bulls clear out of the Stock Exchange."

"Oh, Jesse, do look out. They might be dangerous. And you have so little sense of fear. . . ."

Mr. Rogers roared with laughter. "The bears are the men who try to force prices down and the bulls those who put them up—or perhaps it is vice versa."

"Why don't you say so, then? Honestly, you might spare me the worry—as though I didn't have enough with Zenie. I just left her and no matter what she says, I wouldn't be surprised at anything."

As they sat down to supper, Mr. Rogers tried to look properly worried, but as all his own experiences at fatherhood had turned out well, he was inclined to think that childbirth was something over which women—and Gussie in particular—made an unnecessary amount of pother. More distressing was the fact that for the second evening running, there were only the two of them at the table.

"Norah is taking a tray up to Zenie and that sister of mine is still in Philadelphia. I tell you, Pet, she is up to something."

"As you have observed a few times before. I have been wondering what this business is. . . ."

"Monkey business, you may be sure—and I have my own suspicions. I'm too worried about Zenie, to pay much attention to what Aunt Zena does. After you've done bearbaiting or bull-throwing, I do wish you'd prevail upon Clint to stay here. It would make Zenie happier, and my goodness, why can't he let bygones be bygones? Henry is the one who ought to be angry, after the black eye he got. I never had any patience with a sulker. . . ."

"I saw Clint this noon and he's coming over tomorrow to remain until the baby is delivered. Afterward, though, he's set his mind upon a little house he's seen. You can't blame a man for wanting to start a home of his own."

Mrs. Rogers' lower lip trembled, her shrewishness evaporated in a plaintive wail. "I just can't stand what's looking us in the face. Here we are, only two at table and it's going to be this way the rest of our lives. I can't bear the thought of just staring at you across from me three times a day, with no life or goings-on. There's poor Mrs. Burt. She's got nothing to live for, she's told me more than once, with her children all married and away from home. Oh, Pet, it's awful to grow old—awful—awful. Half the fun of a meal was everyone going at once and knowing they all were enjoying their food as you watched them eating it. Now I've just no appetite. I'd as soon eat dinner in the kitchen as this way and I've always vowed that nothing would make me stoop to not sitting properly at table and making some pretense to being respectable folks."

This was one time that Mr. Rogers did not poke fun at his wife's vagaries. Instead, he combed his beard thoughtfully and when he did speak, finally, it was in a remarkably gentle voice. "I'm not very hungry either, I might as well confess—but if you want to keep

Zenie home, I think it is up to you to work on Clint. I've lived with you years enough to know that you could wind him around your little finger, as you have me, if you wanted to.

"Then when Henry comes home tomorrow, get him to apologize for his remarks and his totally unwarranted assumptions. . . ."

"I've never backtracked to anyone and I'll have you know, Jesse Rogers, that I'm still not certain but that Henry was right about those females," she flared, then subsided into tears. "Oh, all right, I'll try to be nice to him, though it does go against my grain."

"If I know you, you don't hate Clint as much as you think. I've tried to make him understand, but it takes a good many years of married life before a man learns the intricacies of female action— especially when it is further complicated by Italian obliqueness of thought."

Ordinarily, Mrs. Rogers would have been angry at her husband's astuteness. Now she was only surprised at how close he had come to hitting the nail on the head. Hadn't she confessed almost as much to Zena, not many months ago? She pushed aside her plate, almost scampered to the opposite side of the table and embraced him. "Oh, Jesse, you are the most wonderful man. I declare I never can stay angry with you, much as you irritate me, sometimes. And you do see right through me, don't you?"

The admission aroused Mr. Rogers' suspicions that she was being sarcastic, and he gave her a sidelong glance, but she remained with her head buried in his coat until, with the sound of Norah's footsteps on the stairs, she broke away self-consciously.

"Tony is just in, mum—an hour late gettin' the lights on. He says it's freezin' on the sidewalks and his torch blew out twicet."

2

AFTER CLINTON WEATHERBY had left his wife at her home on their return from Florida, he started for Brooklyn filled with conflicting emotions. There would be an advantage to being there for a few days. On the other hand, Zenie naturally wanted him with her and usually he obeyed her wishes. If Mrs. Rogers had not looked at him with such beady-eyed suspicion, he might have stayed, but her attitude aroused all his old feeling. Zenie's mother and brother were against him and the less he saw of them the better for his peace of mind. In spite of this determination, he envied the Rogers' family circle because, until he met Zenie, he had never known the pleasure and comfort of being part of one. He had spent an essentially lonely life, finding companionship among casual acquaintances. He wanted whole-hearted acceptance by the Rogerses and was disappointed—and a bit resentful—that he had not received it.

Desirous of walking off his mood, Clint turned south on Fifth Avenue, striding along at a pace which drew envious glances from passers-by. He was heavily tanned at a time when most New Yorkers were parchment skinned, and his perfect physical appearance made him stand out from the anemic city dwellers. Deep in his own thoughts and worried not a little as to whether he had done right in not staying with Zenie, he found his way blocked, suddenly, by crowds waiting patiently along the sidewalk. The circus parade, of course! He had completely forgotten.

A hurried question established that the procession was due any moment, that it would continue down to Twenty-ninth Street and over to Broadway. There was no need to get to Brooklyn immediately. What better way of forgetting one's troubles than watching from right here? Clint's height gave him an advantage and he leaned against a lamp standard, his face lighting like a small boy's.

The evening was warm and even his light coat seemed unnecessary. Clint began to feel a bubbling happiness well within him. This would be fun—and everything was going to work out for the best. This was the magic of the circus! A disreputable individual pressed a handbill upon him and he began to read the badly-printed message of Phineas Taylor Barnum:

## GOOD WINE NEEDS NO BUSH

Having for fifty years catered to the curiosity, amusement, and instruction of a public which finds no fault with what I offer them, except that I give them more than they can possibly see at a single visit, and many times the worth of their money, it seems superfluous for me to do more than simply announce that THE GREAT SHOW IS COMING.

I will only remind my millions of expectant patrons that my agents are untiringly gathering in all parts of the earth all that is new, rare, amusing, and instructive, carefully avoiding all offensive features.

Eighth Year of the Mighty, Compact, Binding Together Forever Nine Giant Shows of the Universe. Every year a stride further in advance in excellence, purity, morality, greatness, novelty, variety, splendor, and wonder . . .

But here came the parade, and who wanted to read about it when the actuality was to be seen? Bands and clowns and animals —the latter a bit shy of the torches, which were already lit, though it was still twilight. JUMBO, "The most renowned, justly celebrated, grandest and biggest animal on earth," the $200,000 Sacred White Elephant, the lines of high and low caste Hindus, Savages, Idolators, and Guatemalans. The Marimba Band and the two enormous Double Menageries of the rarest of Wild Beasts . . .

Spring weather and the circus! By the time the herd of giant camels turned north on Broadway, Clint watched the passage of the last, flickering torches in the hands of "Wild Central Americans" who looked suspiciously Negroid, and, in a mellow mood, he cut across town toward the Third Avenue Elevated Railroad.

The following day he discussed future plans with Mr. Rogers. Their relations were as cordial as ever and the older man was quite ready to agree that Clint was suffering from mother-in-law trouble. "It took thirty years for me even to begin understanding Gussie. . . . "

"I'd like to like Zenie's mother, but she won't let me."

"My boy, women are like dreams. They go by opposites. When Gussie says one thing, you can be almost certain that she means something else!" Mr. Rogers' observations on the other sex turned out to be long and profound. Before they were half delivered, Clint had to leave with a promise to "stay until after the baby, anyway. I've been looking at a little place here in Brooklyn, but we'll see what Zenie thinks. I'll be over tomorrow and do my best to get along. If the rest of the family was like you it would be easy. Right now, though, I ought to go out to the park and limber up a little."

It was raining and had turned colder before he got back to the room where he was staying.

### 3

The fourth floor rooms occupied by the Angeluccis were always hot when it was warm outside and frigid when it was cold, so

Norah was used to extremes of temperature when she arose mornings to prepare breakfast, first for her husband and later for the family. Today, though, there was more than the usual chill. She put in her prized plates of teeth, felt around on the floor for carpet slippers, enveloped herself in her hand-me-down woolen wrapper and stumbled toward the window. She slipped, but caught herself, on a mound of fine snow that had formed in front of the first dormer. Some of it got into her slippers and tickled and was cold all at the same time. The windows were tightly shut, as they always were, except in mid-summer, but the wind was blowing right around the sash, carrying with it a sieving of icy crystals.

Leaving Tony to sleep a few minutes longer and without waiting to peer out into a world so uncomfortable after the warmth of bed and his body next to hers, she slippered down the four flights of stairs to the kitchen. Her teeth chattered as she performed familiar tasks automatically. She poured out part of the water already in the teakettle, to bring the remainder to a quicker boil for her own tea and Tony's coffee. She opened the draft to the range and began to poke the banked coals. When the fire did not respond as quickly as she thought necessary, she opened the back kitchen door to obtain the coal-oil can which was kept just outside. Involuntarily she braced herself for a blast of cold air, but she was completely unprepared for the drift of snow that collapsed within.

"Holy Mother of Mary," she besought aloud, digging into the mound for the handle of the can. When she had found it, it took all her weight to push the door closed behind her. She held the stove lid expertly in one hand while she poured kerosene with the other. There was a flare among the coals, and in a moment, the roar of flames up the stovepipe.

Measuring the ingredients with her eye, she dumped them into a bowl and beat up pancake batter, then cut a couple of thick slices from the ham in the cupboard. By this time she was almost warm, and a first, barely hot cup of tea completed the process.

Next she bustled into the basement proper, closed the dampers of both furnaces and opened the bottom doors before going back to the stairway and calling Tony. By the time he came down, with eyes still sleep laden, the whole house was fairly comfortable.

The gas jets gave strong yellowed light, so neither noticed the grayness through the front window, or thought that the areaway door might be completely blocked. It was two stacks of hotcakes later before Tony discovered that the whole front of the house was drifted solid!

Aware of the graying dawn, he still took time to make a narrow path from the high-stooped front door down to the sidewalk. It was a path that covered over almost as he made it, but the storm had not yet reached full intensity, and he trudged off upon his rounds, his stick held like a musket over his shoulder.

Mr. Rogers often boasted that he was wide awake long before Norah called him in the morning, so when he was actually roused from sleep he always answered more loudly than necessary to prove the assertion. His wife, usually worn out from household duties, was an even sounder sleeper, but this morning's bellow of her mate brought her awake with a start. "Good grief, Pet, I'll go deaf entirely, with you shouting in my ear.

"Norah, it seems cold in this room. Did you put draft under the furnaces?"

This was a usual wintertime question and the Irish girl answered a bit wearily, "I did, mum, but it's snowin' and blowin' Hail Columbia outside, for a fact. Tony couldn't git out the areaway at all, the way it's drifted. . . ."

"Jesse, hear what Norah's saying?"

"Of course I do. I hope that I am still in possession of all my faculties."

"Norah, look in on Miss Zenie and see if she's all right. If she's asleep, don't wake her. Father and I will take a catnap. . . ."

The ensuing objections could not be heard by Norah from outside, but they were being continued and repeated a little later when Mr. Rogers arrived downstairs, even more carefully dressed than usual. "I'm to write about the Stock Exchange and I propose to do it. A little storm . . ."

"But it's not a little storm. Listen to the wind. And you can't see the front stoop, though Norah insists Tony made a path no more than a half-hour ago. Those cows will wait, I say. This is a . . . a . . . it's a blizzard, that's what it is, if I ever heard of one."

*Chapter 3*

IT HAD BEEN SNOWING all the way from Pottsville and Henry's train was an hour late when it reached the Columbia Avenue station in Philadelphia, where he had to change. Fortunately for him, the connecting train was also behind time and while he waited for it he toasted himself before the potbellied stove.

He heard the long-drawn-out wail of a locomotive whistle and moved expectantly toward the door, but it was not the Bound Brook Express for New York. Instead, a snowplow, pushed by two engines, formed a tornado of smoke, steam, and snow as it roared by.

Henry regretted that last week's warm weather had misled him into wearing a light overcoat, but of course he had not changed his woolens and he'd naturally worn boots, against the deep mud of Pottsville's streets, so he felt reasonably well equipped for the unseasonable storm. Probably by the time he reached New York it would be over or they would have run out of its range.

A train pulled in on the opposite track, its windows, opaque with snow and ice, staring over at him like blind eyes. After it pulled out a group of passengers picked their way across the tracks. Most of them were women, bundled up in furs and long coats. Their skirts flapped in the wind and in a moment they were covered with snow. They burst into the waiting room like white wraiths, although their behavior was far from ghostlike. There were squeals of laughter, shrill cries and excited chatter as they stamped their feet and shook themselves.

Henry watched disapprovingly as the score of women gathered around the three men in the party and vied with each other for attention. Outside a porter struggled with a truckload of baggage and there was more excitement as one of the men insisted that all of it should be brought into the waiting room, out of the weather.

It was an argument which the porter won, merely by walking away and disappearing into the storm, after shouting, "Train'll be along in a moment or two."

The women continued to express concern over the baggage. "May, all our things will be ruined. Humphrey Cartwright, if you were half a man you'd bring them in here for us."

Henry noticed that the trunks on the truck were lettered, "The Saulsbury Troubadours." A theatrical troupe! Humphrey Cartwright looked the part and Henry took an immediate dislike to him. He was overdressed, with a piece of coral as round as a quarter-dollar in a green silk cravat. He had black hair and very noticeable eyebrows and long, upward-curling mustaches, which he kept twisting.

The girl called May was short, with reddish hair and reminded Henry of Norah, at home. She seemed especially friendly with the one addressed as Lizzie, and the way both of them made up to Cartwright was sickening. Henry retreated to the far end of the waiting room, to be as far as possible from these shameless females, but no matter how hard he tried, he found himself looking in their direction and listening to what they had to say.

He learned that the older man, with graying sideburns, who was in charge, was Mr. St. Clair, and the short, youngish one, with the ready smile, was called Jerry. It was evident, though, that the girls were interested only in Humphrey Cartwright.

The porter stuck his head in the door, his face red and his beard whitened with snow. "N'York Express. Trenton, Bound Brook, Elizabeth, and N'Yo-o-ork."

Why did theatrical people have to act off stage as well as on? Everybody was putting on a performance, instead of behaving sensibly and with decorum. Henry showed his disapproval as he crossed the waiting room, for the Saulsbury Troubadours made way for him, either from respect or awe. As the train groaned to a stop, he walked pompously across the platform and boarded the nearest coach with as much dignity as the raging wind allowed.

The lights were on, though it was not yet one o'clock, and he saw that every seat was taken. He moved on toward the next coach, telling himself that he would be glad to escape the theatrical company. There was a struggle with the door and the platforms between the cars were ice covered. He heard an exclamation from behind him and turned in time to see one of the actresses (as he thought of them) slip on the treacherous platform. He reached out automatically and steadied her, while snow from the car roof avalanched over their heads and shoulders.

From some long dormant sense of gallantry, Henry bowed as he held open the further door by main force, and once inside, he became intensely aware that a slender, gloved hand still rested upon his arm.

This coach was empty and the reason was immediately apparent —it was cold as ice! While the rest of the Troubadours trooped in after them, Henry led the way forward and then suggested to his newly-found acquaintance, "Sit there, and I'll see what is wrong with the fire in this stove."

Who could make as much noise as fifteen girls all talking at once? They marveled at the difference in weather of yesterday and today and screamed descriptions of how cold they were. They worried about their finery in the trunks and were not reassured when the little, funny-faced man joined them and insisted that he had just come from the baggage car and that all their baggage was aboard and dry.

All this time Henry worked with the stove and found perfect truth in the old saying that there was as much heat in making a fire as in sitting by one. While he sweated away at it, the conductor came through for the tickets. "No use, young fellow. Something has gone wrong with that stove. My brakeman has been stoking it the whole trip down."

But Henry's apprenticeship in the coal business had included learning how to use the fuel as well as how to sell it. He fussed with the grate, the stovepipe and the damper. He used the poker and cleaned out the ashes. Eventually, he announced, "It's going good now, we'll be warm as toast in a few minutes," and a cheer went up.

Humphrey Cartwright, the center of a group that sat in facing seats next to the stove, cried out, "Well done, my good man." In a high, mocking tone, he continued, "When we arrive in Jersey City I shall reward you fittingly."

There was a snicker from several of his companions, and Henry, who realized they were making fun of him, became even redder than the fire had made him, but he stalked down the aisle, ignoring them. When he arrived opposite the seat of the girl he had assisted, she smiled pleasantly, "Sit down by me, do. And pay no attention to that Mr. Cartwright. I hate him!"

Henry hesitated. It was one thing to help a young lady over a slippery place but quite another to accept a seat next to her. She smiled again and he found himself sitting down though his instinct told him that he shouldn't. "It was nice of you to get that fire started. I was fair to freezing. Indeed I was."

"Nothing but soot or something in the stovepipe." Henry was flushing from embarrassment.

"Humphrey Cartwright would never have found it. We'd have frozen, for all of him." The girl's voice sounded almost vindictive, then softened. "My name's really Ohio Ballou, but it sounded stupid, sort of, so for the profession I changed to Maggie—it's so much more fashionable, for one thing, and prettier, too. People used to tease me and call me Blue Ohio—the way blue and Ballou sounded so much alike when you said them. It was my father's idea, calling me 'Ohio' because I was born there while he was with a medicine show; I've always been on the stage, you see. Don't you like Maggie better, though?"

Henry found himself giving the matter serious consideration. Of course he liked the name. For one thing, every girl who had ever been christened "Margaret" was calling herself "Maggie" for a nickname and the play, "Maggie, the Midget," was at the height of its popularity. Besides, his companion was looking at him with an expression of earnestness in her deep violet eyes, hoping that he would.

"Maggie is a very nice name," he announced, finally. "Ohio sounds a little fly-by-night to me."

Maggie giggled. "I'll say it was. Ma used to say that we were over the river into Kentucky almost before I let out my first yelp."

Gradually Henry was becoming aware that his companion possessed other charms besides beautiful eyes. She had coal-black hair and the whitest skin, though it still retained a bloom of color from the cold. Now she opened her coat, with the remark, "That's a real fire. It certainly makes a difference in here—" She looked at him expectantly, but Henry was busy realizing that she was younger than he had at first supposed, and was not nearly as self-assured as she pretended. Somehow, he liked her the better.

She gave a confused, musical laugh that was not the least forward. "You know my name, but I don't know yours."

For some time the train had been clicking over the rails at half speed, but because of the icy windows it had been impossible to see. Now, the warmth of the fire melted the ice and the windows steamed. Henry reached across, cleaned the glass with his handkerchief, peered outside and answered, all at the same time. "Henry Rogers. The snow is sure getting thicker too. And blowing. Look, Maggie. You can hardly see anything."

"Henry Rogers! It's a nice name. Any relation to the sculptor? The man who does the beautiful parlor pieces, you know?"

Before Henry could answer, the train came to a sudden stop. The other members of the company began to look out, anxiously. The little man jumped up, ran down the aisle and opened the door on to the coach's rear platform. "That's our comedian," Maggie explained. "He's very nice—and a gentleman, which there's one that isn't in the Troubadours."

Henry knew immediately who was meant. "What does he do?"

"He plays the hero, of course. He's the tenor when we give concerts and not plays."

The comedian came running back through the car. "There's a big drift ahead. We are going to back up and try to buck it, the brakeman says."

It was true. There was a crash of drawheads down the train and they were conscious of backing, though the landscape outside was so obscured it was hard to tell merely from looking out the windows. Another crash, during which some of the female Troubadours screamed or shrieked in excitement, and they went ahead again, full steam. Both Henry and Maggie were aware when the engine hit the soft pile of snow. Their speed slowed, they almost came to a stop, then were through and picking up momentum.

Shortly after, the conductor announced Trenton Junction and they stopped before a station that was almost lost in snowdrifts. Mr. St. Clair, the Troubadours' manager, inquired, "Do you think we are safe in going on?"

"The Philadelphia and Reading always gets through," the conductor replied. "You saw what we did to those drifts back aways. Six feet high, they were, but we went through them."

The confident tone reassured Henry as much as it did Mr. St. Clair. His father would have answered in the same way, and in almost the same tone of voice.

Wood and coal were brought in by the brakeman, who also replenished the oil in the lamps. Henry, who had become custodian of the stove, stoked it carefully and then returned to Maggie Ballou's side. They steamed out of Trenton Junction in a whirl of drifting and falling snow. Most of the time they appeared to proceed cautiously, barely crawling along. Occasionally they stopped completely, or backed up, as they had done before, and bucked their way through the drifts.

They were hours late already and the gray world outside was growing darker. Henry realized that his companion was sleepy, for he saw her yawn once or twice, but shyness kept him from proposing that she lean her head against his shoulder. Then he found himself growing sleepy, also, and when Maggie's dark head began to droop in his direction, his blond one almost touched it. The train halted more suddenly than usual, backed and plunged as it had done so often, then stopped again. Everyone sat up, to see what had happened and Jerry, the comedian, again hurried outside. In a few minutes he was back, and in an overcheerful tone announced, "We are stuck for a while, folks—until the snowplow gets here, which shouldn't take long. Let's sing a song, to show that we don't care." He screwed his features into one of the most comical expressions Henry had ever seen. "I have it. Everybody knows the poem about Sozodont Tooth Powder. It seems perfect right now. I'll sing the first verse and you join in on the chorus."

Making up a tune as he went along, Jerry sang the words of the advertisement that Henry had seen almost every day without thinking about it. After Jerry gave full comic effect to the first verse:

> The north wind caught the snowflake
> As it drifted slowly down,
> And whirled the fleecy stranger
> Over the sleeping town

Henry, Maggie, and the others entered into the spirit of the occasion, la-la-ing through any lines they had forgotten:

And on my true love's window
The fragile snowflake lay,
To greet her at the dawning
Of the sullen winter's day.

The old Philadelphia and Reading day coach had never known a merrier moment, stuck though it was, at the blizzard's mercy, than when the full company of Saulsbury Troubadours, assisted by Henry, began the final verse:

And she smiled as she saw the snowflake
For *Sozodont* had given . . .

At this moment, in spite of singing louder than anyone else, Jerry managed to show all his teeth in a most ridiculous smile, then mastered the uneven meter of the last two lines, though the others faltered:

Her teeth to rival the whiteness
Of this snowy child of heaven.

Indeed, Henry was not certain but that the comedian, in deliberately making a burlesque of the lines, was somehow attacking the whole business structure. Undoubtedly the proprietors of Sozodont Tooth Powder had spent large sums in advertising their verses to make them so well known and such an investment was not to be made fun of.

Also, it was good poetry, for which Henry saw immediate application, with Maggie Ballou shyly smiling at him.

2

IN SPITE OF his wife's insistence that he stay home, Mr. Rogers pooh-pooh-ed the storm as nothing to what he'd known in the good old days and likely to be all over and melted in a few hours. Once out in it, he began to revise his opinion. The wind was especially bad, and he tried to excuse his former judgment by telling himself that it was this and not the snow that made the storm seem worse.

Long before he reached the elevated railroad station he was puffing, and he climbed the icy stairs up to the track wondering if he had better not turn back. But that would be an admission to Gussie that he was wrong and she'd rub it in all day. Fortunately a train was steaming into the station, pulled by two engines instead of the usual single one, and he swung aboard as it slowed down.

They were off again as the drivers raced madly, searching for traction on the icy steel, and Mr. Rogers looked out upon a scene that was unrecognizable as any part of America's great metropolis. The webs of telegraph wires that paralleled the railroad were festooned with icicles and here and there a pole had snapped from the weight. Streets and houses were buried under a shifting white blanket. Abandoned streetcars, vans, and drays stood where the drifts had caught them. Just now he caught a glimpse of a brewer's cart, piled high with casks, from which the driver was unhitching the horses.

The black top of a hearse was buried so that only its twin, nickeled carriage lamps peered out, like the eyes of a huge insect. Mr. Rogers wondered if the casket were still within and what might have happened to the mourners and family of the deceased. The scene would have invited further speculation had he not then become involved in troubles of his own.

While the passengers, already late, fumed at further delay, the train came to a reluctant stop midway between stations. Mr. Rogers forced his way to the car door and then stepped down on the footway along the track for a better look. He examined the situation with the professional eye of an ex-railroad man. There was no reason why the engines shouldn't pull up that slight grade. He slithered forward, intending to offer his advice. If the enginemen handled the throttle properly and sanded the rails, they'd make it easily.

Almost immediately his opinion was corroborated, though he derived no satisfaction from the fact. Suddenly the engineers opened their throttles in unison and the driver wheels took hold before Mr. Rogers could jump aboard. He was left behind, completely exposed to the fury of the storm.

Gussie had insisted upon his wearing an old cap with earflaps that he hadn't used since Kensington days, and his felt boots came well up his calves. His face was somewhat protected by his beard, which was partially tucked under his muffler and his coat was the warmest he owned, but as he trudged stationward, he glanced down longingly at the street, wondering if he dared to risk a jump into the snowdrifts.

A train passed, and he vainly attempted to flag it, then was almost drawn under its wheels by the suction. In other circumstances, he might have been amused when he saw it stall a considerable way down the track.

There was something undignified in being thus exposed to the elements, high above the city street, even though nobody appeared to be watching. Mr. Rogers determined to take a chance on a reasonably comfortable-looking snowdrift when he noticed that one of the pillars was provided with rungs for the use of track-walkers, and decided that though slower, they would be less dangerous. He climbed the rail, though in constant peril of being blown off, and cautiously descended the ice-covered iron footholds.

Relatively safe upon a terra firma blanketed under several feet of snow, he sighed with relief, only to be faced immediately by a new peril. A southbound snowplow came by. If the vehicle had been, indeed, a plow, Mr. Rogers would have suffered no ill effect from it. Pulled by four teams of horses, their harnesses jingling merrily, it was actually an open streetcar that had beneath it two very large, rotary brushes, set at an angle and turned by endless chains powered by the wheels. It swept a path considerably wider than the tracks so clean that Mr. Rogers suffered the further indignity of being almost buried under sweepings that contained much more than snow.

There was an immediate silver lining behind this dark cloud of tragedy. While Mr. Rogers was still trying to divest his coat of frozen particles of manure, a southbound car came along in the cleared path. It was jammed to the steps, but he managed to swing aboard and gradually pushed his way inside.

Everything would now be clear sailing down to Wall Street! He crowded up as close to the stove as possible and concentrated upon obtaining a seat, but it was some little while before he was able to drop down into one, completely exhausted from his misadventures.

They stopped for an unconscionable time, but he was absorbing the warmth and paid little attention. Suddenly he aroused himself. The car, which had been crowded so recently, was completely empty. He leaped to his feet and gazed out. The driver and the horses were gone and just ahead was the plow, also deserted and already snowed under.

Mr. Rogers was not one to give up easily. Besides, he was too close to his goal to turn back now. With a sigh at the thought of leaving the stove's warmth, he bundled himself up again and was about to dismount when his way was impeded by an older man, who peered at him shortsightedly. "This car going uptown, mister?"

"When the snow melts you can probably float up," Mr. Rogers shouted above the wind, his good humor restored by the ridiculousness of the question and the patness of his answer. He was still chuckling when he entered the Stock Exchange, just before the opening gong at ten o'clock.

But where were the bulls and the bears? There weren't more than thirty of them present, out of a thousand members. There was nothing to do but suspend business, and all of Mr. Rogers' arduous journey seemed to have gone for naught. But he circulated, nevertheless, conveying the impression that he was an authority on the financial situation.

Most of the members were more anxious to discuss their recent experiences in the storm and the chances of returning home in safety. George Gould was among the missing, but Mr. Rogers tackled a Mr. Kneeland, who turned out to live at Forty-sixth Street, and had therefore endured much the same hardships as he had. After these had been recounted Mr. Rogers inquired: "I suppose the accident on the Erie will cause the stock to recede?"

"No indeed. I should say that was discounted yesterday, in the technical adjustment. As soon as the market can open up again, I look for a rally."

"I've had some information that the western strike of the engineers is affecting earnings? . . ."

"Not at all. Not at all. Though I'd like to know the source of your information. No, you may quote me as saying that the turning point has been reached."

If Mr. Rogers had possessed the ready cash and if the market had not been suspended, he might very well have made an investment then and there, Mr. Kneeland spoke so persuasively. Instead, he questioned another substantial-looking gentleman. "What, may I inquire, is your opinion of the railroad securities?"

"Why ask me? Isn't it obvious to anyone? Look at the Erie accident and the bad report of the New York and New England. In another month the best railroad share in the country won't be worth a plugged five-cent piece."

## 3

AT THE VERY TIME that Mr. Rogers was fighting his way downtown for the glory of *The New York Times*, Clinton Weatherby was struggling against the blizzard in the opposite direction.

He had slept late, unaware that a storm was in progress. When he looked out, his first thought was of Teresina. Why had he left her, even for a moment, at this time? He berated himself for lack of consideration, for being pig-headed about Henry and unreasonable concerning Mrs. Rogers. No wonder she didn't like him!

There was a peculiarity to this storm that set it apart from all others within Clint's experience. He felt partially dazed as he walked to the bridge through ever-increasing drifts, after wasting time in waiting for horsecars that never came. There, the cable cars were out of operation, as the cables were frozen solid. The steam engines that were pulling the cars in the emergency had left for the Manhattan side a half hour before.

"How should I know when the train'll get back?" the attendant replied, in response to Clint's question. He grew more sympathetic when he recognized Clint as a public figure for whom he would have preferred doing some special favor. "You can see the way it's coming down. I can't help it. I was born and raised in Brooklyn —not a mile from right here, and I ain't ever seen anything like this." He grew confidential. "Between you and me, if I was you I'd stay off the bridge, if you don't want that baby you're talking about to be an orphan. All that snow. And you can feel it shake when the wind hits it. Mr. Roebling never thought of nothing like this when he built it. *I* never thought of nothing like this, meself."

Clint nodded. "Guess I didn't either. Well, maybe I had better start walking."

The attendant assumed a hurt expression. "I been telling you how it was, but you just won't believe. They ain't allowing any-body to walk across. For one thing, you couldn't. There's drifts ten feet high and the wind would blow you right off. Why it's been hours since the police closed the footway. . . ."

"I just have to get over," Clint insisted, his voice almost lost under the endless tune which the wind played through the great Aeolian harp of the bridge cables.

"Maybe you could do it down below, like Henry Ward Beecher used to boast he done," the attendant suggested, half facetiously. "It looks frozen all the way across and there ain't any ferries run-ning."

Much to his surprise, Clint seemed to take him seriously. "Thanks, I guess you're right. If you come to see me play next summer, sometime, make yourself known and I'll write my name on a ball for you—on a brand new one."

Even to one as athletic as Clinton Weatherby, the walk down to the shore of the East River was a trial of endurance. This was where he had played as a boy, swimming from pilings or shying stones at tin cans to improve his aim. Under ordinary circum-stances he would have been willing to wager that he could find his way blindfold over the familiar terrain, but now, where there was no curbing to follow, he lost himself more than once before he finally reached the river. It was not only that the snowfall was heavy and almost blinding of itself. More confusing was the way in which the wind changed its direction, blowing first from one quar-ter and then another, so that a five-foot drift against one side of the street was transported to the other within the space of a few hesitant steps.

Clint hardly recognized the foot of Hamilton Street when he reached it, though right over there he had played the game of "one old cat" that had begun his career. With one of the wind's sudden changes, he was in its lee for a minute or so, and although the snowfall never slackened he could see to the further shore.

Undoubtedly the river was frozen clear across. The question was whether it would support his weight. As the attendant on the bridge had reminded him the Reverend Mr. Beecher (for whom Clint had nothing but respect) used often to tell in his sermons of his own crossing over the river's ice, three decades earlier, to

216

prove that it was not the wicked alone who could stand in slippery places.

Somehow, Clint felt that this augured well for his present intention. First of all, though, he had to get down to the ice, which was clear of snow at this point and far beneath him. He was startled to hear a high-pitched voice, shouting in his ear, and was introduced to an example of Brooklyn's native enterprise which he never forgot. A boy, not over ten or twelve, and almost purple with cold, piped again, "You can walk over easy, mister. There goes some now. An' it's only two cents to climb down on my ladder."

Now that they were pointed out to him, it was easy for Clint to see the distant figures, slowly making their way over ice that was continually swept by the wind. He nodded and grinned. "Here's a ten-cent piece and keep the change. Where's the ladder? . . ."

The boy reached his hand out eagerly enough, stopped and looked puzzled. "What's the matter, son. Isn't my money any good?"

"Ain't you . . . sure you are. You're Clint Weatherby. I seen you pitch. . . ."

Clint laughed. "Good boy! I suppose you sat out in the uncovered stands?"

The child shook his head, regretfully. "Through knotholes in the fence, mostly. One time we shinnied the fence and sat on top. You pitched against Radbourne. He won."

This was ridiculous, to be talking baseball in the worst snowstorm he had ever experienced. Clint couldn't help but smile, ruefully, and answer, "That overarm delivery is too much for us Brooklyns, I guess."

"It ain't fair, I say." Here was a stout champion, his little jaw sticking out pugnaciously. "Right down this way, Clint. And I can't take money from you. You go free."

With serious face, Clint slipped the coin back in his pocket. "Fair enough. When you come to the Brooklyns next time there'll be no sitting on fences. How about down on the player's bench with me?"

"You mean it? Honest Injun?"

"Honest Indian. The password will be 'Ladder.' I'll tell the gateman to expect you."

217

Four figures took shape as though the snow had turned solid and become animated. How had they found their way to this particular spot? How had the youngster known that this was the place to take up his stand—or more rightly, lower his ladder?

"It's ten feet down to the river and too far to jump. . . ." Brooklyn's most enterprising young businessman offered his public utility and duly received his fare.

Clint descended first and was quickly followed by the others, each of whom, presumably, was urged by some unusual circumstance to take this desperate risk. They spread out sufficiently to distribute their weight, but kept close enough to go to each other's assistance, if necessary. The bare ice was wrinkled into waves and ripples and proved hard going, but opposite beckoned Manhattan, faintly seen through flakes that whipped into their faces with the sting of hail.

As they felt their way cautiously, Clint looked up at the fairy-like grandeur of the bridge overhead. It was a never-to-be-forgotten sight, the gentle arch of the roadway held aloft by the parallel loops of the cables. It was like a giant confection done in white icing and crystal—the chef-d'œuvre of a celestial maître d'hôtel.

How could the structure bear the drifts of snow and stalactites of ice that clung to it? How withstand the pressure of a wind that buffeted and sent reeling the men below?

The urgency of those little creatures was too great to permit of much speculation. A poet might have been inspired by the grandeur of the scene, but Clint and his companions only pressed on doggedly.

The wind changed its direction and instead of having to struggle against it, Clint was hurled Manhattanward, gaining such momentum that he had to slide, baseball style, to avoid being driven into a row of bulkheads at the Wall Street Ferry Slip. He glanced around for his companions, but they had been dispersed in several directions. He scrambled over to a small icebound craft, pulled himself aboard and crossed its narrow, treacherous deck to step ashore.

So close do human destinies run that in huge, modern New York, with its million and a half souls, Clint and Mr. Rogers were within a stone's throw of each other. When Clint struggled past the vast pile of the Stock Exchange, his father-in-law was still inside, the center of a group of both bull and bear persuasion who waited for the storm to end. Meanwhile, they listened to a discourse upon phases of railroading that were new to them, and highly diverting as well.

Unfortunately for future generations, Clint was unaware of Mr. Rogers' assignment and kept on his way. Four hours later, after he had tramped all the way out to the house on Fifty-second Street, a frenzied Mrs. Rogers opened the door to meet him, careless of the snow that drove into the vestibule. While he floundered on a stoop that was almost impossible of ascent, she screamed, so that he could hear an occasional word before it whipped away, "Father . . . hours ago . . . seen? . . ."

From his expression, she knew that he had not. Sobbing, she plunged toward him and Clint caught her, hoping that they would not go sliding back into the drift. He lifted her as easily as Jesse used to do, years ago, and carried her inside.

"Oh, Clint, I'm so glad to see you. I'm so sorry about whatever I've said, or thought. . . ." Her voice trailed away in semihysterical sobs.

"Come, there is no need to take on. Trust Mr. Rogers to be someplace where it's warm."

Mrs. Rogers pulled herself together. "It's Zenie . . . Norah is up with her."

"Zenie? A doctor? . . ."

"Tony went for one ages ago and Abe is looking for him. . . ."

Clint was already part way up the stairway, while Mrs. Rogers screamed after him, "The Lord knows what's happened to either of them."

He tiptoed into their room, caught Zenie's hand in a fervent, reassuring grasp and dashed out, almost colliding with Mrs. Rogers as he raced downstairs. "I'll be back soon's I can," he cried over his shoulder, slammed the vestibule door and was gone.

Mrs. Rogers was so used to finding fault with him, that out of habit and not from any feeling of exasperation, she observed to the empty hall, "Isn't it like that man! He might have smashed that piece of stained glass into smithereens. He will, too, one of these days."

*Chapter 4*

THEY WERE STUCK FAST, no doubt of that. Within an hour the snow began to bank against the car windows faster than it melted. One of the trainmen asked for volunteers to help dig it away, but Henry, always level-headed, objected. "The way it looks now, we'll be here for the night. The higher the snow gets, the warmer we'll stay. We can save coal, too, and we've none too much."

At the mention of being marooned all night, one of the Troubadour ladies began to have hysterics and screamed for smelling salts. Henry felt perturbed. It was difficult, of course, for modest women to be forced to spend the night in a railroad coach with strange men. No matter what the reason, it affected one's sense of the proprieties. He suggested to his companion, "If you'd like, I'll go back to an empty seat when it grows dark. I wouldn't wish you to . . . to . . ."

Maggie looked at him in wide-eyed surprise. "You can sit with me if you want. Besides, it'll give us each other to lean on when it's time to sleep. And pay no attention to Millie Mullins. She's our leading lady and *always* behaves that way."

For the first time in years, Henry felt a leaping within his chest. He began to look forward to the adventure, instead of merely accepting an inconvenience.

"You know all about me, but I only know your name . . ."

"Oh, there's not much to tell. I'm in the coal business. I came down from Pottsville—where my sister lives. It was snowing when I left, but I thought it would stop. If I had had good sense I'd have stayed over a day."

Maggie waited for the inevitable "But then I wouldn't have met you." When it didn't come, she was pleased, for some wholly feminine reason. "I suppose you live in New York," she prompted.

"Sort of. My family is there. I spend more time in Cincinnati though, where my business is."

"Your own business?"

"My brother-in-law is in partnership with me."

220

"And Cincinnati! What a coincidence, Mr. Rogers. That's where I was born."

Henry started to say something about the world being a small place, but decided that it didn't sound altogether appropriate. He hoped that Maggie wouldn't think he was stupid, for being so unresponsive, but she talked right on. "And a family in New York. I suppose your wife is worrying right this minute. Do you have many children?"

"I'm not married, so of course I can't have any children." This was said so sincerely that Maggie entered a second good mark in her book for Henry. Brightly, she said, "Well, your girl then. *She* must be frantic. I don't believe that I could stand it, if I were in her shoes."

"I've nobody to worry about me that way, either. My parents live in New York, I should have said, I guess."

"Well, it doesn't matter. I just happened to remark, that was all."

This whole discussion seemed unimportant to Henry. He was much more interested in knowing about Maggie, but continued to find himself tongue-tied. Besides, it was pleasant just to sit next to her, without talking. It wasn't only that she was pretty; there was something—well, something about her. Something that Henry couldn't explain. He forgot the storm outside. By now the windows revealed nothing but an opaque grayness and they were insulated from both the cold and the noise.

Like good troupers, most of the Troubadours accepted things as they came, including blizzards, although a few of the girls complained of feeling hungry. Henry was becoming acquainted with his fellow passengers just from overhearing them talk and joke; he began to revise his first opinions of them. The exception was Humphrey Cartwright and his little set. Henry was pleased to note that there were actually only four of the girls who played up to him; all the rest, including the manager and the comedian, shared his own dislike.

Because their car was quite warm, and fearing that the coal might not last, Henry dampened off the stove. In a few minutes, Cartwright jumped up, made some reference to a "cheap toff" and opened the draft. As Henry had started the fire in the first place, he felt a proprietary interest quite apart from their safety. "If you burn coal like that it won't last much after midnight, then what would you do?" he asked, firmly, at the same time shutting the draft again. The situation seemed ripe for a real quarrel and Cartwright jumped to his feet, then changed his mind when he discovered that Henry was several inches taller than himself. No one could say that he was not a good actor, though. He bowed in mock respect. "I withdraw my own attempts to be of service and bow to a better janitor. It is an occupation I never cared to learn."

This was said in a semidrawl which Henry found most unpleasant, but he answered matter-of-factly, "It may prove fortunate that I know about it, if it hasn't already." He walked back toward his seat, when Jerry inquired, "Maggie, you don't mind if I talk to your acquaintance for a few minutes, do you?"

It was plain that Maggie liked the comedian, from the way she smiled, and Henry had a strange feeling which he would have denied was jealousy. It was over immediately; who could feel the least bit unhappy with someone so full of fun?

Maggie introduced them formally. "Mr. Bernstein, this is Mr. Rogers, who is in the coal business in Cincinnati."

The men shook hands. "Glad to know you, Mr. Rogers. We may need a sensible man, like yourself. I'd like to show you something outside."

Henry followed and, when Jerry opened the coach door, was surprised to see that the drifts extended higher than the car roofs, with a kind of tunnel between. He had to stoop beneath the cave-like roof of snow, and observed, "You would hardly know there was a storm, in here. . . ."

"It's snowing hard, outside—and blowing worse than ever. I got through a bit ago and looked. You can't tell now where I dug my way out. This is a real blizzard. In fact, I never heard of one like it."

Henry smiled. "That ought to satisfy my father. He always talks about old-fashioned snowstorms. I'll ask him tomorrow how this compares."

"Has it occurred to you that we mayn't get out of here tomorrow —or the next day?"

"No, it hadn't, but I see your point. If there are drifts like this all along the railroad, with trains stalled in them, we might have to wait until there was a thaw. We could walk out, I suppose. . . ."

"Not right now, we couldn't."

"I wonder where we are. I was talking to Miss Ballou and never thought to look."

"We didn't get very far beyond Trenton Junction. Below Princeton, maybe. There's no sign of a town, or even a farmhouse. I tell you, Rogers, we're as cut off as we'd be in . . . in the Dakota Territory."

"How about food? I heard some of the girls . . ."

"I've thought of that too. The most important thing, though, is fuel. There are only a few passengers in the other coach. The rest got off at Trenton Junction. I think we ought to ask them to come in with us, to save coal. If you proposed it they might pay more attention than to me."

"I'll be glad to, of course. But don't you think it's up to the conductor?"

"The whole train crew pulled out long ago. I could see the path they made—with the fireman's shovel, I suppose, for it's not in his cab. The tender is empty, too. No, Rogers, it's up to us."

"Of course I should have been as aware of what was going on as you were, but why didn't you speak to me before?"

"I didn't want to excite the others, or I'd have said something to the manager. He can't think of anything but that broken-down actress that he's stuck on. And I never talk to Cartwright if I can help it."

The passengers in the rear coach proved to be elderly couples, bound for Elizabeth or Newark, who were aghast at the thought of spending the night away from home. They were readily amenable to Henry's suggestion and trickled forward, expressing concern that relatives would worry at their failure to arrive.

Jerry stayed behind to dump the fire in the stove of the emptied car. When he brought it forward, along with the remaining hod of coal, his cheery briskness, professional though it may have been, did more than Henry Rogers' matter-of-fact manner to accustom the other passengers to their unusual situation. "Just think, folks," he cried, "an evening with the Saulsbury Troubadours free of cost. When next you are in New York come see us at the Fourteenth Street Theatre. . . ."

When Henry sat down again, Maggie asked him, sleepily, "What were you talking about so long?"

"If the storm keeps up we mayn't get out tomorrow, Jerry thinks."

"Keeps up? Hasn't it stopped? I don't hear any wind."

"It is still blowing—and snowing. The trainmen have deserted, apparently, but it is too late for us to attempt to leave. If you ask me, this is the worst snowstorm that this part of the country has ever known. I think it is a real blizzard."

Maggie yawned, clamping her hand over her mouth. "I don't know whether I'm hungrier or sleepier." Apparently it was the latter—or that was the more easily remedied. She laid her head against Henry's shoulder and in a few minutes was fast asleep.

He sat up stiffly, afraid to move for fear of disturbing her. Only someone completely innocent could have been so trusting—someone who didn't know the danger of taking up with strange men in public conveyances. In the morning he must warn her, and in the meantime it was fortunate that she had met him instead of somebody like—well, like Humphrey Cartwright, for instance, who would ruin young womanhood at any opportunity.

A protective instinct was taking form within Henry's breast. A desire to shield Maggie Ballou . . . Ohio Ballou . . .

He must have dozed off, for suddenly he became aware that the car was cold, that the windows were frosting on the inside. There was no sound of the storm and he wondered if, possibly, it might be over. Gently moving his companion's head, so that it rested against the window frame, he walked forward to the stove. All of the passengers appeared to be sleeping. Someone—probably Jerry —had turned out all but two of the oil lamps that gleamed brassily overhead, but there was still enough light by which to see. Henry found himself comparing the appearance of the other Troubadour girls, as they slept, with Maggie's. Some of them had their mouths wide open and others looked haggard and worn, now that they were relaxed and not putting on their prettiest smiles and poses.

Humphrey Cartwright looked especially repulsive in sleep. He was snoring and his mustaches drooped. The girl who shared his seat rested her head against his shoulder the way Maggie had done against Henry's, but this girl's action somehow lacked the restraint and delicacy which had made Maggie's action so charming.

No wonder the coach was cold! The fire in the stove was almost out. Henry added coal as sparingly as possible, then poked and jabbed the embers into renewed life. Who had put on the draft again, after he had dampened it off? He was certain that it was Cartwright. He looked at his watch and saw that it was almost midnight. It would be pointless to go outside to observe the state of the weather. That could wait.

Maggie barely awakened as he guided her head back to his shoulder. There was the merest flash of color as her eyes opened and closed, then she was off again, breathing gently as a child. Henry placed his arm around her for greater warmth, and went to sleep wondering if this were an unfair advantage to take.

2

THE VARYING and often conflicting accounts that Aunt Zena later related about her adventures during the Great Blizzard were never believed by Mrs. Rogers. All of her sly digs and subtle attempts at pumping failed to elicit any statements that were more convincing. Usually the very opposite of reticent, Aunt Zena always became vague when the storm of 'Eighty-eight was mentioned.

She had gone to the Bingham House, that much was known. The snow had started to fall around midnight and she had watched the first, stealthy flakes as they began the conquest of the Quaker City. Over everything that followed hung a veil of secrecy. When, occasionally, there was a rent through which Mrs. Rogers could peer briefly, what she learned was more tantalizing than illuminating. Once Aunt Zena said, "New York didn't have near the storm that Philadelphia suffered. We bore the brunt of it." Did the plural pronoun indicate anything?

In another unguarded moment, Aunt Zena let slip, "Where poor Henry's train was stalled in the snow, ours got through with the aid of two extra engines to battle the drifts, and it was the last one that did. We hardly had enough food—and no milk. I'll never forget the picture, Wednesday morning, when a farmer came into the town on a huge bobsled pulled by three teams of horses and simply loaded with cans of milk . . ." She caught herself, realizing that she was being indiscreet, and finished, lamely, ". . . and me in a spring bonnet—lovely thing, too, that I'd bought in Paris."

Mrs. Rogers' usually sparrowlike expression turned sparrowhawkish, but she inquired, sweetly, "My, Zena, I had no idea that you had gone out to the country. What did you do then?"

But Aunt Zena was not to be trapped. Her high, provocative laugh put an end to Mrs. Rogers' hope of learning just what had happened, and was as close as she—or anyone else, for that matter—ever came to finding out.

Julia, who was East for a visit at the time, broke in to tell of the blizzard's effects in Ohio, much to her mother's annoyance. All during a description of the damage done to Cincinnati the two sisters gazed at each other with glances that were strangely alike, considering how different they were in other ways.

As soon as Julia had finished, Aunt Zena yawned and pleaded that she was tired. Addressing both women, but favoring her sister with a quiet air of triumph, she said, "There was nothing like the Great Blizzard ever before and I don't believe there'll be again, but I wouldn't have missed living through it for anything."

Pressing her lips together tightly, Mrs. Rogers' eyes narrowed as she watched the slight sway of her sister's hips, and she made a vow she was never able to fulfill, "I'll find out what happened to Zena during that blizzard, if it's the last thing I do, so help me."

*Chapter 5*   NORAH measured the coal in the bin with an anxious eye, then opened the doors of the furnaces she'd been stoking all day long. Only last week, when she'd suggested getting another ton or two, Mrs. Rogers had overruled her.

"Good grief, Norah, there's coal aplenty for the rest of the winter, what with spring just around the corner."

Now she took a perverse satisfaction in the knowledge that she had been right and Mrs. Rogers wrong. Not that either of them had expected anything like this, with the frigid winds blowing through the house as though there weren't doors and windows to keep them out. A dozen times Norah had swept drifts of finely powdered snow from the carpet of one or another room. And Miss Zenie's room was just like a barn despite the fact that the furnaces were like insatiable monsters that devoured the shining black anthracite as fast as Norah could feed it to them.

It seemed more economical to scrape the floor of the bin for odd pieces, instead of taking any more fuel from the meager pile in the corner. She performed this task energetically, clanging the shovel over the floor and against the frame of the furnace door. Things had come to a pretty pass, with Miss Zenie ahead of her time, the wind howling and the snow falling as though it would never stop—not to mention what might have happened to her own Tony, who might be lost this minute, while looking for a doctor. There'd been no word from Mr. Rogers either—fool that he was for ever leaving the house in such weather.

But that was the trouble with both him and Mrs. Rogers. Stubborn, they were, taking no advice from anyone. Let anybody say to her that she should have ordered more coal; she'd tell them off and that properly. She banged shut the door of the second furnace, working up a temper. That grinning monkey of an Abe should be doing this, instead of herself. She hated the poor Negro beyond reason. They had both come to the Rogerses at about the same time and Abe was always kindly and willing. Perhaps it was because Mrs. Rogers was so fond of him that Norah so often confided to herself, or to Tony, when he was about, "That naygur gives me the creeps and that's the truth."

She went on fussing about him. "Like as not, he's hiding in some doorway—skulking somewhere to get out of the work I'm doing." Her thoughts veered. Thanks be that Master Clint came back. He'd find a doctor! Which Tony would too, she added, defensively, unless he was lost completely. After all, Tony was of warm southern blood, unfitted to stand such murderous weather. Right now . . .

No, she couldn't think about him, or she'd be done in entirely, which wouldn't do with Miss Zenie the way she was and the coal going fast and no more food in the house than would do for supper. Early in the day she had made the rounds of the Sixth Avenue stores they always patronized and had been amazed to find them cleaned out of everything, with no milk or meat or other perishables coming in. Things were in a state, for a fact, and would be worse tomorrow instead of better, if it kept on snowing much longer. Meanwhile, she had better get back upstairs and see how Mrs. Rogers was doing. She'd be wanting hot water, like as not, just in case . . .

She was diverted from her intention by the rattle of the back doorknob and rushed to it, expecting that Tony had returned at last, but it was the despised Abe who came in, shaking the snow from his coat and stamping it from feet wrapped up in bags.

"Where have ye been, all this time—and me stokin' the hayters, which you should be doin'? Ye brought back no doctor, I'll be bound," she began, shrewishly, then let out a cry of pity as Abe began to empty his pockets and shirt of little feathered objects.

"The saints preserve us. It's frozen to death they are. We may need 'em to eat by tomorrow. It's a pie I could make of 'em, I suppose."

Abe caressed the last of the birds with his slender, chocolate-colored hands and it gave a faint cheep. "I found 'em down the street, 'gainst a house. Birds never been in nothin' like this. Maybe they be all right, come they get warm." He made a nest for them out of the bags he took off his feet, then rubbed each of the tiny bodies in turn. Before he was finished, all but two or three of the birds had revived. Most of them were plump little sparrows; there were several robins and a cardinal—a beautiful red male who languished beside a pink and olive mate that became stiff and cold. "Redbird," Abe said. "Now how do you suppose a country bird like that got way in town here? It's comin' round, too."

Norah watched with the greatest interest, then remembered her duties. Throwing up her hands in a gesture copied from Mrs. Rogers, she complained, "Birds! As though we didn't have troubles

228

enough. Sparrows—most of 'em, and English at that. The dash-hounds will make short work of 'em. . . ." She hurried upstairs while Abe continued rubbing the birds. Soon the sparrows were contentedly chirping and the robins snuggled together in one corner of the nest. Only the cardinal was dissatisfied. After trying vainly to awaken its dead companion, it flew around the kitchen frantically, as though trying to find a way out. Then it perched upon Abe's shoulder and accepted his caresses without fear. Though not even Abe realized it at the time, the Rogerses had acquired a new pet.

2

WHEN THE MEMBERS of the Stock Exchange had tired of hearing how railroads were actually run, and were wondering how they would ever get home through a storm that was increasing in force, Mr. Rogers began to give thought to the problem, although he had been enjoying himself immensely. He put on his boots and over-coat, pulled the flaps of his cap over his ears and stepped out into the street, but the snow was so much deeper and the wind so blinding and confusing that before he had gone a hundred feet he began to wonder if he could even retrace his steps.

Several of the bulls and bears watched with interest while he struggled back to safety, as tuckered out from this short walk as he'd been the whole way down. There was nothing to do but stay where they were. There were none of the cabs and carriages that usually stood in front of the Stock Exchange, and all but one or two of the members were reconciled to the situation. While the exceptions grumbled that the city had not used proper foresight in preparing for such an emergency, the others tried to reach their homes by telegraph or telephone, only to learn that all the wires were down.

Mr. Rogers was impelled to philosophize: here were men of great wealth, but they couldn't buy a fifty-cent hack ride. For the time being, at least, their money was worthless—a pair of snow-shoes was more valuable than its weight in gold. He was still on this train of thought when a remarkable thing happened. These financiers, usually so staid and sober, weighed down by their money and the responsibility it carried, began to realize how poor they really were, and their burdens lifted. Paunchy, graying men cut capers like so many schoolboys. Mr. Rogers found himself playing leapfrog and regretting that he wasn't as agile as he used to be—a feeling that was probably shared by the well-known financier, Sam Chauncey, who was the "frog."

They tired of this and someone shouted, "How about a game of baseball?" Almost immediately the greatest financial institution in the world was turned into a diamond. A broom from a cleaner's closet did service for a bat and a leather cushion for a ball. A man that Mr. Rogers called "Dick Halstead," as everyone else was doing, went through an exaggerated windup while Chauncey assumed a catcher's crouch. "Come on, Jesse," he shouted. "Step up and give it a swipe—bet you strike out."

Almost before he realized it, Mr. Rogers was waving the broom threateningly, desirous of boasting, at the same time, that Clint Weatherby was his son-in-law. It was as well, perhaps, that he didn't get a chance, for with three terrific swings of the impromptu bat he struck out ignominiously.

The game soon palled, for the stockholders began to display another characteristic of schoolboys—they became hungry. By one o'clock, Mr. Rogers, who hadn't missed a meal in years, discovered that he was growing faint. Those who daily patronized downtown Delmonico's, or the Astor House, were in no better position. Whereas thoughts of worrying families had failed to drive them into the storm, memories of the great circular lunch counters of the Astor House did.

By the time that Mr. Rogers had again donned the overclothes that had been drying on a steam radiator, the wind had abated slightly but snow still fell thickly and the drifts were almost impassable. The appearance of the elevated tracks showed clearly that no trains had run over them in hours and the snow in the streets was too deep for carriages but not sufficiently hard for sleighs. Mr. Rogers had not gone very far before he changed his destination from his home to his place of employment.

To describe his adventures en route, as recited during ensuing years, would require a more considerable record than this. But from his account, written at the time, one can gather that he came up

Broadway at least as far as Vesey Street, that he must have turned eastward somewhere, and that he saw more than his share of funerals and fires, of amusing incidents and pitiful ones.

When he arrived at the *Times* office, the blizzard seemed less than no news at all, so he was surprised at the enthusiasm of the single editor in the almost deserted place. Why should anyone who could glance out of a window and see the real thing wish to read about wind and snowdrift in the news?

He protested as much to the editor who practically shoved him to a desk, after hearing about the baseball game in the Stock Exchange. "News," the man shouted. "Rogers, don't be an idiot. This is the greatest news ever. It puts the death of the Emperor on an inside page; it makes John L.'s fight with Charlie Mitchell seem picayune. Good God, man. Here are some pencils—go to work."

Mr. Rogers realized that it would be useless to argue. Where to begin? The pointed pencil made a few meaningless scratches and then Mr. Rogers started to write. By the time he reached the episode where he was left behind by the elevated train, the humor of the situation struck him and he roared aloud as his pencil raced along. As each sheet was finished, a copy boy appeared to take it.

Can Mr. Rogers be blamed if he made a good story better, here and there? Were the handsome Stock Exchange spittoons really used for bases during that famous game? Did a notorious speculator, whom he left nameless, actually attempt to steal third, slide into the huge brass receptacle and receive an unpleasant shower?

Then, remembering how little the financiers' wealth had availed them, he turned philosophic:

"What does civilization amount to when people with thousands of dollars at their command cannot in this great city get food and coal, although tons of each are stored within its confines, whose owners are as eager to sell as the rest of the population is to buy?" The question was a little confused, but Mr. Rogers let it stand, after reading it over. But what about the poor?

"No one unacquainted with the East Side can have any idea of the from-day-to-day manner in which most of the hard-working residents of that densely-populated quarter live. They buy their

231

coal by the pailful, their flour by the pound and their butter by the half pound and their tea by the quarter. The tradesmen with whom they deal keep correspondingly small stocks, which they replenish once a week from the wholesale houses. All day women and children have been running from grocery to grocery vainly trying to buy coal. In many cases they have absolutely nothing except their scanty furniture with which to make a fire. Eggs are 40 cents, wretched butter 60 cents, and beefsteak, called so only by the most barefaced mendacity, is 30 cents a pound.

"Lots of the wealthiest persons are in little better case. Just in the middle of the blizzard, the servant of one, to his horror, informed him that there was little coal left and that the dealer could not send any. Six horses were seen dragging a small cartload of coal to the residence of another well-known citizen. . . ."

Part of this account may have been imagined, but there must have been a basis in fact for his observation that "The Metropolitan undertaker has been robbed of a profitable feature of his business. The cemeteries are interred in snow, the gravedigger's occupation is gone, although grim death has not suspended his everlasting work. . . ."

He waxed lyrical in describing Old Trinity and St. Paul's, richly ornamented with fantastic formations, and took a humorous turn again with the story of a wily store proprietor who had a huge drift shoveled from his front pavement during the height of the storm by the simple expedient of placing on it a small sign, which read:

### LOST

A valuable diamond ring in this snowdrift. Finder will receive a handsome
reward upon returning it to the owner.
Inquire Within

For one of Mr. Rogers' talents, the occasion provided the opportunity of a lifetime. In the throes of composition—and it is to be feared, invention—he forgot that Gussie was probably worrying about him. He forgot his hunger as well, while he forged a tradition of blizzard experiences and tall tales that only came to an end with exhaustion, when he fell asleep finally upon a desk top.

By the following morning, the wind had gone down and the temperature risen, although the city was so shut off from the world that there was no way of knowing whether this was merely a lull in the storm or if there was more to come. Now Mr. Rogers was really concerned over his family—and of his reception. It would be difficult to convince Gussie that it was simply impossible to get home. Perhaps the morning paper, with his account of the storm in it, would help. He began to read through the columns of print with an ever-increasing smirk of satisfaction. He still felt well pleased with himself as he started to leave.

The editor spoke to him, and a grin spread over his face. "Hello, Rogers. That was a good story you did. A wonderful sense of humor, too, that you should be using in your baseball pieces. . . ."

Ever since he had been taken in by that faker who pretended he was going to jump from the bridge, Mr. Rogers had been anxious for a chance to redeem himself with his superior, but now he pretended complete indifference to acclaim. "It was nothing at all, I assure you. I merely put down the facts as I experienced them."

"Oh . . . quite so. But where are you off to now?"

"Uptown. My wife may be upset. . . ."

"But Rogers, it's impossible—the drifts alone! We've less than half a staff, and those are men who live close by."

"I'll make it." Mr. Rogers looked most determined. "Where there's a will there's a way."

Both men walked toward the door, the editor chuckling. "That was a wonderful story. Gad, how did you think it up? We couldn't use all of it, of course, but it was worthy of Bill Nye, any day. You have a real imagination. . . ."

Mr. Rogers drew himself up. "I assure you, sir, that every word I write for the *Times* is Gospel truth. I may color it slightly, for literary effect. I failed to notice which part of my story you didn't use, but . . ."

"No offense meant. None at all. I had reference to where you picked up the policeman's hat."

Mr. Rogers roared. "By the Lord Harry, that was a sight. There was the policeman's bald head under it. His ears were slightly frostbitten and he was mad as hops, but not otherwise harmed—or didn't seem to be after I dug him out."

Suddenly the editor began laughing. "But the horse, Rogers, the horse. I don't know when I so enjoyed a joke."

With a perfectly straight face, Mr. Rogers shook his head. "I'm sure I don't know what you mean. The first thing the minion of the law said, when I asked how he was. 'I'm all right,' he said, 'but I'm afraid my horse has suffocated.' "

"Wonderful, Rogers, wonderful. Oh-uh-uh-hah. And you said, 'Horse? What horse?' "

"And he said, 'The one I'm sitting on.' "

"Delicious! And then you . . ."

"I dug down and there was the horse. Safe and sound. Kept warm by animal heat, I suppose."

"Oh, come, Rogers. A wonderful story, but you don't expect me to believe that it actually took place."

The last thing Mr. Rogers said, before he plunged into the outside drifts, was what he stuck to, all through life. "Of course it took place, and sometime I'll meet that policeman again, with a horse alive and chipper as ever, to prove it."

*Chapter 6*

FORTUNATELY Henry Rogers awakened before Miss Ballou. The oil in the lamps had burned out, but the coach was filled with a gray light that filtered through the snow-covered windows. It was again chilly, but what caused Henry concern was to find that he had done in sleep what he would not otherwise have dared: he held his companion in a close embrace. Furthermore, he was conscious of having experienced the most delightful sensations, which he could remember clearly, although they had taken place during his slumbers.

He found the greatest difficulty in withdrawing his arm from

234

around her waist. Each time he moved it slightly, the sleeper would partially awaken, turn and lean more heavily against him. Suppose she should discover him thus? Desperately, Henry tried the technique for pulling off a plaster—one good yank was the most painless in the long run. It worked! His arm was free. Maggie stirred, and he waited anxiously while her eyes slowly opened. She was wide awake, suddenly, staring with puzzled expression at him. "Oh . . . now I remember. The storm . . . Mr. Rogers . . . I suppose I've been a terrible nuisance?"

While Henry assured her that she had not at all, he felt an inward sense of relief. She had no remembrance of the way he had held her, or she would have protested immediately. Yet he had wronged Miss Ballou nevertheless. He could not look with steady gaze at a girl with whom he had slept the whole night, innocent though their relationship had been.

While Maggie was wondering what was ailing him, Henry began to stammer excuses, and finally, when he managed to suggest, "I better go out and look at the weather," she quite naturally ascribed his embarrassment to a reason other than the real one. Smiling shyly, she said, "Do see. The storm must be over, for we open in New York tonight and have to get there. We just have to."

Henry became aware that someone was standing over them and he looked up. "I'm sorry to intrude upon your pleasant little tête-à-tête. I see, Maggie, that you are not as hard to know as you pretend. . . ."

"I choose my company, Mr. Cartwright."

"Evidently you do not consider that I am good enough. A poor actor, on the way to fame, is not so sure a thing as a merchant in the coal business." Humphrey Cartwright made the word "merchant" sound most unpleasant and "coal business" so positively loathsome that for a moment even Henry felt ashamed of it. He started to rise, but Maggie placed a hand upon his arm. "Mr. Cartwright is somebody I prefer to ignore. I do not care for him or for those with whom he chooses to associate."

The speech proved to Henry that there was, as he had thought from the beginning, a wide gap between the creatures who clustered around Humphrey Cartwright, and his innocent companion. This was no place for a scene, but if the actor were to continue his nasty allusions outside, Henry felt that he would very much enjoy blacking an eye for him.

He was about to make a suggestion to this effect when Cartwright laughed and returned to his friends. "How I detest that man," Maggie whispered, vehemently. "He has made the most unpleasant advances, which I am obliged to resist. . . ."

It made Henry angry, just to think about it. He clenched his fists and might have settled the matter then and there, but the Troubadour's comedian interrupted. Jerry was covered with snow and his nose was red with cold, but he grinned as cheerfully as ever. "Hello Rogers. Hello Maggie. I've just been outside, looking at the storm."

"It's not still snowing?"

"Hard—but the wind has gone down a little. It's still plenty cold, though."

"But Jerry. We open tonight. What will we do?"

"I've been thinking the same thing, Maggie, and I don't know. Nothing less than a thaw will get us out of here. You can't even see the train from outside—except for the head lamp on the engine."

"We must do something."

"Any ideas, Rogers?"

"If you will excuse me, Miss Ballou, I'll go out and take a look. I was about to, anyway, when that Cartwright fellow interrupted."

Jerry's expression took on a calculating look. "You're big enough to handle him. Why don't you? I would if I had a few more inches and another stone of weight."

"He's a complete coward, I think," Maggie added, hotly. "Mr. Rogers was getting ready to put him in his place. I could tell by the way his jaw was setting. Humphrey saw too, so he left pretty quickly. He would pick on a weak female, but fears anyone as strong as Mr. Rogers."

Henry tried to look properly modest, but it was difficult under the circumstances not to swagger a bit as he walked down the aisle between the seats. Out on the car platform he could see a break in the tunnel that led under the snow from one car to the next. This was where Jerry had gone through. He had practically to crawl, and for a surprising distance, before he was out of the drift in which their train was buried. It was still snowing—large, white flakes that fell lazily, drifting to earth like downy feathers, instead of yesterday's stinging, icy particles. So far as he could see in any direction there was only a white, almost featureless waste. There was no sign of the railroad tracks at all. It would have been impossible to tell where they ran, except for the row of telegraph poles that acted as markers. These carried a spidery, icy tracery of their own. Here, close by the right-of-way, the snow came as high as Henry's shoulders. It would be impossible to dig a path very far— apparently they were trapped. The stove fire might last through the day, but what then, with no indication at all that the storm would soon be over? They might burn some of the wood in the coaches, but what about food and water? And the Saulsbury Troubadours were supposed to open that very night in New York. What about them?

"Doesn't look very promising, does it?"

Henry turned around, startled, not realizing that Jerry was behind him. "No, it doesn't. I can't even see the sign of a house."

"Ever hear of people starving to death in a blizzard?"

"Out in the far West, perhaps, but not here—not in New Jersey. Why Mr. Bernstein, we must be less than fifty miles from New York. We can't starve. . . ."

"Maybe we'll freeze then, after the coal's gone—or die of thirst. I tell you Mr. Rogers, I'm worried. We have to do something. On account of the ladies, if not of ourselves."

"If I scouted around—found a farmhouse, perhaps, where we could get food. I don't know about you, but I'm getting hungry. We can melt snow to drink, but food's different." Trust Henry to think about breakfast. He sounded as though the blizzard had picked him out for personal injury. He returned to a previous thought. "If we only had a pair of snowshoes. . . ."

"Maybe we could make a pair out of something—something flat and light, that we could tie on." Jerry was immediately enthusiastic, then thought of new difficulties. "But suppose we did figure out something; do you think either of us could find the train again, once we got away from it?"

This was a poser. Henry knew that in this frigid desert it would be impossible. He suggested hopefully, "The railroad will have to do something. Send through snowplows, maybe, with a lot of engines in back, so they could go right through the drifts. They just can't let people starve."

Jerry looked serious. "That's one of the things I'm afraid of."

"Afraid of?"

"Do you think a special train could see us? Suppose they hit this drift going full speed?"

"Maybe we should clear off the train roof, so they'd see us."

"And freeze when our coal runs out?"

Instead of letting up, the snow was becoming thicker, so that as they watched the whole landscape became hidden behind an ever-changing curtain. "Maybe we better go back," Jerry suggested. "No use telling the others how bad things look. Meanwhile, we'll try to think up something."

Henry followed him into the coach and was surprised that instead of being glum and dispirited, the little man was beaming. "Well, folks, it won't be long now, as the monkey said when it lost its tail."

He was met by a chorus of cries and groans at the lameness of his joke, but Henry noticed that the passengers looked more lively. Evidently a poor jest was better than none at all.

"While we are waiting for breakfast to be served in the dining car let's have a rehearsal. Lizzie and Katie, your opening numbers. Come on Cartwright—snap into it—and you Sadie, there's your cue."

Even the elderly couples from Elizabeth and Jersey City lost their worried expressions as the Saulsbury Troubadours sang and joked their way through the performance. Henry enjoyed it at first, marveling at the way Jerry Bernstein forced them all into a spirit of jollity despite their situation. The high point came when Maggie, as a little seamstress at work over an imaginary sewing machine, sang a plaintive song about the difficulties of her station and her desire for a lover.

When, however, Humphrey Cartwright began to woo her, Henry found his pleasure ruined. He began to think of all the times that the villain must have behaved in similar fashion. Whenever Humphrey Cartwright placed his hand upon Maggie's shoulder, while her body moved to the pressure on the treadle,

Henry would feel a desire to separate them. He tried to tell himself that the whole thing was nothing but acting—that Maggie had given ample indication that she actually despised Humphrey, instead of being taken in by him.

Then it became clear that the whole play was a farce that was making fun of Maggie, sewing away at her shirts, and of the seducer, who really didn't want Maggie's honor at all, but only a proper-sized neckband. Henry didn't know whether to be glad or sorry and ended up feeling that he had been fooled.

Besides, he was growing increasingly hungry. He decided to go outside again and was surprised to find that the hole in the tunnel had closed. He forced his way through. The storm had taken on a new fury. The few landmarks of an hour ago were gone—the telegraph poles had snapped off from force of the wind or weight of the snow and ice on the wires; hills that had been trees, and hummocks that had been bush and shrub, had become indistinguishable in an almost level plain.

Something would have to be done. It would be impossible to push through the snow, though one might be able to walk on top of it. There was no use in bothering the others with his idea; it might not work out anyway. He went into the empty coach and began searching for materials to adapt into makeshift snowshoes.

There were two rectangular, lightweight metal grills to each side of the stove which could be easily removed. They were about a foot wide and almost three in length. How to fasten them on? Henry's eye fixed upon the conductor's signal cord; he cut the cord off with his penknife. He'd need some marker to find the train again, once he'd left it. He pulled the red plush from the back of an end seat, and tacked it to the pole used for turning off the lamps. Throwing aside the poker that had served as a hammer, he seized his banner and started out.

He found it awkward going in the snow, but the grills did support his weight. He planted his flag and as the red plush whipped in the wind, he wondered uneasily how long it might last. He also wished that he had said good-by to Maggie. Suppose he became lost and perished in the drifts? It was quite possible, although he had to take the risk for the sake of the others. Would

Maggie—would Ohio Ballou wonder at all what had happened to him? Might she even miss him?

He decided to head straight away from the train. Stories of men becoming lost and traveling in circles came to mind, so he kept looking back, correcting his course by the marks of the grills. Once he fell and had to undo one of them before he could regain his feet, but on the whole he did better than he had expected. Before long, his red flag was lost from sight and he felt completely alone.

Suddenly he realized that while snow still stung against his face it had stopped falling. The wind seemed to have slackened, and he was perspiring from his exertions. He halted once more, to take bearings. There was no sign of habitation—nothing but snowy desert. It seemed impossible that he could be less than fifty miles from America's three most modern and populous cities. He wondered if the storm were as bad in New York and Brooklyn as it had been in Philadelphia. He felt no worry for his family; none of them would attempt to go out in weather like this.

Then, to his right, a faint plume of smoke arose, blew away in tatters, then puffed upward again. As he focussed anxiously upon it, he realized that it did not rise directly from the snow, as he had first thought, but from a white-blanketed, steeply-pitched roof that blended into the background. A farmhouse! He dashed forward, tripped over his makeshift snowshoes, and plunged headlong. Crying for help, he crawled along, then slid into a narrow path that had been dug between house and barn. Still unable to gain his feet, he crawled to the door, knocked, and pulled himself upright with the aid of the doorknob.

The farmer proved to be typical Jersey countryman, inhospitable and suspicious. Even when Henry explained the predicament of his fellow passengers, the man refused to stir, while his wife stood behind him, nervously chewing on toothless gums. A kettle of soup and pot of coffee were bubbling on the range. When nothing was offered to him, he asked, "I'd like some food—I'll pay for it, of course . . . a good breakfast . . ."

"You can have eggs and sidemeat and coffee for a dollar. Maw'll get it ready. Iff'n you want sandwiches for them others they'll be two bits apiece and the same for hard-boiled eggs. I guess you city folks can stand it."

This was preposterous! Henry paid for his breakfast and while he ate, tried to bargain, but without success. He finally arranged to take a whole ham and several huge loaves of homemade bread, but it cost all the money he had with him. The farmer agreed to follow with pails of soup and coffee, to be sold at whatever price he could get.

Heavily laden, Henry set out on the return trip. He had no idea how far from the train he had come and was surprised, now that the air had cleared, that he could see his plush pennant waving in the distance. The sky was still overcast and threatening, but for the first time it looked as though the storm might be over. The Troubadours might yet be able to keep their engagement for that night.

He found them all outside to greet him, and a cheer went up when they saw his food and were told that soup and coffee were on the way. With a generosity quite unusual to him, Henry announced that the feast was his treat and everybody trooped back into the car to prepare it. Despite the cost, Henry was more than repaid by the look of gratitude and the warm pressure of the hand with which Maggie greeted him. "Oh, you were wonderful, Mr. Rogers. It was most brave of you indeed—but suppose that you had become lost?"

Henry wanted to ask if she would have missed him, but instead he murmured a denial that he had done very much.

"Oh, but you did. Neither Mr. St. Clair nor Mr. Cartwright would have dared and Jerry lacks your tremendous strength. He could never have made it. It was a great thing that you did for my sake—for the sake of all of us, I mean."

Henry could not remember anything more gratifying than the sight of Maggie Ballou nibbling on the oversized ham sandwich he had made for her. With the lull in the storm, rescue seemed near at hand and he sat back and watched her, glad in his heart for the circumstance that had brought them together. When the farmer arrived with coffee, they all complained about the way in which he took advantage of their misfortune. They also learned that they were close to Princeton Junction and not far from the famous college itself. The farmer had underestimated the quantity of coffee to bring, and at Jerry's suggestion, most of the Troubadours accompanied him back to his house. Only several of the old

241

couples remained with Henry and his companion, and Henry quickly forgot about them as he learned of a new world—that of Ohio Ballou during childhood, of Maggie Ballou as a young and (he was certain) promising actress.

There was something charming and pathetically gay in her manner as she told about life with medicine shows and minstrels, as Little Eva in Uncle Tom's Cabin; or merely as a lonely little girl living out of a trunk with parents that were usually but one step ahead of the landlady. The afternoon sped as Henry listened and then told about himself. Good sense made him omit the tragedy in his life, but he made the coal business sound exciting and the family doings so pleasantly human that Maggie cried out, finally, "I know one thing, Mr. Rogers, and that is, I should like your father. I hope to have the good fortune of meeting him, some day."

It was still impossible to see through the windows, and they were surprised when Jerry Bernstein stuck his head in the doorway and announced, "It's snowing again, so we've struck a bargain with Farmer Walton to stay the night. It's two dollars apiece, which is highway robbery for a cornhusk mattress on the floor, but it's better than freezing to death here, now that the coal's gone." While the elderly couples hurried out, Henry and Maggie looked at each other, bewildered. For Henry's part, just to be alone with Maggie was worth freezing for, but he had her to think about. As for Maggie, whatever she desired was left unsaid.

Jerry called once more, "You better hurry, or the snow will cover the path," and then was gone.

Before they followed, Henry, always slow of speech, had something on his mind and struggled for the proper words. He caught his companion's hand and looked deep into her eyes. "Miss Ballou, there's something I've been wanting to say. Now that we're alone . . ."

He hesitated so long that Maggie finally prompted him. "Yes, Mr. Rogers?"

"Well, I've been thinking—I've been thinking a lot since I met you."

"Oh, Mr. Rogers!"

"Well, I have. And you know what I've decided?"

242

Maggie's voice was the faintest whisper as she answered. It was so low that Henry could not possibly have heard, even if he had not rushed on. "Well, I've been thinking about what you asked. Most every girl is named Maggie, or Katie or Lizzie, or something like that. Maybe they are popular right now, but folks will get tired of them. On the other hand, a name like Ohio is different. I got to turning it over in my mind last night. It *is* different—and pretty, too. It's like that Tennessee Claflin's. She worked for a medicine show, too. Now she's famous."

Maggie was about to interrupt, but Henry protested first. "I do like Maggie, understand, it's a beautiful name—but the more I think about it I like Ohio best. Ohio Ballou! It's a name you remember—I would anyway. It's a name I'd never forget."

*Chapter 7*

THERE WAS a tremendous shouting, the muffled beat of horses' hoofs and the brassy clang of fire bells. Norah cried, "The saints deliver us!" and Mrs. Rogers, "The Lord help us!" Anyone with a philosophic bent of mind might have deduced much from these exclamations, but Mr. Rogers, who had that bent, hadn't been heard from since the morning before.

Both women had been up all night and had reached that point of exhaustion where a fire close by would have been too much for shattered nerves. Mrs. Rogers reached a window first and let out an hysterical scream when she saw the plunging horses, the uniformed firemen and the red-and-gold hook-and-ladder truck. "My God, Norah, they're stopping right out front, sure as shooting!"

Norah's scream was even louder, but instead of apprehension it conveyed a feeling of relief. "It's the Mister! Oh, mum, he's safe and not hurt at all!"

It was true! It was really true! How had she possibly missed see-

243

ing him? There sat Mr. Rogers on top of the hook-and-ladder truck, looking large as life and twice as natural. He hello'd to Abe, engaged in shoveling a narrow canyon down the front stoop. Then his eye caught a glimpse of Mrs. Rogers at the window, and an already wide grin broadened. "Hello, Gussie. I call this coming home in style."

Mrs. Rogers' first feeling of thankfulness was succeeded by one of anger. If that wasn't like Jesse—gone all day and night with a blizzard raging and not thinking a bit about how worried she'd be. She began working herself into a temper as he climbed down from the ladders, assisted by two of the firemen. Botherations, he was bringing them in with him! She hurried to the door, fixing her features in a set, polite smile that was undone completely when Jesse rushed forward, caught her in a Gargantuan hug and buried her face in his whiskers as he applied a wet and resounding kiss. "My dear, there have been times since I left this little habitation of ours that I thought I would never see it again. When you hear what I've been through! . . .

"But allow me to introduce two good Samaritans, who brought me home in a really royal coach, Foreman Colby, of Engine Company No. 2 and Assistant Chief McCabe—both doughty firemen and true. My dear wife, Mrs. Rogers. Chief McCabe found the drifts too deep for his steam engine and rode to the fire (at which I found him) on one of the magnificent beasts that ordinarily pull the vehicle. Foreman Colby and his men performed quite as valorously in quenching a most disastrous conflagration on West Forty-second Street. I intend to see that their actions are immortalized in tomorrow's edition of The New York Times. . . ."

When would Jesse ever stop talking, so that she could tell him the great news? He had a pencil and notebook out now, taking down names, but she couldn't wait any longer. "Jesse—Zenie . . ."

"In a moment, my dear. . . . Would you call Mr. Moriarty an axwielder? . . ."

". . . A baby. A darling little girl of five pounds and eleven . . ."

Mr. Rogers was too intent upon his newsgathering to sense immediately the reason for the persistent interruptions. Then his first annoyance gave way to a startled glimmer of awareness.

"Uh . . . what was that? . . . Zenie?"

"Exactly. The doctor just left. He's been here most all night. Clint had a terrible time getting him and Norah's Tony, who was out looking, is in bed with pneumonia or worse and not able to turn on the gaslights last night or put them out this morning. . . .

"Oh Pet, we've had a time and that's the truth. If you'd only been here."

"Tony couldn't put out what he hadn't put on, that's one thing," Mr. Rogers began, his passion for logic almost landing him in hot water, but he noticed his wife's irritated expression in time to shout, "Another grandchild, by the Lord Harry! I'm sorry that there are no cigars in the house, Chief, but if either of you would enjoy wrapping your tongue around a chew of real good plug tobacco . . ."

## 2

AFTER THE HOOK-AND-LADDER TRUCK finally pulled out of the street, with much straining of horses and shouting of men—not to mention good-by's and felicitations back and forth—there was an exchange of experiences that took most of the day and, in the case of Mr. Rogers, at least, grew in the telling. Even the morning's account in the *Times*, which he'd written only the evening before, sounded tame in the reading, compared to the latest acted-out version. Mrs. Rogers shuddered to think of the stories she would have to listen to, during the ensuing years, with the snowfall getting heavier, the wind stronger and the drifts deeper with each recital.

She, in turn, was almost as insistent in describing the details of Zenie's labor, and the Herculean efforts of Norah and herself, their increasing anxiety until Clint's eventual return with the doctor.

"And what we're going to do for coal and food I don't know. Thank goodness it's stopped snowing and the wind *has* gone down a bit, but we'll have to burn the furniture tonight, what with a new-born babe in the house and Zenie the way she is. . . ."

This was an opportunity such as Mr. Rogers hadn't experienced in years. "Mother, how is this house run, anyway? A son in the coal business and our bin not high with the essential fuel? As I wrote yesterday of the shortsightedness of some of our fellow citizens I little thought . . ."

Because she was in the wrong, Mrs. Rogers was more shrewish than she would otherwise have been. "I suppose you've never put coal on the furnace, this past week? That's about the only task I'm spared around this house. If either you or that good-for-nothing Irish girl I have to put up with . . ."

Norah had run downstairs intending to say that Zenie seemed strong enough to see her father for a moment. She heard the last phrase and charged in with blue eyes flashing and each freckle standing out copper-colored against a skin drained of blood. "So it's good-for-nothin' I am, after slavin' the whole night whilst you sit a'sayin' 'Norah do this' or 'Norah do that,' and like as not tellin' the Mister that it was you and not me that done for poor Miss Zenie all night long, besides takin' care of me own man and it's little thanks he'll get for almost losin' his life in a howlin' blizzard such as you've never seen the likes before or will again and it's my fault I suppose that there's no coal in the bin after me tellin' you less than a week ago that we'd better be orderin' some, but no, you says 'The very idea,' you says, 'Gettin' more coal now with the winter nigh over and the price goin' down in another month. Norah, what can you be thinkin' of,' you says and I'll face you before the Mister and tell him the truth and none of your lyin' blarney and tryin' to shove off the blame for the fact that we'll freeze tonight, like as not, on a poor workin' girl that's got no chance to speak for herself. 'That good-for-nothin' Irish girl I have to put up with' indeed!"

She stopped for want of breath while Mr. Rogers roared, which made her all the angrier. With a quick change of target she was off again. "And it's ashamed of yourself you should be, a'makin' game of me, who's done nothin' but the best she can, all her life, after worryin' the heart out of me and the Missus with us not knowin' where you are or alive or dead whilst you're a'playin' baseball with a lot like yourself that ain't got good sense and devil a bit you care. There's not been even a word out of you askin' about Mr. Henry and it's fretted sick about him you should be to say nothin' of the Missus' sister, though she's somebody will always look out for herself, I say. . . ."

Norah's angry words slid past Mr. Rogers with no effect. "Henry and Zena are likely clear out of the blizzard. . . ."

"Oh, Pet, do you really think so? I was expecting them both yesterday and there's been neither hide nor hair of them."

"Henry heard about the weather we are having and stayed in Pottsville, you can count on it. As for Aunt Zena, there are no trains running from Philadelphia anyway, so she's probably safe in a hotel somewhere."

Mrs. Rogers sighed. "If I only knew what Zena is up to. It's something no good, I swear." She sighed again. "I guess I had better get down in the kitchen and see what I can stir up for a meal, Norah having her hands full with Zenie and the baby."

The Irish girl interrupted in her usual placid tones, "If you want to see the blessed creature you better come quick, as I'm not even leavin' her grandfather stay for more than a minute. Hurry, now, Mr. Rogers, tread lightly and no loud talkin'. I want them disturbed as little as possible, after what they've been through this night."

### 3

THE SNOW stopped again before dark. Because it appeared certain that no relief train could reach them until morning, the passengers decided to stay with Farmer Walton, though not without grumbling at the way he was taking advantage of their misfortune. The blizzard was proving a bonanza to him. In addition to breakfast at exorbitant prices, he had charged a dollar apiece for a dinner of ham and eggs. There were cornhusk pallets for less than half the company, but he refused to make a special price to the others. It was two dollars apiece to bed down on the kitchen floor, with the alternative of freezing in a railroad coach. But there was warmth— the range was kept stoked with chunks of good, fat Jersey pine— and there was light from well-filled lamps.

As Henry had spent all of his money on the extravagant gesture of free sandwiches, he was forced to borrow from Jerry, in a transaction that was overheard, unfortunately, by the company's leading man.

With his usual sneer, Humphrey Cartwright proclaimed, "There is your wealthy coal merchant for you. Big talk, but not even two

247

dollars in his jeans. Maggie is welcome to him, I say, though how she'll support him on the magnificent wages paid by the Troubadours is a question I can't answer."

The speech angered almost everyone, from the manager, who was touchy on the subject of salaries, down to Humphrey's special satellites among the girls. The short, redheaded May, who looked like Norah, at home, said, "Fie on you, Mr. Cartwright, after the gentleman treated us so royally this morning. You are just jealous because Maggie has played hard to get, which goes to show what fools Lizzie and I have been."

All these undercurrents were beyond Henry's grasp at the moment. He ignored the actor's outburst, shook hands with Jerry and bade good night to Ohio. He told himself that he liked Ohio, but they were two people who had merely met in a storm and would go their separate ways tomorrow. Then, as he began to make a pillow of his overcoat, in the far corner left to the men, he wondered if things would really work out as easily as that.

A hush fell on the room as the marooned wayfarers tried to make the best of their hard beds. Giggles and whispers from the girls, rustle of cornhusks, scraping of shoes against the floor, and all the other sounds of a sizeable group of people seeking sleep under trying conditions—these died away.

The farmer's wife slippered in, placed another chunk of wood in the range, blew out two of the lamps and carried off the third. Henry listened to the pleasant guttering of the burning pine resin, then dozed off. He could remember nothing further until he was startled by a terrific banging at the door.

He jumped up, thinking that it was somebody else seeking shelter from the storm. A tattoo of kicks beat against the door's stout oak. The farmer's wife appeared, carrying a lighted lamp, her hair straggling down over a red-flannel nightgown, her toothless mouth working in anger. While the passengers scrambled to their feet, she screamed again at the intruders. "You devils go back where you came from—else my old man fills you full of buckshot."

She was answered by shouts of derision. "Open up, let's in, or we'll kick the door down."

Some of the girls began to cry out in fright and there was a whole chorus from outside. "Girls! Fellows, there are girls in there. Girls!"

The farmer rushed in, carrying a second lamp. "It's them young dude students from Princeton. The devils are a pest around these parts." His voice joined his wife's, "Get along now, or I'll riddle you."

Sound of the womenfolk really aroused the college boys. Apparently they made a regular football rush at the door, for its bolt splintered away and a half dozen youths came tumbling in to the kitchen. They scrambled to their feet, a bit taken back to find themselves outnumbered by a group of serious-faced men behind whom the girls cowered in fear. A youth taller than Henry Rogers, though not as broad, appeared to be their leader, and Henry disliked him immediately, almost as much as he did Humphrey Cartwright. A dude, certainly, and of the most supercilious type, though his boastful attempt at a beard was like the feathers on a new-born chick. He had been drinking, evidently, as had the others. Immediately recognizing the Saulsbury Troubadours for a theatrical troupe, he ignored the men and shouted, "Come on, girls. We've two speedy cutter sleighs outside, some warm buffalo rugs and a couple of full bottles. Who's game for a good time in Princeton?"

One or two of the bolder girls looked at each other questioningly. Fun in Princeton was better than sleeping on cornhusks in an out-of-the-way farmhouse. But before they could make up their minds, the leader of the students spotted Ohio Ballou, who was easily the most attractive of the company. Pushing past Henry, he seized her arm. "Ah, there, my pretty madcap, I'm taking you."

For an instant Henry was apprehensive. Perhaps she would be taken in by the young man. Henry was opposed to scenes and the use of his fists—he regretted bitterly the time he had lost his temper with his brother-in-law—but now he wanted nothing more than to give the affected Princetonian a good drubbing.

"Grab your girl—I have mine," the fellow shouted. Ohio cried out, "Stop, you're hurting me. Oh, Mr. Rogers . . ."

Nothing more was needed. With Jerry and Humphrey assisting, Henry sailed into the group of young rowdies with both fists flying. The startled youths, so brave a moment before, escaped out of the door and into the snow. They ran toward their teams, pursued by the three, and as they whipped up their horses, the usually mild-mannered Henry made the loudest threats of what might happen if they returned.

Glass from a whiskey bottle that had been broken in Henry's sudden attack lay on the kitchen floor. Jerry put on an expression that was at once doleful and comic while he read the label. "Old Overholt Pennsylvania Rye. There must have been a full quart, from the smell of it. Rogers, you should be more careful of the way you destroy property. A dollar's worth of good liquor lost! It might have kept us warm until a rescue train gets through."

Everything was a hubbub of voices, in which Farmer Walton's occasionally rose above the others while he inquired, "Who's goin' to pay for that busted door?"

Nobody paid any attention, for he had already made too much from their misfortune. The girls giggled at him and the men ignored his demands.

Then Humphrey Cartwright, nursing a bruised knuckle that he had received in the fracas, stepped up to Henry and suggested that they shake hands. "I'm sorry for being disagreeable earlier. The way you handled that big chap proved you a real man."

Henry thought of the many times that the actor must have played opposite Ohio and would have preferred to go on thinking of him as an enemy, but there was nothing to do but accept the outstretched hand.

Ohio also offered Henry hers—shyly, as she glanced upward through lowered lids. It seemed very small as he held it—small and trusting. He was reluctant to release it and did so only after a longish while.

Someone else had taken Ohio's place on the floor. There was no other spot vacant except at the edge of the section reserved for the women, where she made a kind of pallet of her coat to lie upon.

It happened to be close to Henry, on the men's side—just close enough so that they could reach out in the dark and hold hands again.

They went to sleep that way.

**Chapter 8**

IN THE MORNING, Henry awakened to sore joints and the letdown following an exciting dream. He had stood off a number of men who had not rushed at him in a group, but singly. A blow of the fist toppled each man in turn as though he were a wooden soldier. They were singularly alike—tall and with chick-feather whiskers—and they disappeared, one by one, as his punches landed. He remembered a growing weariness against which he struggled, as new figures took the place of those who had fallen.

He could not recall the next part of the dream, but he knew that a lovely girl—Ohio Ballou, of course, but glorified in such a way that he wondered why he had not appreciated her charm earlier—Ohio was thanking him in the most endearing terms. Then, suddenly—again he didn't know quite how—they were embracing and he felt the softness of her against him, the tenderness of her lips on his.

Before he could enjoy the sensation to the full, he came back to a waking world in which his arms were empty, in which a cold gray light revealed grease-blackened walls, a dismal room and an ugly, squat range. The rest of the passengers were still sleeping, although noises outside indicated that the farmer was already astir.

In sleep, the girls, though fully dressed, had cast off the modesty of waking hours, so that Henry could see more than one trim ankle shod in high-buttoned shoe, more than one full calf in red and white striped stocking that showed it off to advantage. But his glances were for none of these. He felt that sleeping together in this way, although the sexes were separated, was an impropriety born of circumstances over which they had no control. So far as he was able, he had no intention of taking advantage of them. Then his eyes lighted upon the subject of his dreams—the lovely creature for whom he had stood off an army of Princeton students.

She wasn't over three feet away, turned toward him and sleeping with a faint smile on her face as though she, too, were dreaming. An impulse seized Henry which he afterward couldn't excuse.

251

Looking around to make sure that no one had stirred, he crept across the intervening space and then gently, so as not to disturb her dream, kissed her.

Perhaps his lips pressed more ardently than he intended, for Ohio's hand lifted, ran through his hair and drew his head down. It was a long kiss and so fervent that he feared bruising her mouth, as his was being bruised. He whispered incoherent words until her hand relaxed, finally, and Henry, suddenly fearful that they would be discovered, slipped back to his place.

His heart was pounding as it had never done before; then he had a fearful thought. Suppose Ohio were angry with him for taking advantage of her. Of course she had kissed back, but perhaps she had still been asleep and had been thinking of someone entirely different—of Humphrey Cartwright, even. When she realized who it actually was, had she been disappointed? He deviled himself into thinking that she had actually pushed him away, and that even now she was furious with him and would demand an apology as soon as they were alone. He peered over at her from under the elbow with which he pillowed his head and could see that she was also looking at him, but whether in anger he could not tell.

How long did they lie there, each trying to divine the other's thoughts? One and then another of the sleepers stretched arms and yawned. Then the farmer, in heavy boots, disturbed the rest. "It's time for even city folks to be rousin'," he announced, gruffly. "I got some water for the women to freshen up in—kicked in the ice on the waterin' trough to get it. The men can wash out there, if they feel inclined."

While each girl exclaimed over the fright she looked, the men trooped dutifully outside. They splashed themselves with water that almost froze on their faces and then tramped through already broken snow to the little square building next to the woodshed. The reason for its proximity was soon apparent, when the farmer called out to them, "If you bring back a few chunks of wood apiece you'll all be warmer, come breakfast."

Although the skies were still overcast, the great storm appeared to be over. The men returned, ready for breakfast, and with the best manners possible overlooked the disappearance, two at a time,

252

of the women in the group. It cost another dollar apiece for hot-cakes and coffee, but in spite of grumbling, Farmer Walton again reaped a harvest. Finances of the Troubadours had run low, however. They had also missed the opening date for their engagement, which, as a result, might have been canceled. Even Jerry, the comedian, was depressed, and Henry Rogers' sensible, "If the blizzard was as bad in New York as it was here, you would have had no audience on opening night anyway," did little to console him.

"This is in the sticks, out here. A big city like New York would have had the streets cleaned as fast as the snow fell. We might not have had a full house, of course, but if we'd just broken even . . ."

He was interrupted by a shout from the manager, who had been engaged for a time in trying to convince the leading lady that their predicament was not a matter of bad judgment on his part. His relief was therefore greater than anyone else's when he saw a black spot against the horizon and watched it grow rapidly larger.

"Girls! Folks! Everybody! Look! A train! We'll be out of here in no time, now."

At almost the same moment, one of the girls who had been gazing out of the window in the opposite direction cried out excitedly, "An engine! Girls, look . . . I can see the smoke quite plainly."

It was true. Rescuers approached from both Trenton and Jersey City. Their terrible ordeal was almost over. There were no thanks given to their hosts, who had taken such advantage of distress. In pell-mell fashion the passengers rushed over the path toward their train, its location still marked only by the red-plush banner which Henry had placed beside it.

He waited for Ohio, but there was still no chance to talk with her, as he'd been wanting to do all morning. At least he could assist the girls through the drifts, and this he did, while awaiting his opportunity. By this time he was quite certain that Ohio was angry with him, and no wonder, but somehow he had to tell about his dream, shallow excuse though it was for the way that he had behaved.

As the trains approached, it was clear that the P. and R. had made a valiant effort to rescue them, and everyone felt a little pleased to be considered so important. Each train consisted of three engines hitched together and pulling a single coach. Their progress was necessarily slow, for after one drift was overcome there was always another. With a great puffing of steam and blowing of whistles, the trains would back away from the deepest drifts and then head full tilt into the snow, with drivers pounding madly. After either train pushed through in this way, a cheer from the passengers spurred on the crew to still greater efforts.

Jerry and Mr. St. Clair, who were inveterate gamblers, placed bets upon which train would reach them first, but of this Henry did not approve. It was still too hazardous to say which might be the final winner.

There were times when the engines stalled completely and a horde of Italians and Irish would swarm from the coach of one or the other train and dig a way through. For these foreigners the blizzard was undoubtedly a godsend! Poor devils, a couple of dollars for shoveling snow might very well keep them from starvation. Though they were improperly clothed and ill-fed, they attacked the drifts with such courage that they earned repeated cheers from their audience.

When it seemed that the train from Trenton would surely win, and Jerry was demanding immediate payment of his wager, the race took an unexpected turn. The foremost engine of the eastbound train jumped the track as it plunged against an especially solid snowdrift—and Jerry lost. With a lugubrious expression that made all the girls titter and giggle, he paid his bet. Then the "team" from Jersey City dug out their long-marooned coaches and engine.

The passengers climbed aboard, a triple series of highballs from three locomotive whistles, and they were off, forty-eight hours late.

Out of shyness, Henry waited until the very last. He pretended to see that nobody was left behind—as though such a thing could possibly have occurred. When he finally entered the coach, a fire was already roaring in the stove and he took his seat beside Ohio Ballou, who appeared unapproachable. She peered out of the frosted window with great interest and must have watched the

254

white monotony of the landscape for a full five minutes before he summoned his courage. "Maggie—Ohio . . ."

He thought he heard a "yes," muffled by her coat and continued, "About this morning . . ."

"Yes?" Now she spoke quite plainly.

"I'm sorry, awfully sorry about the whole business. It was one of those things that happen, I guess, but I was most unfair, the way I took advantage. . . ." Gradually his voice trailed away. He could see that Ohio was angry with him, really angry, as he'd suspected. She was too wrathy to answer him, but riveted her attention upon a passing scene of which she actually saw nothing.

"Please, Ohio. I am sorry. I don't know what possessed me. I'd dreamt—well—that I was kissing you. When I woke up I wasn't. But there you were—so I did. . . ."

There was the necessity of keeping his voice low so that nobody else would hear his tortured words. Henry found that he was perspiring profusely and he ran his finger under his collar. "It was most ungentlemanly of me and I apologize with all my heart."

Ohio wouldn't hear more. Even in anger she looked beautiful, although Henry shriveled beneath the hatred in her expression. "If that is how you feel, Mr. Rogers, you need never speak to me again. I shan't to you, that's a certainty. Not if I live to be a hundred."

She didn't, either. Not all the way in to Jersey City, though a miserable Henry tried again and again to account to her for his behavior.

2

THANKS to their good neighbors, the Burts, it was not necessary for the Rogerses to burn their furniture to stay warm, as many families had to do toward the end of the great blizzard. Mr. Burt believed in keeping a full coalbin instead of stocking up in early summer, as the Rogerses had done ever since Kensington days.

Mrs. Burt and Mrs. Rogers had been on good terms for a long time. Whether it was the sharing of coal, brought across their joint areaway by Abe, or the exchange of confidences about grandmotherhood that really cemented their friendship, it would be hard to say. Probably it was a combination of both. Because

Julia's children had been born so far away, this was Mrs. Rogers' first experience, whereas Mrs. Burt had been in attendance at the birth of numerous grandchildren. She was in and out a dozen times during the day of the thirteenth. Later, when Mr. Rogers learned that the Manhattan Railway was again in limited operation, and he departed once more for the office of the *Times*, the Burts came over for the evening, laden with jars of food.

They had a merry meal in spite of Mr. Rogers' absence and the weather outside. Mrs. Rogers' talents had always run to pickling and with an end to other food in the ice chest, lunch had been a combination of pickled beets and collared eel, pickled pearl onions and tripe in vinegar, until even Mr. Rogers, who ordinarily enjoyed such appetizers, had cried enough.

Though they still lacked meat, everyone voted that Mrs. Burt's string beans and whole tomatoes were just what was needed, especially when topped off by a special jar of peaches—clings, done whole and heavily spiced.

In the evening, Clint was both toasted and teased over his new daughter, who gave promise of having red hair like his own. Mr. Burt proposed that she should be called "Blizzard" as she'd been born during one. Then his wife cried out, "She dropped to earth during a snowstorm. Why not call her Snow? Or Snowdrop? Snowdrop Weatherby would sound real nice, I think."

It was a good idea, but Clint shook his head. "I'd like to name her Zenie. . . ."

"Good grief, Clint, with Julia's little girl named for her too? And Zenie and Aunt Zena? It is too much of a good thing, I think. A body would hardly know who was being talked about when the name is mentioned. Which reminds me—there still hasn't been a word from that sister of mine."

"With the wires all down, you couldn't expect any. She'll be showing up tomorrow," Clint predicted. "I think I'll run up and look in on Zenie. . . ."

Mrs. Rogers cried after him, "Don't stay too long and get Norah riled at you. The way she's going on you'd think it was her baby. . . ." There was no use finishing what she had intended to say; Clint was already beyond earshot.

When he opened the door a crack, it was to see Zenie nursing her tiny daughter. He caught Norah's eye, questioningly, and when she nodded, tiptoed to the bed and kissed both mother and child. His heart was full. This was his child, his daughter. Born of the blizzard, as had been pointed out so often during the day. Was it a good omen, or a bad one?

Zenie would want to stay at home for a long while and he made up his mind to it. Ever since yesterday, Mrs. Rogers had treated him differently, and he would get along with Henry somehow. Zenie, poor girl, her ordeal had been long and difficult. Her smile was tremulous and worn. He left her after another kiss, and as he went to Henry's room, which he was using for the night, he realized suddenly how very tired he was. He yawned, and hurriedly prepared for bed, but even as he dropped off to sleep a phrase and a question plagued him: Born of the blizzard—good omen or bad?

He was awakened, quite late, by the sound of Mr. Rogers' voice and hurried downstairs in time to hear him say, "I am hungry, woman. Rip-snorting hungry. The storm may be over, as you say, but there's not a restaurant open in all of Manhattan. Except for a few sandwiches of stale bread and cheese, I haven't had a bite since I left the house yesterday."

"I can't help it, Jesse. Abe and Norah both tried to scour up some food, but there's none to be had. In another day things should be normal."

"In another day we'll have floods, like as not, if this snow begins to melt. Meanwhile I'm hungry."

"There are some real nice pickled beets. You've always liked them so."

"I couldn't look a beet in the face. The very word 'pickled' gives me gooseflesh. How about a stack of hotcakes?"

"There's no flour or milk. I never keep much flour in. . . ."

"No chops, no steak. Not even bacon or ham. Mother, what kind of hand-to-mouth existence have we been living all these years?"

"You've done pretty well, I'd say. Good grief, Pet, the storm caught us short, that's all. I'm put to it to get up something for Zenie, who needs strengthening. . . ."

Both became aware of Clint, who had slipped in, unobtrusively.

257

He interrupted a "Clint my boy," from his father-in-law to suggest, "If there is still coffee, I'll have some. Then, soon's I run up and see Zenie, I'll scout around. In the meantime, I hope you don't fall away to a shadow, Father Rogers."

Mr. Rogers sat down heavily in a chair. "My boy, food is something I've joked *over*, many a time, but never *about*. The frigid winds of this storm, unexampled in the history of these United States, never fazed me. I braved Boreas at his worst, but an empty stomach is something I can't stand. It . . . it . . . it defeats me. I fear I couldn't survive another day. . . ."

Clint grinned. "We'll save you sir, don't worry."

Norah bustled in with a full pot of coffee, and Clint was properly grateful that sugar, at least, was plentiful. He scooped three spoonfuls of it into a cup of the black brew. Chow-chow and cucumber rings accompanied it, then he dashed upstairs for a look at Zenie and the baby, and was off.

Mr. Rogers, meanwhile, finished the chow-chow between protests that his gorge rose at every mention of the name, and proceeded to read accounts of the storm from the copy of the *Times* that he had brought home. "It says here that the wind on Monday was only sixty-six miles an hour. That's not much over a mile a minute—and nine degrees Fahrenheit. The man who took those figures must have stayed inside all day. Why Monday morning, when I went downtown, it was zero, easily, and as for the wind . . ."

"There's no more chow-chow, Pet, but there's still a jar or two of cauliflower."

"Pickled, I suppose. Why anyone would want to spoil good victuals with vinegar!"

Mrs. Rogers didn't bother to answer, but called downstairs for Norah to bring up a jar, and Mr. Rogers returned to his reading. "It's a Dakota blizzard, all right, as I said all along. 'It tore down through Georgia, thence up the Atlantic coast and through New York and is moving west again.' Detroit began to feel it yesterday."

There were times that Mrs. Rogers listened, but more often she didn't. "Here's something amusing. A doctor had a smallpox patient in his sleigh, taking her to the hospital on North Brother Island. He was supposed to meet the Health Department boat at

120th Street, but his cutter stuck in a snowdrift and some boys snowballed them. There were a couple of other smallpox cases yesterday, but nothing to be worried about.

"If there were only some bread to go with this cauliflower. . . ."

"There isn't, Jesse, and that's an end to it. What does it say about Philadelphia?"

"Let's see—there's a report somewhere. The telegraph lines were all down, but they got the telephone through last evening."

"Talking all the way from Philadelphia! It hardly seems possible."

"Here it is. 'Philadelphia's terrible condition' is the headline. 'The storm still raging at 10 o'clock last night . . . snow began to fall again . . .' sounds pretty bad. 'Numerous deaths . . . caused by freezing . . .'"

"I'm so worried about Zena. She was up to devilment, I'm sure, but after all she's my only sister. . . ."

Unperturbed, Mr. Rogers let out a shout as his eye caught a humorous item among all the tragic ones. "The Mayor received a telegram from Bismarck. 'Dakota, under a mild spring sun, sends her sympathy to blizzard-stricken New York. Citizens of the Territory are responding liberally. Would you prefer clothes, or food, or both?'"

Jesse had the queerest sense of humor. It was real nice of the Dakota folks to be so helpful; he shouldn't make fun of them for it. Besides, she had to get upstairs and make Henry's bed in case he did get in; he'd be furious at the idea of Clint using it. And there were a million and one things to be done for Zenie and the baby! "It is all very interesting, Pet, and I do hope it is all over, but you've been on the go all night at that newspaper office and not a wink of sleep, I'll be bound. You must be worn out and ought to take a nap." She just had to get him out of the way somehow, to get anything done!

It worked. Mr. Rogers said, "Nonsense. I'm wide awake and fit as a fiddle," but he yawned, and followed to the second floor as she climbed on to the third. There was a moment or two of quiet, followed by a violent shouting. Mrs. Rogers rushed to the banister and screamed down, "Keep quiet, for Heaven's sake, or you'll wake the baby."

259

If Mr. Rogers had not already done so, her screaming did; and as the first plaintive cry was heard, Norah came running, scolding them both. But the shouting from the master bedroom continued. Mrs. Rogers and Norah hesitated in front of its door. Then Mrs. Rogers compressed her lips firmly, seized the knob, turned it and almost gingerly gave the door a push.

Her first glimpse was of Mr. Rogers, his arms threshing wildly in the darkened room. Then, as she recalled that she'd left the blinds drawn to help keep out the cold, she was overwhelmed by the same force that was attacking her husband. Out into the brighter light of the hall flocked a solid cloud of birds! Their cheeping and the whirring of their flight confused her while she struck out indiscriminately at sparrows, robins, and pigeons. When they were all gone, she subsided limply on the bed.

"Woman, what is the meaning of this? Since when has our connubial bedroom been turned into an aviary?"

"Jesse, please . . . till I get my breath back . . ." Unaccountably, instead of explaining, Mrs. Rogers began to giggle, then laugh. Both her husband and Norah shook her, but she kept on laughing until tears ran down her cheeks.

Finally, gasping weakly, she spoke between paroxysms that she could not quite subdue. "Father . . . sorry. I'll never forget your expression . . . long as I live. Funniest thing . . ." She paused, to gain control of herself, then continued more lucidly. "Abe rescued them from the blizzard. I saw a few of the poor things— almost frozen they were, in a box he'd fixed up behind the range. I told him he could keep them, but Norah fussed so this morning about them being in the kitchen. . . ."

"Dashin' out all day yesterday and bringin' in them birds by the dozen—messin' up me place with feathers, just like the good-for-nothin' naygur. . . ."

"That's enough out of you, Norah! . . . I couldn't let the poor things out to freeze again and I was at wit's end about food and the baby and a dozen other things, so I said he could put the box in here, never thinking . . ."

"Box," Norah almost screamed. "He had 'em in ten boxes—not countin' a barrel from the storeroom."

"My heart bleeds for the birds of this city, Jesse. Indeed it does.

There must have been thousands of them perished of the cold and the rest starving. Take this street, for example. There hasn't been a horse through for three days, except those of the hook and ladder, and whatever they did got covered over."

During most of this recital, Mr. Rogers sat quietly, which was unusual for him. Now he jumped up and began to open the blinds. Striving desperately for a reasonable tone of voice he produced a somewhat choked effect. "Has it struck you, Gussie, that there must be a thousand English sparrows loose in this house, not to speak of pigeons? . . ."

Mrs. Rogers tried to answer brightly, "The storm's over, and as soon as we open the door they'll fly. . . ." She stopped in consternation as light flooded the room. Mr. Rogers turned and looked too. Apparently the birds had preferred the greater comfort of the bed to the boxes that Abe had provided, but Mrs. Rogers faltered only a second. ". . . and it won't be anything to do a few extra sheets and pillowcases, what with diapers . . ."

Chapter 9

A SQUAT ICEBREAKER was at work in the river. Its twin funnels belched black smoke while its paddle wheels flailed against the milky water. The heavy ice broke with pistol-like cracks. Humphrey Cartwright posed by the rail of the ferry as near the bow as possible, and pointed out the larger and more dangerous floes that the other vessel was creating. Several of the Troubadours stood by, emitting timorous cries at the approach of each large chunk of ice.

Maggie Ballou was just beyond, seemingly too intent upon every word Humphrey uttered to pay any attention to Henry Rogers. Further along, the rest of the Troubadours were gathered in little groups.

The ferry steamed at half-speed, keeping in the icebreaker's wake, but Henry feared that it would reach the Manhattan side before he could make his peace with Ohio. He had tried three times already, since leaving the Jersey shore, but on each occasion, Ohio had turned her back more determinedly. What was the use of making another attempt?

Suddenly, instead of feeling abject and supplicating, Henry became angry. The idea of her ignoring him for that cheap actor whom she had always hated! And imagining herself so much! Why, she barely came to his shoulder! He reached forward and caught her arm roughly, careless of what Humphrey Cartwright or anybody else might think. With an impatient gesture, he drew her across the passenger section of the ferry, threaded a way between carts, sleighs and sleds—the first to cross the Hudson in more than two days—and found a secluded spot close to the warmth of the engine room. There Henry confronted her, and to the clang of the large, wheeled scoops that carried in the coal, shouted, "I've put up with everything I intend to. I kissed you this morning—yes. And I'm not sorry, not at all sorry. I wish I'd done it twice as long—there, you might as well know.

"I guess in a few minutes we'll never see each other any more, but it will be your fault. I've tried the best I can to tell you, but you won't listen. I love you, I really do. You can take that Humphrey Cartwright, if you want to, but . . ."

Whatever else Henry had intended to say was smothered by a kiss that made the one of early morning pale into insignificance. It seemed to last forever—until the ferry bumped against the pilings of the Liberty Street slip, and Ohio Ballou sighed into his ear, "Oh, Henry. Henry Rogers . . ."

2

IN THE FERRYHOUSE, the agents and porters on duty seemed too tired to care for passengers. Men in various stages of exhaustion were gathered around the huge, potbellied stove in the waiting room and others slept on the benches. Now that they again had an audience of sorts, most of the ladies of the Troubadour company began to put on little acts of their own—queries concerning the whereabouts of trunks, loudly expressed concern over whether there would be a performance that evening. Millie Mullins, the leading lady, was declaiming that she intended to leave the company at the first opportunity.

Mr. St. Clair kept repeating, "No hackneys, imagine. Not a single hansom. I'm going to complain. I'll write a letter that will blister, I tell you."

Henry waited impatiently for an end to all these goings-on; anybody could see that they'd have to check their baggage and foot it. The little comedian grinned over at him. "Don't mind them, they're only actors. From what I've observed, Rogers, you are going to have to get used to them. They all behave the same way, even the nice ones. You should have seen Maggie the day we left Scranton."

"Why Mr. Bernstein!" Turning to Henry, Ohio gave him her widest-eyed stare. "You don't believe him, do you?"

"Of course not. But I've decided on one thing. We're going to get out of here right now. We'll both see you later."

There was a quizzical expression on Jerry's face, but Henry put it firmly out of mind as he escorted his companion through the doors and out into the street.

The scene that met their eyes was beyond belief. Marooned streetcars, some of them blown off the tracks or turned over, deserted drays and other vehicles, were all tangled in a confused web of fallen electric wires and poles. Everywhere there was brick from blown-down chimneys, red-painted roofing tin that had been wound up as though it were still in the original roll, twisted awnings, fallen signs and broken glass.

Ohio exclaimed at the pitiable condition of the waterfront poor, wrapped in rags, with bags on their feet, as they attempted to dig paths from their hovels to the street. A sleigh or two went by, jingling with bells, but the snow was too deep and soft, and the horses floundered. Most of the cross streets were impassable and few of the sidewalks had been shoveled, although it was evident that hours had passed since the snow had stopped falling. It was as though the whole city and its people had been dealt a knockout blow. It seemed impossible that this was modern, up-to-date New York, and Henry began to suspect that they had been as well off in their marooned train in rural New Jersey as they might have been in the Metropolis.

He had thought that possibly his mother might worry about his failure to arrive on Monday, but until now it had not occurred to him to be concerned over his family. As they crossed toward the elevated railroad, Henry made up his mind. Instead of getting off at Fourteenth Street, if the trains were running, they'd go right on uptown. The sooner he introduced Ohio to everybody the better, and this was probably an ideal moment, when they would be too excited over the storm to be much upset over anything else. But an actress might be pretty hard for them to accept—especially after all the fuss he had made about Clint being a ball-player.

Henry had become so involved in his own thoughts, while he broke a path for Ohio through the unshoveled places, that he had unconsciously increased his gait until he heard a plaintive "Please . . . my skirts catch . . . I can't possibly! . . ."

He waited for her, and when she came up he caught her in his arms and kissed her, right there on the street. "Forgive me—I'm just so anxious for the family to meet you that I can hardly wait," he explained.

The elevated railroad was flimsy looking, with its good, solid iron hidden beneath icy, lacelike decoration, but a train steamed slowly by as they approached; and the steps and station platform were sprinkled with ashes to prevent slipping—the first sign they had seen of any effort to repair the blizzard's damage. In the time that passed until the next train, the two stood on the empty platform and discussed a future that bore no relation to the immediate scene.

"I have to finish my engagement with the Troubadours," Ohio protested, when Henry suggested a quick marriage.

"They can get someone else to take your place soon enough. I've thought of nothing but making money for so long that now I want to begin living. Beside, I hate the idea of that Cartwright fellow being around, even if it is only on the stage."

At the beginning of this speech, Ohio had pouted. "If you think they can replace me quickly I assure you, sir, that you are very much mistaken. I ought to be very angry with you, but I can't. You are so sweet otherwise."

Then, as he assisted her into the train she had an unsettling thought. "Henry, suppose your father and mother don't like me?"

### 3

"MOTHER, come listen to this," Mr. Rogers shouted for the third time, and then, when there was no response, "Mother!"

Mrs. Rogers came down the stairs, fondling an object in her hands. "Good grief, Jesse. Won't you ever remember there's a baby in the house?" The dachshunds, who had followed her, were behaving in such a way that Mr. Rogers was immediately suspicious.

"Gussie, I thought this house was shut of birds. I won't stand one of them in here and that's final."

"Abe pleaded so to keep this one—until the weather gets warmer, anyway—that I didn't have the heart to refuse him. Look, Jesse, did you ever see anything cuter in your life?"

"Out with it. I refuse to look at another bird."

"But this is a cardinal, Jesse. Imagine, here in the city. He must have been blown here."

"After this morning I am fed up with birds, completely fed up. . . ." The figure of speech started a train of thought. "Unless it is good to eat. Let me see it."

"I'd let it freeze first—I'd . . ."

"This is not Mr. Quinby, Gussie. You won't need to take in washing. By the way, how is the family pride and joy?"

"Real well, Abe says, but fretting at not getting a run. I haven't seen him yet, but he's getting along beautifully with the livery horses. Abe says they talk together and though he can't quite make out what about he almost can."

During this speech in what Mr. Rogers called his wife's most unlucid style, the cardinal raised his head and eyed Mr. Rogers with a pert and knowing look that brought out his worst impulses.

"A male, I'd say, though I'm no ornithologist. If I have to put up with him I suggest you place him in the cage with the canary and see what happens. If we could raise some rare, salmon-colored offspring we might sell them for a good figure."

Mrs. Rogers, who had long suspected that Jenny Lind was misnamed, decided to ignore all the implications of the suggestion. Instead, she inquired, sharply. "You brought me all the way downstairs? . . ."

"This bird business disturbed my train of thought. Oh, here it is! Who says this wasn't the worst storm ever was? I missed this. All the water was blown out of the harbor at Baltimore. The steamboats were lying flat on their bottoms . . . under many of the piers there was no water at all. You know, Mother, a mere 66-mile-an-hour gale couldn't have done that."

"To hear you talk, one would think it was your own, special snowstorm."

"Blizzard, woman. The greatest blizzard you or I will ever see. I know, for I was out in it. You can't belittle it when I'm around."

"I've no desire to, considering that if Clint doesn't come back soon we'll be without victuals for dinner." As she spoke, she happened to look out the window and saw her tall son-in-law crossing the street. "Speak of the devil . . ." she began to say, and then, considering the way he was loaded down, decided that was not quite accurate, stated more manner-of-factly, "Here he is now, and with food aplenty, or I miss my guess."

Clint began explanations as she opened the door for him. "A stroke of luck, Mother. I've everything for a real feed. Oysters and wild turkey . . ."

"Now where in the world?"

"A provisioner's cart abandoned in the snow. I've been the last hour digging it out." He lowered his packages onto the kitchen table and began enumerating them. "A peck of salt oysters, first off . . ."

"But Clint, that's stealing. We can't. Suppose you had been caught?"

". . . Irish potatoes. Frozen, but they'll be all right if cooked now. I wasn't caught and as Father Duffy says, hunger knows no law. . . ."

By this time Mr. Rogers had joined in an inspection of the

spoils. "Wild turkeys, and fat as they come. Clint, my boy, you are a wonder."

"He stole them from out a provisioner's cart."

Clint grinned, showing his white teeth. "Don't worry, this is a perfectly honest transaction, though I had meant to keep you on tenterhooks a while longer. I stumbled into the cart by accident, and saw that it was loaded. The provisioner's shop was only a short distance away but he had no idea what had become of cart, driver, or horse, and was frantic for food. Why beefsteaks are bringing a dollar a pound. . . ."

"I hope you included several nice, tender ones," Mr. Rogers interrupted.

"I made a bargain to dig the cart out and haul it back, in return for victuals."

"Haul it back! Where did you get the horse?"

"I brought Mr. Quinby from the stable. His feelings were hurt at pulling a cart, I suppose. . . ."

"Of course they were. Mr. Quinby is used to nothing but the most fashionable rigs."

"But it was that or all of us starving. Besides, the workout was good for him."

"Indeed it was. Mother, I think this calls for a bang-up dinner in the old style."

"If only we'd hear from Henry and Zena. Perhaps we better save one of the birds. . . ."

"Nonsense. It will taste just as good cold, when they arrive. Need I remind you that I've had nothing but pickles. . . ."

"Honest, Jesse, you might think we'd all been eating from the fat of the land, the way you go on. Norah, I suppose we better think of getting dinner started."

Her "I'm comin', mum," was followed by the ringing of the doorbell and a shake of the head from Mrs. Rogers. "It's not Henry, as I'd been hoping. I can tell his ring."

It was not, indeed, as they were to find out when they bustled upstairs. Norah was standing at the vestibule door, looking doubtfully at a tall figure in a plaid Dundreary coat, a large carpetbag in his hand. "Come Norah, you're not knowin' an old friend?"

"Duffy, by all that's holy," Mr. Rogers shouted. "Come in, man.

Though you can't blame Norah for not recognizing you in that outfit."

After due explanations, Father Duffy went on. "Remembering your old plan of a genteel home for paying guests, I thought you might revive it for me. I'll be working with the Anti-Poverty Society for some weeks."

"As welcome as spring flowers, after what we're going through —and no question of paying, either. You're in good time for a feast tonight. Oysters and wild turkey."

"A special Providence brought me. I left Pottsville this morning little realizing how badly off the city was. I was too anxious to get back to my work, I kept thinking, but all the time it was one of your delicious meals . . ."

"Oh, Father. I'll not hear a word of your flattery! And we had a new arrival—born at the height of the storm."

"A daughter, and she'll be redheaded like her father, or I miss my guess." In characteristic fashion, both Rogerses were going at once. "All night long, and Clint had a terrible time getting a doctor."

When Father Duffy could get a word in edgewise, he expressed surprise. "When I saw Henry, he said not a word that Zenie was expecting. . . ."

"Henry! When did you see him? Is he still at Gene's?"

"He left Monday morning. I supposed . . ."

"Oh, I'm so worried. Now where could he be?"

"I've already told you, Gussie. A boy as sensible as Henry probably stopped over when he saw how bad things were getting."

"But it's not like him to keep us worrying. He'd have sent word, somehow. I'd expect it of Zena, who'd enjoy nothing better than knowing I was upset, but Henry . . ."

As she left the sentence unfinished, Father Duffy inquired, "Madam Lascalles is missing also?"

"Went to Philadelphia, she said, and not an aye, yes or no from her since. Between the pair of them, I'm most distracted, not knowing whether they may be frozen to death at this very minute." She paused, looked thoughtful, then became her usual bustling self. "Jesse, you make Father Duffy at home while I get down to the kitchen and give Norah a lift with those turkeys. I think I'll make an oyster stuffing, but what to do for dessert beats me. . . ."

## 4

IN THE BROWNSTONE FRONT DISTRICT the city seemed to be trying to throw off the lethargy that the white blanket of snow had imposed. The air was still cold and damp, but there was no longer any wind. An army of small boys and tattered Irish were busily shoveling pavements. One thing about the storm, it was providing a harvest for the poor. At every corner, urchins in rags guarded narrow paths they had dug from one pavement to another, and exacted tribute, not by asking for it, but by being oversolicitous of every pedestrian.

Before they reached his home, Henry had expended his small coins upon these little brigands—proof enough of a change in his character during recent days. Another indication that he was indeed a different man was his stealing a kiss every time a high snowdrift afforded protection from prying eyes.

Ohio's cheeks became flushed from more than cold as she would push him away—after he had achieved his purpose—and protest, "Henry Rogers, if I had really realized the kind of man you were, I should never, never have consented to meet your family. I've a great mind to turn back this minute."

His family! Henry had to explain all over again about them. There was Father and his jokes. Henry was still a little patronizing about Mr. Rogers. "I really keep the family going, although he brings in a little, during the summer, writing baseball scores."

"He sounds nice to me. I'm going to like him, I'm certain."

"Mother is the one to look out for. She's Italian, and to tell you the truth, I've often wondered why Father married her, in the first place. . . ."

"It must have been from love, don't you think?"

"I guess so. But Father is so different; you'll see. I'm not quite sure he used good sense. . . ."

"Well I like that! So you think being in love isn't good sense? I don't even believe you know what it's like and all you've told me is a lot of lies."

Ohio slipped and was almost buried in a snowdrift, and down

went Henry practically on top of her. When they arose again, this particular question had been satisfactorily settled and Henry began to explain about Zenie and Clint. "I've not mentioned him to you before. I haven't been altogether fair to him, I guess. Just walking over here I determined to try and meet him halfway. Most people like him, too, but what I can't stand is someone wasting his life playing a game instead of having a business and getting ahead, especially an able-bodied chap like Clint Weatherby."

"Not *the* Clint Weatherby? The famous one, on the Brooklyns?" Her face turned sad, her voice tremulous. "My father used to think he was wonderful. He loved to see a baseball game before . . . before he . . ."

A pat from Henry showed that he understood while he went on to prepare her for Aunt Zena. Henry had never approved of all the love affairs about which she continually boasted, but his whole life was marked by a tradition of her lavish generosities and he tried to make Ohio see, not the still sprightly but somehow pitiful old woman of today, but the glamorous, fairy-book character of his childhood.

"My, you have a wonderful family. Each one is so interesting. I want to meet Gene. She must be especially nice, for she's your twin and must be like you. Besides, if you hadn't gone to visit her we might never have met."

Right in front of the house—almost on the very stoop—Ohio lost her nerve. "Oh, Henry, this is terrible, I can't. I just can't. Maybe if I could have just one kiss—a little one—to give me courage? . . ."

Henry answered almost gruffly, "Can't here. Mother's most likely watching out the curtains, this minute. There's little goes on in the street that she misses, or anywhere else, for that matter."

He was right, too, for as they climbed the steps, hand in hand, and reached the door—with its imposing iron grille in which Mrs. Rogers always took such pride—it slowly opened for them.

**Chapter 10**

THE FRENCH CLOCK on the mantelpiece struck the half-hour upon its tinkling, unsubstantial chime. Mr. Rogers stopped in front of it, trying to establish a mean time by peering at the round crystal which was set in the belly of a gilt figure of Venus. From one angle it indicated approximately twenty-nine and a half minutes past, and from an opposite one, a hairline less than twenty-nine to. Taking out his own watch by its massive chain, he compared results and then turned it ahead a matter of seconds. "Mother, it's way after five-thirty. Those are wild birds and tenderer than the tame, besides, I'm hungry."

He didn't even draw a reply from downstairs, stood irresolutely and then wandered into the parlor. What was this? The automatic fountain which had stood dry for ten years or more, captured his attention. It was a shame to let so interesting a scientific apparatus go untended, but unless he filled it himself, any mention of it to Gussie would only delay dinner further, so he plumped into his rocker instead, and sighed.

Norah bustled into the dining room, searched uncertainly in the sideboard, then retreated to the stairway. "Will you be wantin' all clean napkins, or only for them as ain't dirtied any?"

From below, Mrs. Rogers' voice floated, "I declare I didn't hear, Norah, between the dogs barking at Tony, who has just gone out, and all."

When the question was repeated, the maid heard the answer without difficulty. "Of course there will be clean napkins. Norah, what ails you? With Father Duffy here, who'll always be Father Duffy to me regardless of what anybody says, and Henry almost frozen to death and that girl of his. Not that I think she's so much, mind . . .

"Not to mention having the Burts over. Norah what can you be thinking of? Of course there'll be clean napkins. And our best china, that Zena sent me, years ago."

The long-distance conversation was too trying for Norah. She had caught no more than the essential information before she began dealing out, like cards, the stiff, folded squares of linen. There went the Mister and Missus and here Master Henry and the girl he'd brought home with him. That was for Father Duffy and those two for the folks next door—who didn't have the good sense to hire an Irish, instead of a German girl. This was for Master Clint, who had a way with him, to be sure, and one went on the sideboard for Miss Zenie and the darling little creature she'd birthed.

Norah was startled to hear the mister clapping his hands. "Wonderful, Norah. I've never seen such aim." She smiled at him, conscious of the perfect beauty of her teeth and showed them, gums and all. "Go along with you, sir. You wouldn't make fun of a poor girl, would you, now?"

She rushed downstairs, almost as conscious as Mr. Rogers of the fleeting minutes. There were still the largest of the oysters to shuck, for serving on the half shell, and some horse-radish root to put through the grinder.

The missus was angry, stirring viciously at a panful of flour that she was browning. "That good-for-nothing Tony might have shucked those oysters . . ." she began.

"And what about the street lights, that's been unlit for two nights because he almost had the pneumonia? What with the electricity out in the bargain? . . . No, I said to him, 'I'll tend to the oysters, which is my business and let any what don't like it say so.'"

This was the challenge direct, but Mrs. Rogers knew well when it was unwise to cross Norah further. While she expertly nicked the oyster shells at just the right spot with the heavy iron back of the knife, and then pried them open with a single twist of its short blade, Mrs. Rogers changed her tone completely. "What do you think of this girl Henry has brought home? Pretty enough looking, I'd say, though not as handsome as any of his own sisters. He's crazy in love with her, it's easy to see that, but I don't know. . . ."

"He's not havin' the long face he's been wearin' ever since I can remember, which is somethin'."

"But less than three days, Norah! What can he know about her?"

"Indeed, mum, it didn't take me ten seconds to know I loved Tony. One look into them big eyes of his—like brown velvet they are—and I was took."

"And no family. None at all."

"I've no family either, exceptin' yourselves, and think I'm as good as those who has."

"Imagine Henry, of all people, taking up with an actress."

"I had me mind set on a policeman, or a horsecar driver at the least—and got a lamplighter."

"Ohio Ballou. Ohio Rogers, if he marries her. What will it sound like? And him insisting on it."

"More credit him, I say. I took Tony with a name I can't even pronounce and have it to wear in the bargain, but I'm not kickin' and neither should he." By this time, the oysters were all shucked and set out in the shed, a dozen big fat fellows to the plate, and Norah was struggling with the grinder, feeding in the scrubbed white horse-radish roots while her eyes bled tears.

Mrs. Rogers was also crying, whether from horse-radish or emotion it would have been hard to say. She threw some cut-up turkey livers and gizzards into the pan, poured in a cupful of white wine and stirred it vigorously, her tears not interfering at all with her skill at the range. "My last child being taken away from me by a little snip of a girl! I don't know whether I can sit at table, Norah, indeed I don't."

"Considerin' you've been wantin' Mister Henry married the last five years . . ."

"But will she feed him proper? You must admit she doesn't look as though she could boil an egg without burning it." With that intuition of good cooks, Mrs. Rogers suddenly set the gravy pan off the fire and opened the oven. One look at the twin, golden-brown breasts was enough. "Done to a turn, Norah." Shielding her face from the heat, with her shoulder and hands protected by pot holders, she pulled out the large roasting pan, scorning the girl's offer to help. "It's all in the way you handle the pan, I say," she commented, as she'd often done before, then repeated another of her kitchen homilies as she spooned up some of the liquor and added it to her gravy, "This way the fowl aren't growing cold while the gravy's being made—the way some cooks do," to which Norah returned an automatic "Yes, mum."

"The potatoes are nice and mealy, too, which I was afraid they mightn't be, frozen like they were. Knock on the wall for the Burts, Norah, and call the others. . . ."

2

CLINT WEATHERBY was the hero of the evening and for the first time felt truly a member of the Rogers family. A transformed Henry had kept a hand on his shoulder while introducing him to Ohio, and when Mr. Rogers expressed distress that Clint hadn't included several good, thick steaks in his bargaining, it was Mrs. Rogers who went to his defense. "Jesse, are you never satisfied? The meat is simply falling off the bones of those turkeys, they were that plump—from eating pine cones over in Jersey, I suspect.

"And did you ever see such fat oysters? I hope you sent a good plateful up to Zenie, Norah. They'll help her get her strength back."

"I did, mum."

Mrs. Burt sighed. "My, I wish I had a son-in-law who thought of us. Once or twice a winter, for dinner, is as much as we see any of them."

"Have some more horse-radish, Mrs. Burt. I bought it last week from a peddler. Dug it before the snow was clean off the ground, he told me. Yes, Clint is a wonderful son-in-law and nobody appreciates him more than I do. . . ."

Father Duffy, while doing full justice to the oysters, which were great, gray fellows, found time to talk with Ohio, who was seated next to him. Mrs. Rogers was in a regular dither of impatience to know what they were saying and what the good man was thinking of her by this time. In her chatter about Clint, which was intended to cover her curiosity, she spoke more favorably than she would have otherwise, but she regretted none of it.

The last oysters had been eaten and were still being exclaimed over, when Mr. Rogers shouted, "Sleigh bells! Hear them, Gussie? By Christopher, we haven't had a good sleigh ride in years. I propose we take one tomorrow morning. . . ."

As the bells grew louder, Father Duffy observed, "That's a spanking team, I'll bet, though I'm somewhat surprised it can get down this street."

Father Duffy was right. It was coming down Fifty-second Street and with such a brave lot of bells, might even be a four-in-hand. Naturally, Mr. Rogers got to a window first, but the others were close behind; there was nothing in the world to look at as thrilling as a sleigh with a beautiful turnout of horses. It was a four-in-hand, in tandem pairs, with a coachman on the box so bundled in furs that he looked like a bear. What was more, the sleigh stopped outside, with a rearing and plunging of the horses.

As the hitching post was completely buried, the coachman was fully occupied holding the horses while two passengers dismounted without his assistance.

Surely nobody but Aunt Zena would have worn a bonnet like that to go sleighing! Mrs. Rogers said, "Pet, do you imagine that can be Zena? Now what do you suppose? . . ."

It was Zena! She was helped to the cleared portion of the side-walk by a man who was almost a head shorter—somebody whom Mr. Rogers didn't know. Henry, standing at the same window, close to Ohio, failed to recognize him.

But Mrs. Rogers did! Her hands itched to be in Zena's hair, although she kept control of her wits. "It is Aunt Zena, Norah— with a gentleman. They're hungry, like as not. Get another leaf in the table and set two more places while I let them in. Hurry now."

The last order was an unnecessary one, as Norah was already flying for one of the table leaves, from the crate of them in the closet, while Clint from one end, and Mr. Rogers from the other, pulled apart the table for its insertion.

At the front door, Mrs. Rogers was enveloped by an exuberant sister. One might have thought that it was a first reunion since childhood, the way Zena went on. It was a greeting which Mrs. Rogers took stolidly, but there was more than enough embracing and kissing on Aunt Zena's part to do for both of them. Finally, when the wells of her affection had drained to a throaty, "My dear, dear sister, to be seeing you again, after all the danger we've been through," she apparently remembered her companion, waiting patiently behind her. "I've the greatest surprise for you—I know you can't guess. . . ."

Mr. Madeira was almost dragged forward and smiled apologetically. "Billy, darling, I want you to renew your acquaintance with my sister. Dear Tina, of course you can't be expected to remember, but you were along when Billy and I first met, in Kensington. Father was alive—do you recall?" She glanced coyly at the youthful sweetheart, who looked more than bewildered. "I returned to Europe with his picture in my heart, but circumstances kept us apart. Ah, the wasted years . . ."

This reflective pause in Zena's histrionics coincided with a stern admonition from Norah. "If you don't get to table quickly, mum, the turkeys will be ruined entirely, if they ain't already."

Along with Mr. Rogers, Henry had always been kept in the dark about his mother's old friendship with Mr. Madeira. To see him come in now, apparently on the most intimate terms with Aunt Zena, was almost too great a shock. Henry sat rooted to his chair when the other men arose, until a low, but nonetheless sharp, "Henry," reminded him of his manners. It was the first time that he had heard Ohio use such a tone and he jumped to his feet, then rushed forward to help Mr. Madeira with his coat. Instead, he found himself in Aunt Zena's embrace. "Henry, I've been hearing the most wonderful things about you. My heart has been bursting with pride! . . .

"And . . . no, it can't be. It can't! Father Duffy, I shouldn't have known you. Billy, Father Duffy is another old, old friend. . . ."

Like a brook, Aunt Zena might have run on forever, except for a last, despairing wail from Norah, "Please, mum, the t-u-urke-e-eys!"

3

MR. ROGERS made a fine art of carving. He cut through joints with the skill of a surgeon and made certain that everyone received similar proportions of dark and light meat. He added oyster filling with an expert flip of the spoon and then passed the plates for Norah to dish the potatoes and rutabagas before Mrs. Rogers deluged it all with giblet gravy. She apologized that there were only two vegetables and discovered that the filling was not quite to her liking, being a little too firm in certain respects and not solid enough in others.

For a while there was no sound but that of food being consumed by a considerable group of hungry folk. Everything else had to wait, although practically everyone at the table was bursting with news of some sort. Mr. Rogers was eager to begin again the tale of his adventures going downtown, the first day of the blizzard, with a few touches that he had thought up since the last telling. Aunt Zena was anticipating the furor which her announcement would cause, when there was an opportune time to make it. Henry wanted to tell about meeting Ohio on the train, and all that befell them. Clint wanted to boast about his new daughter.

Only Mrs. Rogers ate without the appearance of excitement. She played with her food, a polite mask on her face, but her black eyes were at their beadiest. What was on Zena's mind? She had never appeared more vivacious and the bloom of actual youth shone through Eugenie's Secret of Beauty. So far, Jesse knew only that the man sitting opposite her was Mr. Madeira, for whom Henry had worked. Mrs. Rogers told herself that she must be not only discreet, but guide the conversation so that nothing else would be suspected. She attacked her food with little gusto and still had some on her plate when the others passed theirs for seconds.

Now was the time to sauce the remainders of the repast with pleasant conversation and Father Duffy led off with a joke, for which Mrs. Rogers was thankful, as it gave her additional time to collect her wits.

She waited just long enough for everybody to laugh, but not for Jesse to counter with a "that reminds me." "Zena—Mr. Madeira! Everybody has been going at such a rate that you haven't heard about Zenie. Clint is the proud father of a little girl, born right at the worst of the blizzard. He insists on naming it Teresina, after its mother—and my dear sister. . . ."

This was good for ten minutes of talk, while Mrs. Rogers got her second helping. Aunt Zena was restrained from going up to see the infant then and there only by the promise that they could all go up later.

"I shan't be able to wait! Indeed I shan't," she cried. "Clinton Weatherby, you are the luckiest man. Tell me just one thing. Does the baby have auburn hair? It should, you know, with both a father and an aunt so favored."

Mrs. Rogers' lips made a straight line. As though everyone didn't know that Zena's hair was dyed that awful color. She tried desperately to think up some subtle dig, but again it was Father Duffy who picked up the conversation. "And aren't you all entranced with my young companion here? I realize that you've done no more than shake hands with her, while I feel that I really know her. Come, my dear, and blush properly, while I say that you are charming and that Henry Rogers was fortunate indeed to have found you."

"But don't you think they are being hasty, wanting to marry after knowing each other so short a time?" Mrs. Rogers could have bitten off her tongue, both for the words and the tone in which she had said them.

"I don't think so at all," Aunt Zena cried. "When true lovers meet, they should marry immediately, before it is too late. No one will ever know the heartbreak I've suffered through that mistake. Ohio Ballou! What a sweet, sweet name! Is it French?"

"My father was French, I suppose—or his father."

"Mr. Lascalles was French, but I don't hold it against you, my dear. . . ."

"Ohio is one of our states—the one where Julia and Philippe are. A ridiculous name, of course, which the poor girl realizes. She would like us to call her Maggie, I think." In spite of herself, Mrs. Rogers was continuing tart.

"I like Ohio," Henry answered, shortly, and Aunt Zena bore him out. "Of course! It is so musical, so . . . so original. Every other girl you meet, here in America, is called Maggie. Don't let my sister try to manage you—she will, you know."

While she had allowed herself to be maneuvered into this unfortunate position, Mrs. Rogers still felt capable of striking back. Putting on her most elegant manner, she inquired, loudly, "I hope, Norah, that you are taking good care of Mr. Madeira's coachman in the kitchen?" Then, without waiting for an answer which she knew would be affirmative, she let loose her poisoned barb, "I suppose, Zena, darling, that you wouldn't care to give an account of your doings, while we here at home were worried frantic over you?"

"Of course not, my dear Tina. I was caught in the storm's clutches and would surely have perished except for an heroic rescue by a gallant man. Imagine my surprise when it turned out to be Billy, here. Then we were snowbound, like the rest of you, though the details would sound tedious, I'm sure. While Henry found a new love in the storm, we renewed an old one. . . ."

What was Zena getting to? Mrs. Rogers' eyes became gimlets that tried to bore into her sister's thoughts.

Billy Madeira seemed to be trying to convey something to Mrs. Rogers. His face was red as a beet, and though it remained immobile, his eyes were rolling like marbles. She tried to read his thoughts, while the others struggled with wings and other less desirable pieces of turkey.

Aunt Zena was certainly leading up to some momentous announcement. What could it be? She seemed to be overcome, one hand clutched at the edge of the table while the other pressed the general region of her heart. She lifted her head so that the line of her neck and chin became almost youthful. Her mascaraed lashes drooped. It was a highly effective pose, and by this time not a fork scraped against plate.

Mrs. Rogers would have liked to spoil the climax, whatever it was to be, by ringing for Norah to clear the table, but unfortunately her own curiosity was too strong for her.

Pretense seemed to fall away from Aunt Zena. She gave the impression of being simply happy and humble about it, a bit overwhelmed by good fortune. "Billy and I were married this morning. Oh, Tina . . . Jesse . . . everybody—I'm so thrilled. No one will ever know. . . ."

Mr. Rogers cut her off with a bellow that set the punch glasses tingling against their bowl on the sideboard. "Zena! What a grand surprise! And to you, sir, whose sterling worth I know through the reports of my son. . . ."

His expression was a most fatuous one, which Mrs. Rogers

279

would have liked to remove by stating a few choice facts, though she didn't dare. She was almost beside herself when he continued, unaware of her displeasure, "A toast to the newlyweds. May you recapture in mature years all the bliss of youth."

Father was no more than getting started and his lengthened period was only for effect. He sat down with a distinct air of annoyance when Henry, who was rarely given to emotional display, dashed around the table to wring the hands of bride and groom. "Mr. Madeira! The most amazing surprise! I think it is wonderful, of course, but how did you ever come to meet my Aunt? What a coincidence. I wish you both every happiness."

Mr. Madeira seemed to be tongue-tied from joy, so Aunt Zena came to his rescue. "How nice of you, Henry. I do believe you have become my favorite nephew. Philippe has gotten so stout— and stodgy." She turned toward Ohio, who appeared a little confused. "And you shall be a treasured niece, my dear. Billy and I had a discussion on the way from the church this morning that should result in a nice wedding present for you and Henry. Tell them what you have in mind, dear."

Mr. Madeira didn't respond at once and Aunt Zena nudged him. When he looked at her questioningly, she gave him a sharper, but still playful dig. He half arose, began to sit down, then appeared to remember something. "Oh, yes. Things have been happening a little fast for me to keep track of, Henry. Your aunt . . . I . . . we . . .

"I mean that we have decided that I shall retire. . . ."

Mrs. Rogers could see the perspiration starting on Billy Madeira's forehead, but she felt no pity for him. After having been faithful to her all of these years to marry a cat like Zena! There was no fool like an old fool. And would he never come to the point?

"We, er . . . we plan an extended trip abroad. . . ."

"A honeymoon, darling."

"Quite so. We thought . . . I . . . well, Henry, you know the coal business so well. I practically brought you up in it. . . ."

"And now that it is all in the family . . ."

"Quite so."

"You feel . . ."

280

"Quite so. I feel that . . ."

Henry had never known his employer at such a loss for words, and Mrs. Rogers thought that she would scream if he said "Quite so," once more.

"Anyway . . . my, uh . . . my wife suggested . . ." Suddenly Mr. Madeira caught hold of himself. "What I propose, Henry, is that your partnership take over the running of my business."

"I suggested Rogers, Madeira, and Lascalles as a firm name. It sounds poetic, don't you agree?" Aunt Zena inquired. Mrs. Rogers was willing to give her credit for one thing: She could tell from her sister's expression that this whole idea of having Henry run all of Mr. Madeira's business, arose out of one of her truly generous impulses.

Of them all, only Henry appeared not to realize what it meant. It was his turn to need nudging and Mrs. Rogers gave grudging tribute when Ohio acted in truly wifely fashion. It was the business-man in Henry who responded, though. He took on what his mother called his "Quaker expression." "It sounds interesting, Mr. Madeira, although we'll have to discuss terms, of course."

"Interesting! It's wonderful," Mr. Rogers shouted, so loudly that Clint ran upstairs to tell Zenie of the reason for all the noise, so that she wouldn't be upset. He was down again, in a moment, to finish his plate, as the others were doing.

For no reason that made sense to her, Mrs. Rogers began to feel a deep and growing contentment. Suppose Zena had gotten Billy Madeira—she hadn't wanted him anyway. Henry was bound to be rich, from the look of things, and she'd work to make a real woman out of that little hussy he'd picked up. Zenie and Clint would never leave, not so long as the baby was little, that was certain. On the whole, things had turned out quite well.

She realized that the Burts had been rather neglected and pressed them to have more turkey. She heard their refusals absent-mindedly as she thought, "It's too bad that Julia isn't here, with Philippe and the children, or . . ."

Trust Father Duffy to read one's thoughts. Father Duffy—who would always be that to her, no matter what kind of ridiculous clothes he wore—rose from his chair and held up his glass. "From the clarity and sparkle of it, I recognize this for pure Croton water and not any of the Philadelphia stuff all of us used to drink. I'd like to give thanks to God and a little toast in it. . . ."

Mr. Rogers listened with keen anticipation. Whatever Duffy had to say was sure to be good! Aunt Zena pressed close to her husband and Henry put his arm around Ohio's shoulder. Even the Burts, who were not Catholics, felt a new affection for these neighbors of theirs.

". . . Thanks that we were spared during the awful manifestation of His might. Thanks for His power that brought us together here and keeps the thoughts of the absent ones centered in this home. May He give us—and them—food and happiness in the proportions that we are deserving of them.

"And now, a toast. To the Great Blizzard, through which we have passed. I am sure that the oldest inhabitant cannot remember such a storm. Let us hope that the youngest of us, upstairs, will never see such another."

He sat down to a burst of applause, during which Mrs. Rogers again thanked her stars that she had remembered a jar of mincemeat, left over from Christmas. She restrained a desire to slip downstairs and make sure that Norah's pie made from it was all it should be. It was certain to be perfect; besides, she'd lace it with additional brandy before it was served.

While she rang for the table to be cleared, she grew misty-eyed. "You know, Pet, like Father Duffy said, this storm has brought us together again, somehow. It's something we'll never forget, I wager. I, for one, wouldn't want to, either."

The Rogers family, its relatives and neighbors all nodded slowly and seriously. Then, gradually, their faces lightened with smiles, as they waited for the dessert.